The O. Henry Prize Stories 2016

The O. Henry Prize Stories 2016

Chosen and with an Introduction by
Laura Furman

With Essays by Jurors
Molly Antopol
Peter Cameron
Lionel Shriver
on the Stories They Admire Most

Anchor Books
A Division of Penguin Random House LLC
New York

AN ANCHOR BOOKS ORIGINAL, SEPTEMBER 2016

Anchor Books Trade Paperback ISBN: 978-1-101-97111-6
eBook ISBN: 978-1-101-97112-3

www.anchorbooks.com

Printed in the United States of America
10 9 8 7 6 5 4 3 2 1

To Glenn and Kathleen Cambor, with love

Publishing is a profession and also a calling, and the series editor is grateful to the skilled and dedicated editorial, production, and publicity staff at Anchor Books. Each year, Diana Secker Tesdell edits the series editor with grace and patience.

Kelly Luce was the editorial assistant for *The O. Henry Prize Stories 2016*, and the series editor enjoyed her intelligence, broad taste, and keen sense of the importance of literature.

The graduate school and Department of English of the University of Texas at Austin supports *The O. Henry Prize Stories* in many ways. The series editor thanks the university and especially Professor Elizabeth Cullingford.

—LF

Publisher's Note

A BRIEF HISTORY OF
THE O. HENRY PRIZE STORIES

Many readers have come to love the short story through the simple characters, easy narrative voice and humor, and compelling plotting in the work of William Sydney Porter (1862–1910), best known as O. Henry. His surprise endings entertain readers, including those back for a second, third, or fourth look. Even now one can say "Gift of the Magi" in a conversation about a love affair or marriage, and almost any literate person will know what is meant. It's hard to think of many other American writers whose work has been so incorporated into our national shorthand.

O. Henry was a newspaperman, skilled at hiding from his editors at deadline. A prolific writer, he wrote to make a living and to make sense of his life. He spent his childhood in Greensboro, North Carolina, his adolescence and young manhood in Texas, and his mature years in New York City. In between Texas and New York, he served out a prison sentence for bank fraud in Columbus, Ohio. Accounts of the origin of his pen name vary: One story dates from his days in Austin, where he was said to call the wandering family cat "Oh! Henry!"; another states that the name was inspired by the captain of the guard at the Ohio State Penitentiary, Orrin Henry.

Porter had devoted friends, and it's not hard to see why. He was charming and had an attractively gallant attitude. He drank too much and neglected his health, which caused his friends concern. He was often short of money; in a letter to a friend asking for a loan of $15 (his banker was out of town, he wrote), Porter added a postscript: "If it isn't convenient, I'll love you just the same." His banker was unavailable most of Porter's life. His sense of humor was always with him.

Reportedly, Porter's last words were from a popular song: "Turn up the light, for I don't want to go home in the dark."

Eight years after O. Henry's death, in April 1918, the Twilight Club (founded in 1883 and later known as the Society of Arts and Letters) held a dinner in his honor at the Hotel McAlpin in New York City. His friends remembered him so enthusiastically that a group of them met at the Biltmore Hotel in December of that year to establish some kind of memorial to him. They decided to award annual prizes in his name for short-story writers, and formed a committee of award to read the short stories published in a year and to pick the winners. In the words of Blanche Colton Williams (1879–1944), the first of the nine series editors, the memorial was intended to "strengthen the art of the short story and to stimulate younger authors."

Doubleday, Page & Company was chosen to publish the first volume, *O. Henry Memorial Award Prize Stories 1919*. In 1927, the society sold all rights to the annual collection to Doubleday, Doran & Company. Doubleday published *The O. Henry Prize Stories*, as it came to be known, in hardcover, and from 1984 to 1996 its subsidiary, Anchor Books, published it simultaneously in paperback. Since 1997 *The O. Henry Prize Stories* has been published as an original Anchor Books paperback.

HOW THE STORIES ARE CHOSEN

All stories originally written in the English language and published in an American or Canadian periodical are eligible for consideration. Individual stories may not be nominated; magazines must submit the year's issues in their entirety by July 1. Editors are invited to submit online fiction for consideration. Such submissions must be sent to the series editor in hard copy. (Please see pp. 343–44 for details.)

As of 2003, the series editor chooses the twenty O. Henry Prize Stories, and each year three writers distinguished for their fiction are asked to evaluate the entire collection and to write an appreciation of the story they most admire. These three writers receive the twenty prize stories in manuscript form with no identification of author or publication. They make their choices independent of each other and the series editor.

The goal of *The O. Henry Prize Stories* remains to strengthen the art of the short story.

To Jean Rhys (1890–1979)

Some mornings, just to brace myself, I look at the jacket photograph on Jean Rhys's 1976 story collection *Sleep It Off, Lady*. Rhys was eighty-six in Fay Godwin's photo, her fingers arthritic, head cocked, one eye larger than the other, grooves from nose to chin, staring back at whoever dares to stare at her in her chic beat-up hat and jacket. She might be saying, "Go ahead and look if you dare." She looks back just as sharply and with as little expectation as she might have done in life. Her look defines the phrase *gimlet-eyed*.

And so it is with her writing, her brief and searing novels, and her short stories that are delivered like taps that slice the reader at the end.

The title story of *Sleep It Off, Lady* begins with two ladies at tea, Mrs. Baker and Miss Verney, having a chat about a proposed village project, when Miss Verney says that lately she's been thinking "a great deal about death." Here the subversion of the cozy English village begins.

Mrs. Baker answers that it isn't so strange that Miss Verney thinks of death:

> *"We old people are rather like children, we live in the present as a rule. A merciful dispensation of providence."*
> *"Perhaps," said Miss Verney doubtfully.*

Like many of Rhys's stories, "Sleep It Off, Lady" centers on a character who understands very little about the world and is in turn not much understood. Rhys's early heroines, young women alone, lack an instinct for self-preservation and they are always strangers, wherever they are. They trust the wrong person, usually a man, and they end up more isolated and wounded than ever. One story, set on a Caribbean island like Dominica (where Rhys was born and raised), has the same clueless, innocent character missing the niceties of not shooting sitting birds. Whatever everyone else knows and takes for granted, a Rhys heroine will not.

In "Sleep It Off, Lady," even the children are judgmental, mean, and exceedingly unhelpful. In her bitter innocence, the main character has no gift for the sort of politeness that would make a bearable life of tea and non sequiturs. She cannot stand to ask for help and she gets none. Indeed, the villagers condemn her for drinking, which she does often and early. When she needs their aid, they ignore her.

The photographic portrait was taken near the end of Rhys's life when she was rediscovered and republished, rescued by the efforts and publicity campaign of her editor Diana Athill and the writer Francis Wyndham. Her rescue came too late, Rhys told an interviewer.

Jean Rhys's stories would only be painful were it not for the beauty of her prose. She writes simply and clearly. There is never a pretense of style or stylishness. Her tales of alcoholics, petty criminals, and perpetual losers in love are lit by the intimacy of her voice. Her reader is one of her losers. Who in the world that Jean Rhys created would care to be one of the heartless winners?

—Laura Furman
Austin, Texas

Contents

Introduction

This year, as always, when the reading got under way for *The O. Henry Prize Stories 2016*, the stories in the just-published 2015 collection whispered in my ear that this would be the year when I wouldn't find another twenty worthy of succeeding them. The haunting prediction held for a while, and then the first right one appeared. This year, Ron Carlson's "Happiness" reassured me that once again there were more wonderful stories to discover for *The O. Henry Prize Stories 2016*.

A story with that title might be greeted with skepticism. *Happiness? Really?* The word's in our Declaration of Independence but most of us can't say what it means to be happy, though we know the feeling when it's there and we miss it when it's gone.

Carlson's characters—the narrator, his brother, and two sons—are meeting at the family's mountain cabin in October to secure the place for the winter. When the narrator and his son stop for the night in Wyoming, it's five degrees above zero and there are pickup trucks parked in front of Wally's, home of the Wally Burger. The narrator knows that the "smart shepherds and collies" that would in warmer weather be in the trucks are in the motel's warm rooms. Game three of the World Series is on TV.

The narrator lays out these simple and ordinary conditions as if he were describing a moment in paradise.

The unhurried pace of the narration speaks of happiness as the narrator luxuriates in his modest way. He isn't about to rush anything, not his descriptions of the weather, land, trees, water, trout, or deer. Even the cabin's copper Levelor blinds have their moment. Happiness might glow and inspire, in memory and in its presence, but it doesn't last, a truth here not stated but implied by the aesthetics of the story.

The one female character, the boys' mother, isn't there, though she's present. She and the narrator are divorced, and we don't know why or when. A letter she's written to the narrator, which he receives from his son in the course of the story, is protected from the wet and treated with the same care as any other object. When the narrator tells family stories he includes her, calling her "your dear mother." Their parental love, which is also a love for each other, reveals itself in the narrator's careful patience as he instructs their sons.

By the time the vivid, beautifully written story reaches its end, the reader realizes why the narrator is determined to teach his sons how to take care of the cabin and wants them to know how to find a certain place on the land. The reason is more often the cause for tears and not happiness, though Carlson's "Happiness" would have it otherwise.

Joe Donnelly's "Bonus Baby" brings us to the ball game but from inside the very center, from the pitcher's point of view. The story takes place during a game—not just any game but a possible perfect game. We see how the pitcher's life has led him to this moment.

The pitcher's tics, familiar to any baseball fan, are his way of controlling what little he can in the uncontrollable game and in his life. He uses his tug, wipe, and touch to his cap to "harness energy and deliver it."

"Bonus Baby" is in the mythic tradition of Bernard Malamud's *The Natural,* in which baseball is treated as a variant on the Trojan War and the players like demigods and great warriors—but in Donnelly's vision the pitcher is a Midwesterner and speaks with the inherent groundedness and modesty of that region. He's the son of former athletes, homecoming king and queen, whose lives rolled downhill after high school. They spend their adult lives cooped up indoors, his mother as a secretary and his father as an alcoholic mechanic in a textile mill. Their positions are as different as can be from the pitcher's at the center of the playing field. The lesson they teach their son is that glory will not come, and the pitcher must throw beyond his inheritance of failure in order to win. The reader is with him every inch of the way.

In Charles Haverty's engaging "Storm Windows," a son recalls his father's enslavement to a house. Putting on storm windows and taking them down can be a strain even for those who love a house; Haverty's choice of the necessary and tedious chore is a shrewd one, for the twice-yearly task embodies the quasi-matrimonial devotion that some houses demand.

The narrator, Lionel, dislikes the big old-fashioned house, as do his mother and sister. "Only my father, who traveled often on business and spent the least amount of time there, loved the house." As an adult, Lionel is fated to take care of another demanding house because for his wife, "a child of divorce, the house represented a triumph over the chaos of her youth." For Lionel, his own house demands repeated chores and rescue operations performed, with any luck, by others. Lionel has no talent or taste for home repair.

"Storm Windows" reaches through Lionel's marriage with its tenderness and troubles, his daughters' sweetness in childhood and reproachfulness as young adults, his father's near-deaths, and his mother's consistent bitterness. In a crucial scene, the first of his "deaths," Lionel's father asks that his record of "Nessun dorma" from Puccini's *Turandot* be played. The aria ends with *"Vincèro"* (I will win), a moving cry against cold nights, death, and the darkness of the sky. Both Lionel and his father are stuck in the darkness of marriage, adultery, and their imperfect love for each other.

Haverty mixes a protest against mortality with the comedy of a sick man welcoming the ambulance attendants who've come to rescue him and offering them pancakes. The best we can do, the story might be saying, is to try to protect and love one another, as clumsy at it as we turn out to be. The author's combination of the quotidian and the unspoken gives "Storm Windows" its power.

Lydia Fitzpatrick's "Safety" is about danger, and it begins in a setting of sleepy safety, a children's gym class. It would be unfair in this case to give a précis of the story's action. However, it gives nothing away to say that, aside from an intelligent and compassionate dissection of this particular danger, the story's strength comes from the writer's capacity to understand the mature and fantastical lives of children. The story within the story is about trust.

The story is told from the points of view of several children and takes place in an elementary school. Everything in the school has been designed by adults for the children, from the décor to the daily customs, the lining up for phases of the school day, staying silent when asked to be, not speaking out of turn. The children trust in the adults in exchange for the promised safety. It's an agreement that honorable adults work hard to keep. Without the trust children are asked to give unquestioningly, the drama of "Safety" would be negated.

Though the story is about a type of violence that is hard to understand, its focus is not on harm. Rather, it concentrates on the ways in which characters relate, some at their best, others at their worst, and the story demonstrates that even the most evil character is capable of love.

. . .

Even stories categorized as fantastical are based on some level on familiar human life. In such stories it's not only the entertaining and delightful details that keep us engaged but also the shadow of the familiar. In Geetha Iyer's "The Mongerji Letters," the eponymous family has been charged for generations with the preservation of places, weather, and botanical and animal specimens that are extinct or nearly so. New items for the Mongerji collection arrive in envelopes. Another family, the Chappalwalas, explores the world, capturing the rare and the endangered, and sending their treasures to the Mongerjis. So it's been for many years. An ordinary letter in a matching envelope might contain the Arctic Ocean, complete with a polar bear. Storage was no problem for a long while—the many envelopes were filed away—but the world is changing, society degrading, and the Mongerji family is forced to retreat with the collection.

Time is both brief and elastic in Iyer's tale. Extinction puts pressure on those who would preserve the world, yet for these characters years go by as one of our days might pass. "The Mongerji Letters" is told through a correspondence between young Mr. Chappalwala and various Mongerjis, and Iyer gracefully pushes along time and information about events and characters through the various voices. She creates a constant tension between the timelessness of the strange events and our overwhelming sense that we're watching a dying planet, a very contemporary feeling. The tension is gently reinforced by the old-fashioned epistolary form and the style of the dates, for example, "September 7, —18." Is it 1918? 2018? 3018? Iyer's intricate story could be set at almost any time and be just as engrossing and as wise.

Robert Coover, a master storyteller, writes a small-town story that reads like a tale from the Brothers Grimm rather than a chapter of *Winesburg, Ohio*. "The Crabapple Tree" is narrated by a woman no better and no worse than her peers. Her parenting style can be summed up in her credo: "Children have to be allowed to grow up on their own—I've always believed that." The subtext of "The Crabapple Tree" is the power and anarchy of neglect.

Our narrator tells two tales simultaneously, one of magic and murder, the other of the ordinary people in her town going along to get along. The children in question are her own daughter and her peculiar playmates, the possibly magical and probably evil Marleen and Dickie-boy, whose birth caused his mother's death. Dickie-boy is sickly and weak, also lonely, and Marleen plays dangerous games with him, putting a leash around his neck and teaching him to act like a pet dog: "She even taught him to wee with his leg in the air."

Childish meanness is one thing but both Marleen and Dickie-boy have special powers. He can find lost things and she speaks in a bird language only Dickie-boy can understand. Cassandra-like, Marleen tells stories full of casual cruelty and no one believes her. When the narrator's daughter finds her friend playing with Dickie-boy's bones and Marleen explains how and why she came to have them, it's the end of their friendship and the beginning of more severe isolation for Marleen.

Very few children of any age really know their parents. In Marie-Helene Bertino's "Exit Zero," Jo, an events organizer, must deal with her dead father's house and possessions. Jo hasn't seen or heard from her father in years. It falls to her to erase the mess of his life, to clear out his house, and to sort through what he's left to see if there's anything worth keeping. Then she must clean the house—"ranch-style on a prim cul-de-sac"—and put it up for sale. She learns soon enough that she knew even less than she thought about her father.

When Jo tours the house, she finds "workout resistance bands" next to his bed. These surprise her but she's distracted from interpreting small puzzles by planning out her work: one room a day and Bob's your uncle.

More surprises await Jo, a big furry one in particular, and these make "Exit Zero" both funny and poignant. Her father's death is an inconvenient disruption to Jo's life, not least because it forces her into a relationship with him that's badly timed and unwelcome. She must allow it to do what it will.

Strange things are happening in the college town where David H. Lynn's "Divergence" takes place. Jeremy Matthis has just completed successfully his hero's journey: the trials and tests of a tenure review. For the rest of his life, he will be a very privileged person and one who might stay exactly the same.

To celebrate his victory, Jeremy's wife, Shivani, gives him a "blue-and-silver Italian bike" to replace his battered old ten-speed. The very first time Jeremy rides his new bike, his world changes.

Lynn chose well for "Divergence" when he gave his hero the achievement of tenure. The word itself implies not only holding, as in holding on to a job, but also being held by that job and its institution. Divergence isn't always welcome at an institution that depends on the steadiness of its faculty, nor by an anxious academic who assumes that he can finally relax. "Divergence" is an unexpectedly spooky story.

Diane Cook's "Bounty" is an imaginative meditation on privilege. Lust and greed enter the story, and chaos costars, but privilege plays the leading part. The story is postapocalyptic—the world is flooded—and the narrator is self-sufficient, very well prepared, and remains high and dry while all around people are drowning and starving. The narrator is condescending to those who've failed to plan ahead, and unmoved by their filth, illness, squalor, and even deaths. This is not the story of Noah; the well-appointed house is kept locked.

High-minded notions about compassion and charity aren't part of the narrator's outlook on the dying world. Men come to the door begging for food and shelter. Conditions worsen. Where once there were colonies above water, now they are "underwater, most of their inhabitants drowned." As it turns out, the narrator may be right to refuse to help. That way lies disaster.

One of the pleasures of Cook's tale of the nastiness of humanity under pressure is the comedy of possessions, of having just the right thing. The narrator is hopelessly materialistic and comments on the outfit of a drowning man, his nice suit, his interesting tie: "It was a kind of damask rose pattern, but nontraditional. Of course, only designers change designs. It's why we used to pay so much for them. We paid for innovation." Given its provisions of water, wood, gas, food, the narrator's clean and dry house might be the one next door in any prosperous American neighborhood, stuffed with Costco-sized supplies. And that the narrator decides to carry a knife next time someone tries to get into the house isn't exactly the stuff of science fiction: We're a nation armed to the teeth.

The narrator of Ottessa Moshfegh's "Slumming" is a schoolteacher on summer vacation in a derelict house she owns in a run-down town. Daily, she buys drugs from townspeople she calls zombies. She buys one foot-long sandwich per day. There's nothing else to do in the hardscrabble town. The sidewalks are crumbling and the people barely get by. She can afford to own her house and pay the taxes and insurance, even on her salary from teaching high school English in the city. She prides herself on not being her sister, who is rich and has a country house where there is a lot to do in the way of museums and concerts, and more people like her. The narrator isn't looking for neighbors or friends. She doesn't want to be part of the place. She is, as the story's title announces, slumming. The story takes its sinister turn when the narrator, despite her lackadaisical self, becomes involved with a native of the town, a girl much less fortunate than herself, younger and in need of a lot of help. The lure of the story is watching the narrator become a real neighbor, not wishing for it in the least. (See Peter Cameron's words on "Slumming," page 319.)

. . .

The narrator of "Cigarettes," the title and subject of Sam Savage's story, doesn't want to give up what the writer Jean Stafford called her "little friends." They are always with him. They are useful and punctuate time for him. They also separate him from any other friends he might want, and even his own daughter. Savage's brief tale is more tender than a reader might expect from a meditation on cigarettes. It's about choosing and loving.

We shed our cells when we're alive. We become ash when we're cremated. But in between cell and ash, especially if you're Aunt Marjorie in Adrienne Celt's "Temples," there are delicious, complicated cakes to eat, one every week. There's a great-niece to help raise. There's whole milk to drink and chicken cutlets to eat, and the prohibitions of her increasingly vegan great-niece to ignore. There's also the Mormon Church. Marjorie was born in Wrocław, now a city in western Poland, and there she met a boy who once was nothing and no one. After his conversion to Mormonism, he straightened out and performed miracles, inspiring Marjorie to convert also. Though she's a bit slack by nature, she loves the strictness of the church and, it seems, its confidence in its vision of this life and the next.

"Temples" examines the relationship between Aunt Marjorie and her great-niece, who mourns by remembering all the things there were to disagree with, to criticize, to admire, and to love, and all the things, as small as ash and as large as love, that left when Aunt Marjorie did.

The first sentence of Wendell Berry's "Dismemberment" tells the whole story: "It was the still-living membership of his friends who, with Flora and their children and their place, pieced Andy together and made him finally well again after he lost his right hand to a harvesting machine in the fall of 1974." From that sentence, we know that one loss almost becomes the loss of all that Andy Catlett values—work, marriage, family, friends.

And so Berry, a master poet, essayist, and fiction writer, unwinds "Dismemberment." From his first sentence he pulls the threads of membership and dismemberment, falling to pieces, breaking up, straight through the story. The unity of language and thought in Berry's story characterizes all the best short stories.

Even more than his three other O. Henry Prize stories, "Dismemberment" exults in the poet's love of language. Berry brings many meanings to the one loss and shows his main character coming apart and being put back together until he's able to rejoin his family and community. It's very hard to write a story that looks as simple as this one.

Shruti Swamy's "A Simple Composition" is a powerful sexual history of one woman, Arundathi, who tells us from the start that she isn't desirable: "I was shy, with a moon-shaped face and neat black hair, and I was so dark that my marriage prospects would have been grim had my parents not been well-off." Her first crush is on the man her parents engage to teach her the veena, a stringed instrument. Arundathi's teacher is charmless with one powerful exception that elevates him into a seducer: "As he played the veena his face became no more beautiful but it was touched by the grace of the music. . . . A simple composition, like the one he chose for me, became something else in the belly of his veena, something distilled to its essence. A longing for god, or for perfection."

Arundathi has no musical talent and is moved to submission by her teacher's great gift. In time, she marries a naïve boy, and moves with him to Germany. The accomplishment of the story resides in the bell-like tone of the narrative. It is clear and pure, as true as a confession might be at the end of the world, and anything but a simple composition.

Elizabeth Genovise's "Irises" begins with desperate romance and ends in deep and nourishing love.

A young dancer is leaving her husband to run away to New York with her lover, a musician. She's on her way to meet him but she hesitates. The problem is that she is pregnant. The narrator of "Irises" is none other than the baby watching from her mother's womb, telling us that she might never have been born if the day had gone differently. The lover is prepared to let the baby go. The dancer longs for a different life, a better version of the one she used to have before she was injured, and a child is not part of that dream. "Irises" is very much a woman's story, developing from a young woman's romantic dilemma and complicated choice to the deepening of a mother and daughter's relationship. It's natural for a child to think that a parent's fate was always to be a parent. "Irises" tells another tale. Our juror Lionel Shriver called Elizabeth Genovise's story "stunningly accomplished." (See pp. 320–22.)

In Rebecca Evanhoe's "They Were Awake," Emma, Amy, Becca, Carrie, Sabrina, and Liz gather for a potluck dinner. Each woman brings part of the meal, and all are "beautiful dishes," but the real nourishment is their friendship. With a little wine and good food, they begin to exchange dreams, or rather to tell the stories of their dreams. Each comments while narrating, and then they begin to talk about the nature of dreams: "You know, it's funny how we keep describing our dreams. Everyone keeps saying the word *realize*. 'I realized.' But it's not like that in dreams, is it? It's *knowing*. It's only after you wake up that you use the term *realize*."

What the reader begins to realize is that these attractive, intelligent, fortunate women are afraid. They are trapped in their dreams. Some of their fears are based in reality and, all the more frighteningly, some are not. Dreams represent our most vulnerable and personal selves, and also ourselves at our most irresponsible. No one has control over her dreams. The characters in "They Were Awake" exchange their dreams as casually as they might swap gossip, finding refuge in one another's company before sleep begins again.

. . .

Zebbie Watson's first published story, "A Single Deliberate Thing," will kick up memories in any reader who was ever in love for the first time and left behind. The narrator addresses her absent boyfriend, who has enlisted in the military and gone to a different state for basic training. That the lost connection between them is a close one is verified for the reader in every small detail she relates of her months with her dying horse and with her parents, who act as a loving Greek chorus dispensing useless adult wisdom. She tells him about the unrelenting heat and drought. He knows all the places, animals, and the people. He was with her in those places, and he's done all those things. Her summer is colored not just by the drought and her sick horse, but also by his silence in the presence of her words.

Asako Serizawa's "Train to Harbin" is set in Japan in 1939, when China and Japan were already at war. The story's concerns are still contemporary and resonant today. The guilt of civilian scientists who design and carry out torture for the military is a familiar subject. Serizawa's prose is dense, deliberate, and exact. She leads us through different time periods seen in different ways as her narrator works to make sense of his own participation in a dreadful experiment. Its consequences reach deeply into the long life he leads postwar, and for him it's as if the war will never end. Molly Antopol chose "Train to Harbin" as her favorite story, and her commentary is illuminating. (See pp. 317–18.)

Frederic Tuten's "Winter, 1965" gets everything right. The details of New York in the cold winter of 1965, as experienced by a young man who hopes to be a writer, are exquisitely correct and evocative. There are barriers between the narrator as he is and as he wishes to be. Though he works hard at his writing, he is unpublished. He makes a meager living as an investigator at the Welfare Department, a disheartening job if ever there was one. One depressing element is how long he might have the job; it promises him security, which feels like a prison sentence. His supervisor, who's been in the Welfare Department since the Depression, tries to console him by pointing out that his clients might tell him stories that might be useful to his fiction. "But he didn't need stories. What he needed was the time to tell them."

The plot of "Winter, 1965" works its way around a magazine and its editors, but the real story is in the young writer's ruminations: how his work will strike the leading intellectuals of the day (Edmund Wilson, Philip Rahv); his anxiety that nothing will ever change and that he will be forever trying to find more time to write and trying to be published; that he will be without love and without reward for his writing. His day job gives us a chance to see his painful compassion and the helplessness he feels about his clients, one gallant woman in particular. Still, in his anxieties, the writer isn't so different from other young people for whom the future looms threateningly.

Peter Cameron chose "Winter, 1965" as his favorite story of the present collection. (See page 319.)

Another story about a young writer takes place in an entirely different literary scene: our current milieu of writers teaching writing, workshops set in faraway places, and graduate degrees. Elizabeth Tallent's "Narrator," though filled with the precise emotions and moves of a novice writer feeling her way into a new role, is principally about the young woman's affair with an older man. She loved him before they met because she loved his writing, and she was naïve enough to think that loving his work and him were the same thing. When the workshop ends, it seems inevitable that she will stay with him, despite the pull of her husband and dog back in New Mexico, where she has a life. In Berkeley, she has only her lover and his increasingly uneasy company.

One of the charms of Tallent's story is her use of the narrator's misunderstanding of the older man's discomfort and her paralytic incapacity to leave when she knows she should. Though this mistake isn't exclusively a problem of the young, Tallent uses it to reveal the narrator's instability; there are moments when she seems so young and foolish that she could float away. Fortunately, Tallent is a generous writer and lets us see what the narrator becomes—the same person but wiser and all grown up. Without the final section, "Narrator" would be poignant; with it, the story is one that will stay with the reader.

—Laura Furman
Austin, Texas

The O. Henry Prize Stories 2016

Elizabeth Genovise

Irises

I AM EIGHT WEEKS IN the womb and my life is forfeit. It is the first week of October in Chicago; for my mother, wandering the city alone, I am not yet a daughter but rather a subtle shift in the taste and color of her world, unfurling at the edges of her consciousness as the autumn does just before it erupts into deep reds and yellows. She is meeting her lover at the train station at seven o'clock tonight and planning to follow him across the country to a commune in Oregon, where she will change her name and, if all goes well, elude her husband as well as the panic that has been rising in her since her first year of marriage.

Her lover, Joaquin, has promised to help her get me "taken care of," but has also implied that should she decide to keep me, he would be willing to step in as my father. He has not asked my mother to marry him, but this is because he knows my mother: She is not too wild to be loved, but she has been a firefly in a jar for too long. It was her pulsing and banging around behind the glass walls of her life that attracted his attention in the first place, that desperate stunted music that made him think of his first years at the piano, when he had already mastered Brahms on the public library's baby grand but had only a two-octave plastic keyboard at home that kept so many notes ethereal and out of reach.

It is not her pregnancy but my father's announcement of their impending move to East Tennessee that has broken my mother's vows. He does not know about me yet, but wants a child dearly, and so it is a double betrayal my mother is about to commit. The conductor's arm, pulling her onto the train that took her from the suburbs into the city this morning, pulled her away from every promise she had made to her husband and parents; she looked him in the eye as if for affirmation, and he said to her, "Careful, now; don't slip." Falling is exactly what all of this feels like, and she knows that therein lies the problem: She loves this feeling, and her husband's inability to understand it, to bother to understand it, has created the yawning chasm between them that she feels hopeless to span even over a lifetime together.

Her husband is not a bad man. He is a quiet, solid man; his name is Dan Ryan. He shares his name with a Chicago highway that is always thick with cars coming and going to work, and like the highway he is predictable, practical, a man of straight lines. He is a child of the Midwest, hardworking, and his dream (newly revealed to my mother) is to move them to Tennessee where he has family and a small homestead that is his now that his uncle has passed away. Like a father reading a bedtime story to his child, he has shown my mother old photos of the land, the little ranch house, the towering hills behind the big meadow, the goat barn. "Goats, Rosalie," he has told her excitedly. "We'll have our own milk. You can care for them while I'm working in Knoxville. You will love them." What my mother wants is music, coffee shops, paint, and a barre, but she simply nods and tries to smile. My father takes in her smile like a breath to fuel his own speaking and she is overwhelmed by the extent of his plans. She sees the remainder of her life in a flash, like a child's flip book, the pages rushing forward and the pencil-thin illustrations slimming down her choices as the years go by.

My father knows just enough about my mother's past—her years of living alone in different states, her solo travels—to feel confident that she has gotten the wanderlust out of her system. He never asks for details. He came into her life at the tail end of her ballet career, which took her from California to New York to Chicago and came to a shuddering stop when she injured her left knee. As though she had been a stripper or call girl, my father is made uncomfortable by references to her dancing life, but his discomfort is something only my mother and Joaquin can put into words: He has never known immersion in an art, never taken the artist's gamble, and so the sheer foreignness of my mother's commitment to dancing baffles him. A photograph of her onstage is like a memento of a former lover, a dangerous and enigmatic lover, and so my father bans them from the walls and prefers to frame snapshots of the two of them on their small-scale trips to places like Sister Bay in Wisconsin. He cannot imagine that my mother might not be content with spending the rest of her life on a small farm. He cannot imagine that she might want something outside of him, and this is partly her own fault: thrown out of her art like a vagrant from a freight train, my mother is bruised and uncertain, her pack dangling on her back. He is the embodiment of good sense. She is docile with him, a sweetness emerging from some part of herself she hadn't formerly known. It alternately pleases and sickens her.

My grandmother once told my mother that there is a splice of quartz inside each of us, like the quartz inside a compass or clock. We feel the stone glow warm when we find what it is we are meant to do. My grandmother was a singer; voice was her quartz, a second heartbeat that reminded her always of who she was. My mother's quartz is dance and Joaquin's is the piano. The saddest souls in the world, my mother believes, are those who never discover this thing within them. There is a difference between those who wander in search of that glow and those who wander in hopes of evading it. It is frightening, after all—that first awakening when the radiance within threatens to topple you. Even more terrifying is the decision to allow the fire to continue smoldering, because the brighter you let it get, the more terrible the darkness should you ever let it out. This is the analogy my mother has grown up with, and it has saved her in many ways, keeping her spirit alive even five years into her marriage when it seems there are no mirrors left in her world to reflect the truest parts of herself back to her.

Once a dancer, always a dancer. She has repeated this to herself through the thick cottony silence of her domestic life, over the towers of clean linen as she carries them up the stairs, into her cup of stale coffee as she tries to caffeinate herself through another conversation about finances. She has stopped doing her exercises because my father tends to watch her with open suspicion, as though detecting traces of infidelity in her suppleness. She has stopped writing letters to her girlfriends from her performing days because my father hovers over her shoulder, impatient as an excluded child on the playground. His vehement desire to have children terrifies her. Not even now, two months along, can she imagine trading in the weightless grace of a dancer's body for the anchored solidity of motherhood. But the weightlessness of flight alarms my father, who will not even board a plane or a carnival ride, much less try to empathize with my mother's fear of relinquishing her days of spanning half a stage's length with a doe's leap.

My father, who during their courtship was thrilled to discover my mother's love for the color red, had proposed to her with a lab-created ruby. In this final year before meeting Joaquin, my mother could no longer stand to look at her left hand, seeing only a tiny traffic light blinking there, unnaturally pink-red, reminding her that everything had stopped. It was in this year that my father's demand for a child became insistent. My mother could feel the walls closing in around her. The void that had opened when she left dance behind gaped wider every day and she often thought of an Edgar Allan Poe story, a lone man in the dark slowly discovering all the ways he might die if he should make a wrong move: a bottomless pit here, a swinging blade there. She was groping along those walls and she knew she was in trouble. In a final attempt to hold on to herself, she volunteered to teach ballet to impoverished young girls at a community center, and that was where she met Joaquin, a drifter who had been hired on as a pianist for the girls' dance club and choir. She knew it would upset my father but he surprised her by saying little about it. Perhaps he knew her distress; perhaps he was too drained by his own work to vent his frustrations. He ran his own tiny handyman shop just outside the city and he had to fight to keep his customers as better-funded businesses boomed around him. When he came home, he had just enough strength left to eat and shower before falling into their bed.

My mother taught the girls' dance class twice a week, which meant that she saw Joaquin just as often. There had been many chances to fall in love with him. There was the day she first saw him; his looks, not at all exotic as his name might imply, nonetheless startled her. He had softly curling chestnut hair and cornflower blue eyes with impossibly long golden lashes; his mouth was wide and delicate, his bones long. There were rumors that he had been homeless throughout his teens but she did not ask about his background. There was the day she caught him working on a composition, alone in a practice room. She had said nothing and had only watched, a still life herself before the tableau of him bent furiously over the keys, his lashes gold tags on his cheeks, papers with tiny scribbled notes all over the floor and sticking out of the pocket of his wrinkled button-down shirt. There were many days when their eyes would meet as he played for the girls and she led them through a simple routine. He seemed to know that this was only the merest glimpse of what she could do, and she could see the curiosity there along with something like yearning. But it was after months of his playing and her dancing that it happened. He asked her to come into the studio with him alone, before the girls arrived for their class, and she had imagined that he would take her in his arms and kiss her, or tell her that he was in love with her. Instead he sat at the piano and said, "Listen."

The opening notes cascaded down from the treble and arrested her where she was. As he played on, she knew first of all that the music was his own and secondly that he had written this solely for her. It was like singing a piece precisely in one's range; the movements of what he'd written suited her so truly that she began to dance without thinking about her knee or even how she looked to him. As she spun, she recognized that his insight went even deeper than she'd thought; this was a piece that she could dance to without hurting herself again. This realization made her eyes sting. She swayed her way back to him and when Joaquin had played the final chord she put her hand over his. The three notes thrummed there above their hands like a hummingbird and then flew away.

"How did you know—" my mother started to ask, and then the little girls began filing in, and she had to rise from the piano.

In her mind it was over then—her marriage to my father, the domesticity she had struggled to find a place in. Cracked though it was from injury and disappointment, her quartz was sunrise orange again; she was Rosalie. My father's voice over dinner that night was just noise. His socks, as she turned them outside-in before putting them in the washer, were gossamer light in her hands. She rose up on her tiptoes at odd moments, when it was unnecessary, as if to pluck the can of cinnamon down from the low cabinet above the stove.

Over time she learned that Joaquin had been a music teacher at a small academy but had lost his job due to his political views; he was something of a Socialist, he admitted to her, believing firmly that all things could be shared and that too much competition helped people expand their riches but left their souls boxed in the attic. My mother admired his spirit though secretly she found his ideas simplistic. There would always be rich and poor. Some would have a wealth of love, others a wealth of talent. She wanted to tell him that the singularity of his genius would only cause problems in a commune. But she refrained from saying so, because Joaquin was so set on at least attempting the kind of life his childhood had made him long for. They shared histories often. Music and dance, their ravishing force, the madness of the give-over they demanded; the way it felt to reach your stride, to become untouchable yet visibly burning, like a star flickering behind a curtain of clouds; all of this there was no need to talk about. Instead they talked about the places they'd been and the people who had reformulated the arc of their lives.

Joaquin told her that he'd had tiny, unforeseen seizures all his life, moments when he fell away from himself and teetered somewhere between his body and the world. He told her how afraid he was of those moments but how galvanized he was after, as though he had caught sight of someone he'd once loved and had feared he'd never see again. My mother told Joaquin about her obsession with ledges: precipices, points, pinnacles, the lonesome islands and cliff hikes and capes she had sought out whenever she'd had the time and money to travel alone. She told him about the breathlessness of it. The sense of an afterlife or a parallel one in the water below or the air above. The strange familiarity of it all. She fumbled for words; he told her not to worry about it. He knew. It was an addiction to the possibility of loss. The paradox was that it kept them alive. It kept their minds and bones sharp, alert to beauty in its transience.

Even as she walks the well-known streets of downtown Chicago, my mother is standing on this ledge. She has come into the city too early but she has done so for a reason. She needs to think. After all, she is a few hours away from leaving her marriage and a few days away from ending my life. To settle her nerves she is revisiting all her old haunts, most of them on Michigan Avenue and Lake Shore Drive. She never had the money to live here but took the train into the city every day for years to dance in the old Fine Arts Building, which is where she goes first. She walks the halls that smell musty, like old sheet music; she moves gracefully up and down the staircases worn marble-smooth by a thousand slippered feet. The piano rooms are quiet—pools of darkness from which the ivory keys shimmer like moonlight on water. Writers' desks in the studies wear the maps of old pen lines and the hollows of elbows. A bespectacled man attends the ancient elevator and seems pleased to have someone to shuttle up and down the floors. My mother is quiet, remembering.

When she leaves the building she walks to the Hilton, where she once took a lover. She is still amazed at Joaquin's generosity, his willingness to accept this about her past—the other men she has loved, her passionate affairs before meeting my father. She stands in the lobby where she had kissed this lover and fingers the leaves on the potted plants there. She gently loosens a leaf and sticks it in her pocket. Lastly she walks through the Art Institute, hurrying past most of the exhibits in her search for Monet's wall, where the same hut in a field is painted over and over again but at different times of day. First light, midday, a winter twilight. Colors and shifts that have rattled her since she first saw them in a book. She checks her watch. Her hands tremble.

She can hear her mother's voice, and all the arguments her mother would make right now against this decision. *You made a vow to your husband,* she would say. *There are ways to do what you love and still be a good wife.* But my mother is embittered—the memory of my father spreading out a map of Tennessee across her lap is fresh and infuriating—and she walks faster, heading for the stairway. My grandmother would tell her, *You're carrying a life inside of you. It's murder to end it before it can begin. That little soul was meant to come into this world; where will she go if you end her life?* But my grandmother always tended a garden as a hobby in spring and summer, and my mother thinks of evening primrose, how it grows everywhere and anywhere, and she thinks that human souls are this way, too; you cannot stop one from entering this world if this is where it wants to be. If you end a life before it can begin, it will simply find another passageway, another vessel, and it will be back. So there is nothing now to stop my mother from moving forward, and she does: down the stairs, out the door, and back toward the station. The old confidence and grace returning to her, she moves past strangers with ease. She bends to drop a dollar into a homeless man's extended hands. She has seen the Northwest and she can easily imagine this commune so close to the ocean. She sees herself walking the beaches alone, bringing a starfish back to Joaquin. The descending sun will be behind her, framing her with light, as she nears the camp. Making love, she and Joaquin will enter together into a long fall, and wake both heavy and unburdened, having given some memories and taken others.

When she reaches the station and claims her ticket, she shakes herself out of her light jacket and out of her doubt. She scans the crowd for Joaquin but does not see him; it is still just quarter to seven. He is coming with all of her luggage and she knows it might take a little time. She sits down on the floor, against the wall, with her legs crossed in front of her like a much younger girl. She no longer feels the faint weight of me inside her; I am as good as gone. Her life is about to begin again and she whispers to herself, "And I am not taking anything along."

In the end, it is Joaquin who saves me. Unknown to my mother, he too has spent the afternoon pacing the city streets, settling his nerves. He is about to take a woman away from her husband and to help her end her baby's life. He was dumped into foster care at four years old but he still has the distinct feeling that his father would not be behind him in this. For the first time in his life, he purchases admission into one of the city's premier museums—the Museum of Science and Industry—and wanders from exhibit to exhibit, looking at fossils, learning about coal mining and the human heart. It is six o'clock when he starts toward the exit and takes a wrong turn. He finds himself drawn toward an otherworldly rose light at the end of a dark hall, and he takes one last glance at the direction he was supposed to be heading in before starting down this hallway. When he comes near enough to understand what he is seeing, he stops, but he has no choice now but to come closer.

He moves slowly down the line of windows, beginning with the embryo, minute and curled and lovely, suspended in glowing fluid like a tiny snail. At six weeks, three days the child's body is identifiable, the head bowed as though in prayer. At eight weeks, six days the fingers are exquisite, a pianist's dream, and at nine weeks, five days the child is light and airy, a pixie suspended in a silky web like a hammock swinging from the placenta. At fourteen weeks the child is swathed in the amnion, hands curved as though to catch rain, and at twenty-one weeks she has a posture of anticipation with her hands wrung near her face. At twenty-three weeks she is unquestionably wearing an expression of anguished fear, but at twenty-six weeks her face is softened, calm, accepting. As though, in that last moment, it dawned on her that she was not alone.

Stricken, he stands there as others come up behind him. He wonders if he will ever wear that face—that look of peace. It is something he wants for himself, but even more so for my mother, and for me. He cannot imagine any of us having a chance at this if he and my mother do what they are planning to do. He backs away from the exhibit and starts toward the exit, and when he reaches the street, he turns toward home, bypassing the station. There will be a time when my mother hates him for failing to meet her, for vanishing, even after he writes her a letter telling her what happened, what changed his mind. Much later, she will realize that what she loved most was the dream they had together, and what he loved most was her.

But right now, my mother is sitting on the train station floor, chilled and alone. When she understands that no one is coming, she trades in her ticket and takes an evening train back to the suburbs. She makes it home in time to crush the note she had left on the kitchen table and to make my father's eight o'clock dinner. My father has been washing windows in the evenings for extra money, and he tells her of a near-accident, how he'd nearly fallen ten stories. My mother sees a deep mottled bruise on his right hand and imagines him reaching out with a ferocity she has never seen, clinging desperately to something solid. She picks up the injured hand and holds it to her forehead. His obvious surprise at her affection sears her heart; she wonders how much she has withheld, in her own desperate effort to hold on to something. For the first time it occurs to her that he too might be starving. She washes the dishes. She lingers in the kitchen as he showers, holding her hand to her belly as night falls. She comes to bed when he calls for her.

All of this, my mother tells me as we work in her steeply terraced garden behind the house in Tennessee. We are transplanting irises, and it is over the exposed rhizomes thick and bulbous as ginger that I have told her that I am thinking of leaving my husband and son. My son, the bully, the little terrorist who at seventeen has asphyxiated my home and my marriage with the mindless rage that his psychiatrist says puts him at risk for suicide; my husband, spineless, who caters to my son's every whim and to his own whims as well, always at my own expense. As we separate the bulbs and clip their leaves, I talk on, asking my mother why I should go on living like this, afraid of my own child, backed into corners, so lost in their demands that my words are flying away from me like dandelions' skeletons scattered in the wind. I can't write anymore; there aren't poems left in me at the end of the day. I want her to know how to get the words back. My voice gets louder as I demand a solution—from her, from anyone. Then she tells me this story, and when it's over, there is a long pause. I am stunned. I am waiting for the lesson. She has always finished her stories with a lesson, a simple "Now do you see?" But she has gone silent, and I watch her as she bends over the irises, cleaning them one at a time and laying them out to dry before we can move them to new soil. Over the course of her story we have dug out and separated dozens of them. She has become a gardener, my mother; she has found another gift deep within herself. This garden is almost mythical with its wild roses and tiger lilies and fiery lantanas growing in mad spirals. The neighbors have expressed mild disapproval of the disorder here. No doubt the irises will end up scattered where the eye would never expect the bright glow of blue. I decide that if my mother is going to refuse me her advice, she will have to at least answer me when I speak. Shakily I say, "Well? Where are we putting all of these?" But she only takes off her gloves and smiles faintly at me before walking up the stone pathway back to the house. I am left with the irises, the long line of them, each of them meant for some space I can't yet imagine.

Geetha Iyer

The Mongerji Letters

SINCE THE COLLAPSE OF one of the last dynasties of the Common Era and the subsequent end of the era itself, historians have searched for descendants of the Mongerji family, as well as descendants of the scribes who, under their employ, collected samplings of flora and fauna from around the world. The only evidence discovered thus far are the letters that follow. They are from Mr. Mongerji, his wife, Kavita, and two of the three Mongerji children, all addressed to a Mr. Chappalwala, thought to have been the last of the Mongerjis' scribes. Archivists continue to seek Mr. Chappalwala's side of the correspondence.

September 7, —18

Young Mr. Chappalwala,

This once, I wish my family's long correspondence with yours were more of a face-to-face transaction. Your letter telling of old

Mr. Chappalwala's passing has stricken us all. The Mrs. has not spoken more than ten words, and even the children are subdued. They feel their parents' grief. I find it hard to write even now—to acknowledge receipt of goods delivered, to speak of our continued business.

But the polar bear you stuck in the inner envelope suggests you are keen to continue in the family trade. That first explosion of teeth and air bubbles as the creature snapped at my face—what flair! I learned to swim backward that day, you know? It took a week to bail out the living room and pour the Arctic Ocean back into the envelope.

Our three-year-old, thankfully, was in the nursery when I released your capture, and thus spared his first swim. Meanwhile, our middle child, so enthralled by what you'd done, put on a diving suit and plunged right into the water. She stayed there for hours at a time. We nearly wondered if we'd lost the girl, and it was not until the living room was almost dry that the Mrs., in an inspired frenzy, thought to search inside the granary vase in the corner. We tipped out the last of the ocean into the outstretched envelope and grabbed our daughter by the ankles as she tried to follow.

The Mrs. remains put out. After the first shock, she said to me, "I would dearly like to see that young man right now," and I am not sure if she wanted to scold you for your exuberant capture or condole with you for your loss. She could not stop hugging our eldest boy, so perhaps it was the latter. He, you may know, will inherit the Mongerji collection and one day take over my correspondence with you. He did not like the bear—I believe it might have frightened him—but I think he will learn to appreciate your taste just as I learned to appreciate your father's.

Yes, you may consider this letter a renewal of the contract between our families. The unrest in these parts, I assure you, is a trifle, and should not come in the way of our important work. I enclose the usual sum of money. The clutch of purple bellflowers is a token from the Mrs. I believe they are from the collection, something your father must have sent us long ago. We keep him in our thoughts, and watch how you will follow him.

In anticipation,
Mr. Mongerji

June 5, —19

Mr. Chappalwala (Jr.),

Sir, my father requests that I write to you because he is engaged on urgent business in the city, and my mother is busy looking through the collection for important files. He says it will be good practice for me for the future, but I think by then we shall all have to go into hiding. I tried to explain this to my little sister and brother, but they are silly and won't listen to me. Jayu said she would go hide right now, and snuck into the letter with the sleeping octopus. But I stopped her from taking my little brother in with her. I am not irresponsible.

You see, my tutor, Mr. Ali, says the people don't trust us anymore, that they think we own what belongs to them. He says he hears murmurings from the village, and that we should all be prepared to flee. I don't understand it, really. I asked my father why we couldn't just give stuff away if others wanted it so badly—there are so many envelopes in our house that we wouldn't even miss them. He gave me such a look. He said I might as well scatter my ancestors' bones. As if I would do such a thing.

I have been patrolling the grounds with the night watchman, and I think I have another solution. In your next letter, can you send us a stampede? We could use it to frighten people off our grounds. Perhaps, then, my father will see I'm ready for his work—can you believe, he told me to copy from an old letter when writing to you? As if I didn't know how to say "Dear Sir" and "Thank you" for myself.

Sincerely,
R. Mongerji (Jr.)

December 12, —19

Dear Mr. Chappalwala,

This brief note confirms our change of address. The move to the city has been trying. Our new house is a two-story apartment. A top-floor loft, to be fair, and much more than I could have hoped for in our rush to secure a new living arrangement after the riots. But it will be quite difficult to curate the Mongerji collection in such meager environs. I am in conversations with the city's museum directors and the head of the opera house but, until then, most showings of the collection are quite humble affairs, pedestal displays of butterflies and ferns in the living room.

We are fortunate that the brass microscopes survived the move—the mayor was quite impressed with the diatom samplings you sent back from the Great Lakes this summer. It gives me an idea—when you trek the glacial sheets again this winter, would you look out for dark dimples against the blue ice? They are balls of moss collected around dust flecks—the locals call them glacier mice. I am told that entire herds of microscopic, eight-legged water bears lurk in that velvet warmth. It would make a fascinating presentation piece to the mayor. These days I find I need such friends more and more.

In expectance,
Mr. Mongerji

August 28, —22

Dear Mr. Chappalwala-ji,

My name is Abhimanyu Mongerji, but you can call me Abhi, like everyone else does. I am writing because Ammi said I must thank you for sending me the albino gray wolf cub for my seventh birthday. Daddy said it was not really meant to be a present—he wanted it for his work—but Ammi said it was only fair, because when Jayu-dhidhi and Rohan-bhaiya each turned seven, she got a fox cub and he got a baby camel with two humps.

Dhidhi's fox cub letter is lost, and Bhaiya said he sold his camel to someone at his new school, even though I think someone actually stole it off him. I tried to share my wolf cub with them both, except Bhaiya doesn't really like your letters anymore, and Dhidhi, well, she always complains that we should go to the cub's world instead of bringing the cub to us, so they're both no fun at all.

I have been thinking—were the albino cub's mother and father also white? I have looked and looked inside the envelope, but I can't find the parents anywhere, not even their footprints in the snow. Please could you tell me what happened to them?

Thank you,
Abhi

January 5, —23

Dear Mr. Chappalwala,

I imagine you have reached the Caribbean by now. Had I your talent for letters, I would share my winter with you—it hunkers in this city in a blanket of smog so thick I can barely see the streets from up high. Your long journey south through the western continents fills me with a strange dissatisfaction. I long for the old home, though I have tried hard these years to forget those days of warmth.

At any rate, I wanted to note that the release of your latest specimen caused quite a stir around the city. It moves me to critique your delivery in some detail. The instructions you placed within the outer envelope contained a couple of crucial errors. Surely, for example, you meant for us to "direct the mouth of the inner envelope away from the body" before lifting the flap?

I obtained the advised twenty-foot length of strong rope and went up to the roof with my children, as they had never seen such a specimen before. I opened the flap of the envelope and, before I knew what had happened, we were lofted into the upper branches of your bald cypress. We scrabbled for holdfasts among the slender branches while, below, the city swung like a concrete hammock. As I watched our rope slither off a lower tree branch into the fathoms of the cypress roots, I considered writing you a letter, explaining the importance of specificity. Because I should have tied that rope to my waist before venturing into your tree.

My daughter and my youngest, perhaps the world is still new to them for, instead of searching for a way down the cypress, they clambered farther up and out into it. They were in its limbs for hours, hooting to each other as my eldest and I sought our way down.

We were still fifteen feet off the ground when we reached the lowest rungs of the cypress. I will pause to acknowledge that the tree you selected is, indeed, a magnificent specimen. Its trunk is as fluted as a champagne glass, the bark silver whale hide. It must be the last of its size, and I am glad it is now under my care. But this did not strike me then. I looked down into the roil of the tree-beast's roots, snaggled into those distinctive stalagmites, and wondered if we would pierce ourselves upon them as easily as dinosaurs once did when they tried to climb up such trees in the past.

My eldest was impatient to be done with this adventure—he almost dashed himself to the ground in his haste to get down. I am grateful he suffered no injury. He disappeared downstairs, returned moments later with a poker from the fireplace to help stab and shove and stuff the whole tree, knot by knot, back down into its envelope. As soon as I was able to hop down from my branch, I took over for him. The heights of the tree, as the trunk tapered, were easier to pack away. My younger children were eventually shaken out of the upper branches and back onto the roof—they stood blinking like hatchlings thrown from the nest, their fingers tarred with cypress sap.

My daughter said there were fern gardens in the upper branches jeweled with small insects—that we had to climb back up to see. She looked so adamant, just like her mother, that my youngest, poor boy, looking back and forth between his sister's face and mine, started to cry. But I am not one to be swayed by tears or tantrums. It will not do to spoil these children more—they have lost so much already I hate to offer them any false sense that their lives as Mongerjis means what it once did. I continued to bend the cypress branches back into the envelope. By dawn, all that was left was to furl back the topmost twigs, the last pale leaf buds. I sealed the envelope with tape, filed it in the closet. I shall ask at the museum tomorrow if there is room somewhere to display a specimen so tall indoors.

You will find enclosed your payment, which you may note is smaller than it once was. I know your living is incumbent upon my support and, by way of apology, I remind you of our impoverished circumstances here. Take care to enclose better directions with your future dispatches, and to pick specimens easier to contain. This is, I fear, no longer a world for exhibitions of grandeur.

In humbled spirits,
Mr. Mongerji

P.S. Just now the Mrs. informs me, rather briskly, that she had to escort the local police up to the roof to show them we had dismantled the tree in its entirety. She did manage to persuade them that the letter was private property, but we shall soon have to merge the Mongerji collection with the city's to ensure its continued survival.

September 2, —25

Dear Mr. Chappalwala-ji,

Ammi looked through my grade-four textbooks today and her eyebrows became all one line, she was that angry. She asked me if I knew what an axolotl was. Then she asked me if I knew what lots of other animals were, and I didn't know any of their names, so she went to find Daddy and complained to him about my school and how I wasn't learning anything important there. Now it's decided that when I return from school Ammi will take me through the cabinets in the downstairs big closet, the ones with all the amphibians first, next the ones with all the extinct birds.

But Ammi shouldn't worry, I think, because Jayu-dhidhi is already teaching me all sorts of things in secret about your letters. Today she showed me one that came from the last century, from your great-great-grandfather or something. Inside was a rotten fruit—something long and brown. I didn't think it was special—I wanted to see more axolotls like Ammi had shown me before dinner—but then Dhidhi gave me a magnifying glass, and we both lay on our stomachs with our heads right over the fruit and she pulled apart its flesh to show that there was a small fly in there, smaller than an apple seed. Its body was the color of a peacock, and its eyes were the color of gold, and it was laying tiny eggs between the skin of the fruit and the flesh. The eggs were long and white, and under the magnifying glass they looked like tightly closed flower buds.

I asked Dhidhi whether if we left the fruit outside the envelope the eggs would hatch, but she said that everything trapped inside the Chappalwala envelopes was like an axolotl—it would never really grow up.

I know you are in Cameroon right now, and there are still forests there, so I was wondering, Mr. Chappalwala-ji, could you look for some more rotten fruit and send them to me and Dhidhi? She won't ask you herself, because she doesn't like to talk to people she doesn't know, but both of us are very interested in your letters, and we learn a lot from searching inside them. If Ammi or Daddy catches us while exploring we will just say it's because we want to learn more than what they teach us at school. They don't have to know we're doing it just for fun.

Thank you,
Abhi

May 30, —26

Dear Farshad,

You do not know me, and my husband does not know this, but I once met you when you were no more than five. I must have been some twenty-six years old then, married less than a decade, and utterly entranced by you Chappalwalas.

I had visited your home, northeast, beyond the mountain pass. Yes, in your people's fashion, by letter. The air there was so clear I feared my own breath would pollute it. The ground sparkled with little flowers—I forget their name—that hung their lilac heads under weight of dew. I thought I would never return home.

Your father, if I knew him at all, was too discreet to have ever mentioned this story to you, and you will hardly remember my presence yourself. When introduced, you nodded your little head at me without ever meeting my eyes. You had just learned the trick of putting lizards into little greeting cards, and raced off into the woods beyond the village as soon as your father let go of your shoulder.

Nevertheless, I trust you now with the same discretion I came to expect from your father.

My reason for contacting you is to caution you. Since you are a full five years older than my oldest child, I expect you will act with maturity. I am aware you correspond with my younger children, and I know that your trinket specimens to them enrich their lives better than anything else this city can offer. My youngest, my bright star, flourishes in his knowledge of the natural world. He is the natural heir to the Mongerji collection, though my eldest is first entitled to it. My daughter is wild as grass seed, and if not for your portals into the world, she would run away, I am sure of it. She is my blood, after all.

But do be careful as you indulge my children's requests. The Mongerjis have made their name in the world by asking of others, and we have fallen by asking too much. I do not wish my children to follow in the family's fate.

Sincerely,
Kavita Mongerji

July 1, —27

Dear Mr. Chappalwala,

Have you any children? Do you take them on mini-expeditions with you to teach them your trade? How is it among you folk? For as long as I can remember, the Chappalwalas have collected for the Mongerjis, and I never thought to ask my own father how it was our relationship began.

I am attempting to convince my eldest that the great legacy

that is our family's work must remain in our hands, even as we are employed and directed by city officials. It is difficult. He is on break from university and occasionally deigns to listen as I narrate the contents of each letter, specifying when and where they were delivered from, the conditions under which they may be opened. Sometimes he will gesture expansively out the window at the city below. He will say, "It's all for nothing, Father, just look where we live now."

I think the boy resents my employment, collaborating with the museum curators. He expected, I believe, to inherit my work, not my job. He remembers when the Mongerjis hosted galas in the old home, private exhibitions of specimens, immersive snapshots into distant worlds. Only some months before we lost our home to the rioters I had been coaching him to take our guests snorkeling in the coral ponds we had set up in the gardens. Ironic, that we never had a chance to show off those corals. They were to have been a retrospective, after all.

I sometimes envy my youngest one. He does not remember the old home, really. The vast fields, the conservatory, the many libraries budding off the main house. He was not yet four when the riots happened, has no memory of how he was passed, arm-over-shoulder, from handyman to gardener-wala to housemaid, down the bucket chain we made through the old escape tunnels for rescuing family valuables.

My daughter is sullen. Of course she must be groomed, as her mother was, for entry into someone else's home, but she resists such plans. Since the Mrs. is preoccupied with the education of our youngest, and I try as much as possible to expose the eldest to the museum, our poor middle child, I think, suffers. But I cannot take her to work with me. I fear that if she disappears in the museum archives—which are quite substantial, even without the addition of the Mongerji collection—I may never find her again. As it is, most evenings when I return from work I must retrieve her from somewhere inside the diminished family files. That is a task in itself—sometimes she won't even empty the envelopes out, instead she just climbs inside. Tell me, is this wise? I have never questioned your family's craft, but I worry, these days, as my daughter becomes increasingly entangled within the mechanics of your letters, whether she endangers herself.

She used to cry when I took crates of our letters—overstock, I started to call them—for transfer into the city museum. I believe she even stole some of those letters, but I have no way to prove it, as I have never been able to find them on her person or in her room. She only ever seems to be in my study, or in the downstairs closet, exploring what little we still keep in the apartment.

Today I shook her out of your last dispatch, the liana humming with weaverbirds. She seemed to have no memory of what she had been doing in there. I ask her again and again why she goes to a place where she is as motionless, as unconscious as the words on this page, but she cannot, or will not, explain it. Perhaps it is like sleep to her—she always emerges as if wrenched from some dream. I sometimes wonder if you could deliver us something that would terrorize her, in order to cure her of her addiction.

I remain, a devoted father,
Mr. Mongerji

P.S. I would like to request, on the museum's behalf, some more showy examples of miniature homes within homes. The liana was a highlight of the summer exhibition, strung boldly against a blank wall of the museum. The public were thrilled to see the tiny beaks poke out of the weaverbird nests, the little flashes of yellow and black as the fledglings tested out their wings—some even asked if it was clockwork.

A thought occurs—could we market postcard versions of some of the large displays at the gift shop? Perhaps some ornamental beetles, or flowers smaller than fingernails? As loath as I am to see Mongerji-like specimens in the hands of everyday folk, I must admit, this is the way the world is turning, is it not?

April 19, —28

Dear Mr. Chappalwala-ji,

Jayu-dhidhi is trying to discover your secret. Today, I received a small coin envelope in the mailbox addressed from our own apartment. I tried to shake out what was inside, but it was well stuck in there, so I had to hold the envelope open to my eye like it was a kaleidoscope.

Pressed to the inner seam was a plate of tree bark. On the bark was a small oval of lichen, a thumb-peel of orange skin, surface broken by tiny black cups. Along one of the walls of the envelope Dhidhi had scribbled, "The lichen is blooming!"

It was true—the cups would release spores that would stick to more tree bark and slowly new lichens would spread like slow-motion fireworks across the tree. But that might be many years from now and, at any rate, the experiment failed. Dhidhi took me to see the tree from which the lichen had come, an oak in a city park. Now it has an ugly hole in it from where Dhidhi captured the lichen. It is bleeding from the wound. Dhidhi didn't want me to see, but I knew her eyes had tears in them when she saw what she had done.

Mr. Chappalwala-ji, I know it is rude to ask you your secrets, but could you send me a hint of how to make letters like you do? Dhidhi is trying very hard to prove to Daddy and Rohan-bhaiya that she can look after our collection as well as they can—maybe even better. After she graduates this year, Daddy wants her to think about marrying, but I know she doesn't want to. If she could perfect your trick, Daddy might reconsider and let her stay. Nobody else can change his mind, not even Ammi, which is why Ammi never scolds Dhidhi anymore when she does something she shouldn't do, or goes somewhere she shouldn't go. I want to help Dhidhi too.

Can you help us?

Thank you,
Abhi

P.S. I have looked in the little envelope again, and the piece of tree bark just broke in two. I am sending it to you to hide it from Dhidhi.

June 25, —31

Farshad,

Business first. My husband's weak health these months compels me to assist him in his letter writing. He would like to commend you for your current catches off the southeast coast of Africa. He is particularly amused by the electric blue sea slugs, although the museum is rather more interested in the jellies. They wonder if you might postpone your voyage to Socotra till after the midseason spawn. There is a market, they say, in selling juvenile specimens at the gift shop.

I would advise you to think carefully about this. The Mongerjis are not merchants, though my eldest is convinced otherwise. He is beginning to price the remains of the collection—your predecessors had the luxury of capturing herds, not single specimens, and he is convinced he can isolate individuals for private collectors. I know from experience that separating fragments from those letters is not easy, but he will not listen. No one in this family does.

At any rate, your original plan to reach the south seas off the Arabian Peninsula is a good one. Socotra must be exquisite at this time of year, the sun's blaze sending all but the hardiest of creatures into hiding. Your father once told me he spent four months on the archipelago in search of worm snakes. Perhaps you might confirm that there indeed are no more left on the islands. I trust you know the trick of carrying a snowpack letter into the desert? I was quite charmed when your father told me of this.

On to personal matters. I suspect you are aware of my daughter's attempts at delivering herself from the city to—I'm not sure where. Perhaps she wishes to escape to you, as I once attempted when I visited your father. If she does show up, would you reassure her that the unpleasant feeling of being caught in a loop will eventually wear off? When I visited your father, I could not stop rubbing my shoulders, as if for warmth. It was as if my body had been hypnotized into doing what it had remembered doing just as it stepped into the envelope.

I sent myself to your father in a peat bog. A square meter quadrant of mosses and ferns, it was, though I only remember the delicate plumes of vapor coming off it, just as high as my knees. The sample had been collected at dawn, the skin of the bog sweating kisses into the disappearing cold air of night. Your father was an artist. His specimens arrived as though they were caught in three-dimensional paintings of their landscape. I do not blame myself for falling in love.

Your father was very kind. Once I had recovered enough, he introduced me to you, showed me his home, took me around the village to meet the rest of the Chappalwala clan. I met your mother. You have her face, I remember, eyes dark as cherries. Your father explained to me that the Chappalwalas are like skimming stones—you have traveled so much for so long, you cannot form connections to places or people anymore. That you gather together only because you understand each other's displacement—that under-the-skin feeling of being stuck, making the same gestures and decisions, even when you are in a new place, or when you return to an old place and find everything changed.

Have you seen the round pit of bare rock on the west slope past your village where that little creek cuts through? Your father scooped it out. That was what he sent me back with. I keep that letter on my person always. I feel I need to return to that piece of slope more often these days than I did when my children were young. The grass is bent, and I imagine it is still just as warm from the heat of our bodies, lying side by side, saying goodbye.

I have no doubt that my daughter will attempt what I did. It is not my place to interfere with that choice. But please, if you send her back, or forward, send her with thoughts that are happier than sad. She has a particular affection for beetles. Perhaps distract her with one of those as you send her away. The feelings that linger when we reemerge from the envelopes are the ones we entered with, and I would not have her feel as bereft as I did when I came home.

Kavita

December 30, —32

My dear Mr. Chappalwala,

When I was thirteen, I came down with a case of chicken pox so severe I had to sleep in an armchair at night, so afraid was I of turning over in bed, popping open my skin in the process. My father, not normally given to demonstrations of affection, came into my room one evening waving a letter.

"From Mr. Chappalwala," he said, referring, of course, to your father. He crouched by my chair and opened the envelope, releasing a flock of river ducks into the room. I watched them fly back and forth over the floor, their webbed feet grazing the silk carpet, clawing for water.

My father told me the river ducks came from Chiang Rai. He told me your father, old Chappalwala, had stood on the bank where the Mekong met the Ruak, where Thailand, Laos, and Myanmar rubbed flanks like slumbering lizards. The sun rose over Laos, and the birds emerged from the reeds in Myanmar and flew straight across the watery confluence to Thailand. They flew right into your father's arms—he had an envelope stretched open, at the ready.

I often thought about those ducks from Chiang Rai. Were they not in fact Burmese river ducks—and of course, back then, it was Burma—paying a visit to Thailand? But then again, who was to say they were not seasonal birds, migrating from farther north or south, sojourning in the waters of the Golden Triangle before continuing elsewhere? And still, perhaps they were Laotian river ducks, for when they flew out of that envelope, their backs still flashed with bronze coins of sunrise, Laotian sunrise, and surely no one can argue with the sun's claim upon a creature, that soft light burned into its flesh.

Years passed, my father died, and the letter was misplaced—I believe stolen by one of the staff. I had long since given up any pretensions I could run the Mongerji house as my father had. I felt porous with lost memories. On the anniversary of my father's death, I wrote to old Chappalwala, begging him to return to Chiang Rai for more river ducks.

He was gone a month before a letter arrived. He explained that Chiang Rai had greatly changed. From his old spot, where the Mekong and Ruak converged, he could see the lurching frame of a casino, half built, for tourists to Laos. He himself had spent an informative couple of hours in the museum built on the Thai side of the Golden Triangle, documenting the migration routes of ancient opium traders.

Old Chappalwala befriended a woodworker, a small, middle-aged man who plied his trade under the corrugated tin awning of a shop with only three walls. The man claimed it was good business, selling scrap-wood sculptures to tourists wandering out of the museum, the new hotel, the river dock. Chappalwala said the woodworker remembered the river ducks from when he was young. He said they flew so thick across the water that its surface churned into foam. He said the last time he had seen a river duck was five years ago in an old woman's garden, a string tied to its foot and fastened to a mulberry bush.

I could not believe it. I crumpled your father's letter and flung it across the room. In desperation I picked up the envelope, its corners pulpy as cloth from travel, pried it open, and turned it over.

A number of small objects rattled out. I picked one up. A duck, carved from pale yellow wood. Attached to its tail was a pin with a rotating bead, three chicken feathers stuck into the bead like the blades of a propeller. To be hung in an open window, I suppose, so the wind would catch the feathers and make them turn. There were fifty wooden ducks in all. I enclose one in this letter for you.

I wonder, my dear young friend, if you might make the journey your father made. You are on the other side of the world, I know, but I am an old man now, more porous than ever. Could you find me the old woodworker? Could you send him to me? I am curious about him. I wonder, when he was a boy, whether he ever noticed, beneath the sunlight's dapples, what color the river ducks' back feathers were. I no longer remember.

Yours in earnest,
Mr. Mongerji

March 27, —33

Mr. F. Chappalwala,

You have no doubt heard, by now, of my late father's passing, since at least one of my siblings writes to you quite frequently. I have no comment on what the other one does, or even where she is. I wonder if she even knows our father is dead.

I will be brief, as others in my family have not been. As the new head of the Mongerji line, I hereby dissolve the contract between my family and the Chappalwalas. We have no need for your work, as the collection we have amassed no longer carries the currency it once did. I thank your family for their generations of service to us.

On a personal note, do I ask for too much if I request that you cease communications with what remains of my family? They are far too much in thrall with acquisition—as if collecting pieces of the world will help them understand their place in it better. They would do better to be released from the influence of your letters. It seems when you are not peddling plants and animals you fleece us of our hopes. No more, please. Let us be.

Sincerely,
R. Mongerji

June 15, —33

Dear Farshad-bhaiya,

Please find enclosed the latest of the Mongerji collection, the last of what remained in the house. Tomorrow I go to work for the first time with my brother. It will be a while before I have access to the collection archived within the museum, but I am letting you know now so you can remain on standby. The museum will not be long in discovering what I plan to do. Expect one or two fat manila envelopes, and when you receive them, please clear a wide berth around you and open the flaps of the envelopes away from your body.

I almost wish I could be there to see the explosion. All the collection—hundreds and hundreds of years of hard work, so many yellowed envelopes. It makes me chuckle even now.

I have been meaning to ask you—how strong are your muscles? Before Jayu-dhidhi left, she put a whole rat into a letter, and I watched her heave the slim sheet of paper to the mailbox like it was attached to a dragnet filled with whales. It must be so much effort to consider and consider and consider every minuscule little detail of the creatures you capture, to hold all of their intricacies so they stay intact on their journeys. Dhidhi told me things about the rat I would never have known—about the dirt caught between the grooves of its nails, the microfauna within its guts. She said the last thing the rat had eaten was the stub of a pear and its stem. She said it took her five hours of considering to figure that out.

I cannot imagine how heavy the rest of the collection is, and would appreciate any advice you have to offer. If the deliveries are successful, Ammi has agreed to send me to where you and Dhidhi are, though I think Dhidhi must be off somewhere else again—she could never stay still. I asked if Ammi would want to come with me, but she says she has a letter of her own, and will be quite satisfied with where it takes her.

Meanwhile, the next time Dhidhi breezes through to post something, would you tell her to stop? I really like the beetles she's been sending, but the whole point is to return them now, isn't it? When I leave, I want to travel light, and I have beetles from twenty different places in my pocket already—my wallet almost won't close. Just tell her to describe them to me next time.

Thank you,
Abhi

Elizabeth Tallent

Narrator

Near the end of what the schedule called the welcome get-together, two women—summer dresses, charm—stood at the foot of the solemn Arts and Crafts staircase where he was seated higher up, mostly in shadow. That could have been me his silence fell on: I had wanted to approach him, and had held off because all I had for a first thing to say was *I love your work*, and I had no second thing. Brightly, the women took turns talking in the face of his eclipsing wordlessness. *This is you in real life?* I said to him in my head. The women at the foot of the stairs were older than me, in their late thirties—close to his age, then, and whatever was going on with him, they looked like they could handle it, and this was a relief, as if being his adoring reader conferred on me the responsibility to protect us all from any wounding or disillusioning outcome. But they were fine. Unless they let it show that they were hurt, his silence could be construed as distractedness or even, attractively, as brooding, and who gained from letting his rudeness be recognized for what it was? Not him. Not them. They might feel the need to maintain appearances if they were going to be his students in the coming week, as I would not be, having been too broke to enroll before the last minute, and too full of doubt about whether I wanted criticism. I didn't get to watch how the stairwell thing ended. A boy came up to me, and I made my half of small talk: New Mexico, yes as beautiful as that, no never been before—what about you, five hundred pages, that's amazing. Throughout I was troubled by an awareness of semifraudulence; his confidence was so cheerfully aggressive that mine flew under his radar. The full moon would be up before long and if I wanted we could ride across the bridge on his motorcycle, an Indian he'd been restoring for years—parts cost a fortune. There was a night ride across the bridge in his novel and it would be good to check the details. *Long day*, I said—*the flight, you know?*

Enough students were out, in couples and noisy gangs, that I didn't worry, crossing campus. True about the moon: sidewalks and storefronts brightened as I walked back to my hotel, followed, for a couple of bad blocks, by a limping street person who shouted, at intervals, *Hallelujah!* On the phone my husband told me a neighbor's toddler had fallen down an old hand-dug well but apart from a broken leg wasn't hurt, and he had finished those kitchen cabinets and would drive them to the jobsite tomorrow, and our dog had been looking all over for me, did I want to talk to him? *Goofball, sweetheart, why did you ever let me get on that plane?* I asked our dog. When my husband came back on the phone he said *Crazy how he loves you* and *So the first day sucked, hunh?* and *They're gonna love the story. Sleep tight, baby. Hallelujah.*

Though I hadn't done it before, the homework of annotating other people's stories was the part of workshop that appealed to the diligent student in me. The bed strewn with manuscripts, I sat up embroidering the margins with exegesis and happy alternatives—if someone had pointed out that *You should try X* can seem condescending, I would have been really shocked. At two a.m., when the city noise was down to faraway sirens, I collected the manuscripts and stacked them on the desk. They were not neutral, but charged with their writers' reality the way inti-

mately dirtied belongings are—hairbrushes, used Band-Aids—
and I couldn't have fallen asleep with them on the bed. Where,
in Berkeley, was his house, and was he asleep, and in what kind
of bed, and with whom beside him? Before I left the party I had
sat for a while on his step in the dark stairwell. All I had to go
on were the narrators of his books, rueful first-person failers at
romance whose perceptiveness was the great pleasure of reading
him, but I felt betrayed. Savagely I compared the ungenerosity
I'd witnessed with the radiance I'd hoped for. How could the
voices in his novels abide in the brain of that withholder? The
women had not trespassed in approaching, the party was meant
for such encounters. Two prettier incarnations of eager me had
been rebuffed, was that it? No. Or only partly. From his work
I had pieced together scraps I believed were *really him*. At some
point I had forsaken disinterested absorption and begun reading
to construct a him I could love. Think of those times I'd said
not *His books are wonderful*, but *I'm in love with him*. Now it was
tempting to accuse his work of inauthenticity rather than face the
error of this magpie compilation of shiny bits into an imaginary
whole. He had never meant to tell me who he was. Nothing real
was lost, there was no fall from grace, not one page in his books
is diminished, not one word, you have the books, and the books
are more than enough, the books will never dismay you, I coaxed
myself. But the feeling that something was lost survived every
attempt to reason it away.

The days passed without my seeing him again, and besides
I was distracted by an acceptance entailing thrilling, dangerous phone calls from the editor who had taken the story, whose
perfectionism in regard to my prose dwarfed my own. Equally
confusingly, my workshop wanted the ending changed. The ending had come in a rush so pure that my role was secretarial, the
typewriter chickchickchickchickchick-tsinging along, rattling
the kitchen table with its uneven legs; now I couldn't tell if it
was good or not, and I needed to get home to regain my hold

on intuition. At the farewell party in the twilight of the grand redwood-paneled reception room hundreds of voices promised to stay in touch. At the room's far end, past the caterer's table with its slowly advancing queue, French doors stood ajar, and two butterflies dodged in, teetering over heads that didn't notice. They weren't swallowtails or anything glamorous, but pale, small nervous slips dabbling in the party air, and my awareness linked lightly with them, every swerve mirrored, or as it felt enacted, by the consciousness I called mine, which for the moment wasn't. After a while they pattered back out through the doors. Then there he stood, watching them go. And maybe because rationality had absented itself for the duration of their flight, what happened next felt inevitable. I stared. His head turned; when he believed I was going to retreat—when I, too, was aware of the socially destined instant for looking away—and I didn't, then the nature of whatever it was that was going on between us changed, and was, unmistakably, an assertion. Gladness showered through me. I could take this chance, could mean, nakedly—rejoicing in being at risk—*I want you*. Before now I'd had no idea what I was capable of—part of me stepped aside, in order to feel fascination with this development. But did he want this? Because who was I? He broke the connection with a dubious glance down and away, consulting the proprieties, because non-crazy strangers did not lock each other in a transparently sexual gaze heedless of everybody around them, and he wasn't, of course he wasn't, sure what he was getting into. If I hadn't been so happy to have discovered this crazy recklessness, no doubt I would have been ashamed. As it was I was alone until he looked up to see whether he was still being stared at, as he was, greenly, oh shamelessly, by me, and he wondered whether something was wrong with me, but he could see mine was a sane face and that I, too, recognized the exposedness and hazard of not breaking off the stare, and this information flaring back and forth between us meant we were no longer strangers.

We spent the night over coffee in a café on Telegraph Avenue, breaking pieces off from our lives, making them into stories. At the next table two sixtyish gents in identical black berets slaughtered each other's pawns. Look, I told him, how when one leans over the board, the other leans back the exact, compensatory distance. When I recognized what I was up to, proffering little details to amuse him and to accomplish what my old anthropology professor would have called *establishing kinship—We're alike, details matter to us, and there will be no end of details*—I understood that delight, which had always seemed to belong among the harmless emotions, could in fact cut deep. It could cut you away from your old life, once you'd really felt it. The most fantastic determination arose, to stay in his presence. At the same time I understood full well I would be getting on an airplane in—I looked at my watch—five hours. He, too, looked at his watch. Our plan was simple: *not* to sleep together, because that would make parting terrible. We would stay talking until the last minute, and then he would drive me to the airport, stopping by my hotel first for my things. I didn't have money for another ticket and couldn't miss my early-morning flight.

He left it till late in the conversation to ask, "You're, what—?"

"Twenty-four." I stirred my coffee like there was a way of stirring coffee right.

"What's in New Mexico?"

"Beauty." I didn't look up from my coffee to gauge if that was too romantic. "The first morning I woke up there—in the desert; we'd driven to our campsite in the dark—I thought, *This is it, I'm in the right place*."

Another thing he said across the table, in the tone of putting two and two together: "The story that got taken from the slush pile, that was yours."

A workshop instructor who was a friend of the editor's had spread the word. "Someone"—the moonlight motorcycle-ride guy—"told me, 'It's lightning striking, the only magazine that can transform an unknown into a known.' Not that I'm not grateful, I'm completely grateful but what if I'm not good at the *known* part."

"Why wouldn't you be good?"

"Too awkward for it."

"You're the girl wonder."

That shut me up: I took it to mean that instead of complaining, I should adapt. I was going to go on to hear a correction encoded in other remarks; this was only the first instance. "You're chipper this morning, kid"—that was a warning whose franker, ruder form would have been *Tone it down*. "You look like something from the court of Louis Quatorze" meant I should have blow-dried my long hair straight, as usual, instead of letting its manic curliness emerge. When he would announce, of his morning's work, "Two pages" or "Only one paragraph, but a crucial one," I heard, "And what have you gotten done? Since your famous story. What?" I understood that I could be getting it all wrong, but I couldn't not interpret.

Those first charmed early-summer days he put on his record of Glenn Gould's *Goldberg Variations*, which I had never heard before, and taught me to listen for the snatches of Gould's ecstatic counter-humming. When I was moved to tears by Pachelbel's "Canon in D" he didn't say *Where have you been?* He played Joni Mitchell's "A Case of You." He sang it bare-legged, in his bathrobe, while making coffee to bring to me in the downstairs bedroom. One morning, sitting up to take the cup, I asked, "Do you remember at the welcoming party, you were sitting in the stairwell and two women came up to you? And you wouldn't say anything?"

He needed to think. "Esmé and Joanie, you mean. They just found out Joanie's pregnant. Try getting a word in edgewise."

My stricken expression amused him; he said, "You have lesbians in New Mexico, right?"

It seemed easier to make a secret of that first, accusatory mis-reading of him than to try to explain.

I hadn't caught my flight. Instead we made love in the hotel room I hadn't wanted him to see, since I had left it a mess. "Was this all you?" he asked, of the clothes strewn everywhere, and it was partly from shame that I lifted his T-shirt and slid a hand inside. When we woke it was early afternoon and my having not gone home became real to me. My husband had a daylong meeting that prevented his picking me up at the airport—at least he was spared that.

Where he lived was a comradely neighborhood of mostly neglected Victorians, none very fanciful, shaded by trees as old as they were. His place was the guest cottage—"So it's small," he cautioned, on the drive there—belonging to a Victorian that had tilted past any hope of renovation. In its place some previous owner put up a one-story studio-apartment building, rentals that, since he disliked teaching, provided the only reliable part of his income. His minding about precariousness (if it was) was embarrassing. It was proof that he was *older*. Even if they could have, no one I knew in New Mexico would have wanted to use the phrase *reliable income* in a sentence about themselves: Jobs were quit nonchalantly, security was to be scorned. With the help of an architect friend—a former lover, he clarified as if pressed; and never do that, never renovate a house with someone you're sleeping with—all that was stodgy and cramped had been replaced with clarity and openness, as much, at least, as the basically modest structure permitted. This preface sounded like something recited fairly often. The attic had been torn out to allow for the loft bedroom, its pitched ceiling set with a large skylight, its wide-planked floor bare, the bed done in white linen. The white bed was like his saying *reliable income*—it was the opposite of daring. No man I had ever known, if it had even occurred to him to buy pillowcases and sheets instead of sleeping on a bare mattress, would ever have chosen all white—my husband, for some reason I was imagining what my carpenter husband would say about that bed. Sleeplessness and guilt were catching up with me, and there was the slight feeling any tour of a house gives, of coercing praise. I was irritated that in these circumstances, to me costly and extraordinary, the usual compliments were expected. "Beautiful light," I said. The narrow stairs to the loft were flanked by cleverly fitted bookshelves, and more bookshelves ran around the large downstairs living room, off which the galley kitchen and bathroom opened, and, on another wall, doors leading to his study and the guest bedroom that would be mine, because, he said apologetically, he couldn't sleep through the night with anyone in bed with him—it wasn't me; he hadn't ever been able to. Was that going to be all right? Of course it was, I said. I sat down on the edge of the twin bed. *I can get the money somehow, I can fly home tomorrow.* Even as I thought that he sat down beside me. "When I think you could have gotten on that plane. I would be alone, wondering what just hit me. Instead we get this chance." In that room there was a telephone, and he left me alone with it.

He had his coffee shop, and when he was done working, that's where he liked to go—at least, before me he had gone there. Time spent with me, in bed or talking, interfered with the coffee shop, and with research in the university library and his circuit of bookstores and Saturday games of pick-up basketball, but for several weeks I was unaware that he, who liked everything just so, had altered his routines for my sake. From the congratulatory hostility of his friends I gathered that women came and went—"Your free throw's gone to shit," said Billy, owner of the shabby, stately Victorian next door whose honeysuckle-overrun backyard was a storehouse of costly toys—motorcycles, a sailboat. "How I know you have a girlfriend." I would have liked to talk to someone who knew him—even Billy, flagrantly indiscreet—about whether my anxious adaptation to his preferences was intuitive enough, or

I was getting some things wrong. Other women had lived with him: What had they done in the mornings, how had they kept quiet enough? One was a cellist—how had *that* worked? His writing hours, eight to noon, were nonnegotiable. If he missed a day his black mood saturated our world. But this was rare.

The check came, for the story. Forwarded by my husband, who I called sometimes when I was alone in the house. "You can always come home, you know," my husband said. "People get into trouble. They get in over their heads."

The house was close enough to the university that, days when he was teaching, he could ride his bicycle. Secretly I held it against him that he was honoring his responsibilities, meeting his classes, having conversations about weather and politics. My syllogism ran: What love does is shatter life as you've known it; his life isn't shattered; therefore he is not in love. Of the two of us I was the *real* lover. This self-declared greater authenticity, this was consoling—but, really, why was it? The question of who was more naked emotionally would have struck him as crazy, my guess is. But either my willingness to tear my life apart had this secret virtuousness, or the damage I was doing was deeply—callously—irresponsible.

By now I knew something about the women before me, including the Chinese lover whose loss he still wasn't reconciled to, though it had been years. I stole her picture and tucked it into *Middlemarch*, the only book in this house full of his books that belonged to me, and when he admitted to not liking Eliot much I was relieved to have a book which by not mattering to him could talk privately and confidentially to what was left of me as a writer, the little that was left after I was, as I believed I wanted to be, stripped down to bare life, to skin and heartbeat and sex, never enough sex, impatient sex, adoring sex, fear of boredom sex. The immense sanity of *Middlemarch* made it a safe haven for the little insanity of the stolen photograph. Whenever I went back to *Middlemarch*, I imagined the magnanimous moral acuity with which the narrator would have illumined a theft like mine, bringing it into the embrace of the humanly forgivable while at the same time—and how did Eliot get away with this?—indicting its betrayal of the more honorable self I would, in *Middlemarch*'s narrator's eyes, possess. But I didn't go back often; sex and aimless daydreaming absorbed the hours I would usually have spent reading, and when I went up to the loft, I left the book behind—I didn't want him noticing it. He had a habit of picking up my things and studying them quizzically, as if wondering how they had come to be in his house, and if he picked up *Middlemarch* there was a chance the photo would fall out. If I fell asleep in his bed after sex he would wake me after an hour or two, saying *Kid, you need to go downstairs.* On the way down I ran my fingers over the spines of the books lining the stairwell. If you opened one it would appear untouched; he recorded observations and memorable passages in a series of reading notebooks.

My scribbled-in *Middlemarch* stayed on the nightstand by the twin bed, and I had hung my clothes in the closet, but that didn't mean I felt at home in the room, with its dresser whose bottom drawer was jammed with photos. What did it mean that this drawer, alone in all the house, had not been systematically sorted? Near the bottom of the slag heap was an envelope of tintypes: from a background of stippled tarnish gazed a poetic boy, doleful eyes and stiff upright collar, and I wanted to take it to him and say *Look, you in 1843,* but that would prove I'd been riffling through the drawer, and even if he hadn't said not to, I wasn't sure it was all right. His childhood was there, his youth, the face of the first author's photo. Houses and cities before this one. His women, too, and I dealt them out across the floor, a solitaire of faces, wildly unalike: I wanted to know their stories. No doubt I did know pieces, from his work, but here they were, real, and I would have listened to them all if I could, I would have asked each one *How did it end?* When he was writing he would sometimes knock and come in and rummage through the pictures, whose haphazardness replicated memory's chanciness. As with memory there was the sense that everything was there, in the drawer—just not readily findable. Disorder is friendly to serendipity, was that the point? When he found what he wanted he didn't take it back to his desk but stayed and studied it, and when he was done dropped it casually back into the hodgepodge. If I opened the drawer after he'd gone there was no way to guess which photo he'd been holding.

There were things that happened in sex that felt like they could never be forgotten. Recognitions, flights of soul-baring mutual exposure, a kind of raw ravishment that seemed bound to transform our lives. But, sharing the setting of so many hours of tumult—the bed—and tumult's instruments—our two bodies— these passages lacked the distinctness of *event* and turned out to be, as far as memory was concerned, elusive. And there was sadness in that, in coming back to our same selves. By midsummer, something—maybe the infuriating inescapability of those selves, maybe an intimation of the monotonousness sex could devolve into, if we kept this up—caused us to start turning sex into stories. Sex with me as a boy, the one and only boy who ever caught his eye, a lovely apparition of a boy he wanted to keep from all harm, but who one day was simply gone, sex as if he was a pornographer and I was a schoolgirl who began, more and more, to conjure long-absent emotions, tenderness, possessiveness, even as the schoolgirl became more and more corrupt, telling sly little lies, the sex we would have if after ten years' separation we saw each other across a crowded room, sex as if I had just learned he'd been unfaithful to me with one of his exes, sex as if I was unfaithful, the sex we would have if we broke up and after ten years ended up in the same Paris hotel for some kind of writers' event, a book signing maybe, and sometimes it was his book and sometimes it was mine, sex with me in the stockings and heels of a prostitute, with him as a cop, me as a runaway desperate for shelter, with him as a woman, with the two of us as strangers seated near each other on a nightlong flight.

These games always began the same way. Ceremonious, the invitation, somber and respectful in inverse proportion to the derangement solicited. *What if you are. What if I am.* We never talked about this, and though either could have said *Let's not go there*, neither of us ever declined a game described by the other. The inventing of parts to play was spontaneous, their unforeseeableness part of the game's attraction, but a special mood, an upswell of lurid remorse, alerted me whenever I was about to say *And then after forever we see each other again.* In these scenarios where we had spent years apart, the lovely stroke was our immediate, inevitable recognition of each other—not, like other emotions we played at, a shock, not a wounding excitement, but an entrancing correction to loss. All wrongs set right. *And we look at each other. And it's like—*

While he wouldn't drink any coffee that wasn't made from freshly ground Italian dark roast (which I had never tried before) and he had a taste for expensive chocolate, he seemed mostly indifferent to food and never cooked. What had he done when he was alone? Was it just like this, cereal, soup from cans, microwaved enchiladas? Should I try to make something—would that feel, to him, to me, ominously wife-y? He liked bicycling to the farmer's market and would come back with the ripest, freshest tomatoes. He taught me to slather mayonnaise across sliced bakery bread, grinding black pepper into the bleeding exposed slices before covering them with the top slice, taking fast bites before the bread turned sodden, licking juice from wrists and fingertips, the tomatoes still warm from basking in their crates at the farmer's market, their taste leaking acid-bright through the oily mayonnaise blandness, the bread rough in texture, sweet in fragrance. There was at least a chance he'd never told any other lover about tomato sandwiches. After weeks of not caring what I ate, I had found something I couldn't get enough of, and as soon as I finished one sandwich I would make another, waiting until he was out to indulge, and it didn't matter how carefully I cleared away all traces of my feast, he could tell, he was quick with numbers and probably counted the tomatoes.

Really the little house was saturated with his vigilance; there was no corner I could narrate from. When I went elsewhere, tried working in a café (not his) for example, it was as if the house was still with me, its atmosphere extending to the little table where I sat with my books and my legal pad and my cup of coffee with cream and two teaspoons of brown sugar stirred in, and even the music in the coffee shop, which should have had nothing to do with him, caused me to wonder whether he was thinking of me and wanted me to come home or whether he was relieved to have an afternoon to himself, and whether the onset of irritation was inevitable in love, and if it was how people could stand their lives; but look, everyone at the tables around me was standing their life, and I had more than most, I was in love. With *him*, and that was extraordinary, it was surreal—naturally it required adaptation, but I ought to rejoice, day by day, in the revision asked of me, I ought to get a handle on my moods. Two hours had passed; I gave up trying. He was sitting with Billy on Billy's front steps and greeted me by saying, "Everest redux." Billy said, "Can I have a kiss for luck? Leaving for Kathmandu early in the a.m. Oh and forgot to tell you"—turning to him—"Delia's going to house-sit. I don't want to be distracted on the icefall by visions of Fats"—his skinny, hyper Border collie—"wasting away in some kennel. Only good vibes. Last year when I got up into the death zone I hallucinated my grandmother." Deepening his Texas drawl: " 'Time you *git* back home.' Actually one of the Sherpas looked a whole lot like her. Brightest black eyes. See right through bullshit, which you want in a Sherpa or grandma. I lied a lot when I was little, like practice for being in the closet. So, Delia. Fats loves her. So, she'll be staying here." He said, "Always smart not to leave a house empty," but I knew Billy was curious if I would show that I minded, because Delia was his most recent ex, the lover before me, and thinking *only good vibes, right*, I said, "Fats will be happy," and kissed Billy on his sunburned forehead.

I gave up on the coffee shop but when I tried writing in the afternoons in the guest bedroom, sitting up in the twin bed with a legal pad on my knees, he would wander in and start picking up various objects, my traveling alarm clock, my hairbrush, and I would drop the legal pad and hold out my arms. Maybe because he was becoming restless, or was troubled by what looked, in me, like the immobilizing onset of depression, he talked me into going running and that was how we spent our evenings now, on an oval track whose cinders were the real old-school kind, sooty black, gritting under running shoes. If there had been a meet that weekend the chalk lines marking the lanes were still visible, and the infield was grass, evenly mown, where he liked, after running, to throw a football, liked it even more than he ordinarily would have because football figured in the novel he was writing about two brothers whose only way of connecting with each other was throwing a football back and forth, and he needed the sense impressions of long shadows across summer grass and the Braille of white *x*'s stitched into leather to prompt the next morning's writing. When he held a football his tall, brainy self came together, justified. Pleasantly dangerous with the love of competition, though all there was to compete with at the moment was me. When he cocked his arm back and took a step, tiny grasshoppers showered up. The spiral floated higher, as if the air was tenderly prolonging its suspension, and took its time descending. The thump of flight dead-ending against my chest as I ran pleased me. He had trouble accepting that I could throw a spiral, though he might have known my body learned fast. I couldn't throw as far, and he walked backward, taunting for more distance. Taunting I took as a guy-guy thing; my prowess, modest as it was, made me an honorary boy, and was sexy. One bright evening as I cocked my arm back he cried *Throw it, piggy!* Shocked into grace I sent a real beauty his way, and with long-legged strides he covered the grass and leaped, a show-offy catch tendered as apology before I could call down the field *What?*, but I was standing there understanding: *piggy* was a thing he called me to himself, that had slipped out. In my need and aimlessness and insatiability I was a pale sow. How deluded I had been, believing I was a genius lover no excess could turn repellent. The next morning I woke up sick, ashamed that wherever he was in the house he could hear me vomiting, and when I said I wanted a hotel room he told me a tenant had moved out from one of his units and I could have the key.

These studio units, five of them, occupied the shabby one-story stucco box that stood between his house and the street. Flat-roofed cinder block painted a sullen ochre, this building was a problem factory. Termites, leaks, cavalier electrical wiring. With his tenants he was on amiable terms, an unexpectedly easygoing landlord. The little box I let myself into had a floor of sky-blue linoleum—sick as I was, that blue made me glad. The space was bare except for a bed frame and mattress where I dropped the sheets and towels he'd given me. The hours I spent in the tiny bathroom were both wretched and luxurious in their privacy; whenever there was a lull in the vomiting I would lock and unlock the door just to do so. Now he is locked the fuck out. Now I let him back in. Now out forever. After dark I leaned over the toy kitchen sink and drank from the faucet. It was miraculous to be alone. There was a telephone on the kitchen's cinder-block wall, and as I looked at it, it rang. Thirteen, fourteen, fifteen. I slept in the bare bed and woke scared that my fever sweat had stained the mattress; it was light; that day lasted forever, the thing sickness does to time. His knocking woke me; he came in all tall and fresh from his shower. Having already worked his habitual four hours. First he made the bed; with the heel of his hand he pushed sweaty hair from my face; I was unashamed, I could have killed him if he didn't make love to me. "I'll check in on you tomorrow," he said. I barely kept myself from saying *Do you love me. Do you love me.* Nausea helped keep me from blurting that out; the strenuousness of repressing nausea carried over into this other, useful repression. "I'm so hungry," I said instead. "Can you bring me a bowl of rice?" In saying it I discovered that the one thing I could bear to think of eating was the bowl of rice he would carry over from his house. I needed something he made for me. When I woke it was night. Cool air and traffic sounds came through the picture window, and seemed to mean I was going to be able to live without him. Now and then the phone began to ring and I let it ring on and on. Sometime during that night I went through the cupboards. I sat cross-legged on the floor with a cup of tea and ate stale arrowroot biscuits from the pack the tenant had forgotten, feeling sick again as I ate. It didn't matter that I knew that very well, and even understood it; the bowl of rice was now an obsession. It seemed like the only thing I had ever wanted from him, though in another sense all I had done since staring at him that first time was want things from him. In the morning while it was still dark he let himself in—of course there was a master key— with nothing in his hands, and when we were through making love he said, "You're going to bathe, right?" Then I was alone without a bowl of rice, cross-legged on the kitchen floor with the cup of tea I'd made and the last five arrowroot biscuits, locked deep in hunger, realizing that because the hunger felt clear and exhilarating, with no undertow of nausea, that I was either well or about to be. I called and made a reservation on a flight to New Mexico that had one seat left.

When the taxi pulled up before dawn he was sitting on the curb, his back to me, a tall man in a child's closed-off pose, ignoring the headlights that shone on him. Against black asphalt the hopping gold-gashed dot dot dot was the last flare-up of his tossed cigarette. I thought, and came close to saying *You don't smoke*. He stood up and said, "I won't try to stop you," and it was another blow, not to be stopped.

In the novel he wrote about that time I wasn't his only lover. House-sitting next door, the narrator's sensible, affectionate ex affords him sexual refuge from the neediness of the younger woman he'd believed he was in love with, whose obsession with him has begun to alarm him. Impulsively, after the first time they slept together, she left her husband for him. How responsible did that make him, for her? He understands, as she doesn't seem to, that there's nothing unerring about desire. At its most compelling, it can lead to a dead end, as has happened in their case. This younger, dark-haired lover keeps *Middlemarch* on her nightstand, and riffling through the book one night while she's sleeping the narrator finds the naked photograph of the Chinese woman whose devotion he had foolishly walked away from and he thinks, I could get her back. She lives not very far away, and I would have heard if she got married—people can't wait to tell you that kind of thing about an ex. Here the novel takes a comic turn, because now he needs to break up with two women, his house-sitting ex, likely to go okay, and, a more troubling prospect, this girl inexplicably damaged by their affair, turned from a promising actress whose raffishly seductive Ophelia had gotten raves into a real-life depressive who hasn't gone on a single audition. He needs to rouse her from her depression, to talk to her frankly, encouragingly. A tone he can manage, now, because of what he hopes for. Tricky to carry off, the passage where, tilting the picture to catch what little light there is, he falls in love—the novel's greatest feat, also the one thing I was sure had never happened. I don't mean the novel was true, only that the things in it had happened. The likelier explanation was, he'd gone into the guest bedroom while I was out. Farfetched, his coming into the room while I slept—why would he?—though I could see why he wanted, thematically, the juxtaposition of sleep and epiphany, and how the little scene was tighter for suspense about whether the dark-haired lover would wake up.

Twelve years later, on our way home from the funeral of a well-loved colleague who had lived in Berkeley, two friends and I stopped in a bookstore. Between the memorial service and the trip out to the cemetery the funeral had taken most of the day. Afterward we had gone to dinner, and except for the driver we were all a little drunk and, in the wake of grieving funeral stilt-edness and the tears we had shed, trying to cheer each other up. Death seemed like another of Howard's contradictions: His rumbling, comedic fatness concealed an exquisite sensibility, gracious, capable of conveying the most delicate illuminations to his students or soft-shoeing around the lectern, reciting *In Breughel's great picture The Kermess.* If Howard's massiveness was bearish, that of his famous feminist-scholar wife was majes-tic, accoutred with scarves, shawls, trifocals on beaded chains, a cane she was rumored to have aimed at an unprepared grad stu-dent in her Dickinson seminar—*My Soul had stood—a Loaded Gun,* David said; Josh corrected, *My Life,* with the affable con-descension that, David's grin said, he'd been hoping for, since it made Josh look not so Zen after all. Josh was lanky, mild, exceedingly tall, with an air of baffled inquiry and goodwill I attributed to endless zazen, David sturdy, impatient, his scorn exuberant, the professional vendettas he waged merciless. It was David I told my love affairs to, and when I had the flu it was David who came over, fed Leo his supper, and read aloud. Through the wall I could hear David's merry *showed their ter-rible claws till Max said "BE STILL!"* followed by Leo's doubtful *Be still!*

That evening of the funeral one of us suggested waiting out rush hour in the bookstore and we wandered through in our black clothes, David to philosophy, Josh to poetry, me to a long table of tumbled sale books on whose other side—I stared—*he* stood with an open book in his hand, looking up before I could turn away, the brilliant dark eyes that had held mine as I came over and over meeting mine now without recognition, just as neutrally looking away, the book in his hand the real object of desire, something falsely assertive and theatrical in the steadiness of his downward gaze that convinced me he had been attracted to me not as a familiar person but as a new one, red-haired now, in high heels, in head-to-toe black, a writer with three books to my name, teaching at a university a couple of hours away, single mother to a solemn, intuitive toddler who spoke in complete sentences, light of my life, though he wasn't going to get to hear about my son, wasn't going to get a word of my story, and in the inward silence and disbelief conferred by his not knowing who I was there was time for a decision, which was: Before he can figure out who he's just seen, before, as some fractional lift of his jaw told me he was about to, he can look up and meet your eyes again and know who you are, before before before before before before before before he can say your name followed by *I don't believe it*, followed by *I always thought I'd see you again*, look away. Get out. Go. And I did, and though behind me where I stood on the street corner the bookstore door opened now and then and let people out none of them was him. Person after person failed to be him. He hadn't known me. I had known him—did that mean I had been, all along, the real lover? What we had should have still burned both of us. If it had been real, if we had gone as deep as I believed we had, he could never have failed to recognize me. After a while my friends came out carrying their bags, and David told me, "This is the first time I've ever seen you leave a bookstore empty-handed, ever," and we pulled our gloves on, telling each other taking a little time had been a good idea, and our heads were clear now, and we could make the drive home. Of course, that was when he came out the door—long-legged, striding fast. Pausing, fingers touched to his lips, then the upright palm flashed at me—a gesture I didn't recognize, for a second, as a blown kiss—before he turned the corner.

"Wasn't that—?" David said.

"Yes."

"Did he just—"

"When we're in the car, you two," Josh said. "I've got to be at the Zen Center at five in the morning."

"The day before, he told me his biggest fear wasn't that they wouldn't get all the cancer. His biggest fear wasn't of dying, even, though he said that was how his father died when Howard was only nine, under the anesthetic for an operation supposed to be simple, with nobody believing they needed to say good-bye beforehand, and now that he was facing *a simple operation* himself, one nobody dies of, he couldn't help thinking of his father. No. His biggest fear was that he'd be left impotent. Of all the things that can conceivably go wrong with prostate cancer surgery, that was the most terrifying."

"What did you say?" Josh asked, from the backseat.

"'Most terrifying?' I'm wondering why it's me, the gay boy, Howard chooses to confide in about impotence. Because my whole life revolves around penises? I'm a little unnerved, because, you know Howard, his usual decorum, where's that gone? But I want to be staunch for him, I love this man. And he says, 'Not for me. If it came down to living without it, I would grieve, but it wouldn't be the end of the world. For me. Whereas for Martha.'"

"'Most terrifying,'" Josh said. "I'm very sorry he had to make those calculations."

"'Martha can't live without it.'"

"You were right there," Josh said. "You reassured him."

"Of course I reassured him." David checked Josh's expression in the rearview mirror. "But it's not something I imagined, that the two of them ever—or still—"

"Or, hmmm, that she could be said—"

"You idiots, he adored her," I said. "That's what he was telling David. Not, 'My god, this woman, it's unimaginable that I'll never make love to her again.' But 'How can she bear the loss.'"

Josh took off his tie, rolled it up, tucked it in his jacket pocket, and then handed his glasses forward to me, saying, "Can you take custody?" I cradled them as cautiously as if they were his eyes. Once he was asleep, David said, "That was him, wasn't it?"

I told him what happened. "After I'd gone he must have stood there thinking, But I know her, I know her from somewhere. Then he gets it—who I am, and that I'd walked away without a word. Which has to have hurt."

"It's generally that way when you save your own skin—somebody gets hurt."

"Even hurt, he blows me a kiss. That makes him seem—"

"Kind of great," David said.

"Wasn't I right? Walking away?"

"Don't misunderstand me," David said. "There's no problem with a little mystery, in the context of a larger, immensely hard-won clarity." He yawned. "I'm not the idiot." He tipped his curly head to indicate the backseat. "He's the idiot. Did I reassure him. Fuck. I'm the most reassuring person alive."

Oncoming traffic made an irregular stream of white light, its brilliance intensifying, fusing, then sliding by. I held up Josh's glasses and the lights dilated gorgeously. I said, "You know why we'll never give up cars—because riding in cars at night is so beautiful, it's telling stories in a cave with the darkness kept out, the dash lights for the embers of the fire."

"You don't have to tell me any stories," David said. "I'm absolutely wide-awake."

I didn't sleep long, but when I woke he was in a different mood.

"You know, his novel," David said, "—the one about you—is that a good book?"

"If you like his voice it's good."

"On its own, though, is it?"

Mine wasn't exactly a disinterested reading, I said. The style is his style, and like all his work it moved right along, but the novel overall felt tilted in the narrator's favor, and it would have been more compelling if he had made the dark-haired lover—

"You," David said.

—okay, me, but I really am talking about the character now, who is all shattered vulnerability and clinging, the embodiment of squishy need. If he had granted her some independent perceptions, even at points conflicting with his, made her more real, more likable, then her realness would test the narrator's possession of the story, and cast some doubt on the narrator's growing contempt. If it's less justified, more ambiguous, then his contempt isn't just about her and how she deserves it, it's also about him and how ready he is to feel it. If it's not so clear that he's right to feel what he feels, then everything between them gets more interesting, right?

"That's a sadder ending," David said. "The way that you tell it."

"I wasn't thinking it was sad," I said. "I was thinking it was— better."

Joe Donnelly

Bonus Baby

I TUG ON MY BRIM. I tug on it, caress it, and tug on it some more. I take the cap off and slap it against my thigh. I hold it to my chest while I wipe my brow. I pat it, brush it, shape it, and put it back on my head. Then, I tug on the brim again.

I'm not a neurotic, at least not in anything but a typical sense. What I am is a conductor of sorts. I harness energy and deliver it. Mostly my own, but there's also this: The eighty thousand eyes and hands and fists; the voices, the shouting; the sun, the sky . . . But this is no symphony. There is too much that hasn't been orchestrated, too much left to chance. Like how even the slightest change in atmospheric pressure can send a gust across this plane that will tear worlds apart. Not a gust, really. Not even a breeze. A change so small, grains of dirt might barely shift. Nothing anyone else will notice. But I will know. As soon as the object leaves my hand, it will feel like a hurricane on my face.

These tics—they calm me. Because there's so much I don't control once it leaves my hand. So I take off my cap and run my hand through my hair, just so I can put it back on my head and tug on my brim again. I tug and tug and wipe and tug again, until I'm finally settled in that place where there's nothing outside of me and I see only what I have to see.

Now, I come together, folding in upon myself, hugging the object close to my heart, feeling my heart beating through the leather and into the object itself, filling it with whatever is in me that I can use to deliver it with. Then, I kick up my left leg, high in the old ways, high like my socks, and pause for a moment in first position before I lead and point with my toes, shifting everything into the opening up before the snapping shut. Before I lose control.

Before I pitch.

The batter is a right-handed brute, 230 pounds of muscle, emotion, and instinct. He is a naïf, an innocent. He has no nuance, no game, only the desire to launch balls over fences and kill dreams. He is a boy, a destroyer, and I appreciate his earnestness. But I know he'll be too eager with nobody on base. I know he will feel responsible only to his lust. And that's why he gets a fastball, coming in high, sinking low, moving right to left, a little slower and a little faster than he expected. And that's why he's out swinging.

He stares at me long after the ball is safe in the catcher's mitt. He is surprised he missed. He's always surprised, and I appreciate that, too. He'll never know what happened. All that happened. He swung and missed and now he must sit down until enough time has passed for him to be surprised again.

I've retired the first five batters easily and I'm starting to feel something, some gathering of forces. I push it away. Feelings can be dangerous. They can make the ball too heavy or too light. I didn't choose feelings. I chose the solitude of this mound and the mystery of the pitch. What could be more essential than that? If you tell me, I'll follow it, because I know that someday I'll need it. Someday, I will be desperate for it. But until then, I pitch.

The six spot goes down. A curve and a changeup were the killers. Set up by a first-pitch fastball and one throwaway just to see what they're chasing. I can tell by the pitches he's calling that my catcher, Roy Dickey, is starting to feel it, too—the noise stilling, the time between release and catch collapsing, the unknowable becoming slightly less unknown.

I was a free-range kid born into the mythological Midwest at the twilight of the American century. I say mythological not because it was the land that grew Paul Bunyan, bore Casey Jones's track, and sealed Johnny Appleseed's destiny, but because the Midwest that raised me was barren of that sort of damp nostalgia. If it was here once, it had long since dried up with each generation's further remove from the frontier. No Mississippi River adventures beckoned me. Instead, I navigated amid the drudgery of cash-strapped public schools and not enough to eat. I was Tom Sawyer with no Huck Finn, a boy who could hear his own footsteps echoing off the streets of a place that had been dying unattended for years.

My father played ball in high school and boxed at the boys' club. My mother was a varsity swimmer back when the school district could support something so exotic. They were high school sweethearts who couldn't see that the future was growing narrower on those open plains. She worked as a secretary, until it was called executive assistant. My father was a machine-tool mechanic at the textile mill until the postwar prosperity ran out and it closed. After that, he mostly drank.

I can still picture my mother in the breakfast nook at night waiting for my dad to come home, worrying over a puzzle book, keeping company with her coffee, cigarettes, and a snack pack of cheese and crackers.

Our family, like our town, looked best in old photographs.

School was my sanctuary. There, I found in me what had made my dad and mom the homecoming king and queen. And found that in me it was hardened with a cynicism that freed me from the fantastical optimism with which they had been hoodwinked. I used that to my advantage.

All the sports came easy. But I gave baseball the most of me because it asked the most. Even in Little League, I could find traces of some kind of poetry there that I couldn't find in the low hills and fallow fields that formed our dusty boundaries. At times, the ballpark, the diamond, and the mound returned to me a boy that had gone missing ever since I knew myself.

But it was more than that. Baseball had things I could rely on—rules, physics, statistics. It is the world's most quantifiable sport. Yet it still baffles us. The best hitters still miss two-thirds of the time and the best pitchers still lose a hundred times or more before they're done. The game was an enigma I couldn't resist: something I wanted to try to solve even as I knew how far from solving it I might always be.

Mack and Jack try not to sit next to each other in the dugout. It's bad enough that they play shortstop and second base, and that their names rhyme, but to be seen as together—especially in the dugout, where vulnerability is frowned upon—would be more than they could bear. Which is why, whenever possible, the entire team conspires to make it so Mack and Jack have no choice but to sit next to each other in the dugout. Long-running inside jokes are a tradition in baseball, and this is one of ours.

I come into the dugout after my half of the fourth. I've put twelve men down in order. My ball has velocity, movement, and accuracy. I'm hitting my spots like it's on a string. There's flow and economy in my delivery. Something is happening. I've been here before and I know it can be a tease. I approach the dugout the same way I always do, head down, counting to eight and then eight again. Eight is my number, my rhythm.

Near the dugout steps, I look up. Mack and Jack look back at me and quickly avert their eyes. They are aware of what's happening, too, but they don't bother me with it. They're vets and have been here more times than I have. It's way too early.

I take my seat at the end of the bench. I can't get too close to the rest of them or they will drain me. I'm not here for them. I'm here to pitch. I'm here for the game, a vast and infinitely varied game that can be reduced to decimal points. A game that more than all other games inspires songs, poems, and picture shows.

This game is eternal and most of us who play it are dust, here to be forgotten, but here also to sustain its capacity to render the kind of legends that carried this country through the Depression and wars and good times, too. I chased those legends around my hungry childhood, trying to find in baseball the home of Ruth and DiMaggio, Robinson, Musial, Mantle, Mays, Koufax, Clemente, Aaron, Ryan, and Ripken. I thought if I could find them, find baseball, then maybe I could find home, too.

But even with all its countless silent traditions and quiet intimacies, baseball can be a lonely place. Ask a centerfielder when he's sprinting into the deep green nothingness of the right-center gap, knowing that no one else can help him and knowing that the wall is coming up fast, but just how fast he can only estimate based on time and time before, but each time is brand new and that wall means his time is running out.

It can be especially lonely if you're the pitcher. That's why so many of us give in to our tics and idiosyncrasies. We fondle our caps, hitch our pants, talk to the ball, talk to ourselves, pace around the mound like we're looking for messages written in the dirt, tap the dirt, scratch the dirt, rub the dirt . . . anything to feel less alone up there.

There's a commotion.

Mack has hit a double. I hadn't noticed he was at bat, but now he's there on second and Jack is up. They'll never get away from each other. Jack is a master of situational hitting. He's going to work the count. Get a bunt down, or something. He won't give up an out easily. Not when Mack's in scoring position and the heart of the order is coming up.

I close my eyes and try to block it out. But there's another commotion. I look up to see Jack has laid a beauty down the first base line, drawing the catcher, pitcher, and first baseman. There's no play on Mack; he's gone to third. The second baseman is late getting over to cover first and Jack beats the throw. Men on the corners and one out.

This is how we've been doing it. Chipping. Playing smart. These two, in their own ways, have been setting the tone. Showing the young ones, and the ones who never had to pay enough attention before, that there are many ways to draw blood.

On his way to the plate, Dickey takes a look back at me and nods. It's a message. We haven't said a thing about it yet, about how tonight the maddening mystery of baseball seems almost graspable. And now Dickey is signaling a pact. We're chasing it. He's going to do his part and he'll expect no less from me.

Dickey and I are not friends. I'm not friend material. But out here, he knows me as well as anyone has ever known me. He knows what strings to pull. With a simple, quick glare, he sends a jolt through me, a wave of terror and excitement, some reckoning with all the times I've been here before, from Pony Leagues to JuCo, to the minors, and even a couple times here in the big leagues.

I pull my brim down over my eyes and close them, feeling the energy surging through the crowd, rising and falling with each pitch. Dickey's been struggling. There's talk he's past the point of diminishing returns, that he can't turn on the inside fastball anymore. We've been moving him around the middle of the lineup, trying to find that place where his smarts and what's left of his skill can find a groove. It's a short, tough life for catchers in this game.

I keep my eyes closed. I can sense by the rhythm of the crowd that Dickey's worked the count to his favor. I know the pitcher is going to have to go with a fastball and will try to bring it high and inside, jam him up. Dickey will be sitting on it by now.

And then I hear the silence that follows the windup and soon after that a sharp *thwack*, followed by the strange sound of forty thousand people holding their breath—is it fair, is it foul, will it make the gap, will it be calculated and caught? I don't open my eyes until I hear the gasp of relief and then the explosion of surprise and joy that so many things that could have gone wrong somehow went right. And now Mack and Jack are in the dugout getting high fives.

I open my eyes and pull my brim up to my forehead and see Dickey on second base, staring a hole through me.

I was an indifferent student in high school, smart enough to skate by. Math and science could keep my ping-ponging attention, but not much else. Unless I was moving, doing something physical, my brain was flighty and distant. As a boy, I'd go off walking and would find myself miles away from home before it even registered that I'd gone anywhere. I didn't notice anything. Or nothing that stayed with me. I just kept moving, propelled by some instinct I had no words for.

I found solace in the hierarchy and definitiveness of competitive sports. Later, after spending many years examining the nature of my difficulty connecting with life outside the chalked lines—the irony of fleeting chalk on top of dirt and grass being able to contain so much of my life is not lost on me—I came to understand things a little better. How the diamond and the field and the court were where I found escape from the chaos of the house I grew up in.

That house seemed to grow more dangerous as I got older and my facility for connecting things to other things increased. My father got more and more unpredictable—his tempests, his contrition, his stunted love in a pitched battle with his self-absorption. He tried churches, he tried swearing off, he tried going to meetings in the city, he tried college courses, he tried to start things, but nothing stuck and nothing could give him back what had dried up and blown away. His resentment could be explosive. Not knowing when it might erupt was the worst of it.

I grew bigger and faster and stronger than he was when he was my age. I was good, too. He could be proud and encouraging and he could be cutting and cruel. We were pampered and soft, he'd sneer. We didn't know what it was like back in the day. He'd go on about how the equipment and gear and training practically played the game for us these days. Not a particularly original trick, but it's surprising how well it worked. How it made me feel like I wasn't real. So, I started wearing my socks high, like they did in the old days, and took an extra-sized jersey for modesty. I painted my cleats black and stopped washing my cap until it looked a hundred years old. I wanted it to seem as if I stepped out of one of those old baseball cards my dad kept in Ziploc bags inside of shoeboxes inside a chest in the attic.

Sometimes, I'd come home late at night, later than I was supposed to come home—I was out doing nothing much more than staying away—and I'd find him at the kitchen table, thin latex gloves on his hands, going through the cards as if he were handling something made of delicate glass. He'd call me over to sit down and tell me about the people pictured on the cards, names that would mean nothing if I said them now, but names that made those cards worth ten times their weight in gold.

"Do you know how much this is worth?" he'd ask.

I didn't.

"A lot," he'd say, and carefully put the card back in order in the Ziploc bag.

"That's a Tony Taylor rookie-season card. Not many people remember Taylor, but he was one of the first Cubans to come into the league. Nineteen fifty-eight. A solid second baseman. Made the All-Stars a couple years. Remembered best for two things. One was the infamous two-ball, Stan Musial out at third in 1959.

The other is the great play he made at second to save Jim Bunning's perfect game in 1964. Nobody gets a perfect game without one or two of those. He also stole home six times, which nobody seems to care about, but that was enough right there to make his mark."

He'd tell me to grab another beer for him out of the refrigerator and to get one for myself. I didn't care about the beer, but I indulged him. And he'd talk about the people on those cards and their passing through this game, how each left some kind of mark on it, however faint. And it would always end with him packing those cards away and saying, "It might not look like much, son, but these cards are worth more than you think."

Those were the times that worked for us.

When I began moving past him in the high school record books, he tried to act as if he was proud, and I know that in some dim region in the back of his heart, he was. Still, he couldn't keep the spark of resentment from igniting in his eyes or hide the fact that every time my name replaced his at the top of some list, he seemed to age in dog years.

I've retired eighteen in a row. Struck out eight. Three swinging, five looking. Getting them looking is good. It means we've got them all mixed up. Dickey has them all mixed up, I should say. Pitch counts, patterns, locations, rotations—he's running numbers these batters can't begin to fathom. I'm right there with him. Algorithms pass between us in flashes of fingers and nods. The right-handed brute has gone down swinging twice and my admiration for him grows. He'd rather swing at phantoms than get called out with his bat on his shoulder.

So far, only three balls have made it out of the infield, all lazy flies. The rest have been routine grounders, nothing to raise a pulse. But now all our pulses are raised. It started with Dickey: his pats on the back, his glares, his clenched fists, his pointing, his encouraging. He's done the recruiting for this mission. Games like this can get a team on a run to the postseason and Dickey knows he doesn't have too many runs left in him. Mack and Jack signed up early. Now everyone's on board.

The dugout is strange and silent, almost grim. No one has said anything, but after eighteen in a row everyone will be held accountable. After eighteen in a row, only my mistakes can be forgiven. I look over at our third baseman. He's just a kid. He's staring straight ahead, out beyond the centerfield wall into the night. Sunflower seed shells are flying out of his mouth like pulp from a wood chipper.

We lost the state championship finals my senior year in high school because we couldn't win any of the games that I didn't pitch. By then, I had grown to my full height, six-foot-three. I weighed twenty-five pounds less than I do now, barely two hundred pounds. But I was strong and even though I wasn't fast, I had a feel for my body that you could call graceful. I went 10-0 during the regular season that year and gave up no earned runs. I played right field when I wasn't pitching. I didn't much care for it. It reminded me too much of shagging flies with my dad and his red-faced frustration at not being able to hit one out to me after he'd reached into the cooler too many times.

The ball, not the bat, was what I wanted. I needed to hold it, feel it, massage it, coax it, and pitch it with all the intent I could summon. The ball, I believed, held the key to solving the game. But my bat was too valuable for the coaches to keep me out of games. I hit fifteen home runs, eighteen doubles, and five triples my senior year. Drove in half our runs. I lent our team a stature it didn't deserve, and our success pumped some oxygen into our wheezing town. The hopes and expectations were directed at our team, but they landed on me, a conscientious objector. I just wanted to pitch.

I was a mid-rounds draft pick out of high school. The team that drafted me offered me a signing bonus, small by pro standards, but the money would have been a windfall where I came from. When the offer came in, my father's eyes lit up with desire and desperation. He was sick then; asbestos and alcohol had kicked off a parade of cancers. If the money came in, and it came from baseball, he believed he could lay some claim to it.

I turned down the offers and took a scholarship to a junior college in the state capital with a baseball program that fed kids to big-time schools or the minor leagues. I wasn't being spiteful. It was just that if I was going to get a bonus, it was going to be big enough to get my mother and little sister out of there.

In my second year at JuCo, I went 15-1. I had a no-hitter, a one-hitter, and eleven shutouts. I had perfect games going into the ninth inning three times. My dad died halfway through that season. I didn't find out until after, but I pitched on the day he died. It was the one game I lost.

I was drafted in the first round.

I take the mound at the top of the eighth. Twenty-one straight have gone down with barely a protest. It's put me in a dangerous state of mind, one where looking for easy answers could make me alligator armed if I let it. I tug at my brim, toe the rubber, tug and toe, and then step off. I walk to the edge of the mound and tug at my brim some more, but I can't find myself. Dickey calls time and trots out toward the mound. I meet him halfway because I don't want him or anyone else stepping onto my dirt. I don't want to talk. I need to stay in command of time.

Dickey knows I'll turn away as soon as possible, so he puts his gloved hand behind my back to keep me in place. His short arms are surprisingly powerful. He looks past me, into the stands, around the stadium, turns his back to me as if I weren't there, surveys the crowd, and then faces me again.

"You come here often?" he says, straight-faced.

I almost laugh.

"Relax," he says, and lets me go with a pat on the back.

I scale the mound again, feeling lighter, feeling something unfamiliar. Trust, maybe.

Past the outfield, the hills rise above the parking lot in silhouette, palm trees and scrub bushes making sketchbook shapes in black and gray. On the other side of those hills, the city roils with millions of different pulses and prerogatives. Some part of me recognizes that what's going on here is part of it, part of what shrinks the distances between us and makes it all seem slightly less frightening, for a while, maybe.

I tug on my brim, massage the ball and stare out into the shadows, take a few breaths and pull at my brim again. I'm ready.

I should mention that I am not a great pitcher.

In ten years in the majors, I've barely won more than I've lost. My ERA is respectable—above 3.00, below 4.00—and I strike out one in every 4.75 batters. My fastball is good, but I'm no flamethrower. I need location and movement. I've got decent offspeed pitches, but I have to mix things up or I can be caught up with by the late innings.

But I get to the late innings. And that's made me more valuable than my record. These days, when every manager watches the pitch counts of his number-one starter and top closer, lest he be blamed for burning out those expensive arms, you need a workhorse to take pressure off the rest of the staff. That's me. I give innings and I keep us in the game. If our bats are hot, we might win.

Their cleanup hitter is leading off, then the brute, and then a solid bat in the sixth spot. They'll be pressing. Trying hard to break my spell. I can feel them gripping. I can feel each one believing it's up to him. That's how pitching can unravel a team.

Dickey gives me three fingers for a slider. He wants to see if they'll bite on a bad first pitch. I shake him off. It's not time for that yet. I want to go one inside, send a message. When I've been here before, I've tried too hard to hold on to what I had. It made the air too heavy and the ball too sticky. Now, I want to surrender the ball to the night and the city and to everyone in it, including their cleanup batter. I can see Dickey smile behind his mask. He gives me the one, inside and high.

I collect, kick, and unleash. Their cleanup batter swings so hard his helmet comes off, but the ball was in Dickey's mitt before he even started.

They're hacking at anything around the plate now, respecting the game too much to try to work a cheap walk. I return their respect by not cheating too far off the plate, knowing the umpire isn't immune to the buzz filling the stadium. All three go down—the number-six batter on a changeup right down the middle, the ball hidden in plain sight. He could have swung three times before it got there, but he didn't swing at all.

The crowd rises as I walk to the dugout, its cheers muted and wise.

I don't look up.

I live alone in a furnished apartment downtown, close to the stadium. This is my third team and my third city since I came up to the big leagues. I haven't bought a house or a piece of furniture anywhere. I don't have a wife. I haven't had a girlfriend in years. When I need sex, I get it. It's not difficult in my position, but it's nothing more than that. I drive the same car I bought with my bonus. I'm not an ascetic. I just don't care. I don't know why. Or maybe I do. Those things—girlfriends, wives, homes, the artifice or artifacts of life outside the lines—they have their own gravity and logic, their own science and riddles. I don't have room for them. I need to keep my space for baseball. Maybe someday, when this mystery's been solved, I'll want other things. Not now.

I pay for my sister's education. She's pursuing advanced studies in synthetic biology and molecular programming. Soon, she says, we'll be engineered on a molecular level. I wonder how I will feel when science takes metaphysics out of the mysteries that drive me.

I also pay for my mother to live in an assisted-living facility in the city that's a two-hour drive from where we grew up. Dementia came on fast after my sister and I left home. Where she is now is first-rate, as these things go, but she doesn't know me anymore and I don't visit.

The membrane I've built around me, I've worked on my entire life. It's nearly impenetrable. But this crowd, this moment, these teammates, it's all getting so close to me now that I can taste their coughs, hear their laughs, and feel their rising hopes that for once, with them as witness, some tiny prayer might be answered. Time is smashing into my eyeballs like a tsunami hitting land. It's all sending ripples through my skin, blowing my cap back, rustling through my jersey, working its way inside me. It hurts a little in a place I can't quite put my finger on.

We score another run in the bottom of the eighth. We're up 3–0.

I have to stand up. I have to face this. But I can't move. I try to lift my butt off the bench, but it won't budge. Everybody has taken the field. The warm-up catcher is waiting behind the plate. The kid at third base ran out there in a spray of sunflower seed shells. They're ready for me, but I can't move.

Dickey, always the last one out, especially in the late innings when putting on his armor takes all the energy he can muster, comes over to me. I try to get up before he's in my face, but I can't.

"What's going on?"

"I don't know. I can't move."

The ump comes over to the dugout and says something to our manager, who looks down at us and starts in our direction. Dickey waves him off.

"C'mon. You've done this a thousand times," he says. "It's just another inning. It's the same as a first inning, except it's the last. One more and we're done."

"I can't . . ." I point to the sky. "It's like everything is on top of me. Those stars. The night. The black. The air. It feels like it's all on top of me and I can't move it."

Dickey looks up like he's studying something and for the longest moment says nothing, just stares. Then, "Yep, it's there all right. It's on top of all of us. And those stars don't weigh any more on you than they do on anyone else. We all have to get up and do some things whether we want to or not. Now you get up and do this or I'll never look you in the eye again and all those guys out there in the field waiting for you, they'll never wait for you again."

He grabs my shirt with his right hand and hoists me to my feet like I'm a child. I don't fall down. My legs are beneath me. My arms are beside me. I'm standing.

"Take the mound," Dickey says, and walks toward home plate.

I leave the dugout and the crowd rises to meet me.

I tug and caress my brim in a pattern only I can make sense of, the tics seeking a rhythm I can ride. Dickey calls the one, low and outside. I gather and deliver. I can't feel a thing, but the ball is in Dickey's mitt. A strike. Something happens. Some time passes. I tug and pull and caress the brim. Then, same call, same spot, same result. And now a fastball, just off the inside of the plate. The batter chases, misses. Strike three. The ball goes around the infield and back to me. I don't look at anyone. I don't look at anything. I'm not in a hurry, but I have to keep my rhythm. It's eighth notes in double time, the beat of my heart. I've never felt it like this before, the blood throbbing into my earlobes, pounding into my toes.

The eighth batter, their shortstop, fouls off a curve after watching a fastball go right down the middle. With two strikes on him, Dickey calls the three, the ace in the hole we've been holding on to all this time. I nod in agreement. The shortstop waves badly at the first slider of the night and goes down for the second out of the inning. The crowd is on its feet. I can barely hear them roar, but I can feel them on my neck like dragon's breath.

A pinch hitter comes on deck. He's an aging star in his final year. He's on the team to coach as much as to play. It's a good choice. He won't be rattled. Nothing else would be right. He tips his batting helmet toward me before entering the box. I nod back. And here we are, locked inside an equation that has no right or wrong answer, just an irrefutable result. He digs and points the bat toward my mound. He's ready.

I'm square to him. My arms are at my side. Loose and light. For some reason, I feel no urge to reach for the brim of my cap. I just stand there loose-limbed, my hands falling toward the dirt. The crowd is standing straight up like forty thousand quills on a technicolor porcupine. Camera flashes explode in the corners of my eyes.

Knowing the slider has completely shuffled the deck, Dickey goes into his crouch and signals the one, low and inside—surprise the batter by giving him exactly what he wants. I nod in agreement.

I kick up my leg, high in the old ways, high like my socks, and come to first position. I lead and point with my left leg, shifting everything into the opening up before the snapping shut, before nothing else will be known, before I surrender all to the uncertainty of what comes next.

I pitch.

A fastball.

I hear a sharp crack and feel a vacuum rush past me and I know without seeing it that the ball is screaming for the hole between short and third. I turn my head over my shoulder and see Mack diving to his right faster than thought, fast enough to spear the ball before it tears into the outfield. He's on his back with the ball in his glove. There's no throw he can make to first and suddenly everything has stopped. There is no mound, no crowd, no Jack, no Mack, no Dickey, no time. There is only this snake of nothingness wrapping around my gut, buckling my knees. And just as I'm about to go down, I catch a blur at the edge of my vision.

It's Jack, in full stride moving toward Mack like Mack somehow knew he would be, and the ball is already making a perfect arc toward him, and I watch as Jack softly swipes it from the air with his bare hand, pivots, and throws it to first.

And then Dickey's mask is in the air and he's running toward me and everyone else is, too, and I'm being crushed under a pile of bodies. And for the life of me, I still can't figure out why.

Why would they do this?

Why would they do this for me?

David H. Lynn

Divergence

Just as he was swinging his leg over the bike, Shivani brushed past and whacked him on the rump. "Watch yourself," she cried.

Jeremy Matthis bobbed up and onto his saddle. He caught his wife in a few strokes, swooshing past her on the street, and already he was marveling at the lightness of the new frame, the smooth response of derailleur and gears. At the first corner they cruised, slowing for a glance each way. Again he pushed ahead, wobbling lightly—the balance was entirely different from his ancient tourer.

This would take some getting used to. And not just the new bicycle. He was entirely prepared to sacrifice the summer to countless adjustments, now that his book had finally appeared in the spring and, not coincidentally, the trustees of Ransom College had just this past weekend confirmed his tenure in the Classics Department. For months he'd been predicting that his promotion would alter nothing, that he wouldn't feel in any way transformed once it had been granted. Yet already in the stretch of a few days he'd discovered how faulty that reasoning had been.

It seemed that over the course of many years a tightly woven mesh of stress and anxiety had gradually and ever more tightly caged his heart, his lungs. Mostly he'd been unaware of the binding, except for the occasional snapping awake at four in the morning, sucking for air. Over these last few days that invisible harness had finally begun to loosen, to fade, shadow becoming light. Each time his lungs filled with air, it seemed almost a revelation, perhaps the start of a new life.

A decade or more earlier, he'd steal an hour on hard-packed country roads in Virginia, digging with his old ten-speed to grind away the frustrations, dead ends, and humiliations that are the dues paid in grad school, and just such a bicycle as the one he was riding had been his dream. An expensive dream he'd scarcely ever acknowledged aloud. Two days ago, however, he'd arrived to meet Shivani for a celebratory dinner at their favorite restaurant, a trattoria on High Street. She'd spotted him through the large front window and was standing in her black dress and pearls by their special table, with one hand on the blue-and-silver Italian bike, a bright bow on its seat.

Not until today had there been a real chance to get out on the road. They spun down to Main and sliced along an alley to the back entrance of a coffee shop, where their small group of friends was already gathered. Marty, Gretchen, and Lee were there, standing with their own bikes.

As Jeremy swung onto the sidewalk, Owen Thurlow emerged from the shop with a cup of coffee. "Nice wheels," he said, saluting the new bike. "I must be paying you too much."

"Since when are you paying him at all?" Shivani demanded. "I thought he was teaching just for the love of it. Anyway, this baby comes out of my check from the Attorney General."

The provost saluted her in turn.

Everyone other than Owen was satisfied with water bottles and eager to be away. So, soon they were mounted again and cutting over to the Alum Creek path. The day was gray, an occasional faint drizzle keeping them cool but slicking the pavement. It took less than five miles of occasional weaving and dodging before they'd left the city behind, along with its joggers, baby strollers, and dog walkers. They were flying now across the rolling, open country of central Ohio, the river meandering near and away again from the old rail path.

"Hey, fancy pants, quit showing off," Owen grunted loudly.

Jeremy swiveled and tossed him a wave. The machine he was riding yielded such a pure joy that, without quite realizing it, he'd been out front and pressing his friends beyond their usual pace. He eased, coasting so that Gretchen could swing into the lead. As he drifted back to her side, Shivani was breathing hard, but wouldn't grant him the satisfaction of admitting it. She was also smiling broadly.

"So?" she said.

"Yeah," he said. "Nice."

He was feeling strong and swift—he'd remember that afterward. The rhythm of the ride, the entire day, was perfect. There was satisfaction even in the way his sweat was wicking efficiently into the breeze, except for this one annoying patch high on his brow, just under the lip of his helmet. He flicked at it with a finger, and in that instant spied the groundhog ambling out of tall grasses along the river. This too he recalled later. How it raised its snout, spotting them in turn.

Maybe Jeremy was caught up in his own momentum, rhythm, surprise—he hesitated. Had he started to call out? The muscles in his throat tightened when he recalled the instant.

For its part, the animal froze as well. Considered. Then with astonishing quickness hurtled its bulk of rolling muscle and fat across the path. Dodging Gretchen, it rammed heavily into Shivani's spokes.

His eyes were already open. This he realized. But only gradually would they tighten toward focus, and only partly. The pounding pulse in his head throbbed more painfully as his vision cleared. But someone was just then sticking a finger in his eye, pushing one lid up and the other, and he was figuring she was a doctor—who else would poke him with such casual deliberateness?—and so this was a hospital. And he was in a hospital. Okay.

When he woke again he remembered the hospital right off. His own lack of surprise, of curiosity, surprised him. The dimmed light in the room seemed to thrum at the same rate as the thud of pain in his head. A woman was hovering between him and the light, looking for something in his face, studying him. Was this the doctor again? He started to ask and then, the effort too exhausting, fell back and far away. The woman glanced to the side, and then someone else, Shivani, was hovering too, closer. He felt her kiss on his lips.

"Hey," she said softly and held a straw to his mouth.

Water was good. He sucked after more.

"What the fuck," he tried to whisper, water dribbling down his chin.

Next time, or maybe the time after, that's when he began to realize something was wrong or at least different. Though he couldn't put his finger on it. Couldn't put a name to it.

Shivani had been speaking for a while, he realized this too, but his attention was drifting. He tried hard to appear attentive.

"Do you remember?" she asked. She was asking him.

"Not sure," he mumbled. He was proud of that answer—it didn't give him away.

"You saw it just before, right? The groundhog."

The groundhog he did remember.

"Sure," he said.

"I didn't—that's the thing. I felt Gretchen swerve and the thump as it hit my front wheel and then I was pitching over. Darling, brave Jeremy—you tried to catch me. So we were both going down. Owen and Lee ran right into us and down into the mangle. What a mess." She sighed and he could tell she was struggling not to cry.

He didn't know what to say.

He remembered the groundhog.

"Your helmet split on the pavement just like it's supposed to, but you were knocked cold anyway. The rest of us were nothing but cuts and scrapes." Shivani was struggling with her own helplessness.

He closed his eyes. Her voice, its elite Delhi-wallah cadence, more British than the Queen, was scraping, grating—annoying. It had never bothered him before. He knew that. But all this emotion, the concern and guilt, was radiating from her too. Demanding a response in kind. Was he supposed to provide sympathy?

A quick surge of anger shivered him. His head was throbbing harder.

The flame of his little rage expired almost instantly, leaving him frail, a spent wick on the hospital bed. He could not move.

Jeremy groaned. Shivani stroked her cool hand across his forehead.

She had been at his bedside when he woke—he remembered this too—and he'd recognized her right off, her eyes tired, the stylish flair of her short hair, unusually mussed in the non-time of the hospital.

He'd known who she was.

He'd been glad to see her, truly, to sip the cool water through a straw, grateful not to be alone in this strange place.

But now as he considered, and he was panting lightly through his mouth, he realized that even in that first moment awake he'd also felt—what?—different. Distanced. Dislocated. Watching this lovely woman from very far away. His wife. Hugging a silk shawl against the arid chill. Someone he knew so very well. And yet it seemed as though a tether between them had snapped, like a tendon torn at the bone hinge.

A question occurred to him and he opened his eyes once more. "How long?" he whispered.

She hesitated, searching his face. "You've been here two weeks."

That stopped him. It took a while to make sense.

"Two weeks? I was out for two weeks?"

Shivani nodded, and now she was looking sad and worried and guilty again, and relieved all at once, tears in her eyes.

He turned his head. He figured the groundhog must have got away free and clear.

"You remember the groundhog?" This time it was Owen Thurlow, his pal the provost.

He managed not to roll his eyes. "Sure," he sighed.

And all he didn't remember: the shell of his helmet splitting. Cell calls to 911. The medevac copter. It had become a crazy therapeutic catechism, his wife and friends reciting the sequence over and over. Chanting the story of all that had swirled about while he remained an unconscious witness. As if capturing it in ever-finer detail might somehow penetrate to the heart of the matter. As if grasping precisely what had happened would bring him to himself. His old self.

It was beginning to drive him crazy.

Did they sense the truth?

He would listen graciously, or pretend to, hiding his boredom and occasional flaring annoyance as best he could. The flashes of emotion, unwilled, unprovoked, unreasonable, were also unnerving. All his life he'd prided himself on his cool. Unlike other teenagers years before, unlike many adults to this day, he'd never allowed his emotions to run riot. This was one reason he'd been convinced that the silent libraries and controlled classrooms of the academy were his destiny.

Of course, the recitations did also obviously help Shivani and Owen and Gretchen feel better about the outcome. That annoyed him too. So this time it was Owen Thurlow resurrecting the damned groundhog.

A question struck him only now. "Why the hell did it take me so long to come out of it?" Jeremy demanded, as if he needed to get to the bottom of some truth buried from his gaze, his voice both hoarse and sharp.

Owen seemed startled. "Well, you just didn't wake up, not that first evening. The neurologists wanted to stabilize you. So they induced a coma to play it safe." He hesitated before going on, as if this next verged on something more intimate. "I mean, Jesus, Jeremy, your brain was all bruised and swollen—it needed time to heal. But even that turned out not to be enough," he said, trying to convince the patient after the fact. "Dr. Wainwright finally persuaded Shivani you needed surgery—she opened a patch of skull to relieve the pressure."

He lay still and considered. The image struck him as odd, as eerie: contemplating his own head laid open. It dizzied him. Tears welled up out of nowhere, trickling onto his cheek. He'd never been one to weep, certainly not in front of others. He swatted at them with one hand, an IV tube rattling awkwardly along. Thurlow seemed not to notice.

From his first waking, nurses had been swabbing a wound on his head and changing the bandage every few hours. He'd assumed a gash from the original accident.

And all along there'd been this headache behind his eyes, radiating deeper and deeper still, and it had never entirely disappeared. Now its presence seemed almost reassuring. Along with the thrum of his blood and the steady breaths in his chest, one after another.

He'd never felt so fully the fragility of this enterprise. Living. He blinked away at a fresh rush of tears.

A day or two later he was being examined by Dr. Wainwright, the same neurologist who'd brought him back into the world. She must have been forty or forty-five, he guessed now, her tinted auburn hair cropped short. She was checking his eyes again, the stitches in his itching scalp. As she bent close over him in a lab coat and hospital fatigues, he smelled a faint mix of sweat and detergent and peppermint.

"There's this thing," he said.

"Mmm, hmm," she said, shining a pocket flashlight into his other eye.

"It's hard to describe, to explain."

"Mmm, hmm."

"I just don't feel like myself."

She flicked the flashlight off. "Are you experiencing discomfort? Nausea?"

That distracted him for a moment. "Well, yes, actually— there's some nausea. And sort of a constant headache. But that's not what I mean."

"Okay." She seemed only partly listening.

"The thing is, I don't feel like my old self. It's like I'm not the same me anymore, if that makes sense. Something's gone all haywire." He was speaking softly. Could she even hear him now? His lips were dry.

This was hard. He closed his eyes. But the struggle to mold words around it was already helping him grasp the slippery thing itself—the strange feelings of dislocation. As though he was staring out at the world from an angle slightly askew to what he'd ever known before. At least trying to explain the deeply unnerving sensation to Dr. Wainwright made it more real, more than just a vague unease.

If this had also taken on the tones of a private confession, as much as a plea for advice or explanation, it was because he felt, well, guilty—as if he were somehow responsible for what had happened. Though he couldn't imagine how. It occurred to him suddenly that if he were Catholic, he'd be having this chat with a priest—that notion provoked a snort of laughter. Which shot a bolt of pain through his head.

He winced and lay silent, panting lightly, for a few seconds while she was making notes on his chart.

"For one thing," he murmured, taking up the thread again,

"I've been having these crazy, veering emotions—wild swings, from rage to a kind of weepy sadness. It's pathetic." He sighed. "I've never been that kind of guy."

Still no direct response from the doctor. She was glancing at a bank of monitors.

"Yeah," he went on. "And it's also how I'm seeing my friends. Even my wife. Like they're strangers. I mean, I do know them. I'm just not relating the same way. About them. Even about myself."

A flash of heat flushed through him as he lay there. His cheeks burned and his brow was slicked with sweat. It might have been another burst of emotion, but it felt more physical than that. He wanted a sip of water. He wanted this woman to stop examining him for a moment and demonstrate some concern or at least pay him some attention.

He wasn't sure she'd even been listening. But now she did step back, a hand on the stethoscope draped over her shoulders. She studied him seriously—an odd look, almost as if she hadn't until this moment taken him in as a whole person beyond patched head, bruised brain, dilated pupils.

Nodding, she shrugged. "Yes," she said. "I hear what you're saying. This is all very uncomfortable and confusing—I can well imagine. But given the trauma you suffered, these feelings of, let's call it disorientation, aren't uncommon. And each case is so different. How symptoms manifest—there's never any predicting." She patted him on the leg.

"My guess is you're experiencing a response to a severe concussion. Believe me, Professor Matthis, it could be so much worse. As the injury fades, as your brain heals, many of these unhappy feelings will almost surely lessen and even disappear entirely."

"Okay," he said, wanting to believe her. "But it sure doesn't feel like it's heading in that direction."

She hesitated, fumbling a roll of mints from her side pocket and slipping one into her mouth. Glancing at him again, she considered. "I do have one piece of practical advice, if you don't mind my offering."

His eagerness was only too clear.

"Now understand, this part lies outside my expertise. One of the clinicians or the chaplain may say something different. But I've seen other situations resembling this, and my suggestion is, keep these feelings to yourself, at least for the time being. Think of yourself as having been wounded—recovery is always going to be slower than you like. And for better or worse, confusion is part of that process. It's understandable. Everyone understands."

Jeremy lay quietly, considering as best he could. His energy had already spent itself again, and weariness was beginning to crush him.

She looked at him directly. "What I'm saying is, if you rush to share your—what?—your sense of all these emotional changes with your wife and friends, isn't it likely they'll only feel hurt and rejected? Not to mention more guilty because they're all right and you're not.

"So," she became brisk and businesslike again, picking up his chart. "What's the point in upsetting everyone at this stage, when things may go back to the way they were?"

"Sure," he whispered, closing his eyes. "You're right."

"What I can say with some confidence is that you're healing very nicely—as rapidly as we could hope."

Even the shaded light in the room had begun to throb through to the back of his head.

At some point Dr. Wainwright must have drifted away to other duties.

Oddly—it seemed odd to him—whenever he woke alone in the night, he never doubted his own sense of himself. His consciousness would tug free of the suck of heavy, vivid dreams that vanished without a trace, even as he broke through their surface. For a few moments he'd lie still in the dry air and dim light, thirsty, taking stock, trying to recapture for an instant an image, a feeling, that had already faded beyond his grasp. He was also relieved to be alone.

The last monitor and IV drip had been detached, leaving him untethered. He moved his legs up into the sheet, lifted his arms. Their heavy thinginess, the constant need to pee despite the catheter, these were reassuring. They implicated him in being who he was, lying there, and the me-ness of the self he was considering. It provided a kind of animal certainty of the here and now. He might doubt everything else, but not that.

On one such occasion he awoke deep in the night and his head felt clear, with an alertness, a sharpness he'd forgotten could exist. Exhilarated, he sat up and breathed deep. He was hungry. It was cold in the ward. And a new thought struck: Wasn't *himself* some sort of amalgam of memories collected from boyhood on? Were the ones flicking about in his head still his? What a bizarre notion, he thought. Who else's might they be?

Almost without volition, a haphazard inventory flared, wild, charged with no little terror and fretting, leaping from one memory to another. What traces of himself might have disappeared entirely, lost forever? One recollection chased and tumbled into another by chance or association, or no reason at all.

That ugly moment when Sandy Greenwalt, like him twelve years old and training in the same bar mitzvah class outside of Pontiac, had one day opened the desk drawer in his friend Jeremy's bedroom. Who knew why? Looking for a pencil? But there lay exposed before the two of them the complicated army knife he'd swiped off Sandy's bedside table some weeks earlier, naked and accusing. All the little blades and screwdrivers and bright red shell with its silver cross. He could no longer recall why he'd taken it, or even the scene of the theft. But, oh, how vivid that scalding instant of discovery and shame had remained.

Without citing that precise example, Jeremy had often spoken over the years to his students about such peculiarly human capacities, often displayed or discussed in the very texts they were studying. The Greeks delved especially deep. That the memory of something shameful or embarrassing might eternally kindle a blaze of the original agony, piercing if brief. Stranger still to consider that the events themselves, distant in time and space, no longer existed anywhere except within the precincts of an individual skull.

Sandy Greenwalt, and this too Jeremy never mentioned to students, had died long ago. A terrible death in a ditch, the rainwater only inches deep, him having crawled from a car wreck he hadn't caused. So no one alive could testify against Jeremy any longer. No external correlative to the theft or the terrible instant of exposure in his bedroom survived. Even that damned Swiss knife was surely lost forever, buried in some unknown landfill. He alone remained custodian of the sin and shame after all these years.

Except now there'd been a singular, revolutionary adjustment: cracking his skull on an asphalt bike path had apparently cauterized the memory. Oh, the original scene could still be summoned in detail—Sandy Greenwalt, long limbed and thick lipped, shaggy red hair, opening the drawer. The jerk of recognition and accusation in his eyes. Jeremy not saying anything, just closing the desk and walking away. But the burning guilt that had haunted him for twenty years and more had vanished. Not even a shadow of it lingered, almost as if the memory did indeed belong no longer to him but to someone else entirely. No matter that it existed only in this head wobbling on these shoulders. It was an eerie sensation, as if he were peering in on someone else's private life.

His skin itched. He'd already sat up in the hospital bed and flung off the sheet. Now he slid awkwardly down and sat heavily in a padded chair by the window. His legs and feet were cold. He realized he was trembling and also that a flood of panic unlike anything he could remember was welling into his chest and throat.

Another memory came unbidden to test him, one with higher stakes: his first glimpse of Shivani Chatterjee nearly eight years earlier. Its details had been reliably seared into his synapses.

Hot and frustrated, he'd been killing time on a block of dumpy bookstores and run-down bars across from the university, instead of laboring in the library's unairconditioned stacks. The decisive chapter of his dissertation lay waiting, half-drafted in a spiral notebook, half-scattered about the airless carrel on note cards. An hour riffling through the same boxes of dusty books that had been on limp display for many months yielded nothing. Not that he expected any treasures. At last he was pushing open the shop's front door and stepping warily into the ferocious sun, when this tall, thin figure strode past him purposefully on the sidewalk, arms swinging, bangles tinkling, fresh and light and oblivious to any heat. She wore a sleeveless sundress like all the Southern girls, but a silk scarf, magenta and bluebird blue, rippled at her throat.

And he's following her. He finds himself *following* her, trailing along behind. It's already something more than curiosity. He's never done such a thing. It's not at all who Jeremy Matthis is or has ever been. Yet it's so matter of fact, as if he's been waiting for this all along and never had a choice. Turning into an alley, she tugs open the side door of the Methodist church, and before the screen can slap shut he scoots forward and slips inside too, right on her heels. Where wouldn't he have followed?

She's arrived, it turns out, to attend a monthly meeting of the local Amnesty International chapter. Some ten or twelve other good and earnest souls have fluttered in as well. Okay, he's all for this—he's decided in an instant. He'll pen letters of protest to all the oppressive governments on the planet, just so he can share the same musty air with this woman.

A cascade of dark brown with a hint of henna, Shivani's hair reaches her waist—she's still unmarried, of course—with a ribbon of the bluebird blue gathering it at the back of her long neck. A trio of delicate gold bangles, the ones that had captured him on the sidewalk with their tinkling dance; they dance, sliding up and down at the wrist of one elegant arm.

Had she noticed him before the meeting began? Eight years on and he still didn't know for sure—she'd laugh, treasuring the mystery of her own thoughts in that Methodist church and the question of whether she'd even been aware of his presence. She never let on.

More important, whether he was recounting the tale at a dinner party or the memory was scratched alive by a certain scent of rose (or mildew), it had always conjured as well a trace of his original breathless desire. Of the sexual dazzle. The delight in his own bold chutzpah. Something, too, of the dismaying worry throughout that interminable Amnesty session—there'd been so much political outrage to set down on paper—that when the instant finally presented itself and he mustered some brilliant *hello*, she might simply dismiss him out of hand like some furtive stalker. However faint, these feelings flashed along the sinews of his being, part of the fabric of his identity.

Tonight the images of that faraway moment did flare vividly—sharper, cleaner than anything he'd seen or remembered in the long, fuzzy days since the accident. Tall and slim and elegant, Shivani came striding past him, turning at last into the church's screen door. He remembered his own shoes sinking into the asphalt on that torrid afternoon. He must have followed her down the stairs—that he couldn't recall—but he certainly did remember the musty basement and the smoky rose of Shivani's cologne. Only later did he learn that her sister faithfully supplied it twice a year from a certain stall in Connaught Place.

Jeremy sat panting in the padded chair. And as he spied now the further truth, a new truth, seeping through, he drew his legs up in the hospital gown to his chest and squeezed tight, as if to shut it all away. For it came to him that, vibrant or not, this memory, like the other, had been leeched dry of emotion at its heart. Though he might recall every detail, he felt nothing. The magic that had drawn him to Shivani and bound them together from that distant start, the fatedness and wonder of it all, had belatedly flashed out, fading gray, ashen, leaving behind only the tatty, worn shell of habit and everyday life.

He might have moaned, but that seemed too dramatic. He felt too little. A strange distance or mutedness had been draped over his past, creating a chasm between a former Jeremy Matthis and the person he felt himself to be in the here and now. He had changed. That was the thing. His life had changed. Not a lot. But enough.

It now seemed to him that from the very first moment of waking days earlier, before he'd known where he was or what had happened to him, he'd been flung out stumbling on a journey over which he had no control or compass or guiding star. All he could manage was a kind of awkward staggering forward in the dark. Yet in this late night of the hospital ward, an unmapped land lay stretching before him.

He was slightly dizzy and his head ached. He realized he was shivering again. Pushing himself up from the chair, he climbed back into the bed. He was breathing hard, and he wrapped his arms about himself. Sleep offered no refuge. His mind remained sharp and clear, and it was racing.

Only two hours later, never having slept, Jeremy Matthis rose once more and showered for the first time, with difficulty, in the tiny bathroom. He dressed in clothes that Shivani had brought several days earlier to cheer them both with the anticipation of his release, whenever that might be, back into the world. But it was a new world he now intended to enter, making a place for himself as best he could. He carried the largely empty suitcase with him.

He announced his intentions at the nurses' station, and after they had remonstrated and warned as he knew they must, they pointed him to the office where he would sign his release, absolving them, the hospital, its doctors and administrators, of all responsibility. Responsibility for himself was precisely what he intended to assume. When the final form was presented for his signature, he wrote the name Jeremy Matthis with a sense of eagerness and a bit of fear, because he suspected it might be the last time. He hadn't yet decided what would take its place. Or what he would say to Shivani when she surely found him. He knew only that this was the journey, that this was the right path, wherever it might lead him.

Shruti Swamy

A Simple Composition

WHEN I WAS SIXTEEN my parents decided I should take up the veena, and I began to receive lessons from a great musician who had fallen on lean times. I had little talent, and he was a strict teacher. He often yelled me to tears. "These are the fingers of a princess," he would say, examining my hand for calluses and dropping it with scorn. My palm felt hot as I brought it back into my lap. "Again," and as I began to play he would take up his instrument in a fit of irritated passion and override me with his music. "Like this." He had thick brows and a fat, jolly nose that seemed out of character with the rest of his features; he always appeared to be scowling. As he played the veena his face became no more beautiful but it was touched by the grace of the music. His black eyes closed and his fingers moved with a subtlety I could never hope for. A simple composition, like the one he chose for me, became something else in the belly of his veena, something distilled to its essence. A longing for god, or for perfection. A longing for childhood or mother, a longing for lost days, or for a lover. His notes were never singular; he bent them into each other, playing just as time passes, one moment blending into the next. When he finished I could see tears in his eyes.

I started to practice for hours in the evenings, and my finger-tips toughened. I began to love the veena like I would a living thing, feeling tenderness as she lay in my arms, my fingers moving up and down her slender neck. But I could feel my lack of talent as my skill grew. Even to my own ears the music I produced sounded flat and rigid. I could bend the notes and quiver them, but the animating spirit that was supposed to be there underneath never appeared; it was like manipulating a puppet. But I felt it, that ache. Perhaps this is why I fell in love.

The lessons took place in the sitting room of my house, where my mother sewed clothes for the poor while my teacher scolded me. It was dark in the sitting room—the curtains were always drawn to protect the furniture—and stuffy. The overhead ceiling fan turned too slowly to do more than stir the hot air, and often went off altogether with the power cuts. I had been left alone with my teacher only three times: when the cook had needed special instruction on the night's meal, when the leather-sole repair-man returned with our shoes, and when my youngest brother had fallen from his bicycle and came crying home with a scraped knee. During the first two instances I was tense, but my teacher hardly seemed to notice any change. During the third, he told me, "You're improving."

"Not much."

"I can still see the work in your fingers."

"You have a gift so you can't imagine what it's like not to."

He looked at me sharply. He was not a young man. I knew almost nothing about him, where he lived, if he was married. Yet in that look, some knowledge passed to me, innocent as I was, about how he was thinking of me. He was considering me the way men consider women, with a grudging appreciation, even deference to their beauty. I could feel myself grow hot, not just my face, but my entire body, alone in that close room with him.

"You give yourself an excuse that way. You're too easily distracted."

I can remember being sixteen and feeling that love heavy in my chest. I was shy, with a moon-shaped face and neat black hair, and I was so dark that my marriage prospects would have been grim had my parents not been well-off. At school the girls thought I was dull and ignored me. At home, I had three brothers, all younger, who filled the house with noise, while I, even with my music, occupied the rooms very quietly, taking up very little space and demanding no attention. But attention mattered little to me, and less now that my desire for it was concentrated to a single source.

When the afternoons became hotter my mother dozed in her chair during my lessons. There was a growing awareness between us, my veena teacher and I. He began to scold me even more fiercely for my ineptitude. But I started to realize that his sharp words were a substitute for something else, and I did not cry. In fact, it was all I could do to keep from smiling. One day, he asked if I could meet him at a park that evening. Not so much asked as told me, quietly but with no sense of wrongdoing, as my mother slept. The park was on the other side of the city, one I had not been to before. I didn't think my mother would let me go, and in the intervening hours I became more and more agitated trying to think of an excuse. Ultimately, it was simple: I told her I was meeting a schoolmate to study. Since the days were long in summer I would likely be home before dark. She took no notice of the wild look my eyes had. I bathed and put flowers in my hair and wrapped myself carefully in a fresh milk-blue sari. My hands were shaking from excitement as I paid the rickshaw wallah.

My veena teacher was waiting for me by the entrance. He had not changed out of the clothes I had seen him in last, and was soaked through by his own sweat. He was smoking a beedi, and when he saw me he stubbed it out carefully and put it in his pocket. His face looked rough and unshaven. He asked immediately if I was skipping my evening practice in order to meet with him. I told him I would practice when I got home. We began to walk in the park. It was lush, full of flowers and green trees, but it seemed oddly empty, especially for this time of day. The evening light was becoming a heavy orange, almost metallic. As we moved through the park I realized it was not empty: There were lovers hidden in every corner, behind bushes and low walls, and leaning against the pillars of the crumbling ornamental buildings. Yet he didn't touch me. He told me that he was four years old when he picked up the veena for the first time: his father's. His arms were not wide enough even to span the instrument, yet after he managed an awkward hold on it music came to him effortlessly and pierced him with joy. It was the joy, he said, of a loved one returned to you—one thought dead, lost forever. He knew he had only to wait for the skill of his body to catch up to the music inside him.

Nothing felt like that to me. I didn't want to tell him so. To me, music was the unity and division of tones, like a painting was the arrangement of colors. Beauty was a mathematical certainty that arose from a precisely correct combination. It was impossible for me to imagine him as a young boy.

"You didn't tell your mother where you were going?"

"No."

He nodded. I studied him, his curls, his slender, beautiful fingers encased by rings, which he would take off with a kind of ceremony as he settled down for each lesson. His gaze was directed straight ahead of him, yet I knew that he was aware of me by how he seemed to ignore my presence. Somewhere in the distance, there was an odd sound, like a rusty gate opening.

"What is that?"

"A peacock," he said.

"No, is it?" I said. I knew the mewling cry of peacocks.

"There's something wrong with him."

The noise sounded again. And now there was something animal, ragged in it. Then the peacock came into view, brilliant and absurd. He had a strange, almost drunken gait, and when he got closer we saw knots of pink flesh where his eyes should have been. He heard our footsteps scuffing in the dust, and began to panic, running a wide, wavering arc through the dust of the path.

"What's happened to him?"

"Someone's cut out his eyes."

"You think a person did it?"

"Not a peacock."

"Why would anyone do that?"

He shook his head. "Poor fellow."

We walked for some time and it began to grow dark. The evening had swollen around me, I had sweated through my blouse. I feared I was utterly ordinary. The air smelled thickly of flowers, and in my desperation it became a cloying smell, smothering, and I wanted to pull the jasmine from my hair and throw it on the ground. He took me suddenly by the arm and led me behind a low wall where ten or twenty feet away two people moved against each other in the growing dimness. They made no noise, but I could see them: an unbuttoned blouse, hands that gripped tightly to the naked flesh. The sky was low, pinking. My veena teacher kissed me and put his hands on my breasts. His mouth tasted like the beedi he had been smoking, and some other, sweet-bitter thing— alcohol, I realized later. This should have been the moment of my truest joy, the kind of joy he had described as a young child first picking up the veena. But it felt like nothing, worse than nothing. I did not expect pain—but what had I expected? I started to feel for my voice, at first curiously, then frantically, as he pulled at the fabric of my sari and pressed his flesh into mine. At first I couldn't find it. Then it was there, small but there, like a little white moth. I felt it come up in my mouth as he moved against me. I swallowed it down.

.   .   .

So I was not a virgin when I married Hritesh, though I led him to believe differently. On our wedding night we fell asleep in the petaled bed as soon as we removed our elaborate clothes, consummating our marriage four days later, shyly, and with genuine ineptitude during the afternoon. Whatever I had worried about disappeared when I saw his bashfulness and inexperience. It made me gentle toward him, holding him in that act of love no differently than a mother holding her boy; it is pity, I thought, the way a mother holds her boy. In the morning I woke before him and watched him sleep, this half-stranger who had grown up in my neighborhood and whom I had passed by walking to or from school. Love had not come yet, though they told me it would, growing slowly over the years of our lives together. What I felt was a kind of detached fondness, which often I drew out of me to hold up and inspect like an X-ray, looking for signs of growth or change. Once, when he placed a sweet in my mouth, I thought I observed a change, a new tender shoot. He took my braid in his hand and wrapped it around his fist, marveling at its strength. And wept during our first true fight, tears that startled, even frightened me, as his eyes got so red. I touched his hair, saying, "A husband shouldn't cry." And then after a while he stopped.

"Will you play something for me?"

But I would not touch my veena. Sometimes when my husband was at work I walked by the home of my veena teacher. He lived in a small bungalow behind a wall that was topped with shards of glass: Through the gate I could see a garden, and I could hear children's voices coming from the other side of the gate. Once, I saw a woman going through, a young woman with flowers in her hair. After that I stopped walking there. Each day that summer, the heat that collected in the small rooms of our flat was intolerable, and we brought our mattresses up to the roof and slept without blankets. Then my husband received a scholarship and we went to Germany. The air in Mainz was thin and dry, not like the heat of home. It was lighter and deadlier, this fall air. My husband was studying particle physics at the university, and I spent my days in the apartment they rented to students, which, though it was not much larger than our flat at home, seemed set up for a kind of life I didn't know how to live yet. I had thought that I would feel like a new person when I came to Germany. It was not that I was lonely. I was no lonelier than I had ever been. But I had some difficulty sleeping. I missed those nights on the roof, lying on a thin cotton mattress. I missed the looseness of those nights, watching the stuck kites in the trees shifting as a breeze came through, the fat orange moon.

We went one evening to the house of my husband's adviser, who was Gujarati, and his German wife. This professor had been living in Germany for so long that he now ate meat, and there was no food for us at the dinner because even the salad had bacon. I didn't know whether it was less polite to keep some food on my plate and not eat it, or to not put any food on my plate at all. I was afraid to look at Hritesh because I was sure that whatever he was doing was the wrong thing, and he would be doing it with a smile at the center of his burning face. I was hungry and watched the professor and his wife eat. The professor's dark face had taken on a German look, a frowning, inward expression.

"You don't like German food?" said the wife, finally, as I sat in front of my empty plate.

"We are vegetarians," I said.

"It's only chicken." Her arms were white and bare and looked soft, but she was plain and wore a shapeless blouse. "Here."

I covered my plate with my hands. The professor looked at me with a smile on his face—what could have been called a smile. Sometime later he said a phrase to me in German, but I didn't know he was speaking to me, and kept my eyes fixed politely away. He said it again. This time my husband said, "He's asking you how your German is coming."

I said the one phrase I knew in German, "*Ich spreche kein Deutsch.*"

The professor replied in English. "Smart man, your husband. He's picking it up."

"You like this city, Mainz?" said the wife.

"I haven't seen much of it," I said.

"*Sie hat immer Angst,*" he said to Hritesh. "Do you tell her about your research?"

"I don't want to bore her."

"You don't bore me." And I noticed, now, that he had grown thin, my husband. His face especially. It had a restless quality to it, and his eyes were unusually bright. After dinner, we walked home in the cold, what felt like bitter cold to me, though it was not yet winter. At this time of night, the city was lit yellow, spilling over with students, laughing and arguing in their harsh, orderly language. "Why didn't you tell them that we were vegetarians?"

"I thought he knew."

"Is he a good man, this professor of yours?"

"I think so. He's brilliant."

"What did he say about me in German?"

"He said you were scared."

"Scared? Scared of what?"

But he didn't know. "We'll have to have them over for dinner," he said, with a kind of despair.

My husband glanced often out the window when we were at home. He had acquired habits I found odd. First thing when he arrived, he ran his finger under the rims of the three lampshades in our apartment, and sometimes he took the framed picture of his father off the wall and removed the back. Then he would replace it and clean the glass, almost apologetically, freshly anointing his father's forehead with kumkum and sandalwood paste, as we did to honor our dead.

"What are you looking for?"

"No—nothing. It comforts me."

He did seem comforted by his actions: They eased him. After dinner we would watch the one channel on TV that sometimes showed English movies. When I was alone, I began to go on long walks. I wanted to get my skin used to, or even immune to the cold. I wanted my body to accept Germany, its new home. It was true, I had spent so much time in the flat because I was scared to leave it. I was constantly worried I was going to be made a fool. And as the days grew colder and shorter, the flat seemed to grow smaller and closer, contracting around me like a fist. I walked around the university, which was hundreds of years old, and decorated with the statues of serious-nosed men. But for all my worry, hardly anyone seemed to notice me. I bought coffee at the cafeteria and drank it slowly as I sat. This is the future, I thought, I had wondered so much about. It was here now. I could stop wondering what would happen to me.

"Arundathi?" When I looked up, it was my husband's professor, carrying his food on a tray. An odd hour to eat, not a mealtime at all, nearing four.

"Where is Hritesh?"

He shrugged. "You imagine he is always with me. Were you meeting him?"

"No." Then I said, "You eat here?"

"Yes, on occasion. It's not bad."

"Your wife doesn't make—?"

"No, she's not a good wife like you, packing lunches. I'm going to eat this in my office if you'd like to join me."

His office was in a squat, modern building that looked out on the river. It was warm in the room, and he sweated as he ate, wiping at his forehead with a napkin. Again I watched him eat. He had thick, sensual lips and intelligent eyes, near black, and cutting. But there had once been a softness I could make out in his face, in his eyes. I thought I could see the kind of boy he had been, brash and loved, and happy. When he was finished, he belched into his closed fist.

"Your husband is transferring out of my department."

"What?"

"He's going to mathematics. Or trying, at any rate."

"He didn't say anything about it."

"Your husband," he said, shaking his head. "Your husband is coming up with some strange ideas."

He placed his tray on the stack of trays he had accumulated in his office. The books on the shelves were not just science—I spotted three slim volumes of Urdu poetry.

"You speak Urdu?"

"Not anymore. I used to."

"I studied it in school."

"I've never read more beautiful poetry. I can't read those books anymore but I remember what they were like. I've lost the language." There was something about the way he was looking at me. I had never felt physical desire before, and was not sure I felt it now. It was my heart coming up in my mouth. Beating loud in my ears, my heart.

"Are you happy here, in Germany?"

"Yes," I said, automatically. "Are you?"

He went to lock the door. Then he came to where I was sitting and leaned down to put his mouth on mine. I could taste the meat in his mouth from his sandwich. I stood up and pressed my body against him. I was on my period, but he said he did not mind. There was nothing in it, no shyness. There was no anger. It was deliberate and almost tender. At one point, realizing we would be visible to the students below, he went to turn off the light. Outside, the river was a flat sheet of silver, shining so hard it hurt to look at it, even as the sky was dimming, the thick gray clouds seeming to absorb all that brilliance. Without giving anything back.

. . .

At home, I washed myself and made supper and waited past dark for my husband, who now kept irregular hours at the lab. I was not altered, my hair was still neat, my clothes and my face. It stunned me, my own neatness, my lack of change. I thought, this is not the woman I have become, this is the woman I have always been. When Hritesh finally arrived, I looked hard at him, wanting to feel pain. What a tired face my husband had for someone so young. His skin was a rich nut-brown but darker and delicate under his eyes. "You didn't tell me you were transferring departments."

"I didn't think you'd be interested."

"I saw Professorji at the cafeteria."

"Oh god," he said, "we still have to invite them, you remember? To dinner."

"Look at you. You're working too hard."

"I'm close," he said. "I'm close to something."

"Close to what?"

But he wouldn't—or couldn't say. Later I found him standing worried at the window, looking out at the street.

"You see that van?"

I looked. There, parked across the street, was the white delivery van of the bakery around the corner.

"What is it?"

He stood there for a long while. Then he came away from the window. "Nothing."

The van was gone in the morning. As he was leaving for work he said, "Tell me if the van comes back."

"You want me to call you at the lab if the van comes back?"

"No, no, don't call. Just write down the time." Then, at the look on my face, he said, "Forget it. Forget it, *na*? Don't do anything."

But there was, quite suddenly, a miracle that was happening outside: It was snowing. I had seen snow in movies, but it was fake snow, only soapsuds, and looked different than this. Real snow was so small, and came all at once, but gently, and fell in a way I had never seen anything fall before, with none of the weight and force of rain, with profound and unhurried silence. We stood like children at the window. The snow touched every-thing we could see, like light. We were afraid only because we didn't know how it would feel in our fingers and our hair and on our faces. But after a while Hritesh became brave and handed me my coat. Outside, there was a quality of silence I had never heard before, even in this quiet country. I caught a wafer of snow on my finger. I licked it. It was a pure drop of water, tasting of nothing, holy water. Hritesh, I saw, was standing quite still, like I was, as the white gathered shaggy in his hair and eyebrows and eyelashes and on the shoulders of his coat. There was something absurd about the way he stood there, almost unblinking, but I was so glad. He had sensed, as I had, the sacredness of the living moment, the sacred quality of that silence, and become, like me, utterly still.

Yet we bore no resentment toward the children who broke into the quiet with their shrieks and their snowballs and their stamping feet. We went inside, shook the snow from our hair, and wiped our dripping faces. He was smiling, my husband, he had a good smile, the smile of a shy young girl. "You'll be late," I said.

"Arundathi—"

"You'll be late," I said, pushing him lightly toward the door. When he was gone, I sat down on the sofa. I thought I would cry. But I didn't cry. I just sat there.

For two weeks, I watched myself. I cooked the meals, as I always had, making the sad substitutions with German vegetables and spices that made my own cooking unfamiliar to me. The snow melted and the world became ordinary again, even drab, with all that mud. I walked around the university, but I didn't see the professor, except for once, talking to a student outside the physics building, and I quickly turned around and walked the other way before he saw me. My husband during this time pulled further and further into himself. I saw him once, too, on campus, through the lighted window of a classroom where he sat in the last row, furiously writing notes. At home, he seemed almost apologetic, and talked to me gently, as if compensating for some hurt he had caused me. The matter of the van was not mentioned. Some days it sat parked for hours when he was at the university, but left before he got home.

Then one evening the van had not gone when my husband got home, and he became very agitated. He was frightened, I could see, and I began to feel frightened, too. He kept walking to the window and looking out at the van. He wouldn't tell me what was the matter. He was suppressing tears: They trembled on the lids of his eyes and wet his eyelashes. I sat with him, talking to him very quietly, in our mother tongue, which seemed to calm him just a bit, to make his suffering just bearable. When I ran out of things to say he begged me to keep speaking, so I recited the poems I had learned in school, and then, when I came to the end of those, nursery rhymes. I talked and talked for what felt like hours, until my throat and tongue were tired, even my jaw. Sometimes I would fall into a light doze, and wake to see him in such a terrifying state of despair I would rouse myself completely and begin talking again. Then it was dawn. He was tired out. He stretched his body on the bed and slept. I washed my face in the sink with cold water, put on a clean sari, and went to the office of his adviser. It was too early, and the building was locked; I waited outside for some time. It was cold, and it was good to feel cold. In my tiredness I leaned against it, pressed it close to me to keep me awake. I felt love for my husband all at once, bright as sunlight, breathtaking. I thought of him on our wedding day, his smiling face surrounded by red and white flowers. After a while a janitor came and unlocked the door and I went to the third floor and sat opposite the professor's office, and, in the warmth of the hallway, dozed until he came and prodded me awake. We went into his office. He was angry to see me and said that it "looked bad" for me to come there. As he lectured me I began to wonder at the little tenderness I had felt for him. He now looked so self-satisfied, his face the wide, fleshy face of a frog. With his frog's tongue he wet his lips. He made no allusion to the last time we had seen each other, as though our physical awareness of the other had shifted back to its original, blank state. But I remembered him, his wide shoulders, his soft belly. Then he said, "Well?"

"What is my husband researching? Is it dangerous?"

"Dangerous? In what way?"

"Something has happened. I don't know quite what, he won't tell me. Is he in some kind of trouble?"

"No, no. There is nothing dangerous about his research. Dangerous maybe for his career, nothing else. He believes that he's found a fundamental error in the basic precepts of mathematics that disproves everything that came after it. He believes he is on the cusp of developing a new system of numbers that will change the way we understand the world."

"What is it?"

"What is what?"

"The error?"

"Two and two is not four."

"Two and two is not four? What is it, then?"

"For that, you'll have to ask him."

"Why didn't you tell me?"

"To be honest, I didn't quite know the extent of it until a few days ago. The maths chair and I had a long chat."

"Two and two is not four. Could it be true?"

He answered me with a look.

"Will you help him? My husband?"

"How can I help him?"

"I don't know—there must be some way—"

"I'm a professor, not an ayah. I can't force him to study this and not study that, to do this but not to do that."

I was pleading. "He needs help."

"Go home to your husband. He needs a good wife to pack him lunches. That's how you help him. You be good and gentle and kind to him and make him feel like a man." He fixed me in his gaze. A brilliant man, but not a good man, I knew that now, too late.

Then I was back outside, in the widening morning. The sunlight was sharp and dripped into my eyes. They were having a parade, the city of Mainz, another parade, for there had been two or three already this month. The parades, my husband told me, would stop only in March, after Lenten time. The thought of him waking embarrassed or frightened clenched around me. I didn't want him to wake alone. But though it was not very far to the flat, the streets were dense, nearly impenetrable with people. There was a marching band, loud brass, and the music was meant to be cheerful but it hit my chest with a booming menace. I remembered the firecrackers that went off in the streets at home during parades, a wild scattering of noise that was so unlike the orderly racket of the marching band—it had never occurred to me that it would be a noise I'd miss. In the heart of this noise I thought: My life is starting. For a moment I felt a frenzy that was like happiness. Then the marching band moved farther down the street and the clamor lessened. In its place was a hideous group of Punch-and-Judy puppets, larger, even, than human-size, with enormous red noses and fat cheeks. But there were no strings—people, I realized, in painted masks. The masks were large and heavy looking, three or four times the size of the true heads underneath, but the bodies bore them lightly as they ambled down the street, clowning for the children who sat on the shoulders of their parents and clapped their hands and laughed with delight, pointing their chubby fingers. I let my terrified heart calm, thinking, people not puppets. The expressions on the masks were contorted with delight, delight that came like an agony upon them, and I could not calm. I could not calm and I could not hide my face.

I could not pass until the procession was finished. I could not stand still. But what choice did I have? I stood and watched as the puppets made their way down the street. I stood there until the procession was finished and the street was cleared, and then I walked home to my husband.

Charles Haverty
Storm Windows

BY SEVEN-THIRTY MY FATHER hadn't come home, so we sat down to dinner without him. My mother didn't touch hers. She kept very still, her hands folded in her lap, her cranberry-colored dress crowded with the Twelve Days of Christmas—lords-a-leaping, maids-a-milking, geese-a-laying, the works. The saddest thing of all was that my father would miss her in that dress. Now and again, with a swish of silk, she'd step away from the breakfast-room table to stare down the telephone on the kitchen wall, returning silent and stricken, her eyes fixed on the back of his chair. When my sister, Margot, and I had cleaned our plates, she told us to take the dog outside.

It was Christmas Eve and white beyond the dreams of Irving Berlin. I was eight years old, Margot was six, and I'd stop at nothing to make her laugh. Before dinner we'd made a snowman in the backyard, and now, to amuse her, I endowed him with breasts—massive breasts—so that he became a she, and when her breasts got so heavy they dropped to the ground, I reinforced them with wire croquet wickets and wooden stakes whose rounded tops protruded like nipples. As the breasts grew bigger and bigger, my sister laughed and laughed until Trixie ran around us, barking, churning up a muddy circle in the snow.

"Stop it, Lionel," my mother called from the back door. "You're making her wild." Coming closer, she saw what I'd done and went back into the house. She emerged carrying a broom. With the glare of the porch lights behind her, she swung hard at those gravity-defying breasts, and I could almost feel the shock run up her arms when she made contact with the wood and wire within; I could see it in her face and her body. She let go of the broom and tore at the breasts with her bare hands. She closed her fists around the stakes, drew them out like daggers, and let them fall at her feet. Breathing hard, she looked at me and said, "You make me sick."

When she was back inside, I set about repairing the damage, but the fun had gone out of it. It had become a chore. Soon headlights swept over us. "He's here," my sister said, and followed Trixie into the garage attached to the back of the house. I stood still, waiting, until I heard the rise and fall of my mother's shouting through two layers of window glass. I returned my attention to the snowwoman.

After a while, my father came out in his shirtsleeves with Trixie close behind. "Your mother's upset," he said in his sad, reasonable voice.

"She's upset with *you*." I wouldn't look at him.

"I'd like you to stop that now. Would you please cut it out?"

I continued restoring the breasts in my workmanlike way.

"You know what night this is, don't you?" he asked. "You know who's watching?"

I knew there was no Santa Claus, but I didn't want my father to know I knew—this seemed somehow important to me—so I stepped away from the snowwoman. He looked her up and down and shook his head. "For Christ's sake, fix that, will you?" Then he turned around and went back to the house.

The snow had stopped. The only sound was Trixie's heavy, humid panting as she watched and waited for what I'd do next. I dug into the snowwoman and tossed the snow behind me. Trixie caught it in her mouth, gnashing her teeth in the air. Our big, old house loomed in the dark.

We'd moved in at the end of August, and my mother, my sister, and I hated the house, each for our own reasons. I hated its oldness. On Long Island our home had been built just for us, whereas this one had been constructed before the First World War. Innumerable strangers had lived in it; some might even have died in it. In my new school, our third-grade teacher, Sister Alexandra, taught us that in the course of a single day, the human body lost almost a million skin cells, that over a year we each shed more than eight pounds of dead skin. "And where do you think it all goes?" She ran a fingertip across the desktop. "Dust," she said and offered it to the air. "Here's a little bit of all of us." I imagined a blizzard of past lives drifting through the rooms. Only my father, who traveled often on business and spent the least amount of time there, loved the house.

My woolen gloves were wet and heavy, and I dropped them on the ground. Trixie retrieved the left one, brought it to her hiding place under the evergreens planted along the foundation, and tore it to shreds. I scooped snow from the snowwoman's ravaged torso, packed it dense and smooth, and pelted the side of the house. The icy air seared my lungs, and my hands felt raw, but the solid slap of snowballs against brick was pleasing, and I hurled them harder and higher, until I heard the splash of breaking glass. The back door opened, and my father stepped out onto the porch. He gazed past me up at the lighted window of his bedroom, where my mother appeared in her bathrobe, staring down at him. When the light went out, he said to me, "Don't say I didn't warn you." He didn't sound angry.

I stayed out there as long as I could stand it and then went straight to bed without saying good night. When my father checked in on me later, I pretended to be asleep.

My parents' door was shut when my sister and I woke the next morning. She padded down the stairs ahead of me. Turning the corner into the living room, she cried, "Trixie ate the baby Jesus!" Under the Christmas tree, the nativity scene was in disarray.

"No, she didn't." I fetched the mangled Christ child, still wet with saliva, from in front of the fireplace. "She just chewed him up, is all."

"Smart dog."

"What's so smart about that?" I was distracted. Something was off about the scene, some asymmetrical something.

"Other dogs would eat a wise man or a shepherd," she said. "They're bigger." She wrapped her arms around the dog's neck. "But you picked the baby Jesus, didn't you?" Then glancing up at me, she asked, "How did she *know*?"

Colored lights sizzled on the tree. My Christmas stocking hung flaccid and empty from the mantel beside the cornucopia of my sister's, and suddenly I understood what was wrong. They'd given me no presents, nothing. I remembered the snowwoman, the shattered window, my father's sad face, and I felt like throwing up, though mostly I felt embarrassed.

Margot knelt before her pile of presents. More than anything, she'd wanted an Etch A Sketch. She already knew the size, shape, and weight of the box and moved from package to package until she located the right one and began to unwrap it. Without a word, I went to the foyer, put on my boots and corduroy coat, and walked out into the morning and away from that hateful house. With the mutilated Jesus pressed into my palm, I bore this colossal injustice like a cross and might have walked all the way to Calvary had the sidewalks been shoveled and I not been wearing pajamas. At the end of our block, I turned around and went back.

Inside, the house was silent but for Andy Williams singing "It's the Most Wonderful Time of the Year." From the foyer, I could see my father stretched across the living room floor, his head cradled in my mother's lap, drawing ragged breaths through bared teeth. I stepped into the room.

My mother's face was a mask of anger, a leopard's face. "Laugh now," she said. Then, casting a panicked glance at my sleety boots, she shouted, "For God's sake, take those off!"

I sank to the carpet beside my sister and did as I was told. Fingers fiddling with the knobs on her Etch A Sketch, Margot said, "Daddy says he can't *breathe*." The gray screen displayed a tangle of fine black scribble, and I sensed that whatever was happening here was my fault.

My father tried to speak. I scooted closer.

"Change that," he said.

"Change what?" I was trying not to cry.

"That." He gestured toward the stereo.

"Oh, what does it *matter*?" my mother said.

"This—" he took a great gulp of air and swiped his hand at Andy Williams. "This can't be the music I die to." The word jolted through me.

"Turn it off," my mother said.

"No." My father slapped the carpet. "I said *change* it." Then he looked up at me and said, " 'Nessun dorma.' "

"In *English*," my mother wailed, but I knew what he meant, and he knew that I knew. I went to the turntable and replaced *The Andy Williams Christmas Album* with *Favorite Italian Tenor Arias*. On the third drop of the tone arm, my father raised his hand.

"There," he said, "leave it," and the aria began. Evenly, the singer sang the phrase "Nessun dorma," then he sang it again. The tenor went on, his voice building, rising on a tide of music, rising and rising and then breaking, tragic and ecstatic.

My mother got up to phone for an ambulance, and my father called me to him. "Closer," he whispered. "I don't want your sister to hear." He hadn't yet shaved but smelled of lime aftershave. Trixie lay beside him. I smoothed her fur with the flat of my hand, not to calm her so much as to calm myself. "Upstairs. My bedroom. The walk-in closet."

"What am I looking for?" I didn't want to stop petting Trixie; it was all that kept me from crying.

"You'll see." He nudged me. "Go."

The music swelled, spreading through the house, following me up the carpeted staircase, licking at my heels. It was strange to be inside their bedroom—we weren't supposed to go in there—and as soon as I entered the closet, I saw the presents, wrapped in paper patterned like my mother's dress, with tags that read, TO LIONEL, FROM SANTA. Across the room, through the intact window, I saw the jagged hole my snowball had punched through the lower-left corner of the storm window, a many-pointed star against the morning. Relieved I hadn't broken *both* windows and let the winter in, I loaded my arms with packages and carried them down to the living room, where my mother was back on the floor with my father. She held herself with the tragic dignity of the president's widow, back straight, eyes downcast, lashes like wet black petals. One hand played in my father's hair, the other clenched in a fist, tight as a grenade.

"That's not all," my father said, rising to his feet. "That *can't* be all. Fetch the rest." It took me two more trips up the stairs. "Now, open them." I unwrapped the smallest one first: a waterproof, shockproof Timex wristwatch with a Twist-o-Flex band. My father sat in his armchair by the window. "Go on." He watched with an almost cannibalistic intensity as I unwrapped the next present and the next and the next—a junior deluxe chemistry set, the Aurora Thunderjet 500 HO slot car track, the works of Franklin W. Dixon—but I took no pleasure in it, and by the last package, the ambulance had arrived. My father met the paramedics at the door, and though Christmas Mass still lay ahead of us, he welcomed them inside for Belgian waffles made on the waffle iron my mother hadn't yet unwrapped.

Thirty-two years later, my wife and I bought our own brick house, a round-shouldered colonial outside Boston even older than the one I'd grown up in. Though it was a stretch for us and needed lots of work, Jane portrayed it as a shared adventure, and I gave in. For her, a child of divorce, the house represented a triumph over the chaos of her youth, whereas all I could feel was a suffocating sense of responsibility; all I could see was a never-ending plague of peeling paint, dripping faucets, buckling shingles, and rotting railings, whose repair fell mostly to Jane. When I was growing up, my father had spared me such chores, performing them himself while I watched from a safe distance. He believed that a man who couldn't replace a sash cord couldn't be a real man, and in time, Jane too came to see my neglect of our house as a kind of betrayal.

It was the night before Halloween, and though it was past their bedtime, I'd promised our girls, Caroline and Vanessa, that we could carve jack-o'-lanterns. As I plunged the knife into the second pumpkin, the whole house went dark. Jane was still at work, and I had no idea what to do, so I called our friend Martin, who arrived within minutes. We've known Martin and Claire since Caroline and their daughter, Julia, attended preschool together. A dozen years older than I, Martin was a professor of political science and as handy around the house as my father.

Flashlight in hand, Martin explained to the three of us how electricity works. "It flows through a pair of wires called a circuit, and each circuit is protected by a circuit breaker. Old houses like yours often have fuses instead." He went on, chanting the words into the dark like a psalm, like one of my father's arias, lyrical, rhapsodic, incomprehensible. He disappeared into the basement; my daughters and I stayed at the kitchen table.

When the lights clicked on, Vanessa, who was five then and has always been afraid of masks and makeup and any manner of disguise, said, "I hate Halloween." Caroline, who's six years older than her sister and has never been afraid of anything, asked why. "'Cause it's about death," Vanessa said, and I laughed to hear her little voice wrapped around that big word. The laugh was still in my throat when my sister phoned to tell me that our father had been taken to the hospital. She recited the litany of symptoms: the chest pains and nausea, the burning sensation in the upper abdomen, the sense of impending doom.

"Impending doom?" The knife was in my hand. One jack-o'-lantern wore a raggedy gash where its grin belonged; the other had no mouth at all. Between them sat a blue mixing bowl brimming with pulp and seeds and stringy membrane. "Dad said that—impending doom?"

"What does it *matter* what he said?"

"What if it was just something he ate?"

"Come on, Lionel. This is classic heart attack stuff."

Once Martin was gone and Jane was home and the girls were in bed, I called the airlines and packed my suitcase. Before driving me to Logan the next morning, Jane zipped a sober-looking suit into a black vinyl garment bag and laid it across the backseat. I could still feel the slime between my fingers and the pumpkin flesh under my nails.

As I waited to board the flight from Boston to Chicago, there was an announcement that it would be delayed on account of a malfunctioning toilet in the plane's rear lavatory, but when at last we boarded, the guy in the seat next to mine leaned in close and said, "Toilet, my ass."

"Sorry?"

"The delay. That was no busted john. Guy died in here."

"Died?" I said. "In the bathroom?"

"Not in the bathroom—in *here*. On the red-eye from L.A. Heart attack, stroke, whatever. Girl at the counter told me. Took 'em that long to haul him out of here and clean up the mess."

I thought of the pumpkin guts sloshing in the blue bowl and of my father, my poor father. It was Halloween, and flight attendants roamed the aisles in witch hats, their faces painted ghoulishly. Vanessa was right: It was about death, *all* about death, and there was nothing cute about it. On a yellow legal pad, I scribbled notes toward my father's obituary but found that I could barely trace the outline of his public life; his private life, his *real* life, remained an even darker mystery.

When we landed at O'Hare, I rented a car and drove deep into the suburbs. The hospital was new and ungainly, a high-tech purgatory grown up out of a cornfield. I took an elevator to the cardiac care unit, but when I stepped into the room whose number my sister had given me, I found a stranger in the bed. He pressed a button and a nurse appeared. "Can I help you?"

"Detweiler," I said and pointed to the whiteboard on the wall behind her, where traces of my father's name, partially erased, hovered over her shoulder. "Richard Detweiler?" It was hard to breathe. "My father?"

"Mr. Detweiler's *gone*," she said and turned to scrub the ghost of his name with the heel of her hand. I leaned against the wall and started to cry. "Oh, no," she said. "He left on his own. Mr. Detweiler's fine. Really." She brought her face close to mine and whispered, "I really shouldn't be telling you this, but it might have been something he ate."

Traveling west, away from the hospital and toward the big, old house I grew up in, I felt lightened, reprieved, immortal. Compared to the occluded streets back East, the roads here were straight and wide, and in my mind's eye I pictured the red rent-a-car as a robust little corpuscle pumping unimpeded through a network of veins and arteries and into the healthy heart of my history. In a couple of weeks, I'd turn forty. I was home.

When I pulled into the driveway, my father was standing at the top of a ladder set up high against the house. A stack of storm windows leaned against an oak tree. The bottom of the ladder was planted among the evergreens where our dog, Trixie, used to hide and where her ashes were now buried. High above it all, my father appeared embarrassed.

I called up to him, "You think this is the best time to be doing this?"

"It's late." He wouldn't look at me. "Tomorrow's already November."

"But it's so warm. Wouldn't you rather—"

"The women are inside," he said. "You should let your mother know you're here."

I found her talking with my sister at the breakfast-room table, filling orange and black paper bags with peanut butter cups, Mounds bars, and Snickers and stapling them shut. Margot was in the thick of a divorce—her husband wanted out of their childless marriage in order to marry his pregnant girlfriend—and as soon as she saw me, she went silent. I stood in the doorway and said, "Trick or treat."

Like our father on the ladder, my sister wouldn't look me in the eye. She seemed to be holding her breath, hiding in plain sight, and when I bent to kiss her she said, "What was I supposed to do?"

"Did I reproach you? You were being a good daughter, a good sister."

"But I made you come such a long way," she said, warmer now. "And for what?"

"Consider it a sort of dress rehearsal."

"A dress rehearsal?" my mother said.

"For the real thing."

The dent of her smile disappeared.

"Go help your father," she said. "For God's sake, the man just got out of the hospital."

So I asked him how I might help, and he told me to go upstairs and unlatch the screens. Though this was a ritual we'd performed every spring and fall until I moved East, time hadn't abated the sense of trespass I felt on entering their bedroom. This was a place of secrets, of heated words and shouts. Once, when I was fifteen and Margot hadn't yet turned thirteen, we found ourselves standing together outside their door, heads bowed. She said, "You know it's about a woman, don't you?" I nodded stupidly. Later, when the coast was clear, I snuck into their bedroom and rummaged through their nightstands seeking confirmation of The Woman's existence. My father's nightstand housed a small library of travel guides and foreign phrase books, though he never left the continental United States; my mother's contained a cache of the sexual self-help classics of the 1970s—*The Sensuous Woman, The Joy of Sex, Any Woman Can.* I found it all so achingly hopeful and sad that I called off the search then and there.

A shadow moved behind the window shade, my father's silhouette cast by the Indian summer afternoon. Still giddy with a sense of reprieve, I decided that the time had come to settle the question of The Woman. I raised the shade as if opening a confessional window, but as soon as I saw his naked, frightened face through the wire mesh, my courage fell away. As an ex-altar boy, I knew that the latticed screen of the confessional was designed to hide the priest's face as well as the penitent's, and as a practicing lawyer, I'd learned that the first rule of cross-examination was never to ask a question you didn't already know the answer to. So I slipped the hook from the eyelet, butted the bottom of the screen with my fist, and moved on to the next window.

In the dozen years since that Halloween, my parents had, between them, been hospitalized at least a dozen times, including an actual heart attack, a ministroke, and a tumble down the stairs. They were both eighty-two now and still living in that big, old house, but my sister and I had convinced them to sell the place and move into an assisted-living facility. When I flew out to discuss what needed to be done, I arrived to find a scatter of storm windows propped up one to a tree in the backyard. These were less than half of the ground-floor windows—either my father had run out of strength, or my mother had put her foot down—but they seemed a sort of offering to me, a gift. *Welcome home.*

The four of us were gathered around the breakfast-room table, seated in the same places we'd occupied for as long as I could remember, when my father announced that they'd changed their minds; they'd decided to "stay put for the time being." I could tell this wasn't news to Margot and felt betrayed.

"Lionel disapproves?" my mother said, her wide mouth smiling her small smile. "Lionel's displeased?"

"I didn't say a word." But of course I was displeased.

"You don't have to say anything," my mother said. "It's written all over your face."

"I think you're making a mistake, is all." My eyes were on my sister, who was writing on a yellow legal pad with a purple felt-tipped pen. Since her divorce, she'd gone to law school and joined a practice specializing in so-called family law. "A big one. Now's the time to act, to make your move—while you still have the luxury of time." But even to myself I sounded like a television commercial, and when Margot finally met my gaze, I asked, "Are you going to help me out here, or have you gone mute?" She tilted the pad of paper so that only I could see it. In big block letters, she'd printed, SOMEBODY PLEASE SHOOT ME!!!

"Now, now," my father said. His voice had become wispy, and he could see that I heard it. "I know I *sound* bad," he said, "but I don't *feel* bad—at least not as bad as I *sound*."

I pushed my chair back from the table and stood up. "Not that this hasn't been perfectly delightful," I said, "but some things need doing, whether you stay here or not."

"Such as?" my mother asked.

"I'll start with the rest of the storm windows." I'd come there to be useful, and now I needed to channel that energy elsewhere. "It's like a mausoleum in here."

"But it's still *cold* at night," my mother said.

"If you think I'm going to haul myself back out here in a week or two just to—"

"Are you really *that* anxious to put us away? Can't you wait just a little longer? Maybe we can do you the favor of dropping dead and spare you the bother."

"Enough already," Margot said. "Go do what you've got to do before you give us all an ulcer."

I went down to the basement, my father close behind, docent

on my tour through the museum of my childhood. Between a paneled wall and a Ping-Pong table stood a group of tall Mayflower movers' cartons, yet to be unpacked after half a century. It was like the end of *Citizen Kane*: stacks of board games, yellow canisters of petrified Play-Doh, tubes of Tinkertoys and Lincoln Logs, my sister's Spirograph and Etch A Sketch and Easy-Bake Oven, a broken one-armed bandit and a scuffed, white plastic Stetson whose band read, "All the Way with LBJ."

"Boy, oh boy, I don't envy you having to get rid of all this stuff," my father said. I'd heard this before. As if for the first time, he led me past the enormous cast-iron furnace into what was once the coal room, where the screens and storm windows were stored. I carried the screens upstairs two at a time. A fine layer of dust, a little bit of all of us, had settled on their top edges.

While my father went from room to room, unfastening the inside catches on the storm windows, I fetched the long extension ladder from the garage, planted its feet among the evergreens, and drew the rope through the pulley, hand over hand, the sound of metal scraping metal, until the top touched the bricks above my parents' bedroom window. I climbed the ladder like the mast of a ship and saw shoals of snow still banked along the edges of the driveway and the shadows of the shrubbery, the leafy curve of the earth. After what seemed a very long time, my father came out of the house and took his position below, squinting up at me. I lifted the big storm window out of its frame, but after carrying the flimsy screens, my muscles weren't prepared for its sudden weight, and it slipped from my grasp and plunged down through the April air, a guillotine of wood and glass.

My heart seized. I looked down. My father stood at the bottom of the ladder, unfazed. The window lay intact across the tops of the evergreens. He looked at me, then at the window, then back up the ladder, and then he laughed, and I laughed to hear him laugh.

By the time I reached the ground, we'd both stopped laughing, and to divert attention from the fact that I'd nearly killed him, I held forth on how insane it was to perform this high-wire act year after year; how he should have the storm windows converted, replaced, modernized; how this improvement would make the house that much more marketable. "Or do I sound too anxious to put you away?"

"Go easy on your mother," he said. "The woman's had to put up with a lot of nonsense over the years." This seemed to me a strange accusation, strange and unfair, until I realized he was talking about his own nonsense, the Sixth Commandment, The Woman. He was inviting me, however obliquely, to draw him out. His confession was something I'd waited a lifetime to hear, and now I found myself terrified at the prospect. "You know, we're not so different, you and me," he added. "Not as different as you think." He watched my face with a look of acute expectancy, sipping the air through parted lips, seeking any sign of encouragement.

It was my move—all I had to do was ask—but a sudden shyness had overtaken me, and I shifted my attention to the nearest available prop. The storm window was of a long-antiquated design, divided into quadrants whose glass, by force of time and gravity, poured thicker toward the bottom. I pointed this out and said, "You know, it's liquid."

"What is?" he asked, mildly annoyed. "*Glass*? But it's not. It's not liquid *or* solid. It's—" His fingers moved over the lower-left quadrant, while his eyes continued to search my face. "It's something in between." His expression softened. "Some things are like that."

I recalled a visit to the glassworks of Murano with Jane and the girls ten years earlier, and I'd begun to describe it to my father when I remembered the kernel of regret at its center, the disgrace I'd crossed an ocean to escape, but this wasn't the story I wanted to tell there among the evergreens. Suffice it to say that there was a woman in it and that I'd behaved badly, and though

Jane had forgiven me, dismissing the affair as the classic male hedge against death, I knew even then that there was no such thing. When the glassblower stepped away from the furnace, twirling a dollop of molten fire at the end of his long metal pole, I felt my heart twisting there, my guilt. With a pair of primitive pliers, he worked at the orange-yellow hive—prodding, pinching, pulling—until it assumed the form of a horse frozen in mid-gallop, and though I mentioned neither my heart nor my guilt to my father, without these my story was hardly a story. He listened politely, but I saw that he'd grown bored and sad. This wasn't what he wanted to hear; he wanted to be *heard*, to tell his own story, share his own shame. But shame, like prayer, is a solitary pursuit. I steered the conversation back to the here and now of converting the storm windows, how this would save energy and lower his heating bills.

"I couldn't if I wanted to." His tone had turned resigned and distant. I knew I'd disappointed him. "The house has been declared a historic building. They won't let you change a thing, not even the color of the shutters. It's against the law. Imagine that."

He took his hand off the quarter-pane, and I noticed that its glass was thicker, clearer, of a different consistency than the other three, and it occurred to me that this was the one I'd broken half a century ago, its replacement. "That's from the night Santa Claus didn't come," I blurted out. He regarded me without expression. "You know," I insisted, and as I recounted the events of that evening and the following morning—my mother's party dress, the snowwoman, "Nessun dorma"—the muscles in his face twitched, and he swallowed.

"Sorry," he said, "but I don't remember any of that."

"Oh, come on, Dad." I was embarrassed by the edge of desperation in my voice, and I smoothed my fingers over the feathery evergreens to calm myself. "It was operatic. I mean, an ambulance came, for Christ's sake."

But the moment had passed; the confessional window slid shut.

"I remember the dress," he said, pressing his hand flat against the newer pane. "A partridge in a pear tree—well, that you don't forget. But the rest?" He smiled. "No, that was somebody else's life, not mine."

Year after year, we've declined my parents' invitation to celebrate Thanksgiving with them in the big, old house, opting instead to spend the holiday weekend on Nantucket with Martin, Claire, and Julia. It's the closest thing we have to an actual family tradition. Though modest as traditions go, these long, late autumn weekends make me inordinately happy, in part because I love these friends, but more, I think, because I love that Quaker island, which I've seen only at its least temperate. I find that I am happiest on islands, perhaps because I was born on one, and because, consciously or not, my daughters leave their catalog of grievances behind on the mainland, and for the space of three days, we revert to the same trio that used to carve jack-o'-lanterns at the kitchen table.

Last year, though, the girls didn't come. Julia was spending the weekend at her fiancé's parents' house in upstate New York, and then my daughters begged off, claiming that it would be "weird" to go without her, leaving just Martin and Claire and Jane and me. That last Friday, as always, we drove down to Hyannis, took the afternoon ferry across the sound, checked into the bed and breakfast we've stayed at for twenty-four years straight, and settled into our rooms, each named for an old whaling vessel. At dusk, the inhabitants gathered at the top of Main Street to light the town Christmas tree, followed by the carol sing, and as always, we were among them, though I was acutely aware of the voices missing from that chorus.

After dinner we returned to the inn. Martin opened the first of two bottles of Malbec he'd brought along. Though he is Jewish—

or maybe *because* he is Jewish—Martin takes almost guilty pleasure in the trappings of Christmas. The holly and the ivy, Alastair Sim's Scrooge, the carol sing. The four of us were sitting around the glass-topped kitchen table, talking about the origins of Santa Claus, and I somehow got on the subject of my family's first Christmas in the big, old house. Martin found this funny, and it pleased me to make him laugh (though none of the others was laughing). By the time I got to "Nessun dorma," he was laughing so hard that he seemed beyond listening. He's probably the most controlled person I know, but now he was out of control, and it was strange and unnerving to behold.

Finally I said, "It wasn't *that* funny."

"It's not funny at *all*," Jane said. "It's depressing. Pathetic, really." But this only made him laugh harder.

"He laughed to humor Lionel, and now he can't stop himself," Claire explained. Her eyes were fixed on Martin. "This isn't the first time this has happened."

"Maybe he'll stop if I tell him something *really* pathetic," I offered. "Maybe a little tragedy's just what the doctor ordered."

"It's not *funny*, Lionel," Claire snapped. Then, realizing how fierce she'd sounded, she added, softer now, but with a terrifying catch in her voice, "The last time this happened, he fainted."

Martin's face had become a purple mask, his smile a rictus through which he gasped for breath, and I feared a blood vessel would burst, that he'd suffer a stroke or an aneurysm, that he might literally die laughing, and it would be all my fault. The rest of us sat by helpless, watching and not watching, saying and doing nothing, scared to move. A passerby glimpsing the scene through the window would assume we were torturing him.

At last, his laughter became less breathless and then lifted altogether. He began to breathe normally, and wiping the tears from his cheeks, he apologized. He picked up the bottle and offered to refill our glasses, but something had gone out of the evening. We soon said good night and retired to our respective rooms.

Upstairs, Jane finished unpacking and prepared for bed, but I'd been spooked by Martin's laughing fit and wanted to talk about it, or at least to try.

"Well, that was close," I said.

She pulled back the covers on the four-poster bed. "What was?"

"*That.*" I nodded toward the door. "Martin. Downstairs. I really thought he might—" I couldn't say it.

"Oh, Lionel." She came closer and touched my cheek. "No one ever died laughing." She spoke as to a child afraid of the dark, but with the authority of loss, and I felt even more childish, though no less afraid. I pressed her hand, warm against my face. From the bathroom behind us came the persistent sound of a running toilet. "Do something about that, will you?" Jane said, turning, yawning. "I want to go to sleep, and it's driving me crazy."

It was a simple repair—a matter of untangling the chain connecting the lift arm to the tank ball—but by the time I'd finished washing up and brushing my teeth, Jane was asleep. I lay beside her in that old bed where God knows how many others had lain, and I felt Nantucket Sound still roiling under me, along with the sudden notion that death could come smiling, even laughing. Trick or treat.

Outside, the wind had picked up, rattling the ancient windowpanes. A car door slammed; a scrabble of voices and shouts rose from the cobblestones. I got out of bed and sat in a rocking chair by the window. Carefully, I raised the shade so as not to wake Jane. The pane was unprotected by a storm window, letting in the night sounds and the cold and the wind. My reflection flickered in the wavery glass—a frightened face, my father's face—and I looked past it at the night, which, in spite of the old-fashioned streetlamps and the illuminated steeple of the First Congregational Church, felt darker and deeper than before. A dog barked in the distance, and I remembered Trixie running around my snowwoman, her lopsided orbit scarring the lawn for years to come, and I realized, with a pang, that somehow I'd left her out of the story I told downstairs. I sat there thinking of her running and running, her pink tongue flapping, and as I pressed my palm against the cold glass, my cell phone buzzed on top of the dresser. A shock ran through me. I knew without looking who it was and what she would say. Still, I picked it up and whispered, "Hello?" in the dark, and my sister said, "He's gone."

Asako Serizawa
Train to Harbin

I ONCE MET A MAN on the train to Harbin. He was my age, just past his prime, hair starting to grease and thin in a way one might have thought passably distinguished in another context, in another era, when he might have settled down, reconciled to finishing out his long career predictably. But it was 1939. War had officially broken out between China and Japan, and like all of us on that train, he too had chosen to take the bait, that one last bite before acquiescing to life's steady decline. You see, for us university doctors, it was a once-in-a-lifetime opportunity. We all knew it. Especially back then.

Two nights and three days from Wonsan to Harbin the train clattered on, the lush greenery interrupted by trucks and depots manned by soldiers in military khaki. Despite the inspections and unexplained transfers, this man I shall call S remained impassive, shadowed by a dusky light that had nothing to do with the time of day or the dimness of the car's interior; he sat leaning against the window, face set, impervious to the din around him. Later, I would come to recognize this as a posture of self-recrimination, but at the time I had barely recovered from our initial journey by sea, and I was in a contemplative mood myself, in no condition to pause over the state of others, much less engage with my colleagues, who by now had begun drinking in earnest, liquor still being plentiful then, loosening even the most reticent of tongues. So I excused myself and must have promptly nodded off, for the next moment it was dawn, the day just beginning to break, the long length of the train still shrouded in sleep. I was the only one awake, the only one woken by the sudden cessation of rhythm, which drew me to the window, still dark except for my reflection superimposed on it.

We had apparently stopped for cargo, the faint scuffling I could hear revealing a truck ringed by soldiers, their outlines barely visible against the paling horizon. Later, I would learn the significance of this stop, but for the moment the indistinct scene strained my eyes, and I pulled back, hoping to rest for another hour.

Forty years later, this scene returns to me with a visceral crispness that seems almost specious, when so much else has faded or disappeared. Perhaps it is simply the mind, which, in its inability to accept a fact, returns to it, sharpening the details, resolving the image, searching for an explanation that the mind, with its slippery grasp on causality, will never be able to find. Most days I am spared by the habits of routine. But when the air darkens like this, turning the windows inward, truncating the afternoon, the present recedes, its thin hold on consciousness no match for the eighty-two years that have already claimed it. If hindsight were more amenable, I might long ago have been granted the belated clarity that might have illuminated the exact steps that led me into the fog of my actions. But hindsight has not offered me this view; my options and choices are as elusive now as they had been then. After all, it was war. An inexcusable logic, but also a fact. We adapted to the reality over which we felt we had no control.

For what could we have done? After seven years of embroilment and two years of open war, the conflict with China had begun to tax the everyday, small signs of oncoming shortages beginning to blight the streets, thinning out shelves and darkening windows, so that even menus at the fanciest restaurants resembled the books and newspapers blatantly censored by the Tokkō thought police. Then, when officials began making their rounds of sympathetic universities, seeking candidates disposed to patriotic service, our director submitted a list of names, eliciting more visits from other officials, this time escorted by military men. Were we alarmed? Some of us were. But the prospect of a new world-class facility with promises of unlimited resources stoked our ambitions, we who had long assumed ourselves dormant, choked off by the nepotism that structured our schools and hospitals. If any of us resisted, we did not hear about it. Flattered and courted, we let ourselves be lured, the glitter of high pay and breakthrough advancements all the more seductive in the light of our flickering lives.

So the day we set sail, we were in high spirits, the early sky heavy with mist, the hull of the *Nippon Maru* chopping and cleaving as the sound of rushing water washed away our coastline, leaving us to wend our way through our doubts and worries to arrive in Wonsan, stiff and rumpled, but clear in our convictions. After two turbulent days, we were grateful to be on steady ground, overwhelmed by new smells and sounds, the bustling travelers and hawkers broken up by the young, bright-eyed representative dispatched to meet us. This youth was energetic, if brashly so, and perhaps it was this, along with the sudden physical realization that we were no longer in Japan, that reminded me of my son, but it plunged me into a mood that would last the rest of the trip. Of S I have no recollection at this time, not until a few hours' gap resolves into the memory of that cold window of the stilled train, my eyes pulling back from the soldiers and the truck, their dark outlines replaced by the reflection of my face, above which I caught another face, its eyes watching me.

No doubt it was the hour, and the invasiveness of having been watched, but the shock colored all my subsequent encounters with

S, so that even decades later I am left with an ominous impression of a man always watching as the rest of us adapted to our given roles and fulfilled them perfectly. Did we exchange words? I regret that we did not. For by the time I gathered myself, he was gone. Two hours later we pulled into Harbin, our Emperor's celebrated new acquisition.

From Harbin we were to head twenty-six kilometers southeast to Pingfang. But we were granted a few introductory hours in the famed city, and we set about familiarizing ourselves with the cobblestone streets flanked by European shops and cafés still festive with wealthy Russians and a few well-placed Chinese, all of whom politely acknowledged our entourage. If people were wary, they did not show it, and we, for our part, acted the tourist, taking turns deciphering the familiar kanji strung together in unfamiliar ways on signs and advertisements as onion domes and minarets rose beside church steeples and pagoda roofs, obscuring the city's second skyline: the "Chinese" sector of this once Russian concession city. Once or twice unmarked vans stole by, but overall our impression was of wonder and delight as we strolled through the crowd, the hot sun on our backs coaxing out a healthy sweat despite the chill in the October air.

If not for a small incident, Harbin may have remained an oasis in my memory of China. But our young representative had irked me from the start, and the farther we walked the more he chatted, pointing out this or that landmark we *must* have heard of, and soon his loud voice, lilting with presumptions, began grating on me, and I snapped back with an energy that surprised even me.

My colleagues were quick to intervene, rallying around him like mother hens, clucking at my lack of magnanimity. But, you see, my son and I had been getting into it just like this, and I could not abide the youth's hooded eyes; I lashed out, admonishing his audacity, his misguided courage and naïve ideals—the very things that I believed had pushed my own son to run away, presumably to enlist. I might have lost my head, save for the tether of my wife's face, her pleading terror checked by her refusal to blame me every day I failed to find him. I dropped my voice and let myself be pecked back, the sun-dappled street once again leading us on, this time, to our first proper meal in days.

The day's specialty was duck. Despite our meager group of thirty-one, the restaurant had been requisitioned, its large dining room conspicuously empty, its grand floors and walls cavernously echoing the stamps and scrapes of our shoes and chairs as we accepted the seats arranged around two large tables set in the center of the room. S was observing us, his stolid face amplifying the garishness of ours as our tables brimmed with plates and bowls, exciting our chopsticks to swoop and peck, securing a morsel, punctuating a quip, our cheeks growing rosy as platter after platter crowded the wheel ingeniously fitted at the tables' centers. At last the duck was set before us, its dewy skin crisped and seasoned, the complex aroma of fruit and game emanating from it. For most of us, this was our first taste of the bird, and the pungent flesh, voluptuously tender, provoked our passions, prompting us to trade stories of our youthful lusts. But I for some reason found myself remembering the days I had spent toting siblings who never tired of feeding the ducks that splashed in the pond behind our house. I earned my title as the group's sentimentalist that day, but I believe it was at this moment that we fell in with each other, our shared pleasure piqued by our unspoken guilt at gorging on such an extravagance when our families back home had mere crumbs grudgingly afforded by the patriotic frugality demanded of them. Perhaps this is why Harbin has stayed with me, nostalgic and laden, edged with a hysteria I would come to associate with this time.

I believe few of us forget what we keep hidden in our memory's hollows. True, many of us are capable of remaining professionally closed-faced, tossing out facts of our wartime accomplishments the way we toss our car keys, casually and full of the confidence of important men who have worked hard and earned their keep, rightfully. But forgetting?

My two colleagues and I have been debating this point over our yearly meals taken here in the rural outskirts of F City, where by chance we converged fifteen years ago. They claim that, if not for these meals, they too might have forgotten, these memories, stowed for so long, buried by a present that discourages remembrances so that trace feelings, occasionally jostled, might momentarily surface, but nothing more. For why dig up graves from a banished past, selfishly subjecting all those connected to us to what can only amount to a masochistic pursuit? Isn't it better to surrender to a world populated by the young, who, taught nothing, remain uncurious, the war as distant as ancient history, its dim heat kindling the pages of textbooks and cinemas, occasionally sparking old men with old grudges, but nothing to do with them?

I would like to disagree. But life did move on, the war's end swallowing us up and spitting us out different men, who, like everyone else, slipped back into a peacetime world once again girdled by clear boundaries and laws meant to preserve lives, not to destroy them. And yet, for me, S has continued to tunnel through time, staying in my present, reminding me of our shared past, which we, with all our excuses, have been guarding as tightly as the walls that surrounded us in Pingfang.

You see, you must understand something: We had always meant to preserve lives. A few thousand enemies to save hundreds of thousands of our own? In that sense, I hardly think our logic was so remarkable or unique.

What was remarkable was Pingfang. Its imposing structure looming in calculated isolation, its vast grounds secured by high-voltage walls, its four corners staked with watchtowers overlooking its four gates armed with guards whose shouts were regularly drowned out by the clatter of surveillance planes circling the facility. Approaching them for the first time in jostling trucks, the walls of the fortress compound seemed to unroll endlessly, each additional meter contracting our nerves so that our faces, initially loose with excitement, began to tighten, eliciting a lustrous laugh from our young guide, who turned to remark, *Of course, we don't bear the Emperor's emblem here.*

Sure enough, when we stopped for authorization at the northern gate, we saw that the walls were indeed ungraced. In a world where even our souls were expected to bear the mark of the Emperor, the absence was terrifying, and perhaps this was when I *saw* Pingfang, its forbidding grandeur, cloaked by its unmarked walls, presaging what it was capable of. By then it was clear that the warning emanating from it made no exceptions, even as it opened its gates and saluted us in.

In increments we would become privy to the extent of Pingfang's ambitions. But first we were dazzled. Our days snatched away by seminars and orientation tours, we scarcely had time to unpack, our bodies as well as our minds collapsing into white sleep always flooded with sunlight, so that even the hardiest of us grew weary, dragging from conference rooms to auditoriums, the occasional outdoor tour whisking us off in rattling trucks that clattered our teeth and fibrillated our brains until we developed an aversion to Pingfang's astigmatized landscape. After a fortnight, we reached our threshold. We broke down, all of us mere husks of ourselves, our individual drive wrung out of us. Until then we had been accustomed to mild routines with little expectation; to be inducted into a life ruled by the exigencies of war proved transformative. We readjusted, our senses and sensibilities recalibrated to accommodate the new demand. After all, humans are remarkable in their ability to adapt. Time and again we would find ourselves reminded of this fact, which, I believe, was at the root of what came to pass at Pingfang.

Had I understood what I glimpsed that night from the train window, would I have turned back, returned to the circumscribed safety of my home and career? I would like to imagine so. And in my right mind I am certain I would have. But, you see, there is the problem: the issue of "transgression." In peacetime lines are clearer; even if proceedings are flawed and verdicts inconclusive, one can and does *know* if one has transgressed—certainly, the court need only assemble one's intentions to make that determination. But in war? Does transgression still require intent? Or is it enough for circumstances to conspire, setting up conditions that pressure one to carry out acts that are in line with, but not always a direct result of, orders? I do not know. Yet I find myself looping through memory's thickets for that exact bridge that let us cross our ambivalence to another side.

My two colleagues believe it happened in Harbin. They claim that, as tourists, we were set up to accept the exotic and so dismiss what would have been, in another context, obviously amiss. I do not dispute this view. Yet I wonder whether we hadn't been set up—inoculated—long before we set sail for Wonsan. By then the mood of war, long since gathering in the air, had precipitated into crackdowns, the once distant patter of the jingoists' tattoo pounding down doors, sending us scurrying under the official wing. Even our mandatory participation in the bucket brigade, as well as our patriotic duty to look the other way, had already become two more chores as seemingly unavoidable as the war itself. Resisting would have been foolhardy, the hard-line climate a meteorological fact, its terrorizing power mystical in effect. Yet I am a man of science; I have never been swayed by weather's mystical claims. Nor have I been captive to its blustery dramatics. So I was arrested. My son, Yasushi, was six then, a bright child already fiercely righteous. He never mentioned my arrest, but I believe it left an impression. He became rebellious, his childish disobedience erupting into full-scale mutiny by the time he was fourteen. My wife urged me to confront him; I did nothing of the sort. Because, you see, I recanted my beliefs. True, I was thinking of *them*, my wife and son, their torturous road if I refused to cooperate. But finally, I could not bear it, the dark shapeless hours sundered by wood and metal and electricity; in ten meager days, I gave in.

Four decades later I do not have reason to believe Yasushi is still alive, but every so often there is news of yet another Imperial Army straggler emerging from the jungles in Southeast Asia, and I am unable to let go.

The latest straggler, one Captain Nakahira Fumio, is currently on the run. His hut, discovered on Mindoro Island two weeks ago, had evaded detection for thirty-five years. Widely speculated to be the last repatriate, the authorities finally released his picture.

What could I do? I bought up the newsstand. The image, a grainy reproduction of a school portrait, showed a hollow-chested boy with an affable face. A little thin-framed, he was nevertheless generic enough to be any youth. Could Yasushi have taken his identity? Because, you see, Yasushi had been too young for service. Needing my consent, he had approached me with the forms. I, of course, refused, taking precautions to prevent him from forging them. But forms are traceable; Yasushi, realizing this, opted to trade in his identity. What name he assumed we never found out. Even then the military was eager for soldiers, and I, despite my connections, had a record: An official charge of treason.

Comparing the images for quality, I tucked several newspapers under my arm and hastened into the street still burnished with morning light. That's when I saw him—S—his old man's shape bearing the shadow of his younger self, his ornithic neck bobbing forward, his once languid gait sped up to a near footloose shuffle. I opened my mouth to call out. But what could I have said? Had I been a different man, able to withstand the eyes of those eager to condemn me for what they themselves might have done in my position, I might have mustered the courage to catch the attention of the one man who may yet have the right to judge us. But

I am not that man; I did not call out. Humans may be adaptable, but that has no bearing on our ability to change.

All told, I spent twenty-four months in Pingfang. Officially, we were the Boeki Kyusuibu, the Epidemic Prevention and Water Purification Department, Unit 731, a defensive research unit. Materially, Pingfang spanned three hundred hectares, its fertile land dappled with forests and meadows, its innumerable structures—headquarters, laboratories, dormitories, airfield, greenhouses, pool—luxuriously accommodated within its fold. Locally, we were known as a lumber mill, our pair of industrial chimneys continually emptying into the impending sky.

I remember the first time I stood beneath one of these chimneys. Having finished a procedure, we had followed the gurney out, the damp air white with frost, the bare earth crunching underfoot. S, like the rest of us, was in a morose mood; our work, bacteriological in nature, was making useful gains, but we had not succeeded in developing the antidote we had been after, and I, for one, had become increasingly restless. By then the war, in gridlock in China, was beginning to fan southward, and I was convinced that if Yasushi had indeed enlisted, he would end up in the tropics, where the fruits of our work would be most vital.

I do not know why I risked airing these thoughts. Perhaps it was my way of acknowledging my son. I approached S. Until then we had all been careful to keep to the professional, repeating stock answers whenever we strayed. But S was sympathetic. He replied openly, agreeing with my prognosis, adding only that the war was likely to turn west before pushing farther south—an unentertained notion at the time. I was about to press him on the feasibility, indeed the audacity, of such a course, but just then a flare of heat drew our attention, and the gurney, now emptied of our *maruta*—yes, that's what we called them: "logs"—pulled us back to our duty.

Because, you see, that was what Pingfang was built for, its

immaculate design hiding in plain sight what we most hoped to control: the harvesting of living data. For how else could we compete? Our small nation, poor in resources and stymied by embargoes egregiously imposed by the imperial West. Our one chance lay in our ability to minimize loss, the most urgent being that of our troops, all too often wasted by war's most efficient enemy: infectious diseases. But war spares no time. We found ourselves beating against the very wall that had always been the bane of medical science. In other words, our problem was ethical; Pingfang sought to remove it. Its solution was nothing we dared imagine but what we, in medicine, had all perhaps dreamed of. All we had to do was continue administering shots, charting symptoms, studying our cultures—all the things we had always done in our long medical careers—except when we filled our syringes, it was not with curatives but pathogens; when we wielded our scalpels, it was not for surgery but vivisection; and when we reached for sample tissues, they were not animal but human. This was perhaps Pingfang's greatest accomplishment: its veneer of normalcy. We carried on; the lives of our soldiers, indeed our entire nation, depended upon us.

I do not know who came up with the term *maruta*. It is possible that its usage preceded us, though I do not recall hearing it used in those introductory days. The first time we saw them we were in the hospital ward, where they looked like any patients, supine under clean sheets changed daily. The second time we saw them it was at the prison ward, where they looked like any prisoners, uniformed and wary. Both times, I remember the brief hush that fell over us as we registered exactly what we were being shown before we were briskly ushered away. By the time we were given full rein over our research, we were using the term, counting up the beds, tallying our *maruta* in preparation for our next shipment, always by train at night. Indeed, I believe it was a cargo transfer that I witnessed that morning on the train to Harbin.

I was asked to accompany the inspection of such a cargo just once. Woken abruptly, I was summoned by an officer who, for this occasion, had driven his private jeep. Throughout the ride, I had been bleary, my mind cottony with sleep, and once I gleaned the purpose of the trip—a preliminary health scan—I shut out the chatter and arrived unprepared for the secluded station, the small squadron of military guards patrolling the length of the curtained train, the cargo's white tarp peeled back to reveal twelve prisoners strapped to planks and gagged by leather bits.

My first reaction was morbid fascination, my mind unable to resolve the image of these people packed like this, and the term *maruta* acquired an appropriateness that struck a nerve. I began to laugh, a sputtering sound that elicited a disapproving glance from the officer who pressed me forward. How they managed to survive I could not imagine. Trembling with exhaustion, they lay in their thin prisoners' clothes, wet and stinking of their own unirrigated waste, until one by one they were unstrapped, forced to stand, their movements minced by the shackles that still bound their hands and feet. No one protested, the only shouts coming from the guards as they stripped and prodded them, the tips of their knives shredding their garments, exposing them first to the cold, then to the water as a pair of soldiers hosed them down.

Had I been able to, I would have abandoned my post, and perhaps I made as if to do so, for the officer gripped my arm, his placid face nicked by repulsion, though it was unclear by whom or what. As the water dripped away, and the *maruta* were toweled off, I was led to the nearest plank, where four women, now manacled together, sat shivering. They were all in their twenties and thirties; their eyes were black with recrimination and their bodies so violently pimpled by the cold I could hardly palpate them. The second plank was an all-male group, each man, wiry with work, radiating humiliation so primal my own hands began to shake. The third and final plank was a mixed group, perhaps a family. One woman grew so agitated by my attempts to minister to a limp girl, I barely registered the man pulled from the train and added to the cargo. This new prisoner was my age, in good health and spirited enough to have risked the curtains to "spy" from the train window. He was brought to me to be tranquilized, and though I must have complied, I remember nothing else, only the leering heat of the soldiers snapped to attention behind me, and then later, the vague relief that flooded me when the next day I stepped into my ward and did not recognize a single face.

Lumber mills?

I do not believe anyone was so naïve.

Pingfang's operation expanded with the war, its defensive function superseded by its natural twin: the development of biological weapons. This offensive capability had been pursued from the start, mostly in the form of small-scale tests surreptitiously deployed as creative endnotes to our ongoing anti-insurgency missions, but it did not peak until the war took that fatal turn west. By then, many of us had been dispatched to newly conquered regions or strategic teaching posts back home, but news continued to reach us, mostly as rumors but sometimes through odd details we recognized in otherwise ordinary news reports. As the war entered its last throes, Pingfang rose in importance. By the time Germany began its retreat, Pingfang, already anticipating a Russian offensive, had begun testing, for example, the human threshold for the northern freeze. How they planned to use the data I do not know. With so few resources and so little infrastructure left, there would have been no way to manufacture, let alone distribute, any new equipment. Why these tests struck me as crueler I also do not know. Perhaps the obvious brutality of the method touched my conscience. Or perhaps it was simply a defensive reflex, the mind's protective instinct that indicts another in the attempt to save itself. After all, had I been in their position, I too would have likely carried out these experiments, meticulously freezing and thawing the living body to observe the behavior of frostbite or assess the tactical viability of a literally frozen troop. While some of us still insist on our relative human-ity, I do not believe we can quibble over such fine points as degree.

I, for one, return to the fact of the cargo inspection, and it was this that finally drove me from my practice, a quiet family clinic discreetly set up for me after the war. Despite promises, we had become an inconvenience for the university, and the direc-tor had found ways of paying us off. For a while the setup suited me fine. The clinic, bankrolled by the director, yielded enough to survive on, and I was able to keep to simple diagnoses and treatments. Even so, the body does not forget. A clammy arm, a quivering lip—my hands, once recruited for their steadiness, began to jump.

So fifteen years ago, following my wife's death, I ventured to F City. At the time China had just normalized its relationship with Japan, and my two colleagues and I, having respectively come to a similar juncture, found ourselves reunited at the K noodle shop known to connoisseurs for its duck. To say we were sur-prised would be an understatement. It took us a moment before we could attempt a greeting, our old hearts fluttering like scat-tered chickens. Once again we ate with a greediness we dared not explain and parted with a gaiety that consoled us. But I believe we would have preferred to have sat apart, if not for our curiosity and relief that this moment, dreaded and yearned for, had finally come to pass. Since then, we have had an unspoken agreement to reconvene on the same day every October, the fateful month we boarded the *Nippon Maru*.

Only once did S and I manage a sustained conversation. That day I had gone in search of a colleague, T, a man of considerable promise, who had taken to visiting the female prisoners. Soft-spoken and decorous, he had become the most vicious among us, his increasing notoriety forcing us to take turns to restrain him. But T was not in the prison ward that day, and I made my way to headquarters, thinking he had gone to request more "matériel," but nobody had seen him there either. I was about to retrace my steps when I glimpsed S emerging from a restricted office, slipping a sheaf of papers into his laboratory coat. When he spotted me, he paused but made no attempt to explain himself. Instead he fell into step with me, convivially opening the door to the underground passage that connected all the buildings in Pingfang.

"Who knows what'll happen to him now," I said, trying not to glance at the papers.

"T?" S shrugged. "Who's going to miss him?"

"He could have had a whole career—a whole future."

"Future?" S looked at me. "You think this is going to last?"

"I don't think that's anything we're in a position to say."

"What? That we're going to lose?"

"Look." I lowered my voice. "We're just following orders."

"And you expect the world to be sympathetic?"

"What choice do we have? T, on the other hand, is being excessive."

"And you think that makes you different from people like T."

"I'm saying the world will have to consider that."

"And if it doesn't?"

I was silent. It was true: The world had no obligations. What chance did we have in what was likely going to be a Western court? True, we were obeying orders, but we were the ones carrying them out; we could not look at our hands and plead innocence, dusting them off the way our superiors did, passing off their dirty work, expecting it returned to them perfectly laundered "for the sake of the medical community." From the start this had been an untenable situation we were expected to make tenable; forced to be responsible for what I felt we should not be, I had become resentful. I began misnotating my reports. Small slips, easily dismissed until the accumulation became impossible to ignore. Instead of 匹, the counter suffix for animals, I began writing 人, the counter suffix for humans. I worked systematically, substituting one for the other with a calculated randomness befitting Pingfang. I glanced at his laboratory coat. "I suppose it depends on if anyone finds out," I said.

"We all have to do what we have to do, don't we?" S patted his coat, grinning.

"After all this, maybe they'll have no choice but to protect us," I said.

S did not disagree. "There may already be interest in the matter beyond our small military and government," he replied.

And he was right. That was more or less how it played out, with the Cold War descending on the infernal one, and the Americans, fearful of the Russians, agreeing to negotiate with our Lieutenant General for sole access to our research, the objective being the advancement of their own secret bio-program stymied by medical ethics. The result? Our full immunity in exchange for all our data, human and otherwise.

Few historians have unearthed, let alone published, evidence of Pingfang's abuses. Those who have, have been divided over the problem of numbers. At one end, Pingfang's casualty rate has been estimated at several thousand. At the other end, the number hovers closer to two hundred thousand, mostly Chinese but some Russian and Japanese deaths as well. I believe both figures tell a certain truth. While it is true that our furnaces saw no shortage of logs in their five years of operation, our goal was never mass extermination. Our tests, contingent on the human body, its organic processes and upkeep, were costly, and even our field tests, aerial or on-site, were limited to small villages and hamlets optimally secluded for tracking our data. But Pingfang cannot be confined to its five years of operation. Its construction took two years, fifteen thousand laborers, six hundred evictions; and afterward, when surrender triggered the destruction of the compound, whose walls were so thick special dynamite was needed, the final blasts were said to have released only animals, common and uncommon, the only witnesses to escape alive. And the gain?

Militarily, history has shown the regrettable results, with reports of odd casualties surfacing now and again, if only in the half-light of prevarications. Medically, it is harder to assess, our research having pushed our field to the cutting edge, landing many of us influential positions in the pharmaceutical sector, where some of us are still directing the course of medicine, or the money in medicine, in not insignificant ways.

The irony of it all is how well we ate within those walls, our *maruta* fed better than us to maintain optimal biological conditions. This prurient coupling of plenitude and death, so lavish in its complicity, has lent a kind of heat to my memory of Pingfang, compressing its eternity into a vivid blur coalesced around two towering chimneys, their twin shapes always looming, gone the moment I turn to look. These days it is this collusion of the mind with Pingfang's irreality that terrorizes me, the fog of the entombed past threatening to release a hand, a face, a voice.

My colleagues are more fortunate. Our annual meals seem to have done them good, churning up old soil, mineralized by the years, the new exposure letting them breathe. I, on the other hand, find myself hurtled back to people and places lost in time but not lost to me. At my age it is time, not space, that is palpable, its physicality reminding me of the finality of all our choices, made and lived.

This morning they deemed the story of the straggler a hoax. Captain Nakahira Fumio, whereabouts irrelevant.

So it goes, all of us subject to the caprice of time as it releases not what we hoped for but what it does before it closes its fists and draws back, once again withdrawing the past from the present. And perhaps that is as it should be. For what would I have done? Would I have risked showing myself, braving the eyes of idle journalists, braving those of my son? I have not even had the courage to visit my wife's grave.

. . .

I mentioned S to my colleagues for the second time last year. After the first time, I should have known better, but the urge had taken hold of me. Over slivers of duck prepared to our specifications, I once again gave my account of the papers he had stolen, the exchange we had had. As before, they listened patiently, commenting on his courage, his uncanny foresight and reckless integrity, wondering how they could have forgotten such a character. Again, I described his solitariness, the way he had observed us—so quietly, so persistently—until they finally remembered, not the man himself, but the previous time I had given this account. Should he have exposed the papers? I asked. As before, my colleagues turned on me, asking me why I returned to this, what stake I had in these moot moral questions, nothing but a masochistic exercise—was I certain I hadn't made him up?

I defended myself, reminding them that we had each mentioned one person the other two hadn't been able to recall, and frankly, I said, wasn't the point to see if we *could* imagine it—another life, another self—because look at us, I said, year after year, three old men uselessly polishing stones.

The silence was prickly. For the first time we parted uneasily, our forced gaiety failing to hide what we must have all been dreading. Indeed, the last few times we convened, we had gone through our menu of memories rather mechanically, and despite our appetites, our bodies had grown less tolerant of the fowl's fattiness, and I am not sure that we haven't lost our taste for the bird now that we have exhausted our staple of remembrances. Perhaps at our age it is only natural to want that release, to move once more in time with the clock.

As for S, he may as well have not existed the way things turned out; he never exposed those papers. Yet he had offered me a chance, and perhaps that is my final offense. I did not take that chance. Instead I carried on, watching, as the world marched on—another war, another era—with fewer of us left every year to cast a backward glance.

So perhaps this is why I continue to return, tantalized by those moments during which it might have been possible to seize the course of our own actions. Because, you see, we all had that chance. That day, just before we walked to the chimney, we had performed a surgery. I was at the head of the table, logging the charts, while T glided the scalpel over the body's midline. Y, my noodle shop companion, was tracking the vitals, calling out numbers, the beat of the pulse measured against the ticking of the clock, as the body underwent all the characteristic spasms—the fluttering of the eyes, the shaking of the head—the once warm flesh rippling with tremors as the skin grew clammy, its tacky surface soon sliding beneath our gloved hands, as we wrestled the mutiny of the body. Perhaps if Y had stuck to procedure. But, you see, Y was monitoring the vitals; he was looking at the body, its special condition, and it occurred to him that he should be tracking not one pulse but two—the second, unborn beat. So he pressed his fingers in; the *maruta* bolted up. Fixing her eyes on us, she opened her mouth, stilling us. Few of us had acquired the language beyond the smattering of words we kept in our pockets like change, but we did not need language to understand her, her ringing voice a mother's unmistakable plea reminding all of us of our primary duty: to save lives, not destroy them.

Needless to say we did not save anyone's life in that room that day. Instead we went on to complete a record number of procedures, breaking down bodies, harvesting our data, the brisk halls and polite examination rooms only reinforcing the power of omission as we pushed to meet the demands of a war that had heaved us over one edge, then another, leaving us duly decorated but as barren as the landscape we left behind.

As for S, his story began irrecoverably to diverge from ours the day he slipped the papers from the office. While the rest of us hunkered down, he continued to plan and plot, imagining a justice that seemed inevitable. When the war ended and the proceedings began, he too must have waited, hoping and fearing that justice would find itself. But the sentences never came, and he, more than any of us, must have felt its weight doubled back on him. Yet he never disclosed the papers. Instead he stowed them away, perhaps planning to donate them someday to one or another bookstore frequented by frugal university students. Then, fifteen years ago, he retired to a house in the rural outskirts of a city, where an old cedar gives its shade to a backyard visited by birds in the spring and blanketed by snow in the winter. There he spends his days tending to the saplings he has planted behind the shed, where he keeps the papers stashed in a crate of old textbooks. Now and again his mind wanders to the crate, and he marvels at his own resistance, the unrelenting human will to preserve itself.

But today, with spring softening the breeze, and the birds abundant in the yard, he finds himself compelled to visit the papers. After all these years, it is a wonder they have survived, slightly yellowed but otherwise intact, and he places them on a workbench he keeps outside the shed. In this light, the pages are clear, and the neat script, painfully familiar, has the power to jolt him, once again invoking the face of the woman, her wide eyes and gaping mouth, silenced by the wet sound of the fetus slapping the slop bucket. For days he had smelled it, the sweet scorched scent drifting beneath the common odors of cooking and laundry and disinfectant, and he inhales, filling his lungs, as he steps back into the shed, pausing to appreciate his rake and shovel, the long-handled hedge shears now corroding on the wall. Reliable for so many years, there is comfort in this decay, evidence of a long life granted the luxury of natural decomposition. He untangles a knot of rope, empties the crate that had held his papers. The rope is sturdy, as is the crate. He drags them to a spot beneath the arching cedar and sets the crate's open face squarely on the ground. He briefly wonders if his colleagues will meet this year. He hoists the rope, faces the wall. Once again creepers have scaled it, their dark leaves ruffled by a breeze eager to spread the fragrance of the neighborhood's peach and plum blossoms. He grips the rope; the crate wobbles, and while I never tested the precise time it takes for air to be absorbed by the lungs, the brain to starve of blood, and the body to cease its struggle to save itself, I am hoping that, in that duration, I will be able to wrest from myself the snatch of consciousness necessary to remember once more my siblings and those ducks that swam in the pond back home.

Wendell Berry

Dismemberment

It was the still-living membership of his friends who, with Flora and their children and their place, pieced Andy together and made him finally well again after he lost his right hand to a harvesting machine in the fall of 1974. He would be obliged to think that he had given his hand, or abandoned it, for he had attempted to unclog the corn picker without stopping it, as he had known better than to do. But finally it would seem to him also that the machine had taken his hand, or accepted it, as the price of admission into the rapidly mechanizing world that as a child he had not foreseen and as a man did not like, but which he would have to live in, understanding it and resisting it the best he could, for the rest of his life.

He was forty then, too old to make easily a new start, though his life could be continued only by a new start. He had no other choice. Having no other choice finally was a sort of help, but he was slow in choosing. Between him and any possibility of choice lay his suffering and the selfishness of it: self-pity, aimless anger, aimless blaming, that made him dangerous to himself, cruel to others, and useless or a burden to everybody.

He would not get over the loss of his hand, as of course he was plentifully advised to do, simply because he was advised to do it, or simply even because he wanted and longed to do it. His life had been deformed. His hand was gone, his right hand that had been his principal connection to the world, and the absence of it could not be repaired. The only remedy was to re-form his life around his loss, as a tree grows live wood over its scars. From the memory and a sort of foreknowledge of wholeness, after he had grown sick enough finally of his grieving over himself, he chose to heal.

To replace his lost hand he had acquired what he named contemptuously to himself his "prosthetic device," his "hook," or his "claw," and of which he never spoke aloud to anybody for a long time. He began in a sort of dusk of self-sorrow and fury to force his left hand to learn to do the tasks that his right hand once had done. He forced it by refusing to desist from doing, or to wait to do, anything that he had always done. He watched the left hand with pity and contempt as it fumbled at the buttons of his clothes, and as it wrote, printing, at first just his name, in letters that with all his will it could not contain between the lines of a child's tablet. With two fingers of his pathetic left hand he would hold the head of a nail against the poll of a hammer, and strike the nail into the wood, and then, attempting to drive the nail, would miss it or bend it, and he would repeat this until he cursed and wept, crying out with cries that seemed too big for his throat so that they hurt him and became themselves an affliction. He was so plagued and shamed by this that he would work alone only where he was sure he could not be overheard.

To drive a stake or a steel post, he would one-handedly swing the sledgehammer back and forth like a pendulum to gain loft and force, and then strike. At first, more often than not, he missed. This was made harder by the necessity of standing so that, missing, he did not hit his leg. For propping, steadying, and other crude uses, he could call upon the stump of his right forearm. To avoid impossible awkwardnesses, he shortened the handles of a broom, a rake, and a hoe. From the first there were some uses he could make of the prosthetic device. So long as he regarded it as merely a tool, as merely a hook or a claw or weak pliers, he used it readily and quietly enough. But when some need forced him to think of it as a substitute for his right hand, which now in its absence seemed to have been miraculous, he would be infuriated by the stiffness and numbness of it. Sooner or later—still, in his caution and shame, he would be working alone—he would be likely to snatch it off and fling it away, having then to suffer the humiliation of searching for it in tall grass or, once, in a pond. One day he beat it on the top of a fence post as if to force sentience and intelligence into it. And by that, for the first time since his injury, he finally was required to laugh at himself. He laughed until he wept, and laughed again. After that, he got better.

Soon enough, because spring had begun and need was upon him, he put his horses back to work. By wonderful good fortune, for often until then he would have been starting a young pair, he had a team that was work-wise and dependable. They were six-year-olds, Prince and Dan. Andy's son, Marcie, who loved the horses and was adept at using them, was in his twelfth year then and could have helped. But Andy could not ask for help. His disease at that time, exactly, was that he could not ask for help, not from either of his children, not from Flora, not from his friends, not from anybody. His mode then was force. He forced himself to do what he required of himself. He thus forced himself upon the world, and thus required of the world a right-of-way that the world of course declined to grant. He was forever trying to piece himself whole by mechanical contrivances and devices thought up in the night, which by day more often than not would fail, because of some unforeseen complication or some impossibility obvious in daylight. He worked at and with the stump of his arm as if it were inanimate, tying tools to it with cords, leather straps, rubber straps, or using it forthrightly as a blunt instrument.

In the unrelenting comedy of his predicament he had no patience, and yet patience was exacted from him. He became patient then with a forced resignation that was the very flesh and blood of impatience. To put the harness on the horses was the first obstacle, and it was immense. Until it is on the horse, a set of work harness is heavy and it has no form. It can be hung up in fair order, but to take it from its pegs and carry it to the horse's back involves a considerable risk of disorder. Andy went about it, from long habit, as a two-handed job, only to discover immediately, and in the midst of a tangle of straps, that he had to invent, from nothing at all that he knew, the usefulness of the prosthetic device, which was at best a tool, with an aptitude for entangling itself in the tangle of straps.

When, in his seemingly endless fumbling, he had got the horses harnessed and hitched, he became at once their dependent. He could ask help from no human, but he had to have the help of his horses, and he asked them for it. Their great, their fundamental, virtue was that they would stop when he said, "Whoa." When he dropped a line or had too many thoughts to think at once, he called out, "Whoa!" and they stopped. And they would stand in their exemplary patience and wait while he put his thoughts and himself in order, sometimes in the presence of an imminent danger that he had not seen in time. Or they would wait while he wound and rewound, tied and retied, the right-hand line to what was left of his right forearm. A profound collaboration grew between him and the horses, like nothing he had known before. He thought finally that they sensed his need and helped him understandingly. One day he was surprised by the onset of a vast tenderness toward them, and he wept, praising and thanking them. After that, again, he knew he was better.

His neighbors too, knowing his need, came when they could be of use and helped him. They were the survivors, so far, of the crew of friends who had from the beginning come there to help: Art and Mart Rowanberry, Pascal Sowers and his son Tommy, Nathan Coulter, whose boys by then had grown up and left home, and Danny Branch, usually with one or two of his boys, none of the five of whom ever would stray far or long from the Port William neighborhood.

The first time they came, to help him with his first cutting of hay, their arrival afflicted Andy with an extreme embarrassment. He had not dared so far as to ask himself how he would save the hay after he had cut it. He cut it because the time had come to cut it. If he could not save it, he told himself in his self-pity and despair, he would let it rot where it lay.

He did not, he could not, ask his friends to help him. But they came. Before he could have asked, if he had been going to ask, they knew when he needed them, and they came. He asked himself accusingly if he had not after all depended on them to come, and he wavered upon the answer as on a cliff's edge.

They came bringing the tractor equipment they needed to rake and bale his hay. When they appeared, driving in after dinner-time on the right day, he was so abashed because of his debility and his dependence, because he had not asked them to come, because he now was different and the world was new and strange, he hardly knew how to greet them or where to stand.

But his friends were not embarrassed. There was work to do, and they merely set about doing it. When Andy hesitated or blundered, Nathan or Danny told him where to get and what to do as if the place and the hay were theirs. It was work. It was only work. In doing it, in requiring his help in doing it, they moved him to the margin of his difficulty and his self-absorption. They made him one with them, by no acknowledgement at all, by not crediting at all his own sense that he had ever not been one with them.

When the hay was baled and in the loft and they had come to rest finally at the shady end of the barn, Andy said, "I don't know how to thank you. I don't know how I can ever repay you." He sounded to himself as if he were rehearsing the speech to give later.

And then Nathan, who never wasted words, reached out and took hold of Andy's right forearm, that remnant of his own flesh that Andy himself could hardly bear to touch. Nathan gripped the hurt, the estranged, arm of his friend and kinsman as if it were the commonest, most familiar object around. He looked straight at Andy and gave a little laugh. He said, "Help *us*."

After that Andy again was one of them. He was better.

The great obstacle that remained was his estrangement of himself from Flora and their children. He knew that in relation to those who were dearest to him he had become crazy. He had become intricately, painfully, perhaps hopelessly crazy. He saw this clearly, he despised himself for it, and yet he could not prevail upon himself to become sane. He looked at Flora and Betty and Marcie as across a great distance. He saw them looking at him, worried about him, suffering his removal from them. He understood, he felt, their preciousness to him, and yet he could not right himself. He could not become or recover or resume himself, who had once so easily reached out and held them to himself. He could not endure the thought of their possible acceptance of him as he had become. It was as if their acceptance, their love for him, as a one-handed man, if he allowed it, would foreclose forever some remaining chance that his lost hand would return or grow back, or that he might awaken from himself as he had become to find himself as he had been. He was lost to himself, within himself.

And so in his craziness he drove them away, defending the hardened carapace of his self, for fear that they would break in and find him there, hurt and terribly, terribly in need—of them.

For a while, for too long, selfishness made him large. He became so large in his own mind in his selfish suffering that he could not see the world or his place in it. He saw only himself, all else as secondary to himself. In his suffering he isolated himself, and then he suffered his loneliness, and then he blamed chiefly Flora for his loneliness and her inability to reach him through it, and then he lashed out at her in his anger at her failure, and then he pitied her for his anger and suffered the guilt of it, and then he was more than ever estranged from her by his guilt. Eventually, inevitably, he saw how his selfishness had belittled him, and he was ashamed, and was more than ever alone in his shame. But in his shame and his loneliness, though he could not yet know it, he was better.

At that time his writings on agriculture had begun to make him known in other places. He had begun to accept invitations to speak at meetings that he had to travel to. On one of those wanderings far from home, and almost suddenly, he became able again to see past himself, beyond and around himself.

Memories of times and places he had forgotten came back to him, reached him at last as if they had been on their way for a long time. He realized how fully and permanently mere glances, touches, passing words, from all his life far back into childhood, had taken place in his heart. Memories gathered to him then, memories of his own, memories of memories told and retold by his elders. The wealth of an intimate history, belonging equally to him and to his ancestral place, welled up in him as from a deep spring, as if from some knowledge the dead had spoken to him in his sleep.

A darkness fell upon him. He saw a vision in a dream. It was much the same as Hannah Coulter's vision of Heaven, as she would come to tell him of it in her old age: "Port William with all its loved ones come home alive." In his dream he saw the past and the future of Port William, of what Burley Coulter had called its membership, struggling through time to belong together, all gathered into a presence of itself that was greater than itself. And he saw that this—in its utterly surprising greatness, utterly familiar—he had been given as a life. Within the abundance of the gift of it, he saw that he was small, almost nothing, almost lost, invisible to himself except as he had been visible to the others who have been with him. He had come into being out of the history and inheritance of love, love faltering and wayward and yet love, granted to him at birth, undeserved, but then called out of him by the membership of his life, apart from which he was nothing. His life was not his self. It was not his own.

He had become small enough at last to enter, to ask to enter, into Flora's and his children's forgiveness, which had been long prepared for him, as he knew, as he had known, if only he could ask. He came into their forgiveness as into the air and weather of life itself. Life-sized again, and welcome, he came back into his marriage to Flora and to their place, with relief amounting to joy.

He came back into the ordinariness of the workaday world and his workaday life, answering to needs that were lowly, unrelenting, and familiar. He came into patience such as he had never suspected that he was capable of. As he went about his daily work, his left hand slowly learned to serve as a right hand, the growth of its dexterity surprising him. His displeasure, at times his enmity, against his stump and his left hand slowly receded from him. They rejoined his body and his life. He became, containing his losses, healed, though never again would he be whole.

His left hand learned at first to print in the fashion maybe of a first-grade boy. And then, with much practice, it mastered a longhand script that was legible enough and swift enough, and that he came to recognize as his own. His left hand learned, as his right hand once had known, to offer itself first to whatever his work required. It became agile and subtle and strong. He became proud of it. In his thoughts he praised its accomplishments, as he might have praised an exceptionally biddable horse or dog.

The prosthetic device also he learned to use as undeliberately almost as if it were flesh of his flesh. But he maintained a discomfort, at once reflexive and principled, with this mechanical extension of himself, as he maintained much the same discomfort with the increasing and equally inescapable dependence of the life of the country and his neighborhood upon mechanical devices.

And so the absence of his right hand has remained with him as a reminder. His most real hand, in a way, is the missing one, signifying to him not only his continuing need for ways and devices to splice out his right arm, but also his and his country's dependence upon the structure of industrial commodities and technologies that imposed itself upon, and contradicted in every way, the sustaining structures of the natural world and its human memberships. And so he is continually reminded of his incompleteness within himself, within the terms and demands of his time and its history, but also within the constraints and limits of his kind, his native imperfection as a human being, his failure to be as attentive, responsible, grateful, loving, and happy as he ought to be.

He has spent most of his life in opposing violence, waste, and destruction—or trying to, his opposition always fragmented and made painful by his complicity in what he opposes. He seems to himself to be "true," most authentically himself, only when he is sitting still, in one of the places in the woods or on a height of ground that invites him to come to rest, where he goes to sit, wait, and do nothing, oppose nothing, put words to no argument. He permits no commotion then by making none. By keeping still, by doing nothing, he allows the given world to be a gift.

Andy Catlett and Danny Branch are old now. They belong to the dwindling remnant who remember what the two of them have begun to call "Old Port William," the town as it was in the time before V-J Day, 1945, after which it has belonged ever less to itself, ever more to the machines and fortunes of the Industrial World. Now of an age when Old Port William might have taken up the propriety of naming them "Uncle Andrew" and "Uncle Dan," they fear that they may be in fact the only two whose memories of that old time remain more vivid and influential than yesterday evening's television shows. They remember the company of Feltners, Coulters, Rowanberrys, Sowerses, Penns, Branches, and Catletts as they gathered in mutual need into their "membership" during the war years and the years following.

Andy and Danny are the last of a time gone. Perhaps, as they each secretly pray, they may be among the first of a time yet to come, when Port William will be renewed, again settled and flourishing. They anyhow are links between history and possibility, as they keep the old stories alive by telling them to their children.

Sometimes, glad to have their help needed, they go to work with their children. Sometimes their children come to work with them, and they are glad to have help when they need it, as they increasingly do. But sometimes only the two old men work together, asking and needing no help but each other's, and this is their luxury and their leisure. When just the two of them are at work they are unbothered by any youthful need to hurry, or any younger person's idea of a better way. Their work is free then to be as slow, as finical, as perfectionistical as they want it to be.

And after so many years they know how to work together, the one-handed old man and the two-handed. They know as one what the next move needs to be. They are not swift, but they don't fumble. They don't waste time assling around, trying to make up their minds. They never make a mislick.

"Between us," says Danny Branch, "we've got three hands. Everybody needs at least three. Nobody ever needed more."

Marie-Helene Bertino

Exit Zero

B EFORE THE RINGING PHONE startles Jo into upsetting a
stack of crackers she'd been matching to cheese, before the
man asks for Josephine and she says *No one calls me that*, before he
identifies himself as the executor of her father's will and inhales
sharply as if bracing for collision, Jo sits at her kitchen table, listening to her landlord's children pretend to be astronauts. Two
floors down in the courtyard, they've improvised robes for space
suits. Her ritual is to eavesdrop for indications that the bigger two
are excluding the little one. She likes to imagine herself interced-
ing, lifting the bullied child into her arms while admonishing the
bigger two. Today the children are getting along, so Jo enjoys an
off-duty feeling. It is Sunday. She assumes her father is still alive
in that she is not thinking of her father at all. After the phone
rings and the crackers vault, the children yell *Blast off!* and the
executor, braced, delivers the news that her father is dead and had
lived in New Jersey, in a house that is now hers.

The will is practical, matter-of-fact. The house is to be
sold, her father cremated. Whatever money is left after funeral
costs and whatever is left of him—*cremains*, the executor calls
them—are hers. Cremains. Though it sounds like a cross

between a dried cranberry and a plastic comb girls use to gather hair, the word enacts violence. An unseen force yanks Jo's shoulder blades, as if someone has pulled to smooth her the way you would a bedsheet.

The worst of the news conveyed, the man relaxes into chat. *Rio Grande*, he says, *is a one-strip mall town. The Econo Lodge is the only motel. The other side of the peninsula is Cape May, where the beach is beautiful, even now, in midwinter. Exit Zero on the Parkway.* He promises to leave the key in a lock box hanging on the front door if she will go soon, like tomorrow. *It will be up to you to clear the contents of the house before it sells, and your father has a few . . .* she hears the nervous click of a pen *. . . sensitive items. Will you have help? Siblings or . . .*

Only child. Jo stares at the address on the pad of paper. She is an event planner for a national organization of doctors. Right now, one hundred cardiologists are beginning their initial descent into Miami for a drug conference. She has coordinated accommodations and activities for their free time: massages, art deco tours, twilight snorkeling. *I'll have to take a leave of absence at my job.* She expects the executor to sympathize. She thinks she knows his character because he is the purveyor of news that produces immediate intimacy. He remains silent. *Sensitive items?*

It's on a cul-de-sac, he says. *Please go soon, like tomorrow.*

They have famous fish tacos, don't they? she says, meaning the town.

He says, *They have what?*

Jo follows the executor's directions four hours south to a marshland town overrun by sea reeds and canary grass. She parks in front of her father's house, ranch-style on a prim cul-de-sac. Bright windows. Exhaust stews around the idling station wagon.

The workout resistance bands arranged next to his bed are a surprise, as are the razors in the medicine cabinet. A few of his hairs remain in the hollow of a blade. Coarse and black like hers. Jo closes the mirrored door. His bedspread, a halfhearted floral, is perforated by an array of precise divots, as if it has recently been the resting place for a constellation of stars. Later, Jo will pinpoint this as the moment she should have suspected. Instead, she ticks through a plan: She will empty one room each day. She will not take one thing—not one thing—home. She will not use her father's possessions to puzzle out an image of what his life looked like before he succumbed to the disease she hadn't known was hollowing his kidneys. Professional cleaners will arrive in a week, the house will be put on the market, and Jo will rejoin her life in New York. Already her phone vibrates with messages from work.

The refrigerator contains several jars of apricot juice. Lined, labels out. Jo transfers them to the counter. No milk or crusted ends of butter. Only these jars.

The drawers are stuffed with brochures for zoos from all over the world. A zookeeper's card is fastened to the fridge with a magnet for the Cape May Wildlife Association.

Jo jerks the chain for the pantry light and finds hundreds of boxes of matzo stacked in uniform rows. Apricot juice, zoo brochures, and matzo. Were these the sensitive items?

By the end of the day, the contents of her father's kitchen have been transferred into trash bags she bought at a Shop and Save. A week ago, Jo did not know where her father lived. Now she is dragging the most delicate part of what kept him alive to the curb. The sun has retreated behind the water tower that reads: RIO GRANDE: A GREAT PLACE TO GET FROM HERE TO THERE! The false daylight of Atlantic City hovers behind it. The mailboxes glow blue in a trick of dusk. The basalt smell of a neighbor's fireplace. A faraway seagull laments. Jo pulls the sides of her coat tighter and checks her messages.

Her assistant, calling about a cardiologist who forgot his conference ID.

Her assistant saying never mind, he found it.

Her assistant saying never mind the never mind, please call.

The last message is her mother's sister in California, apologizing for a change in plans that will prevent her from attending the funeral.

Jo slips the key into the lock box, imagining the satisfying crack of opening a beer in her room at the Econo Lodge.

I didn't like him but I wanted to come for you, her aunt says. *I appreciate that you have no siblings to help.*

Jo hears a sound in her father's backyard and halts. Behind a green slatted gate, something animal stomps and haws.

Your mother hoped you'd have a husband or boyfriend when the time came. Of course, she never imagined she'd go first.

Jo walks toward the yard as whatever lurks there quiets, detecting her. She hesitates before unlatching the gate. A motion sensor illuminates the driveway. She blinks to clear her vision, steadies herself against the flimsy tangle of plastic fencing.

On the other end of the line, her aunt sighs. *Kiddo, there is never a perfect time.*

Jo opens the gate. The yard is half-bathed in synthetic light. Dark humps of mowing equipment, planters, and rakes abandoned near the back. A picnic table warped by years of weather relents against the earth.

In the center of the yard, a silver unicorn stamps in place. Seeing Jo, it exhales sharply through its nostrils. Cold breath pillows above its head.

The motion light quits, plunging them into darkness. Jo loses her grip on the phone.

Back inside the house, Jo hunts the trash for the discarded zoo brochures. She calls the zookeeper and gets his voice mail. *Howdy,* he says. *You've almost but not quite reached me.* She hangs up, calls again, and leaves a message. She repeats her phone number three times.

The unicorn has followed her inside. It hooves open the pantry door and pushes a box of matzo to the floor. The fulgid, metallic hair that covers its body appears purple from certain angles, like the reed fields that turn and change color in wind. Its mouth is perfunctory and lopsided, and arranged, even when it's chewing steadily, like it is now, into a smirk. It does not seem violent or aggressive. It seems unenthused. If it weren't for the horn—the only pleasant thing about it, Jo thinks—navy-colored with flecks of glittery mineral issuing out from an active, spiraling core—it would look like a pissed-off donkey.

Jo understands why it has been left in the backyard. It chews several crackers at once, leaving a mess. It gnaws the knob to the silverware drawer. She cannot leave it here to destroy the house before it goes on the market. It follows her into the yard where she relatches the gate with it inside. She walks to her car and turns the key in the ignition. Heat sighs through the vents. Jo resents the added responsibility this creature brings and the havoc it could wreak on her schedule.

Thanks, Dad, she says, to no one. Her voice sounds tried on, two sizes big.

Jo drives to the strip mall, where she finds the taco shop and stands in line. Except for her father's orderly development, nothing in this town seems governed. Thin teenagers glare by the shop, curled like parentheses. Restless zoning restrictions permit a Kmart next to a real estate office next to an apartment complex. Jo cannot see the ocean but the ocean is everywhere: pooling in the swells between foxtails, frizzing the hair at her temples. Its mascot, the horseshoe crab, appears in decal form on car bumpers, motel signs. Seagulls holler over her as she walks back to the car. Anything left out in this night will be demoralized by cold and salt. She will not think about the creature standing alone, hunching its back against the wind, shifting its weight from hoof to hoof for warmth.

· · ·

Her return to the yard summons the motion light. She peers through the gate slats to where the unicorn stands, unsurprised, regarding her.

Jo converts the backseat of her station wagon into what the manual calls an after-antiquing space. The unicorn climbs in and rests its chin on the console between the front seats.

I can't drive with your head there, Jo says.

The unicorn snorts but doesn't move.

It's a short ride, she bargains.

The unicorn repositions but leaves a rough hoof where it will brush against her hand when she shifts gears.

Jo and the unicorn drive to the Econo Lodge in silence. It spits when she attempts to help it unfold from the car. She leads it to her room, grateful that no one is in the reservation office or the pool decorated to look like a tropical island. Jo uses extra pillows and one of the motel's unfriendly blankets to hew a makeshift palette. She fills the miniature coffeemaker with water and places it on the floor. The unicorn sniffs but does not drink. Jo retrieves a bottle of apricot juice from her bag and refills the coffeemaker. The unicorn laps it up. Jo refills it and the unicorn drains it again. Satiated, it flicks a critical gaze to the television, the bathroom, her clothes. It soundlessly swallows her hairbrush. Jo scrambles to zip her suitcase but the unicorn is too fast. It ingests a tube of mascara. Its tail twitches and an elegant line of feces plummets onto the thin carpet. The room fills with the tang of leather and armpit. The unicorn lowers itself onto the blanket and falls asleep.

Jo checks for balls and finds no balls. A girl, then. A feeling of solidarity shivers over her but is quickly replaced by the factual odor of dung. Jo turns on the television set. A newscaster named Jasmine reads tide reports for the Delaware Bay as Jo uses motel shampoo to scrub the feces out of the carpet. Jasmine. A fragrant kind of rice.

. . .

Later, wet hair wrapped in a towel, Jo checks in with her assistant. The cardiologists are enjoying cocktail hour. They have complimented the ice sculpture she ordered to be cut in the shape of a heart.

Jo dials California and defines the term *cremains* for her aunt. She doesn't mention the unicorn farting in its sleep by the bed, its flatulence sounding like the upper notes of a xylophone, operatically high. *Cremated and remains*, she says. *A hybrid.* The over-specificity feels like a gut punch. Hocked spit after your opponent is already down.

And I will tell you what I told your father, the zookeeper says when he calls the next morning. *You are not equipped to take care of a creature of this nature.*

Jo is driving and swatting the unicorn away from chewing the upholstery. *This morning it defecated on my suitcase.*

She, the zookeeper corrects her, *defecated on your suitcase.*

Jo says, *I thought unicorns would be peaceful and calm.*

His laugh sounds like a mean bark. *You have a lot to learn about unicorns.*

Jo crouches inside her father's bathtub, scrubbing grout. Her father was a retired electrician with no history of whimsy. What was he doing with a unicorn? Was it a gift meant to ease her grief? Was he holding it for someone who will show up to collect it, a wizard, or . . . ?

His bathroom is neat but not clean. It takes three tries to whiten the tub.

Jo returns to the living room covered in bleach. The unicorn has gnawed through one of the packing boxes filled with wrapping supplies and has strewn ribbon and tissue paper across the carpet, making it look like the aftermath of a party. She bats the unicorn's nose with an empty roll of ribbon.

Bad Jasmine, she says.

. . .

That evening she meets the zookeeper at Applebee's. He is a squat man in high-waisted jean shorts with erratic facial hair. His speech is punctuated by the nervous, barking laugh. They sit in a padded booth and order dinner. It's been over two days since Jo has interacted with a live human being and she is giddy and talkative. She details the unicorn's eating habits and bad behavior. *Today, Jasmine kicked out the heating vent and broke the bathroom mirror.*

Jasmine? The zookeeper chuckles. *That's a little girl's name. Her name is* _____. He makes a sound like a breeze moving through plastic tubing in an open field.

He is part of a team working to repair beach erosion after a recent hurricane. Without enough sand, the horseshoe crabs won't have room to mate. This affects the Red Knot bird population arriving from Argentina expecting to refuel on crab eggs.

Everyone here seems obsessed with horseshoe crabs, Jo says.

They're as old as dinosaurs, he says. *Their relationship with the Red Knots is important.*

Suspicion deepens his eyes to a mean green. Jo is aware he is drawing lines around himself and this town, but she's too tired to care about little birds.

What is it you do, Jo?

I plan events.

He uses his fork to lift his steak as if he will toss it over the bank of booths. *You know how to make God laugh?*

No, she says.

You make a . . .

She forks the last piece of chicken into her mouth and chews. She doesn't feel like participating in a joke about her work.

Plan? he says, finally.

In the lull between entrées and desserts, he hitches up his pant leg to reveal the silver slap of a gun. *I have one in my car, too,* he says.

Jo experiences simultaneous desires to laugh and run. *Who are you going to shoot at Applebee's?*

No one, hopefully. But you'll be happy if we get robbed.

If we get robbed?

Mistaking her question for interest, he places the gun on the table for inspection.

When are we getting robbed? she says.

I wouldn't know exactly, would I? Go ahead. Try the grip.

No, thanks. Like collecting items into a purse, Jo gathers herself inside of herself.

People get robbed here, he says. *We carry guns for protection. We care about the relationship we have to our surroundings. And the names we use matter. Your unicorn isn't an "it," she's a "she." Even your father understood that.*

My father? Now Jo is suspicious. *Did you spend a lot of time with him?*

I did. He leans against the hard plastic of the booth. *We were getting to be friends, maybe.* He seems to be gauging whether she is ready to hear something. *He was a good man.*

The waiter approaches, balancing apple cobbler on a tray. They look up from the gun on the table.

On the way back to the Econo Lodge, Jo stops into a liquor store. On a television hanging over the counter, the announcer named Jasmine reports on what she calls the *ongoing horseshoe crab situation.* The Red Knots are expected to land in a month. If the horseshoe crabs haven't produced enough eggs the birds won't be able to gain enough sustenance to endure the second leg to Antarctica. They will fall out of the sky somewhere over Canada. A Red Knot appears on the screen. It is smaller than Jo would have guessed—the size of a Ping-Pong ball. *Even now, trucks from Texas are hauling tons of sand through the night*, Jasmine reports. Jo imagines the zookeeper shooting bullets into a mound of sand.

. . .

At the motel, the unicorn is restless. She balks and pivots, drags her neck along the floor. Something red winks near her hindquarters. When Jo tries to investigate, Jasmine figure-eights out of her grasp. Jo traps her in the bathroom between the sink and shower and looks closer. A few inches of ribbon hang from the unicorn's sphincter. Wrapping ribbon from her father's house. That he used to wrap presents. For whom? She closes the door, trapping the whining unicorn in the bathroom. The unicorn has ingested an unknown length of ribbon that now wants out. Jo could cut it but has no idea how much is left inside the creature. She pours whiskey into a glass and takes a long drink.

She returns to the bathroom, closes the door, and kneels by Jasmine's side. She pulls the tail aside so it does not impede the opening and takes the ribbon between her thumb and forefinger. She tugs, revealing another half an inch. The muscles in the unicorn's legs constrict in discomfort. Jo has never been this close to the creature. The fur that looks bristly from afar is soft and parts easily to reveal improbably pink skin. A current of cool air circumnavigates her body—light jacket weather. Jo pulls and the ribbon emerges slow inch by slow inch. Jasmine tenses. A prolonged, high-pitched cry ripples through her long throat. Jo slows her pace. The unicorn shudders as the end of the ribbon finally emerges. Jo flushes it and allows Jasmine to back out of the bathroom and sink into her makeshift bed. Jo dry heaves into the bathroom sink.

The next morning at her father's house, Jo finds a sleeve of Polaroids and, after initial hesitation, flips through them while sitting cross-legged on the floor. The bay at sunset. Two women, hips against his old LeSabre, rigid as coworkers. The girlfriend he left her mother for, wearing a sombrero. His parents smiling over eggs at the diner, when everyone was still alive. Jo in a bank vestibule, brandishing a lollipop. Jo honking the LeSabre's horn. Leaping a sprinkler. Holding a turtle. Always alone. The sunset again, from a different vantage point. The sunset again. The sunset again. A tag of thumb at the corner of the photo. His thumb.

Jasmine rests on her father's bed, licking her hoof. When she's not chewing doorframes or urinating on Jo's clothes, the unicorn is good company.

Jo holds out the lollipop photograph. *Look*, she says. *This was me.*

Jasmine climbs down and stretches her front legs. The bed-spread is perforated by her rump, chin, and leg joints.

He let you sleep with him? Jo feels punctured, as if this would nullify an unacknowledged arrangement between her and her father, that he would stay isolated from other living creatures, as she had.

Family can slough away from you like bones shed meat in boiling water.

Jo's mother thought daughters and fathers should talk, no mat-ter how unwilling the daughter, no matter how disputatious the father. After she died, there was no one to force them around a table. Their twice-annual phone calls ceased. Jo never called and he never called, afraid or unwilling to disturb the quiet that Jo convinced herself was peace. She didn't know he had been refus-ing dialysis for two years because they hadn't spoken in three.

At the Econo Lodge, Jo pauses over her crossword, filled with inexpressible relief. In the gentle, rented space, amidst the fwip of television, she realizes her father's death has canceled only his life. Their relationship, albeit one-sided, continues. When he was alive, there were times she forgot about him. Someone would mention his or her father, or the idea of fathers, and everyone would think of their own. Jo would wait the topic out, with no more emotion than one uses to write *not applicable* on a medical form. Existing condi-tions? History of diabetes? Father: NA. Then, something would catch and she'd realize, I have one of those. When he was alive, Jo never knew where her father was. Now his existence is irrefutable, his location exact and near: in incinerated fritters, sealed in the plastic depository on the coffee table, next to a box of matzo. Belief can create existence, but tonight the opposite is also true. For the first time, Jo believes in her father. This family is closer than ever.

Later, the zookeeper examines Jasmine, then he and Jo share a six-pack.

Pulling it out was the worst possible thing you could have done, he says about the ribbon. *It could have been tied up in her intestines.*

It wasn't. Jo is sulky, guilty. She finishes a beer and starts another.

It's easy to mistake her size and attitude for strength. He sits on the edge of the bed next to her. *But there's a tranquility inside her that must be protected.*

He takes her hand with surprising delicacy. Jo perceives a cue in his earnest, fixed gaze. She leans in and presses her lips against his. She answers what feels like hesitance with certainty. His hands hover but don't land on her body. She unbuttons her shirt and pushes his hand inside. Curled on a pile of blankets, Jasmine sighs, bored. Jo insists with her mouth though the zookeeper has no interest. Finally, he peels away from her grip and stands.

Don't be upset but I'm going to leave.

Stay. Her blouse is open. Her bra is white and practically designed.

Sometimes when we're grieving we think we want things we don't. It is obvious he is accustomed to talking unmanageable animals into things they're not interested in. She is not a wounded bird.

His coat sags on a chair. She roots through it and pulls out his gun. It is a cold, dumb bar in her hand. It doesn't seem capable of something as sophisticated as a kill. She aims at his chest.

He raises his hands, smiling. *I give up.*

She lets it fall to the bedspread with an innocuous thump. *Bang bang*, she says.

He palms it and replaces it in his pocket.

Did my Dad ever . . . Jo says. Every word she could use to finish the sentence leaves her mind. *Say . . .* she manages *. . . anything?* She knows how pathetic she looks, unarmed on the bedspread.

About you? the zookeeper helps. *He said you were as stubborn as him.* She thinks he will reach out to her, but he nuzzles the unicorn's ear, crosses to the door, and with a look in Jo's direction she can't decipher, leaves.

In Jo's dream, an apricot asks her a series of difficult questions. She gets most of them right. Frustrated, the apricot lapses into a paroxysm of hooting.

Jo awakens, slick with sweat. The hooting has followed her out of the dream, transforming into a flute coming from the next room. Someone is practicing scales with the ambition of a newbie. That can't be, thinks Jo. Practicing an instrument is something one does in a permanent home. Motel rooms are for transitory activities like preparing for a meeting or dressing for a wedding. Do people live in the Econo Lodge? A breeze through the open door chills her. The open door that, Jo realizes, is open.

Jasmine is not in the parking lot or the motel store that sells car-specific items like replacement windshield wiper blades. Wearing pajamas and motorcycle boots, Jo runs through a copse of ever-greens that connects the motel to a service road. She sprints the service road, streetlights switching on above her. Seagulls make erratic arcs over a figure in the distance. Teenagers jeer and throw cans. They've tied a rope around Jasmine's neck. They've fisted a newspaper into her mouth as a bridle. One of the boys mounts and sinks his heels into her hide. They close ranks. Jasmine blows and canters, attempting indifference. They kick out her back legs. The unicorn does not defend herself. She falls gracelessly against the asphalt.

Hey, Jo yells.

One of the kids registers her with a quick slip of his tongue while another throws a broken bottle that pierces Jasmine's skin. Pain storms through the unicorn's body. Jasmine rolls her eyes toward Jo, who recognizes a familial sense of disappointment. Jo doesn't know how to put herself in between something she's responsible for and something that wishes to do it harm. Her people were withholders.

The unicorn lifts her head to the electric wires fretting above them and bays. The sound begins as the whine Jo has become familiar with but then it grows mythically, emergency loud. Jo covers her ears. The boys scrabble across the lot into a waiting truck and yell, *Go* to the driver. The unicorn's cry grows louder, splintering the back windshield. The truck screeches away as its windows concuss.

Jasmine quiets. The lot is silent. Mackerel-colored bruises bloom along her shoulders. Blood pushes through the skin where the bottle hit; slippery and silver, like mercury. Jo rests her hand on Jasmine's neck. The unicorn shudders but doesn't protest. Halting occasionally so the unicorn can steel herself, they walk the service road back to the motel.

The expression of the Kmart cashier sours as she turns to the line and asks, *Who smells like horseshit?*

Jo holds a heating blanket, bandages, a jar of apricot juice, a tube of mascara, and a hairbrush. Jasmine waits in the car.

Me, she says.

Jo and Jasmine drive to the Econo Lodge in silence. Jo cleans the unicorn's wounds and they watch television. Seeing her in pain is like seeing someone in a bathing suit for the first time. Too much exposed softness. Jasmine seems unfamiliar now, as she places her chin in the crook of Jo's elbow and heaves a relieved sigh. Jo is surprised by how much this intimacy pleases her. She runs her hands through the creature's silky forelock. She rests her head against Jasmine's and falls asleep.

On the last day, only the items in her father's bedroom closets remain. The first holds his casual clothes; sweaters folded and arranged by color. Jo slides them into trash bags, relieved to be almost finished.

Despite her best efforts, she has pieced together an image of her father's life: He lived on an impeccable cul-de-sac in an organized house, eating diet dinners, shaving regularly, exercising his bi- and triceps with products ordered from television, and ignoring advice from doctors and zookeepers, with a drawer of old photos and a flatulent, possibly Jewish unicorn. It was maybe not the most thrilling life but it was at least as happy as hers. She thinks of her second-floor apartment, the din of other people's children in the courtyard below.

The last closet holds his work clothes. Twenty or so replicas of the same evergreen jacket. Pockets for his tools. His name tag gleams on each left breast—she flips through them and it is as if her father is standing in front of her, repeating his full name. Jo lifts as many coats as she can over the clothing rail. The collars press against her neck. The smell of his skin: cardboard and licorice. She stands and inhales into the gruff fabric, his battered sleeves gathering her.

Jasmine's irritable nature, briefly anesthetized by pain, returns and, as if to make up for lost time, worsens. She takes proud dumps where it is hardest to clean, kicks through the door when Jo is in the shower. She belches and farts to fill the room with the odor of minty trash. She refuses to sleep, neighing and pacing by the foot of the bed until dawn.

After making the last of the funeral arrangements, Jo returns to the Econo Lodge to find that Jasmine has eaten most of the Polaroids. Those she has not subsumed she has mauled unrecognizable. The creature dozes in the corner, exhausted as Jo surveys the scene, mute with shock. She paces over the mutilated photos. A corner of sunset. Half of the Buick. She grips the unicorn's head unkindly. Jasmine tries to corkscrew out of Jo's hold but Jo is stronger and accustomed to restraining unmanageable things.

She screams into her face until the unicorn's cheeks quake and her eyes fill with pearly liquid. The unicorn cowers in the kitchenette. Jo hurls herself around the room until she collapses onto the skin-thin bedspread and dials the number by heart.

By the time the zookeeper arrives, Jasmine is trying to repent. She cozies against her. She laps up her juice, taking care not to spill. When none of it works, she leans against the kitchenette, blinking and panicked. Jo sits on the bed, dismissing television channels. They both startle when he knocks.

Even though she called him, Jo glares through the peephole.

It's cold out here, he says.

Jo opens the door and attempts aloofness. *How are the Red Knots? Has anyone heard from them?* He doesn't answer but makes the breeze-moving-through-plastic-tubing sound. Jasmine perks and trots toward him. Jo cannot anticipate the damage this act of recognition wreaks in her heart. Before she can protest, the zookeeper unfurls a gold leash and collar from his bag and secures it around the unicorn's neck. Jasmine knickers, flirting.

What did you do to her forelock? he says.

Jo feels accused. *I braided it.*

He rolls his eyes and leads Jasmine out of the room to his truck. The unicorn follows his unapologetic gait, which annoys Jo, though she follows too, her breath coming in quick punches. *She's too much for me*, she says, though she is suddenly not certain. A ramp extends from the flatbed and the unicorn back-walks into the kennel. *She doesn't have room to turn around.*

It's only ten minutes to the zoo. He snaps the door in place.

I was wrong to think she could ever fit into my life. The other night she got out and kids attacked her. Jo knows she sounds desperate. She has failed her father in a way she doesn't understand. She wants the zookeeper to tell her she is making the right decision.

Sounds like you could have used a gun. He starts the engine. *Look.* His eyes stay trained on the roof of the Econo Lodge where a fistful of shorebirds gathers to watch. *You did your best, but there was no way you could handle it. I told him that but he wouldn't listen.*

The truck joggles across the lot. The unicorn stares whitely toward where Jo stands in the doorway. Under the slate sky, her metallic coat debates gray and purple, and appears to rise. The truck turns onto the service road. Jo waits until she can no longer see the wink of it through the trees. Until she forgets she is a person leaning against a doorframe, until she remembers, and is still unable to move.

At the funeral home, Jo places the cremains like a vase in the center of a platter of cold cuts. She and the executor sit on a mannered loveseat and she signs the paperwork that concludes a life.

Were you able to take a leave of absence from your job? he says.

She is pleased he remembered. *I can work from anywhere. What I do doesn't require me to be present.*

And what is that? he says.

Someone pushes through the front door. They look up in greeting but it is a churchgoer, mistaking the entrance. *I make God laugh*, Jo says. She thinks he will look confused, or get up and remix the dips stiffening in the parlor's stilted air. Instead, he smiles.

That's what we all do.

No other mourner arrives. Jo and the executor wrap the cold cuts and seal the extra rolls in bags. *He was a good man*, the zookeeper had said. It's been bothering her for days.

Can I ask a question?

Yes, the executor says.

Would you call my father a good man?

He pauses transferring cold cuts to a bag. *He always sent contracts back promptly.*

The executor resists taking the leftover food, but accepts after Jo insists, voice breaking over the words. *Leftover food at my father's funeral.*

Can you think of a reason your father wanted you to have a unicorn? he says. *He took wild risks to get it. Did you like them growing up? My girls love them. They have figurines, brush their hair, make waterfalls for them in the sink.*

No doubt these are the girls who crafted the #1 DAD keychain that hangs from his belt loop. Jo admits she's considered every possibility and has arrived at no conclusion. *Sometimes a unicorn is just a unicorn.*

You did the right thing, giving it to the zoo. He is already looking toward the parking lot where his car waits to take him home.

She, Jo says.

Jo eats tacos and steers with her knees. She sits on the damp sand and watches the ocean hoist itself into the air. It is unapologetic and there are glints of anger in it and Jo appreciates this as she eats. She's alone. It's Sunday. Hundreds of miles south on another, warmer beach, one hundred cardiologists are being secured into life preservers. They will snorkel by the light of the moon then enjoy a champagne toast. Even with its detours, the week has gone according to plan.

This ocean, however, is not one you can see the bottom of. Aggravation frills its waves. A hard-tailed horseshoe crab rudders through the sand and muck. One force pushes toward the shore while another pulls, clearing the previous wave's under-layer of silt. A seagull beats against calm air, arcing and holding, arc and hold, battling pressure only it feels.

But where are the Red Knots? Legs tucked into plumage sheared from struggle. Their gaze alert, expectant. Neutralizing their ache by communicating to one another in flight: a little more, a little more, a little more.

That morning, Jo was charged one thousand dollars in room fees for the carpet, the mirror, the drapes, the vent, the shower curtain, the coffeepot.

The motel clerk rang her up with a pitiless look. *Rough night?* Embarrassed, Jo had lied. *My sister gets a little nuts.*

Jo finishes her tacos and balls the wrapping. She would like to see a unicorn charge across the sand. *My sister*, she thinks, watching the shoaling waves.

The unicorn leaps from the brush and gallops across the field. Jo and the zookeeper watch her under the darkening sky. Her wounds have healed. Her coat shines. Jo realizes—how had she missed it?—that the creature advances and retreats in the same movement, obeying two instincts, the way her father would, even in the midst of his worst tirades, pause to drag his cheek against his shoulder, as if asking himself for pardon.

You gave her to me, the zookeeper reminds her, *because you couldn't handle her.*

A decision I regret, Jo says. *However my father left me everything he owned, and he owned her, so she is mine.*

She needs room to run. He gestures to the field. *Do you have a big apartment in New York?*

I have a junior one bedroom, Jo says.

The nervous, barking chuckle. He points to the walking path where goldenrods flex in the cold breeze. *How about this? I'll go over there. We'll both call to her.*

This can't be how it's settled, Jo thinks. A simple call and response. But the zookeeper is already walking to his appointed spot. *If you know what's best for her, you shouldn't be worried.*

Jasmine reclines in a thatch of foxtails, chewing the bulb of her heel. Darkness blots out the bordering trees making the field seem endless. Somehow they both know he will go first.

_____, he calls. A vestibule where chimes hang, a benevolent sound that mothers out background noise. For the first time since entering this town, the scream of seagulls doesn't fill Jo's ears. The unicorn looks up but doesn't move. He calls again. The unicorn rises and takes a few skittering steps. Jo envisions her drive home alone, mile markers flipping silently by. But Jasmine halts, investigates an infraction in the grass, and doesn't move again.

The zookeeper jockeys from foot to foot. He rattles his keys to get the creature's attention. He tries again, but Jo knows—it is no longer her name.

Jo stands in her appointed place, working up the correct voice. The air is so crisp it seems about to crack. Dusk hovers, carrying the threat of snow, but it's just another worry on the field. *She won't come to you, either*, the zookeeper assures her, sounding uncertain. The unicorn reclines, unconcerned by the clash of wills being wrought over her name. Jo is battered by the desire to protect this heavy, unwilling thing and understands that this battering is love. She must allow it to do whatever it wants to her when she calls: *Jasmine, come to me.*

Sam Savage

Cigarettes

My LANDLADY STANDS IN the doorway, one hand braced on the jamb, breathless from climbing the two flights of stairs to my room. She's come up to bum a cigarette. It's the same old story. Her doctor convinces her to kick the habit, scares the shit out of her, sends her home full of virtuous resolve. All she can talk about for the rest of the day is how she's finally quit smoking, how this time she really means it. Next morning, stepping into the kitchen, the first thing I see is her coffee cup on the counter, a couple of soggy butts disintegrating in the saucer. "It's not worth it," she says. "Next time I decide to stop, you need to tell me it's not worth it." I know how she feels, so I refrain from wisecracks and just hand her one. She lights it, takes a long drag, and sighs. The smoke drifts from her mouth and nostrils. "Shit," she says. I twist my chair around to face her, tip it back against the desk, and light my own. We smoke a while, not talking. We are two-packs-a-day smokers, the landlady and me. Same for her brother, Clement, who has a separate apartment in the basement but spends most of his time upstairs in the kitchen or in the living room in front of the TV smoking. Clement rolls his own. It's a house of smoke. One of us is always at it. Sometimes we are all three smoking at once, and the smoke gets thick as fog. There is a sticky film on all the windows. The landlady says there is no point wiping it off. There are not that many real smokers left. We are the last of a dying breed, Clement says. We stick together even though we don't have much to say to each other. They don't let you smoke in restaurants or bars anymore, so we never go out at night. Starting next year we can't even smoke in the parks. I remember when you could smoke in movie theaters. Same with friends. Nobody gives parties where you can smoke anymore, and if you drop in for a chat they want you to stand outside in the rain to smoke, or in the freezing cold. Thrift shops are full of ashtrays that nobody wants anymore. If people have ashtrays, it's to hold paper clips and the like. So we spend a lot of time together—me, Clement, and the landlady hip to hip on her little sofa, watching television and smoking. Of the three of us, Clement is the expert smoker. He can blow rings, one after the other. I can blow a ring now and then, but success is haphazard, and the rings are raggedy, not perfect *O*s like Clement's. He can't explain how he does it, says it's just a knack. I'm not upset that I don't have the knack. In my view blowing rings is not an important part of smoking. I told Clement he could piss off with his rings. I visited France when I was young, lived there for almost a year. France was paradise in those days, but I was so down-and-out I had to buy the cheapest cigarettes. They were called Parisiennes. They came in packages of four and were so loosely packed you had to hold them horizontal while you smoked or the tobacco would fall out. The bums, who were most of the customers for those cigarettes, called them P4s. I was in France for so long without cash that I was calling them P4s, too. Nowadays the three of us spend most of our money on cigarettes. My daughter won't come to my place. Tipped back in the chair, facing my landlady, whom I don't particularly like, the two of us not exchanging a word, just smoking—that's as good as it gets. My daughter says she can't get the smell of cigarettes out of her clothes, even after several washings. I can't make her understand.

Adrienne Celt

Temples

H ERE, YOU CAN SEE Aunt Marjorie's pillow, heavy with the
cells of the dead. She wouldn't consider any offers to replace
it, remaining insensitive to the argument that cushions collect
shed skin, gaining up to a pound over time. For ten years she slept
on this pillow, boasting about it as a luxury. Down feathers. Soft
cotton slipcovers. So plump. Now that we've ashed her remains
and tossed those ashes out over the salt flats, this pillow is the
weightiest piece of her that exists on earth.

There is an argument to be made that her soul, wherever it
landed, is heavier still. But naturally we can no longer measure.
At this point we've done all we can do.

To get to the salt flats in Tooele County, where Marjorie swept
out on the wind, bitter clean, we must first pass through a more
complicated terrain. We must, in fact, go back in time and look
at Marjorie at the height of her strength. It's the only way to see
just where that strength failed.

It's bright outside, summer, and she's walking into a bakery.
She gave up alcohol when she converted, abandoning the glass of
brandy her mother and father each indulged in before bed. But

although she enjoys the lucidity, the all-time clearheadedness of teetotaling, she is not immune to pleasure.

Behind the glass counter, the cakes are sweating. Or perhaps not—but it is a hot day, and everything seems to exhibit a sheen, a glow. Particularly these beautiful cakes, frosted to resemble flower gardens, little girls' bedrooms, the Taj Mahal. The colors are bright and moist, the iced edges precise. Little placards explain what lies inside each sugar-wrapped package.

Sweet cream and raspberry jam. Lemon with slivered almonds. Chocolate ganache on a bed of candied walnuts.

Marjorie's hands are aloft in an attitude of delight, fingertips pressed together, palms tented. She buys a cake for herself every Sunday—an almost hysterical indulgence—and eats it slowly over the course of the week. Generally she chooses something unusual: a vanilla bean body with a layer of sliced strawberries and an outer shell of marzipan, for instance. But really, anything will do as long as she doesn't know how to bake it herself.

When Marjorie knows how to bake a cake, the illusion of its individual perfection is spoiled. Plain chocolate cake, for instance, is out, because all Marjorie sees when she looks at one is two eggs, cocoa, two sticks of butter, a few cups each of flour and sugar, and a pinch of baking powder, baking soda, and salt. On the other hand, pear galette filling over Peruvian spiced butter cake carries a whiff of the eternal, the slices of pear laid out with the geometry of ammonite fossils, of star formation. That's what she told me. What I used to believe.

Let's look at Marjorie's hips, encroaching on the band of her skirt. Her hands have been gnarled by time, but still evoke a certain cream-fed health. Her face is round. Her teeth stick out. Her body would be beloved, beautiful, if you didn't focus in on the particulars.

When we had Aunt Marjorie cremated we asked that the crematorium take care not to leave any bits of unburned bone. I didn't want to recognize a femur, a finger, something from my freshman anatomy textbook. I didn't want to recognize any piece of Marjorie in that pile of smooth gray ash.

There is an art to cremation, with different schools of taste and judgment. For instance, it's traditional for Japanese cremation to take place at lower temperatures so the family can recognize the form of the skeleton and place their deceased feetfirst in the urn. I felt it was important to know these things, in order to make the right requests for Marjorie. Temperature, density, duration. It's always better to know what you're doing, to be in control.

Because I was interested, the technician let me watch the beginning of the process. He even let me push the button to start up the fires. It's like being in a jet engine, he told me. You need a fuel that will burn at extreme levels. I watched them place the bag in the oven. I pressed the button with my thumb.

Marjorie wasn't really my aunt, she was my mother's. But she helped raise me, and after a couple of arguments over the niceties of terminology—did our relationship make her my great-aunt, or my something-once-or-twice-removed?—it was agreed that Aunt Marjorie had a sweeter ring than any of those more specific titles. In Wrocław her name had been Margita, but that she shed on Ellis Island along with all her traveling companions.

I always liked the idea: stepping down from the dingy steamer where you've spent a frightened month and shaking everything off. The body scent of vinegar and soap, the late-night conversations with strangers. The strangers themselves, turned into circumstantial friends. Even your name. Get rid of it all.

Walk away clean.

Here is Marjorie in her kitchen, a wax cloth thrown over the table. She is rolling out a wad of dough and tearing off hunks, fashioning them into little animals and people and mushrooms, to the delight of the small girl beside her. The girl is on her knees, on a chair, elbows grinding into the spare flour strewn across the tabletop.

Each of their bread-pale creatures is loaded onto a tin baking sheet and popped in the oven, emerging rock-hard and flavorless to be painted with acrylics. Marjorie and the girl sip glasses of cold water and work in a glow of concentrated attention long past the point of hunger. The longer they work, the nimbler their fingers, so the last character Marjorie fashions looks just like the little white dog from the girl's favorite cartoon. Its fur is riveted, its nose and eyes distinct.

Their facility is a gift.

But then Marjorie sees the clock and is dismayed. She wipes her flour-and-water-crusted hands on her housedress, leaving streaks. From underneath a tall glass dome she produces her weekly cake—a deceptively simple one, seven thin layers of gingerbread with a honeyed buttercream frosting. Dusted with nutmeg.

For herself and the girl she cuts two gigantic slices, breaking the spell of their holy focus. These are pieces of cake as large as men's shoes, and will certainly spoil dinner for both parties. But according to Marjorie, it's all right, they skipped lunch. They may each plunge fork-deep into the butter softness of the layers and eat until their eyes glitter with sweetness and their bellies bell out like women with child.

My mother always told me that Aunt Marjorie was converted to the Mormon Church by a boy back in Wrocław, himself transformed by missionaries from an indifferent type into a community pillar: a kind of miracle. Where once he'd slept all day and pilfered cigarettes from the corner store, after his baptism the boy worked for his father as an apprentice carpenter and building contractor. He told his neighbors the good word of Joseph Smith while dangling from great heights, hanging shingles.

Marjorie was moved to see the boy translated from apathy to energy incarnate. But her conversion became official only after she witnessed the boy save his father from a pile of collapsed boards at a build site, lifting him so easily that it seemed neither the man nor the lumber weighed anything at all. Another miracle. She left Poland in the thirties, on the rising tide of war, and always felt that her faith brought her safely to America—the carpenter's rescue an appropriate premonition of her own salvation.

So, she was Jewish before she converted? I asked once.

No. My mother laughed. Where did you get that idea? Lots of people left then. The place was deadly.

I should be clear: It wasn't that I really thought Marjorie was Jewish, not the Marjorie I knew. But you get a certain sense of things from school, a tidiness of history. You imagine the throngs of people escaping from disasters as all having, in some sense, the same face. The monsters as uniform, the blameless as uniform, and the possibility of good in the world as existing in the pure separation between those two units.

Marjorie approaches the temple of her adopted church with the look of someone being baptized. She appreciates the way that the church's temples—even in America, where buildings so often blur into functional boxes—aim for style. She stands on the lawn, making her small companion wait, so she can admire the view. Sleek white, clean corners. A spire—or is it an obelisk?—on top, tapering off into an ideal point.

Secretly, Marjorie even likes the way this temple mimics the severe lines of Soviet architecture. The thought betrays how far she's come from Wrocław, where the Russian troops did no favors. But she admires discipline, and if she can only access it at church—through her commitment to God, through the structural engineering of His house—then she will do so with gratitude.

The lawn is precise and green and it springs back under Marjorie's footsteps as she strolls across it, struggling somewhat against the tightness of her outfit. Her dress today is gray and blue—you can see how it once fit her figure, although now the seams are strained. Marjorie holds the hand of the young girl to whom she has fed cake, whispered secrets. The girl is attired in lavender and her dress is shapeless as a bag, showing off the roly-poly nature of her childhood body.

As she's tugged into the lobby, the girl is making a decision. She will not, when they get home, accept a slice of cake to "start off the week." They never end up having time for breakfast before church—I'm not exactly an early bird, Marjorie says—and the girl likes how she enters and exits the temple with a feeling of pure ascendancy. She wants to spend the whole day like this, vibrating with the light of God.

Marjorie chatters happily with other members of the congregation, who ask after the girl's mother—so sad, she has to work on a Sunday. It is sad, but Marjorie's face is alight; her love of the church is transfixing. Outside, Marjorie is just Marjorie, but here, her beauty shines through. Her commitment. She knows all about miracles and transformation. And so, standing in the vestibule and watching dust motes rise on the heat of sunbeams, the girl makes the mistake of thinking that Marjorie will understand.

Another thing my mother has always said is that loveliness is not everything, but it helps. I appreciate the way this point of view makes her sympathetic to what I have to do. She takes me grocery shopping, and we skip by the aisles of milk and bread and cheese and pick out gorgeous slender celery and organic oranges. With a good orange, you can suck the juice right off the pulp, so you never have to swallow more than the pure nutrients, the ones you need to stay alive.

I tell my mother, then you're not weighed down by extra fiber, see? If you know the tricks, if you know how to plan, your muscles can stay long and sinewy, like they're supposed to. Your ribs won't be hidden under thick layers of fat, as if you were a penguin hunkering down in the arctic cold. My mother nods. Though as I turn, I think I see her shake her head.

Part of planning well is not wasting energy on too much analysis. Even the thought of, say, a pastry, exhausts me. It's just a whole mental effort. Picking apart the ingredients and weighing them out on a scale in your head so you know what you're eating. Like math homework.

When Aunt Marjorie died I saw her house with entirely new eyes. It was different without her in it. Everything dusty, the kitchen rimed with oil and peelings. Scrubbing it down for sale was a team endeavor, and I remember sweeping behind the stove and finding the papery shell of a garlic clove. Who knows how long it had been there? Who knows what meal it made, however many years ago? Perhaps Marjorie knew, but with her gone the pieces of her life were just pieces. The pieces were just trash.

I picked up a little white dog from the mantel, made out of flour and water paste. It had calcified over the years, and shrunk. Its stomach squeezed, as though by a corset. I put it in my pocket, and it was so light I could barely feel it.

Back at home my mother baked cookies, which is not the kind of thing she does. She sat with a plate of them in front of her while I made tea, and she watched me.

You could have one, she said. They're not that bad for you really. They're oatmeal.

She never used to say things like that. Aunt Marjorie would, though, any chance she got. My mother is easy—she backed off with her plate of sweets as soon as I closed my eyes and told her no. But Marjorie wouldn't leave it alone. Just one bite? she'd say. You used to love cakes. Red velvet, orange pecan, double espresso hazelnut chiffon.

Look at her, choosing one: a bubble of a woman with a cheeky smile, telling the man behind the bakery counter that this is her one great opportunity to be naughty. But really, is that true? Doesn't she eat chicken cutlet, doesn't she eat garlic bread? Doesn't she drink whole milk, on the argument that it is healthier despite the little plug of cream that sits at the top of every bottle?

The girl and Marjorie have gone to the shopping mall, hoping to buy the girl's mother a gift. It has been a long day, and the girl and Marjorie are in a tiff. They couldn't find nice shoes in the shoe stores—everything was patent leather, wedge-heeled, ticky-tack. They couldn't agree on a scarf or a lipstick shade, tending toward different colors and styles. The girl likes everything diaphanous and bright, whereas Marjorie is looking for something just a little practical, for a woman, after all, who has to wait outside every afternoon for the bus.

Now it is getting close to closing and the girl is tired in her knees and her spine. She tells Marjorie her ankles are getting swollen and Marjorie snaps at her to sit *down* then. Just wait on the bench, and she will find the one object they can come to terms on: a charm for the mother's charm bracelet. Both disapprove of the bracelet itself, where it comes from, but they know the gift will please her.

In her early life, the mother was a beauty. She got married just out of high school, choosing a husband a few years older than herself—one who'd already been on his church mission. She had her pick of men to fall in love with, and that was an important criterion. If she missed a few others, well, never mind. It was of great concern to girls she knew, their beaus leaving to travel the world while they sat at home, writing letters. They were like fishwives, all of them, doomed to it. So the girl's mother had sniffed.

Her husband did his mission work in Istanbul, walking or biking around the city wearing a crisp white shirt. Temples, though not his temples, loomed above him. Bells rang, and voices called the world to prayer, but not his prayer. He showed her pictures. In them, he looked very young, and very happy. After a year of marriage, he melted back into those images, this time for reasons of his own. Proving that there are no safe choices, not in marriage, not in the world.

The girl has never yet seen those fabled pictures of her father—the disappearing man, the vanisher—though she has seen the charm bracelet from him that her mother still wears everywhere. We've already *looked* in the jewelry store, the girl tells Marjorie. She's sitting on a bench that wraps octagonally around a planter, in the middle of the mall's throughway. The bench is made of slats, and bits of the girl's legs keep getting stuck between them.

I'm just going to pop downstairs and check the bargain area, says Marjorie.

But it's her *birthday*.

Just *sit*. Marjorie screws her lips up to the side, making herself look somehow garnished. Her mouth a vegetable sliced up like a flower. You never know, she says, what you'll find down there.

This late in the day, Marjorie is the only one going to the basement, and so she seems to be the engine driving the escalator down, sinking the steps with her bulk. Who knows what she will do there, how long she will dawdle? The girl can only guess, inventing interactions between Marjorie and exhausted merchants: Marjorie tossing out uninvited banter and standing in the middle of a walkway to consider a spritz of discount perfume. Marjorie peering one-eyed through a glass paperweight, as though, on the other side, another world would reveal itself.

She won't find anything, the girl knows. By now, half the bargain counters will have been locked up and prematurely abandoned. Perhaps, by the time Marjorie gives up her quest, the escalators will even have been disabled, forcing her to trudge, step-heavy, up the immobile staircase. The girl smiles; she thinks it's funny: Marjorie tricking herself into getting some exercise.

Families hurry around her, mothers checking their children's arms for the requisite number of packages. A threesome of teen-age girls scurry by, their hands held up over the mouths, eyes alight. The girl is about to abandon her post to take a closer look at a store window—she's drawn by its display of slender dummies, draped with summer whites and seersucker. But then she hears it:

Ha!

There's Marjorie, rising, rising, on the escalator, one hand held over her head. She's pinching something gold—a charm—which catches a flicker of fluorescent light and glints. Like a polestar. Like a signal. Marjorie is beaming, her mouth spread wide enough to show the fillings in the back of her jaw, but she doesn't care. She's laughing, smiling, coming up in triumph from below.

Aunt Marjorie went to church every week, and for many years ran the Relief Society. If she were a man, she would certainly have been a bishop, but she was content to serve as God saw fit for her. She took care of me when my own mother could not, and helped me see the clean lines of the church, the sweetness of discipline, the possibility of miracles.

Let's look at heaven: a place of perfection, weightlessness. The ideal mathematics of celestial planets, one person on each, living as a god of light. That is something people don't understand, if they don't go to church, study the scriptures: that our God was once a man like us who earned his radiance through strict adherence to the Gospel. By living a life that was strictly good—good in every measure.

And now let's look at Marjorie, fleshy from bottom to top. She wouldn't listen to my explanation of why I only wanted a dinner of crackers and apples, the lightest possible food, the simplest vitamins. No matter how I tried to make her see, she turned ashen when I talked about the beauty of bones, how they are like volcanic rock—so much more delicate than they appear.

Bones are full of fatty marrow, Marjorie told me. People in Wrocław would boil them and scoop the marrow out, and spread it on toast. Like lard.

That's what she said to me, that's what she believed. Marjorie whom I loved. Marjorie, with her heavy feather pillow. Marjorie who dipped one pinkie into the cream of a tiramisu and stuck it in her mouth with such a glow of pleasure that she appeared to be self-cannibalizing. Marjorie, hungrily stripping the flesh off her hands to feed the rest of her heft, the fat marrow of her bones. Marjorie, massive.

I promised that we would end up on the salt flats in Bonneville, that somehow Marjorie would lead us there. But in fact it was my idea to go to Tooele County, and on the drive out I held Aunt Marjorie's ashes in my lap. My mother drove barefoot, her black shoes kicked off and thrown onto the backseat in a jumble.

The salt flats are moonlike, with the incandescent glow of a night-light even at high noon. In life there was little about Marjorie that was tidy, and I'd made it my mission to fix that, to the best of my ability, now that she was dead. Marjorie refused to understand me, couldn't see that I was enacting a marvel of my own. A transformation. Sometimes her cheeks would hang off her face and jiggle a little. Sometimes she had jowls.

I imagine being a teacher, using Marjorie as an instructive example of how to save a falling soul. Here we see the droplets of sweat that polluted Marjorie's brow when she exerted herself. Here is the back of Marjorie's knee, creased like a marshmallow crushed between crackers. But then: We see her cleansed into ash, cool and gray and soft.

At Bonneville, the ground is self-disinfecting. Salt leeches out the moisture, evaporates into the air all possibility of mildew and blooming mold, leaving the landscape white and uniform, the wind whistling across it unimpeded. I told my mother: It will be pretty. It will be a nice place for her to rest. To meet with God.

I wanted to believe in Marjorie's ascension into heaven: a last miracle, for her. Rising up into the arms of infinity. I wanted to believe I had the ability to make such a thing possible. My mother slipped back on her shoes, and we crunched out over the dry earth of the salt flats until we were in the middle of a great white nowhere. I knelt down and tried to pry the lid off of the box, the Marjorie box, but my fingers shook.

Let me, my mother said. Honey, let me help you.

She took an old pocket knife out of her purse, a knife with a yellow body and a slightly rusty blade. Her charm bracelet made a sound like ice when she jammed the blade into the seam of the box and then the hinge. Sharp, clean movements. One, two, three. With a pop, the lid came free and released a little puff of Marjorie around us.

God bless her and keep her, my mother said.

The sun was hot; there was very little breeze. I picked up the bag of ashes and turned it upside down above my head, downwind of my body, and watched Marjorie fall. I was a little disappointed—she was supposed to catch on a breath of air and fly to the Lord. But Marjorie remained in death what she was in life, even after all my planning: so heavy, so physical, so full. She drifted onto the salted earth and moved across it like a wave, like a twister. And then the wind changed.

The dust of Marjorie rushed back at us, a sudden gust hitting our faces and billowing my skirt. My mother covered her eyes, but I didn't move quite fast enough. We were in a cloud, and then the cloud was gone. In the stillness that followed, I looked down at my arms, which were coated in gray. The color grit stuck to my eyelashes, and to my teeth.

Mama, I said.

She was all over me. Marjorie in my ears and under my fingernails. Sitting lightly on my collarbone and dusting the part in my hair. Marjorie, swallowed, no matter how I tried resisting. My mother used her shirtsleeves to clean off my cheeks, bent my neck down and scratched the ashes off my scalp, then flipped my hair back up and over, for volume, the way she'd shown me when I was a little girl still learning how to be in the world. How to be good, and how to measure it.

Safety

Lydia Fitzpatrick

IN THE GYM, THE children are stretching in rows. Their arms are over their heads, their right elbows cupped in left palms. Class is almost over, and this is the wind-down—that is what the gym teacher calls it—though the children move constantly, flexing their toes inside their sneakers, shifting their feet, canting their hips, biting their lips, because they are young, and their bodies are still new to them, a constant experiment. The gym teacher counts softly, one, two, three, four, and before five there is a sound that reminds a boy in the back row of the sound a bat makes when it hits a baseball perfectly. In the front row, a girl thinks it is the sound of lightning, not lightning in real life, because it is sunny out and because she can't remember ever hearing real lightning, but like lightning on TV, when the storm comes all at once. Next to her, her best friend thinks it is a sound like when her mother drives her into the city and the car first enters the tunnel, only this sound is sharper than that one and stays within its lines, and she is not inside it. One boy recognizes the sound. He has been to the range with his father and brother, and he has worn headphones and stood a safe distance and watched the sound jerk his father's arm and push his brother off balance. This boy is the first to let his elbow drop.

The gym teacher is thinking *five*, and then he knows. He looks to the door that leads to outside, to the ESL trailers, to the walkway that connects the elementary school to its middle school, because that is where the shot has come from, and there is this throb of hope for the girl who teaches ESL, who has just moved here and still bakes brownies for the teachers' lounge. The gym teacher is calm, and in his wind-down voice he tells the children to be quiet, completely quiet, and to run into the boys' locker room. The gym teacher is old, has been at this school for decades, and with each passing year, the children like him more and listen to him less, but they know to be afraid from the carefulness in his voice— they are not talked to carefully, except when they ask questions about death and divorce—and at first their fear is only for the tone of his voice, but then they remember the sound. They run, and their sneakers are the sort that light up with each footfall and their shoelaces whip against polished wood, and the gym teacher is not worried that they will trip, but that they will stop—because they are that age when rules are God and shoelaces must be tied—but they don't stop, and they don't trip. There are eighteen of them. They are as fast and graceful as he has ever seen them.

When they reach the locker room, one boy grabs the gym teacher's sleeve. It is September, and he has not yet memorized their names, but he knows that the boy's brother was a student of his years ago and that the boy's father is back from the war. The boy whispers, "Gun." He is the one who recognized the sound and he has worried, as he sprinted across the basketball court, that the gym teacher might not know. The gym teacher nods, puts a finger to his lips. He is thinking means of egress. He is thinking police, hide, gun. He is thinking of his cell phone, which was a present from his son last Christmas, a tongue-in-cheek present, a comment on character, and it is in the pocket of his windbreaker on the back of the ladder chair in his kitchen at home.

The children have gathered around him when usually they scatter, and he can see in their eyes that they want to be picked up and held. One girl has forgotten the sound. She smiles and raises her hand. She has a question. She wants to know whether they should change out of their uniforms, but before she can ask, the gym teacher points to his office, which is in the middle of the locker room, and he tells them to lie on the floor behind his desk and to be quiet, and the carefulness drops from his voice—he can't help it, there are more shots, inside the school now, and a yell cut short.

As the children file into his office, the gym teacher turns out the lights in the locker room and looks out into the lighted gym. The floor is perfectly bare, perfectly clean, glowing like the surface of a planet seen from afar. The cones and Frisbees and Hula-Hoops are back in their bins, and there is nothing to show that a class meets this period. Through the windows of the double doors he sees pale yellow wall tiles (they are the color of butter, of winter sun, but the tiles are more a constant in his world than butter or pale suns, and so when he sees those things he thinks that they are the color of the school). The boy whose father is just back from the war, the one who recognized the sound, watches the gym teacher look to the doors, and he wishes that the gym teacher were his father, because the gym teacher is old and afraid, and his father has only been afraid twice and both times were at the war, never at home, because here, he says, is paradise compared to there. This boy is the last into the office, and as he lies down next to the girl who thought of lightning, he goes on wishing for his father in the fervent way that children wish for things because they think those things are almost in their grasp.

On the teacher's desk is the blue parachute that the children play with on Fridays. On Fridays, they grip the silk and make it ripple and buck, they run underneath it and around it, but one of its seams is split, and the gym teacher meant to take it home to his wife, who would stitch it up as she has dozens of times before. Behind his desk, the children are lying in two neat rows, and he has seen children lie this way before, on the news, in other countries, but not these children, his children, and he almost tells them to get up, that it is tempting fate to lie this way, but there are more shots, closer, in the cul-de-sac of classrooms across from the gym, and the gym teacher grabs the parachute and spreads it over them, and they are so small that it covers all eighteen of them easily, and at the thought of them—of how many and how small—his chest seizes, and he thinks that he will be the one to make a noise, but then he hears the clang of the gym doors opening and the long sigh of them swinging shut and his fear becomes the biggest thing he's ever felt. It is so much bigger than him that for a second it eclipses him entirely.

The gym teacher cannot think, and then, just as suddenly, he can. He turns out the lights in his office and the parachute is not quite as dark as the shadows around it—the silk has a gleam—but it is the best he can do. He crouches under his desk. He is between the children and the door, and he whispers to them one more time, "Do not make a sound. Do not move." Under the parachute, a girl pees without thinking of holding it. She feels it hot and soaking the seat of her gym shorts, and the parachute is light on her face. On Fridays this is the best feeling, and she thinks of that, of how she is getting to feel it today even though it is not a Friday. There are footsteps moving across the gym. A boy thinks, Dad. A girl thinks, Mom, Mom, Mom. One boy thinks it is the principal, because the principal is the only one who walks through the halls when they're empty. One girl begins to count silently. She panics sometimes—when she sees the road disappearing too fast under the car's tires; when the train cuts through their town, its whistle blaring; when she is in the swing at the park and finds herself too high—and her parents tell her to count, to breathe, to count and breathe, and they count with her, lead her from one number to the next.

The footsteps are slow. The gym teacher knows that this means it is the man with the gun and it means something about him too. The gym teacher is curled around his own knees. He has never made himself so small. Behind him, the parachute moves with each of their breaths.

There is a new noise. A clang of metal on metal. The boy who recognized the shot does not know what this sound is, and he realizes now that there was comfort in knowing. He does not love Fridays and the parachute. He does not love anything that hems him in, and his mother tells him that even as a baby he did not like to be held. He edges out from under the parachute. He is between the wall and the girl who thought of lightning, and it is dark, but he can see the gym teacher's coat rack branching over him and he can see the windows that line the walls of the office and look out into the locker room. Deep in the dark there is a red haze from the exit sign over the door that leads to outside, to the ESL trailers, and to the walkway to the middle school where his brother is, and the boy could run that walkway in twenty-two seconds—he has timed himself on a watch that is both waterproof and a calculator—but his brother does not like him to come to the middle school. Instead, his brother meets the boy on the hill above the soccer field, where there is a tree with peeling bark and a path that leads through the woods to their house.

The clanging noise shakes in the air and gives way to the footsteps. The girl counts thirty, thirty-one. The man with the gun is close, the gym teacher thinks, by the showers, whose dripping is the metronome of his days. The showers are separated from the office by three banks of lockers, and as he thinks of the lockers, he realizes that that was the clanging sound, metal on metal—the butt of the gun or the muzzle. The children's things are inside the lockers and strewn around them, their backpacks and jackets and lunch bags and dioramas—they are that age, when teachers tell them to pick their favorite place in the world and fit it in a shoebox and they can—and the man with the gun will see these things, and he will know that they are here. The gym teacher shifts into a squat and one of his ankles cracks. He doesn't know what he'll do when the door opens, but he keeps his eye on the dark square of the window next to the door. The footsteps are closer and closer and closer and far away there are screams, and a girl—the youngest in the class—has heard these screams before, at the hospital, when she was having an arm set and down the hall someone else was having something worse. Next to her, a boy wishes for something to hold on to. His palms burn with the need, and he finds the girl's hand next to his and grabs it, and she thinks this is like the hospital too, where everyone was holding hands.

He is here. There is a change in the darkness in the window that the gym teacher feels more than sees (just as he feels his wife's absence some nights, when she is sleepless and moves through the house below him), and then the change is clearer: He can see the man's glasses catch the red light of the exit sign. He can see the nose of the gun moving toward the window. There is a clink, a knife on a plate. Fifty-six, the girl counts, and the gym teacher knows the glass will splinter, he knows how this ends, but behind him the boy crouched under the coat rack sees something different: A half-foot down the gun's barrel, where the shoulder strap attaches, there is a dangling medal, a slim silver oval barely bigger than a thumbnail, but big enough for the boy to recognize it. It is a saint medal, the saint whose job it is to protect soldiers, and the boy knows the saint's name because it is the same as his own, and he knows the medal because his mother gave it to his father years ago, before you were born, she tells him, before your brother was born, when your father left for the first time.

The gun drops from the window, and the boy does not hesitate. He is up. He opens the door and slips through it, his body filled with the certainty of it, with a wish fulfilled, his father, and as he turns the gun is ready for him. It is inches from him. Dad, the boy thinks, even as he realizes that the man is not tall enough to be his father, is not tall enough to be a father at all. In life, the boy has been fearless—he trusts the dark, trusts the slimmest branch, trusts that he alone can fly—but he looks at the gun and his mind goes cold and cavernous.

"Where's your class?" the man says, his voice muffled by a ski mask.

The boy hesitates for a moment—he does not think of protecting his class, of protecting the girl who is his favorite, who is under the parachute, trying to remember the prayer that her grandmother mumbles in Polish each night—for a moment he hesitates because he cannot speak. Then that moment is over, and he is still alive, and he says, "Outside."

"Outside," the gym teacher hears, and he thinks that this might save them, but the silence grows long and he does not know what it means. He is listening for sirens, wishing for sirens in the fervent way that children wish, as though his chest is opening to dispatch some part of him that will find the sirens and usher them here. Behind him, the children know that for the first time they are hiding without wanting to be found.

The boy raises his eyes and looks up the long line of the gun to the medal. It *is* his father's gun. The boy can see it here, and he can see it locked in the case in the hall between the door to his room and the door to his brother's room, where it glows in the way things precious and forbidden glow—the grandfather clock with the damp brass gears and the ostrich egg with foreign letters inked on its curves and the tiny crystal bottle on his mother's dresser—and the constellation of these things is as sacred and eternal as anything up in the sky, and the boy cannot believe that the gun is here and that its case is empty.

"Let's go," the man says, and his voice is muffled, but there is something strained in it that the boy recognizes. The boy looks up, past the medal, to the mask, which is a ski hat with holes cut for the mouth and nose and eyes, and over the eyeholes are glasses that could be anyone's, except that they are his brother's. They are across the table from him every morning, slanted toward a book whose pages are dusted with the crumbs of the toast his mother makes. They were across the table from him this morning.

The boy reaches out and puts a finger to the nose of the gun, and it is warm. He has never touched the gun before, and his brother yanks it away, and the medal jingles, this tiny silver noise, and his brother grabs his hand.

Under the desk, the gym teacher listens to them walk away and he begins to cry. He has always thought that you could *know*, that right and wrong were like bones beneath the skin—hidden but there, waiting to be laid bare—and his hands are empty and he cannot weigh the one against the seventeen. The girl who is counting hits a hundred and starts over again at one, and the boy's brother pulls him toward the emergency exit, and the boy has dreamed of this, in certain stretches of homeroom, when he is filling a sheet with cursive *L*s, he has dreamed of his brother taking him out of class and letting him sit on the back of his bike as they coast down the hill into the town to the store with the miniature models of helicopters and tanks and dragons that are all the color of flour, waiting to be painted with brushes whose bristles are thin as eyelashes, but even as he has dreamed this, he has known it will not happen because his brother prefers to be alone, likes to have space, though their mother says that as a baby his brother was the one who liked to be held.

They are at the door, and his brother pushes it open with a hip so that he can keep one hand on the gun. The gym teacher watches a wedge of light stretch across the locker room, the benches, the book bags, and he is waiting for a child to speak, to cough—it is that season, when their noses run and their lips chap—but they are silent, and the light recedes, and he tells the children to stay quiet and that he will be back.

Outside, the air is cool and sweet. The light is too bright—it makes the boy think of Sundays, when their mother takes them to the movies, and the boy loves the movies, cannot sit close enough to the screen, and when the movie is over and they step out of the theater, the fact of the world outside is a shock to him, an insult. The boy's brother lets go of his hand, and the bell rings, blaring from loudspeakers in the corridors and classrooms, from speakers mounted on the corners of the ESL trailer. It is time for lunch, but no one comes out of the trailer, and the school is still. There is the soccer field. The grass arches away from the wind, and they cross the parking lot to the field, and the boy looks back over his shoulder and sees a girl lying on the sidewalk next to the ESL trailer. She has fallen with one ear against the pavement, and the boy recognizes the girl. She is two grades above him, with dark hair and a red birthmark on her cheek in the shape of a cloud. Her face has gone so pale that even the birthmark is drained of color, and beyond her, on the steps of the trailer, there is a woman and from the way she is lying the boy can tell that her face will look the same.

Under the parachute, the girl who thought of lightning is thinking of her grandfather, who is the only person she knows to have died—his heart had been good but turned bad—and her own chest hurts, and she wonders if it is her heart turning inside her. A boy begins to shake. His teeth are chattering and he puts a finger between them because the teacher said not to make a sound. He has never thought of himself as truly separate from his mother, and yet he is sure that at her desk in the office in the city she does not know what is happening to him and cannot feel his fear. In the years to come, he will think of this over and over, of how she did not know.

The boy's brother is breathing fast behind the mask, and the boy knows that he shot the girl and the woman. The tip of the gun was warm, but the boy cannot make sense of it or of why he is following his brother, crossing the field at the same angle he does every afternoon. From the door to the locker room, the gym teacher watches the two boys—they are both boys, he can see that now—as they walk up the hill toward the woods. There is a dead girl on the pavement and on the steps of the trailer a woman moans, and when the boys are far enough away the gym teacher runs to the woman. It is the ESL teacher, and he puts his fingers to her neck and says, Please, please, please. Under the parachute the girl counts, her lips careful with the numbers: eighty-eight, eighty-nine. The silk is so hot that it begins to stick to them, to foreheads and noses and knees.

At the top of the hill, where there is the tree with the peeling bark and where the path to the boy's home begins, there is a cross stuck in the ground. It is two pieces of a yardstick that the boy recognizes because his mother used it to stir a can of paint—one end is the blue of their kitchen—and now it has been broken in two and nailed together. The boy's brother stops at the cross and says, "They'll ask you why." Every word comes out like a splinter, like he is in pain, and the boy says, "Are you crying?"

The gym teacher hears sirens, faint as wind chimes, as he puts his mouth to the woman's and exhales.

"Listen to me," the boy's brother says, and he gets down on his knees. "They're going to ask you why."

His brother's glasses are fogged. The ski hat is their mother's. It is the one she wears when she shovels snow and it smells of a dog, though they've never had one, and he does not know how to square these ordinary things with the way his brother is shaking—not gently, but wildly—as he pulls the gun over his shoulder and points it at him.

"Are you going to shoot me?" the boy says.

The girl counting reaches one hundred and stops, because her fear has dissolved, is a memory now. The gym teacher puts his fingers to the woman's neck again, and this time there is nothing. Another girl hears the sirens and thinks of her dog and the way he howls with his throat arched whenever he hears a siren and of how he will be howling now, in her house, which is nearby, pacing the halls and filling the empty rooms with that sound.

The boy begins to cry. Not because he is afraid of being

shot—he cannot think what that might feel like, though he has seen it in games and on TV, though he has seen the holes burned through the paper targets at the range—but because he is afraid that his brother hates him, has always hated him. That must have been why, one time, his brother held his palm open and ran the blade of a knife across it.

The gym teacher looks up the hill and he sees that the boys are the same height—the boy with the gun is kneeling—and he sees where the gun is pointed, and he gets up and begins to run across the soccer field. The seventeen are safe, under the parachute, but already he knows that it won't matter against this one, that that is not how the scales work.

"I'm not going to shoot you," the boy's brother says, "because I'm not crazy. You tell them that. That I'm not crazy."

The boy nods, but he will not tell anyone what his brother said, not his mother, not his father, not ever. He will insist that his brother was silent, that his brother was crazy, and he will dream of the girl with the cloud-shaped birthmark. With the gun, the boy's brother motions for him to turn toward the tree with the peeling bark, and the boy turns. He is facing the path that leads home and he has timed himself on this path, too. In two minutes and seven seconds he can be home, where his mother is pulling clothes from the drier. She straightens, hearing the sirens, and it takes her a moment to unravel the sound, to register how many and how close, and she thinks there must be a fire—it has been a dry summer, a dry fall—and she goes to the window and looks toward the school. The boy can't tell if the sirens are getting closer. They seem to be carried on the wind, like they are coming from the trees, and even though he knows this isn't so, he looks up at the leaves that are red and brown and thrashing.

The gym teacher is halfway across the soccer field, and in two months, when the school reopens, his wife will walk from goal to goal for hours, eyes on the grass, looking for the gleam of a bullet in the dirt. Under the parachute, the children think of lightning and tunnels. They think of the gym teacher who said he'd come back and of mothers and fathers and of the sound of the man's voice when he said, "Let's go," and how you are never supposed to go. Later, when the policeman finds them, when he pulls up the parachute, and tells them they are safe, he will not be able to forget it: how still the children were, how silent, how they didn't move a muscle.

The boy looks from the trees to the school. The gym teacher is running across the field, and he is old and slow, and from this high on the hill it seems like he is barely moving. The gym teacher's heart is battering at his lungs, his chest is burning, and the boy only watches him for a second, but it is too long—his brother turns toward the field. The sirens are everywhere now. His brother is breathing in the way that means you're hurt. The gym teacher is across the field, and he is afraid, but with his next breath his fear goes, and he does not know why, because the gun is aimed at him now, but he thinks of a morning years ago, when his son got a shoelace caught in the mower, and the gym teacher cut the lace with a pocket knife and watched the panic roll out of his son's eyes, and an hour later, in the hospital, he will die, whispering to his wife about a knife through cotton.

The boy hears the shot. He begins to run, and the leaves slide under his sneakers and he keeps his eyes on the path because there is a root up ahead that tripped him once, walking home, and his knee had bled, and his brother had looked at him and kissed his knee and said, "What's the point in crying?" The boy leaps over the root. He is running fast enough that the trees blur around him, and the gym teacher feels the hot rip of the bullet, and up on the hill there is another shot.

Diane Cook

Bounty

A DEAD MAN TWISTS AROUND one of my Doric columns.
I chose these columns for their plainness, their strength. I
liked imagining people looking up at my home, its smoky leaded
windows reflecting their city back at them, the classical Greek
proportions held up by simple, democratic design. Tasteful. No
frills. The dead man's arm trembles oddly in the water, out of
rhythm with the rest of his body. It's most likely dislocated at the
shoulder. Perhaps more than dislocated, but I won't investigate. A
brown gull does a number on his eye.

The man doesn't look familiar, so I don't believe him to be one
I've turned away.

When the world first flooded, the men who came to my door
asking for handouts calmly went away when I said no. They'd
survived once before and would do it again. There were other
options still. Colonies remained above water with homes to take
refuge in. They speckled the rising sea. Now those colonies are
underwater, most of their inhabitants drowned.

The other day a man in what looked to have once been a
pretty fine suit knocked on my door. The suit, now, was in ruins,
the arms shredded like party streamers from his shoulders. Sea

salt ghosted his face. Some sand, or maybe a barnacle, clung to his neck. A blue crab scuttled under his pick-stitched lapel. But I mostly noticed his loosened tie because it was definitely designer—it was a kind of damask rose pattern, but nontraditional. Of course, only designers change designs. It's why we used to pay so much for them. We paid for innovation.

This man in the nice suit asked for food and water, then tried to strangle me, choked back tears, apologized, asked to be let in, and, when I refused, tried to strangle me again. When I managed to close the door on him he sat on my veranda and cried.

I've gotten used to these interruptions. I don't blame these men. If I'd been one of the unprepared, I'd be desperate, too. They come to my door, see that I am clean, are dazzled by the generator-fed lights. They sense I have rooms full of provisions, that my maid's quarters are filled with bottled water, cords of wood are in the exercise annex, and gas is in the garage. They ogle my well-fed gut. I am dry. They are embarrassed, filthy, smell of fish. They get back on their driftwood, or whatever they use to keep their heads above water, and paddle next door to my neighbor's. If I were them, I would overtake someone standing dry in the doorway of a fine home. I wouldn't give up so easily. But these men are not me. For starters, they're awfully weak from not eating. But still. I don't like the change. I miss the old days when, though they happened to be begging, they were gentlemen who understood that hard work was their ticket to success. I'll need to carry a knife to the door next time.

It was happening just like they said it would. Things never happen like they say they will. That I was living to see it felt kind of special, truth be told. Like a headline. HISTORY IN THE MAKING!

My neighbor's house still stands, and across a new tiny sea in turmoil from trapped fish and unprepared people, one additional cluster of houses remains, perhaps four in all. Day and night, people hang out the windows waving white bedsheets and shouting. What kind of message is that? Surrender? To whom? I'll bet they have no food or water. My neighbor's house shakes from the extra people crammed inside. Each of the ten bedrooms probably holds a small village of newly homeless vagrants he's rescued. I told him to prepare. *I know this sounds crazy,* I said. We haven't always gotten along, but I decided it was the neighborly thing to do. You'd think he'd have been grateful. But instead he just crowds our last parcel of heavenly land with bums. If I open the windows I will smell the house, its burdened toilets and piss-soaked corners. The shallow but rising sea moat between our homes is rank with sewage. The tide takes it away, but more always comes.

In the old days, I would have left a letter in his mailbox about this or that neighborhood issue. The mail carrier once warned that it was illegal for non–mail carriers to put things into mailboxes. She held it out for me to take back. *It's just a note,* I snarled. *See how overgrown his hedges are?* She stared unbudgeably hard, held the letter steady between us. *Why can't you just leave it there for him?* I fumed. I slammed the door in her face and the next morning I found it stuffed in with my own mail, in my own mailbox. On it she had scrawled petulantly, *Only I can put this in the mailbox, and I won't do it!*

Through my great-room window, I can see that his grand staircase, with those audacious carved-pineapple finials, is littered with men, women, and children. The way they lie about, it looks as though there's one whole family to a stair. A boy dangles from a dusty crystal chandelier. I watch an old woman topple over a railing while maneuvering through the immense spiral shantytown. What a shame. But you can't let everyone in. There would be no end to it.

I run a finger over the great room's mantel. Dead skin, infiltrated ash. Too bad the housekeeper has most likely perished.

. . .

Someone knocks on my door—insistent and angry rather than timid and begging. I grab that kitchen knife.

On my veranda stands a man holding himself up by the door knocker, his muscles about to tense themselves off his bones. His face is unshaven, neglected. He has the skinny corpse and fat face of a drunk, and when I pull the door open he attempts to keep hold of the knocker and falls in, face-plants on my entryway Oriental.

"Whiskey," he groans, reaching for an imaginary tumbler.

I think about swiping his open palm with my blade, but there is something about him that I like. His request is original. At least he's trying.

Where my driveway used to break into a grand circular turnaround, the waves are mincing: they hiss, churn up crud and fish parts. But the ones farther out, nudged upward by some bar—probably the submerged cul-de-sac lower on the hill, the one I drove through on my way home every day—are large and smooth. They roll long like bedsheets drying in the wind, and I can feel their break.

I never thought I'd get tired of the crashing waves, but it never ends. It holds your attention like someone who can't stop coughing. It grates. It might be nice to listen to something else for a change. Plus I'm tired of my music.

I know I probably shouldn't, but I kick his feet toward an ornamental umbrella stand, get him full-bodied into the house, and close and lock the door. He wants whiskey? I don't care for it, and I have too much as it is. Besides, I've always liked having drinkers around. They often surprise.

The man—he grumbles that his name is Gary—doesn't even take the stack of crackers I offer him, flings them like dice, messily pours another glass.

"Ice," he slurs.

I shake my head. One of the first things I did was unplug the fridge and freezer. My food is canned.

He's so at ease in his stupor. Though he arrived sopping wet, if he asked me what's with all this water, I wouldn't be the least surprised.

Now he wears one of my bespoke suits. He wears it like he's a metal hanger, but it's a bit tight on me. I'm not ashamed. I live a good life.

I make a list of chores for him.

"If you're going to live here, you're going to work," I say, and slide it over for him to sign. He does so without reading. Irresponsible.

So I summarize it for him. "The contract states that in exchange for room and board, Gary will guard the house, take care of any beggars or intruders. He will fill the flush buckets with seawater when they are empty so we can flush our toilets like civilized people. He will throw our empty cans, bottles, and uneaten food out the back door each night to avoid smells. He will help the owner with weekly cleanings of the house. He will perform all other duties the owner asks."

There are plenty of extra rooms for him to stay in, but it's my house. So for the first night, I set him up on the study love seat with some fine sheets and a goose-down pillow. He scrunches into it, keeping one eye open as he sleeps, one foot up on the coffee table and the other leg bent, perfectly right angled, foot flat on the floor, ready. For what? To run? Though the water is creeping closer to the house, I'm not sure that's it.

The far stand of houses is gone. Where there should be rickety multifamilies, I see water flat like a prairie, occasional whale spouts on the horizon, the glare off all that water like looking at the sun.

I see my neighbor padding around the sleeping bodies in his halfway home for derelicts. He is dressed in a tattered robe, his beard is long and unkempt. I can practically smell him.

I catch his eye across the moat and mime a drowned body,

limbs, head, tongue hung and bobbing, and then point to where the houses stood. He looks, rubs his eyes, then drops to his knees. Some of the criminals he's invited into his home take this opportunity to rob him. Their hands work him over, dig in his bathrobe pockets, his hair, while he shudders with tears. Something is yanked from under his arm, and they disperse so quickly it is like they were never there. I shiver. My neighbor is taller than I am, and stronger. Who knows what would become of me if I had hundreds of people crammed into my house? I'd have no food left. I'd be bullied out of my master suite. I might even lose my life. I am once again grateful for Gary. He wants nothing from me except my whiskey, and has the build of a welterweight or a thief: small and wiry, someone who can put you in a headlock before you feel his touch.

As my neighbor wipes his tears, I shrug in commiseration. But he just shakes his head at me, like I'm the one who robbed him, I'm the water that tore those houses down.

Unless he's sneaking into the pantry late at night, I doubt Gary has eaten a morsel since his arrival. I notice no dent in my supplies, except the whiskey, which is already half gone. The other night, I crumbled some crackers into a half-full bottle to see whether he would take to the sustenance, and he roared, smashed the bottle against the marble table on which we dine. The noise was exhilarating. Normally the only sound is the constant murmur of the sea around us. Some nights I hear displaced loons calling out to their mates, or human calls from the boats of survivors looking for a place to dock. Their voices travel low across the water and get trapped within the walls of my bedroom. I hear music from my neighbor's house. Not often. In all, it's dreary, but on occasion a piano is played, accompanied by some squeaky string instrument. People stomp feet and call out. It's rustic. One night I heard a wavering wedding march and imagined a bride, in a dress of pinned white towels, making her way through the mob to stand with her groom, two people desperate to have what they think is love before the big end. It was hard not to feel something.

Gary doesn't always hear noise or even conversation. He sleeps undisturbed in strange intervals, like a pet. It's pleasant enough. When I need him, he is a great bodyguard. When a knock echoes through the house, I send him to the door with instructions to gut-punch the supplicant men. And he does it. They fall backward from shock and he slams the door. Once, a woman came to the door, bent like a hook, and Gary paused, turned to me miserably. I shrugged. Most bands of vagrants send the men, as is proper, but clearly they were beyond propriety. They hoped we might treat a woman differently. I saw two tense shapes in a rowboat just beyond the south wing of the house. What could Gary do? Some people hang on to old ideals. I do not. But I couldn't make a man like Gary do something he didn't feel good about. He has integrity. I pointed to my knee. He gave hers a halfhearted kick and she crumpled. He shut the door gently. I hope he feels like this is his home, too.

Gary has allowed me to shave him. He sits on the edge of my tub and snoozes while I hot-towel him, lather his face and neck. I'm careful not to nick him; I wag the razor clean in a silver bowl of mineral water. He looks more and more like a businessman in my suit; his graying temples lend him an executive air. He wears my suits and sometimes I add a tie for color. The world outside is gray, black, and blue, dotted by faded plastic garbage. A bit of color brings out Gary's eyes.

I leave him to clean up, and a while later he tumbles through the bathroom door with a bottle in his hand and knocks into the armoire. He is dangerously intoxicated and half dressed.

He crouches before me as I sit in my reading chair, sticks a soiled finger into my mouth, claws my lower jaw open. I'm stunned and let him. He strokes the caverns of my back teeth. I taste sour salt.

"Where's *your* gold?" he asks, like a child who thinks everything is his mirror.

I lean back from his brackish finger. "I have porcelain fillings."

He is blank.

"You can't see them. They blend in with my teeth. They're better."

His face threatens a smile, which would be a first, but instead his mouth gapes wide; it's like a California riverbed, shallow gold in every hole.

He taps one. "My bank," he says, and howls irresistibly. Then he gulps more from the bottle and falls into my bed. He's wearing a pair of my paisley silk boxers, his legs knobby and bowed like a baby bird's, and a hand-stitched dress shirt, the French cuffs gutted.

"Gary."

He murmurs from just below sleep.

"Did you ever think you'd be sleeping under down, in a well-appointed room, clean-shaven, in tailored shirts and silk underwear?"

He strains an eye open, seems to ponder it, like maybe he can see where I'm going with all this.

"I'm just saying, I think we have a pretty good thing here. We are at the height of land. We have a beautiful house. It doesn't smell, doesn't leak, isn't crowded. Think of the wind. It sweeps over the entire sea, gathers all that fresh air just to deposit it at our doorstep. We have loads of food. More than we could ever eat, really. We drink imported water."

I suck at a bottle to demonstrate.

"The whiskey won't last, but I'm sure we can think of something. There's other liquor. I have port. Several vintages. All told, Gary, we have a pretty nice life."

He yawns. Perhaps he'll take this moment to drain another bottle of whiskey. He looks toward the neighbor's house.

I'm wondering whether he's heard me when he mumbles, "We're homeless."

I don't know what he means. "Don't be absurd," I say. I'm certainly not homeless. And neither, now, is he.

But then I think maybe I do understand his meaning, looking at the lapping endless sea, which for once stretches beyond metaphor and actually is endless.

Homeless is a term of destitution. We're not hanging out of windows, waving blankets; we're not trod on by pruned feet like my neighbor. But undeniably we are experiencing a lack. I respond, "Friend, we are *worldless*." I let my new word linger. Gary sniffles and paws at his face, and then I see a glistening on his cheek.

"Gary, are you *crying*?" I mock tenderly.

He scowls and pulls the blanket right under his nose, clutches the whiskey close to his heart, and pretends to sleep.

I hear murmuring outside the house. A boat creaks a hundred yards offshore.

A multicolored sail of ragged cloth, swatches crudely stitched together, barely registers the wind. I can make out the figures of two men swim-walking their way to our door while others wait in the boat. They gaze admiringly at the house. As they should.

"Gary," I hiss.

A minute later, he shuffles into the entryway, bringing with him a scent of something savory. Not whiskey, I notice, and think it odd.

"Men are coming. See what they want."

Gary peeks out from behind the drapes, allows his eyes to adjust, nods his head. I hand him a knife and he slips out the front door to meet the men.

He returns with a note in a bottle.

"They're from next door," he says, slurring slightly.

"They have a boat next door?" Should we have a boat? I hadn't thought about surviving outside my home. Would I even want to? It seems so awful out there. But maybe it's something I should get Gary on, just in case. The note is scrawled on the back of a soup label:

Dear Neighbor, might you have some food and water to spare? My men will ferry it over. We are running dangerously low. Might you have some room to spare? I'll send clean women and children. We're greatly overcrowded and I am concerned. Respectfully.

I crumple the letter. The nerve. "No way to this."

Gary looks surprised, which surprises me.

"But we have spare food."

"What do you know about food?" I yell.

"You said we had more than enough."

"I did not!"

"You did."

"That was before. We're running very low. You eat too much."

"We have a lot of food," he mumbles again.

"I suppose you know best. I suppose you're the decision maker now. I guess you'll be telling me we should invite them over."

"Would it be so terrible to let some in?"

"Yes!"

Gary looks up at the grand staircase, considers each wing. "There's room."

I throw my hands up. "You're unbelievable! He's scamming you!" I'm ashamed of the squeal in my voice, but I can't control it. "His house has always been a wreck. Always a cracked window. Bricks crumbling. *His* vines growing over *my* side of the fence. And that's just the outside."

Gary stares longingly at the upstairs hallways as if fantasizing that they are crowded with laughing children and pretty women.

"They'll ruin everything. Our life. They'll eat more than their share. They'll waste water. They'll drink your whiskey, you know they will."

Gary blushes and looks down at a smudge on the golden maple floors, licks a finger, squats to rub it out. "I don't care," he mutters into the smudge.

"I'll make it simple for you, simple guy. If you want to be with them, then leave." Even as the words come out I want to take them back. The rest of this life feels impossible without Gary. But I shouldn't have to give up a life I enjoy to harbor the foolish masses. What's the point of living if you can't have the life you want?

Gary turns toward me and I don't like the look. It's like we don't even know each other. He slips the knife from his pocket and strides out the door.

They are having words. I can't tell if Gary's is one of the voices. Maybe the men are begging to be let in and Gary is merely listening, hearing them out. That would be so like Gary.

But maybe the men are begging to be let in and Gary is saying yes. That would be a different Gary, I think.

Then I hear yelling and grunts from a struggle. I run to the coat closet and hide inside. A lone jacket hangs above me. I pull it down and wrap myself in it.

A cry of pain leads to the sound of men splashing in retreat.

The front door is opened, then gently clicked shut, as though I am a child and Gary is taking care not to wake me. Feet shuffle away. I crack the door and see the knife lying in the center of the rug. It is smeared with blood and sea scum. I would like to dress his wounds if he has any, but I don't move.

From the study comes the clinking of bottle to glass. A glass this time. What civility. I'm ashamed for doubting him. He is a loyal friend. All is well.

A terrible crash wakes me. I reach across the bed, but Gary is not there.

I see nothing through the window, but hear the sea lashing at the side of the house, frantic and high. The clouds are thick like insulation and hide any evidence of a moon. Is it large and full and pulling the tides higher, or is this some kind of grand, irreversible shift in things?

I sink into the cold middle of the bed. Then comes another crash, and yelling, and the unforgettable cracking of heavy beams of wood, of walls collapsing. Screams, splashes, cries for help. If I had to guess, I'd say my neighbor's house has just fallen to pieces. I don't want to look, in case I'm right. The surrounding sea would clog with the lifeless, faces down, a simple burial for those who had survived longest. A passing thought: Must I shoulder some blame for this tragedy? I'd believed our stories were separate. I'd begun to think of this earth as my own private sanctuary. Shared with Gary. We could climb higher and higher as the water rose and live out our days in that quaint, functionless widow's walk, until it, too, was swallowed. I'd always thought it such a romantic scenario. But with our neighbors washed away, I'm suddenly curious what other story we all might have told together. We're each of us survivors, after all. What a pathetic end. How desperate. I fall asleep in a surprising state of grief.

In the light of day, my neighbor's house is still standing. The top of the building has caved in on itself. Some bodies float in the surrounding waters, but not many. The bobbing corpses lack the gravitas I imagined. I leave bed to fix myself a plate of crackers and peanut butter.

As I approach the landing, I hear hushed voices and see my neighbor in the entryway with Gary. They lean into each other, whispering. It all looks quite friendly.

"Howdy, neighbor," I force.

They look up, caught. I scan Gary's face for clues. Then my neighbor's.

He has tried to clean himself up a bit. His clothes look pressed in spots, like they have been lain between stacks of books to mimic the effect of steamers. But they are pieces from different suits, clashing directions of stripes on the jacket and trousers, and a gingham shirt. His beard is roughly trimmed, big chunks of hair cut shorter than other chunks. He looks to be wearing some kind of makeup, a powder or rouge.

My neighbor nods in greeting. "We had an accident," he wheezes haltingly. "The roof. Fell in. Top floor. All dead."

"I know, we heard," I say, mustering horror. Gary looks distraught. Then I say, "We heard it fall, I mean," so that my neighbor doesn't think we heard from someone else, as though it were gossip.

"I saw the bodies in the moat," I say.

My neighbor looks ashamed and sputters, "We had to. The disease. All the others."

I notice Gary's suit is rough and wrinkled. I reach out, fondle the fabric. It's damp.

"Have you been *swimming*, Gary?"

My neighbor coughs. "Neighbor," he says, beginning a plea.

"What do you want?" I ask, trying to sound friendly, but I can tell by their faces that my tone is pure stone.

"We have to hold up the ceiling."

Gary clears his throat. "I found big posts in the basement."

I'm looking right into his eyes and they are mossy green and clean like he is fully awake. We are so close; his breath in my face smells sweet like milk. I'm about to hypnotically say I don't have any posts when I remember that I do, from a renovation last year. Why does Gary know my house better than I?

I glare at him, preparing to accuse him of something, when my neighbor begins to cry. Gary clamps a hand on my neighbor's shoulder to comfort him. I'm alarmed. Those are my hands.

Sea foam curls around my neighbor's galoshes and I suddenly feel woozy. I step back, hug my cardigan close, and realize I've become pointy, emaciated, swimming in this sweater, the cuffs hanging on me like I'm wearing my father's clothes. Is this even mine? Haven't I been taking care of myself? I look at Gary. He's lean. But I don't think he's leaner than usual.

"He's going to borrow the posts," Gary says, making it sound utterly ordinary to give something away. He tightens his grip and guides my shell of a neighbor inside. "Watch the rug," he says absently, and instinctively I'm grateful. He's thought of me. Of us. Of our things. I think to offer him my most thankful expression, but he is already leading my neighbor through the basement door. "I'll help him," he calls back over his shoulder.

Of course my neighbor will need help. The posts are big and long and were almost too much for the builders to get down there in the first place. And my neighbor is clearly starving. When he and Gary come out of the basement, I notice that Gary isn't stumbling. He appears strong, almost. He is speaking in full sentences, not slurs. He's concerned and not angry. He directs my neighbor, who is bent and shaky, barely able to hold the post up, toward the door. Gary stands tall, the post balanced easily on his shoulder, like the weight isn't even felt. I almost want to check my food supply, but I know that would be wrong. It's his house, too.

I watch them float the posts over and disappear into my neighbor's house. I bolt the door. When they come back, they'll have to knock. But then I think, no, it's Gary. I draw the bolt back.

I stoke the fire all night and wait for the splash of someone crossing the moat. I deserve an explanation. I can't sleep without him.

Across the moat, in my neighbor's house, lit by candlelight, I see a crowd gathered around Gary as he appears to give a speech. His gestures are humble. He is not throwing bottles and sulking. And when he begins to weep, the masses gently reach to comfort him, place hands on him. My neighbor steps through, the people break apart for him, and he and Gary embrace. Gary sobs into his neck.

I crawl to the liquor cabinet. One bottle remains. I cough down half and then hurl the bottle at the great window. I check my food supplies. They don't appear diminished beyond reason, but I suppose there is more food gone than there should be. Didn't there used to be one more pallet by the bed? Had Gary started to eat? I couldn't remember his ever sharing a meal with me, though he always kept me company while I dined. I could live off this food for a while longer, definitely till the end, which feels closer than ever before. But that's not the point, I think, as I urinate into the fireplace. Smoke, thick like clouds, smothers my mouth. I double over, breathless. I wrench the window wide and gasp in the fumes from the putrid moat. The sun is breaking. A bloated cow drifts by, its hide rippling with bugs, its tail end chewed off by some animal, its belly intact but about to burst. That will be me. Pale, bloated, and raped in some feeding frenzy by what still lives.

Why did he leave?

Did I say he could leave?

The water in the moat has an eerie heft like it is about to become slush. I find firm ground near the corner of my neighbor's house, and soon I emerge. Water sloshes out from under my clothes and from my pockets; salt and sand grit my mouth.

I hear the noise of much life inside, hundreds and hundreds of people, but as I pass in front of a window the commotion stops. When I knock on the front door it's like the whole world holds its breath. I press my ear to it. Nothing.

"I know you're in there," I yell. "I can see you all from my house."

I hear a cough from inside and a quick rush to stifle it.

"You stole my food."

Silence.

From my pocket I pull a note card, kept dry in a plastic baggie. It's an eloquent reminder for Gary of our comfortable life at home, and of the contract he signed. I find a crack at the top of the door, try to push the note through. Something stops it mid-slide and pushes it back out.

Gary.

I palm the door and press my cheek against it. It is slimy and cold. I feel painted onto it.

"Gary!" I yell. "Let me in! I'm cold and wet."

The moon is full. The water is waiting for orders. I think it wants this house as much as I do.

I could still make it home. But for what? People begin moving around again inside my neighbor's house. I hear the piano, and the march of many feet up and down the staircase. They are carrying on. I notice for the first time that my neighbor's house sits slightly lower on the hill than mine. We truly were at the height of land. It was not my imagination, or merely a boast. I'm awash in sadness.

"Gary. We had it all."

I sit down on the stoop and the water rises to my knees. Small fish circle my legs like they are playing a game. Hawks circle high in the pinking sky. I don't know much about birds but I imagine they need land somewhere nearby. If they are gulls, they can float on the water. I don't think hawks can do that. Or buzzards circling a kill. If they were albatross they could fly the length of one giant ocean and never get tired. I've heard they keep ships company on an entire journey.

I had never thought that somewhere beyond my sight the world might be continuing as normal. If those are hawks they'll have to return to their treetops, high above houses full of sleeping families, husbands and wives, children lucky enough to have been born. Just beyond the curve of the earth, out of my view, sky-scrapers could be creaking slightly in the newly blistering wind. Newscasts could be reporting about us, the ones who perished.

I'm surprised how easy it was for me to believe I was one of the lucky few left. If people are watching this sunset all over the world then I wouldn't be so lucky after all, sitting up to my chest in cold ocean water cluttered with debris and oily with human waste. What makes me so special? I had a house. I had Gary. It felt like enough for the end of days.

Soon someone will need to open the door. They have flush buckets to fill. Cans, bottles, batteries to toss. Don't they? I could wait.

I try to imagine it: *me* in *there*. Pressing palms, talking about the lives we lived. Being nostalgic for what? Eating crumbs together? Of course, if they were to let me in, I'd be expected to give over my house and supplies. They'd paw my antiques. They'd mess all the beds' bedding. I'd never again enjoy that morning echo of solitary me padding across the floors in my empty house.

But if I go home, I'll live longer. It is indisputable. I don't know what more I could ask for.

"Okay, Gary. Last chance. I'm leaving," I call out. I wait a beat, listening for the door to creak, for curiosity to win out.

Instead, I hear laughter behind my neighbor's door.

I know that soon they will come. Gary will lead them. It could be any minute now. They'll wade, swim, selectively drown their way across the moat and break through my great window. Eventually they'll splinter open the locked front door. It's a quality door. It won't be easy.

The water and weather will soon get in, eat the house from the inside. They'll be left with nothing yet again. I could warn them, but do I have to think of everything?

I wait in the widow's walk, surrounded by soft down pillows, a tower of blankets. I have with me water, crackers, tinned meat, and my two biggest knives, but I hope it won't come to that. I don't think Gary will let it. True, I feel betrayed. He knows all my secrets, what I'm most afraid of, all the combinations, and where anything of worth is hidden. But I will still be his friend. If he'll have me.

The moon rises, dips, rises, dips. The tide rolls in and out. I wait for the end. The wind pries itself inside. Even shrouded in blankets, I'm folded over from shivering. I wait for them. Pieces of my neighbor's house are letting go, dropping into the sea; some break windows as they fall. Is that a piano I hear tinkling, or glass shattering? Is that the sound of singing or of wood creaking to its breaking point? The whole house leans. The sea is knocking, but his door remains shut.

Zebbie Watson
A Single Deliberate Thing

IT HAD BEEN A long, rainless July and before that, a dry June. The pastures were brown, the grass chewed to stubs and coated in dust. The horses stayed in all day and if I tried to turn them out before dark, they stood by the gate and sweated and stamped. Most farms got the corn planted early enough that it grew shoulder high and deep rooted, but the second cutting of hay would be late and small and the soy beans were doing poorly, their leaves chewed by the deer and withering on the stem. I was counting swallows and waiting for the letter from Kentucky that might let me know if you still loved me.

There were more swallows that summer than I can ever remember seeing. In spring there had been the usual number of mud-daubed nests—one under the eaves in the front of the barn, one in Otter's stall, and one on the side of the garage—but somehow, come July, the fields positively crackled with the glint of the sun off their blue-black backs. Most days I counted more than thirty of them. They would perch in a row on the telephone wire that ran up the drive, and when I passed under them, they'd peel off one by one in all directions, sleek and made of angles, to swoop across the fields and turn their wing tips vertical. Dad said it was because there was no mud for a second nest; there was nothing else for them to do.

When you told me you were enlisting, you said we should just break up then because you would probably be sent someplace out of state. That made sense, but then the night before you left, when you came over to say goodbye, you hugged me on the front porch and pressed a folded paper into my palm with your address at boot camp and left without coming inside. I wasn't sure if that meant you wanted me to write or not, and if that was your way of letting me choose, I didn't get it at the time.

I wrote you mid-June. I think now that I shouldn't have, but what can I say, it was habit to want to tell you things. When I saw fox kits playing in the field, when I counted thirty-seven swallows on the wire, when Grace jumped her first full course without refusing a fence, I wanted to tell you. I also wanted to apologize for saying you looked dumb with your head shaved, you know it would have grown on me. And then I added that I didn't care if you were giving up college or if we would have to be apart a lot because I didn't need that much from you anyway. And I didn't get why you thought staying together would be hard when it had always been easy before. And finally I told you that I wouldn't mind waiting most of the time, which, I realize now, is funny, because after a couple weeks the waiting started to drive me crazy. I knew the mail would be slow but the relentless heat made the days longer and they eventually began adding up and summer dragged on indefinitely.

I should have kept busy riding but Mom and I were only riding in the late evening when the flies were more bearable. You know how grumpy the mares get in the heat, some days I didn't even bother. One night I was riding Grace behind the house and she was already so annoyed to be out that when a horsefly landed on her rump she bucked once and launched me right over her head. She was good for the most part, but that night not so much. Maybe I'd have ridden more if you were home to come out with me, my mom never wanted to. She's even less tolerant than the mares. I never told her I had written you but sometimes I swear she knew by the way she'd say *why don't you do something different with your hair*, or *you'll meet so many cute boys in college*. Other times it seemed like she'd forgotten, she didn't ask, as if hearing from you was never on the table to begin with. Family dinners were spent mostly just complaining about the lack of rain and worrying about Notes.

We took Notes in March from a friend of a friend. They told us he couldn't be ridden due to his age and his heaves, but as soon as the summer humidity set in, it was obvious that his breathing was so bad he should have just been euthanized. We saw that and acknowledged that but still he was already so dear and familiar, and Otter, who in seventeen years had never bonded closely with the other horses, loved Notes instantly and fiercely. The two of them grazed nose to nose although Notes barely came up to Otter's chest, and Otter would chase the two mares if they came close to his pony. Notes lost weight quickly when summer came; he wasn't too thin when you saw him last, but by the end his ribs showed with every breath and his hollow neck tied into bony withers. My parents would talk about it every time the temperatures rose, watching in the late evening as Otter's tall dark shape moved in protective circles around Notes's small white one, and we were all guilty of too much hope. It became a pattern of *maybe this summer won't be too bad*, and then *we got him through the last heat wave, we can't give up now the humidity's broken a bit*. But July dragged on and I was still waiting for your letter and drenching Notes with cold water every afternoon to keep him cool.

I wish now that I could have just made a decision for him. That's a lot of afternoons in the barn with sweat between my shoulder blades and nothing to do but listen to Notes's wheezing and think about when your letter might come. I imagine that summer in Kentucky must have been even hotter than Virginia so I thought of you every time sweat soaked through the back of my shirt, knowing you were wearing combat boots and fatigues. I thought of how easily your nose and ears sunburned, and how dark your freckles would be. I thought that maybe it had taken a long time for you to get my letter, and that maybe you were too tired each night to write back. At some point I realized that I hadn't even told you to write back, I was just leaving it up to you to decide, I was only ever asking you to decide. My parents must not have known or else they would have kept saying things like *teenage love will die naturally anyway* or *you two would have eventually grown apart at college.* They assumed my worry was about Notes, which makes sense because he was the one I sat next to as I waited.

The day before he died, looking back, I think we knew. It was an unbearably heavy week, the air was so thick and the temperature barely dipped into the eighties at night. When Mom brought the horses in that morning, Notes ate his small handful of grain and lay down, already tired and heaving. I confess we were so used to his flaring nostrils that it didn't seem much worse than usual, but I could tell she was worried when she left for work. She asked me to check on him in the afternoon, reminding me about his medication, as if I didn't do it every day.

I checked on him every day but that day I avoided it, waiting until after lunch when it would be time for his medicine. I remember that I went out on the porch to water the plants and saw a dozen or so of the swallows gathered in a low dip in the driveway that would become a puddle were there any rain. They moved so unnaturally, their bodies stooped and narrow, it was striking. I watched them, amazed that some deep instinct drove them to this low place—that they knew if there were mud to be found it would be there—and yet somehow was ashamed to see them that way. I loved the tiny sharpness of their hunched shapes when they perched, but on the ground they groveled, moved like bats in daylight, it made me feel so helpless. I took the watering can to soak the dust they were pecking and they scattered before me. It was a relief to watch them skim away across the pasture.

I went out to the barn after lunch. The place where I'd poured water for the swallows was dry; I hadn't seen them come back. The barn was dark and still, no air moving despite the open doors and windows. Notes was standing up eating his soaked hay, but I could hear the rapid pace of his breathing. Otter was napping with his head in the corner and a hind leg cocked, bits of straw in his tail from having lain down earlier. Grace and Sassy were sleeping too. Their flanks were already dark with sweat despite the box fans in every stall that were always on those days. I refilled the water buckets then crushed Notes's albuterol pills and mixed them with his Ventipulmin in a syringe. Otter woke up at the sound of the feed room door so I grabbed mints from the bag and gave him one. Notes came to the front of his stall and nickered. His nicker was an unbearable choking noise. His eyes looked bright though, glinting out from his thick forelock, his small, sculpted ears alert. I fed him a mint and his lips were damp and green from the hay, leaving slime on my palms.

He was used to the routine and allowed me to hold his head with an arm over his neck and squeeze the medicine into his mouth. I could feel the strain of his breathing through his whole body and he was drenched in sweat underneath his heavy mane. We'd clipped his coat twice already that summer, Mom did it in the spring and then I clipped him again in June since his hair was so thick, but he sweated and labored anyway. In that moment I felt suddenly desperate, as if all summer I'd been telling myself he was dying but didn't see it until then. It wasn't a decision, not really, I just grabbed scissors from the shelf and began to cut his mane off in chunks, twisting bunches of it in my fists and letting them fall to the ground. Otter watched us over his stall door and chewed his hay in tense, intermittent bites. Notes didn't move, just stood with his head low, looking out from behind that long white forelock. I cut that too.

I fetched the electric clippers from the cabinet, unwound the cord, and knelt down next to him, feeling the cool of the concrete spread up through my knees. I started between his ears and ran the clippers down the crest of his neck in one long stroke, watching the jagged tufts of hair pour off. I clipped more slowly down each side, evening out the edges meticulously, my free hand over his neck and pulling him closer to me as I shore off the remains of his forelock, carefully moving between his ears and following the swirl of a cowlick. When I was finished, Notes's skin showed black and dusty through the stubble.

I sat back on my heels. Notes turned and nosed my hand for a treat and I gave him another mint. The roached mane did not flatter his thin neck. You know, he was actually only about twenty, but he looked so old and sick. I don't know what could have happened to make him that way. His gray coat was dingy and yellow from sweat and dust. I took him outside to the water pump, Otter watching us suspiciously, and washed him, spending a long time with my fingertips working suds into his coat and tail until he was clean. The swallows swooped and chattered in the sunlight as I worked. The medication had kicked in and Notes was breathing a little more freely when I put him back inside. I swept up the hair and threw it away.

I didn't even bother checking the mailbox that afternoon. I think my parents were used to me doing it because they asked me where the mail was but I just answered *Notes is bad today* and they forgot about the mail. I wish I'd added *we should do it tomorrow*, but I knew they'd realize that themselves. I heard them in the kitchen after dinner talking about him and they both came out to the barn that evening to help me feed and turn the horses out. They commented on how clean he was but didn't mention the haircut. He was clean; he glowed in the dim late-evening light walking across the pasture with Otter shadowing his steps. As I washed my own hair that night, I thought that Otter should be with him when we put him down, and that you weren't going to write back.

Notes died sometime that night. We found him not far from the barn, in the spot where he and Otter always stood. His body looked very small. Otter was still next to him and wouldn't come to the gate, but when I took him in on a lead he didn't protest. Dad called a friend with a backhoe and they buried him on the edge of the field behind the house, by the woods, with two of Dad's old foxhunters and my first pony. I stayed in the barn while they did, watching Otter chew hay and feeding him mints. I didn't cry until Dad came back with a banded lock of Notes's tail he'd saved, and I thought about the feel of his mane in my fists as I cut it. Otter was quiet all day but when he went back out at night, he whinnied once and looked back toward the barn as if waiting.

The next day, it finally rained, one of those wicked summer storms that can only come after weeks of relentless heat. The worse the weather, the bigger the snap, and this one broke with a rare violence. We could feel it coming, all morning the air crackled and the swallows were nowhere to be found. It finally came early afternoon, like something out of an ancient mythology. It was then that I realized I'd done nothing all summer but wait for rain, that I hadn't done a single deliberate thing. The electricity went out and we watched from the house as waves of rain swept through like fists, wind bowed the trees, and the sky flared a sick, tornado green in the distance. When it was over, I turned the horses out and they went like new colts, all high-kneed and quivering. Grace dropped right to her knees to roll, then ran off bucking and nipping at Sassy's flank. Otter sniffed the ground where Notes had lain, then trotted off after the mares.

The storm brought down trees all over the place. Dad and I were at the end of the driveway clearing branches a few days later when the mailman brought your letter. I took the bundle from the mailbox and riffled through it and when I saw my name in your handwriting, I didn't know what to do anymore. You'd decided to have your say after all, but I'd stopped waiting. Dad asked if there was any interesting mail and I answered *Nothing*.

The swallows flitted from the wire one by one as I walked back up the drive to the house, my back sticky with sweat and your letter tucked between other envelopes in my hand. I wondered when you had sent it and why it took too long to arrive.

Briefly, I held the envelope over the trash can, but that felt too impulsive. Instead, I put it in the bottom drawer of my desk, under some old school papers. Notes's tail was still on my dresser and I didn't know what to do with that either, so I put it in the drawer as well.

I just wanted you to know, that's what I did.

Robert Coover
The Crabapple Tree

Tᴴɪꜱ ʜᴀᴘᴘᴇɴᴇᴅ ʜᴇʀᴇ ɪɴ our town. A friend of mine—we were on the cheerleading team together—married a local farmer, and right away they wanted to have a baby, though the doctor said she shouldn't. She was a bleeder, he said, and if she started he might not be able to stop it. But she didn't listen. She went ahead and got pregnant, then bled to death during childbirth and was buried out by the farmhouse, under a crabapple tree. It was very sad. I cried for a week. But the baby survived, a pretty little boy; his dad called him Dickie-boy, but I don't know if that was his real name.

His dad was a hard worker and a nice guy—I went on a movie date with him once when we were young—but he sometimes drank too much and he was hopeless at ordinary household chores and raising babies. So pretty soon he found another wife, either through a dating service or else he picked her up in one of his bars somewhere, because none of us girls knew her. She was a tough, sexy lady, a hooker, maybe. She made no effort to be one of us or to make us like her. I guess she considered us beneath her. We called her the Vamp. She got around, and it was said that she'd taken half the men in town to bed, my own ex included.

They all denied it, like cheating husbands do, but, when the subject came up, little shit-eating grins would appear on their faces and their eyes would glaze over as if they were remembering the wild time they'd had.

Maybe Dickie-boy's dad knew about all that, and maybe he didn't. He was mostly either drunk or out in the fields, and he left the raising of the kid to his new wife. He loved Dickie-boy to the extent that the child reminded him of his dead wife, but resented him for the same reason, just as he resented the boy's mother for selfishly dying on him. He had hoped for a sturdy fellow to help around the farm, but Dickie-boy was a sickly, fine-boned child who had trouble lifting a finger to pick his nose, forget pitchforks and shovels. Certainly he didn't get on with the Vamp, who had a mean temper and slapped him around, with or without an excuse.

The Vamp had a daughter from a previous relationship, a cute kid with big dreamy eyes, called Marleen. I never knew what to make of her. Marleen seemed to live in a storybook land of her own. When she spoke, she spoke to the world, the way singers do, and what she said seldom made any sense. You probably had to be a kid to understand her at all. My little girl—she's a young woman now and has her own little girl—was the same age as Marleen, and sometimes the two of them played together, my daughter pedaling her bike out to the farm and back, or sometimes I took her and picked her up. My daughter had a lot of stories about Marleen, but I didn't always understand those, either.

Marleen settled right in with her new little stepbrother. They were as tight as crib siblings and had a way of talking to each other that didn't use words. My daughter said it might be bird talk, which Marleen had offered to teach her. Some people said that Dickie-boy wasn't all there, others that he had something almost magical about him. Once, for example, he somehow crawled up onto the barn roof, and they had to call the Fire Department to get him down. The fire marshal said he had no idea how the boy could have got up there, unless he flew. Marleen said he did it because the birds wanted him to. She told my daughter that the crabapple tree had helped him, though it was over near the house, not the barn. I had no idea what she meant. My daughter didn't know, either, and Marleen never announced it in her peculiar way of speaking.

My daughter and Marleen played dolls and house and nursie, just like all little girls do, and sometimes they used Dickie-boy in their games. In nice ways and maybe not-so-nice ways. Strange Marleen might get up to anything, and my own daughter had a mischievous and curious streak, so things probably happened. Kids are kids, after all. I figured it was best to mostly look the other way. Children have to be allowed to grow up on their own—I've always believed that.

Marleen wanted a doggy, for example, so she put a collar and a leash on Dickie-boy and walked him around on his hands and knees with his clothes off and did circus tricks with him. She even taught him to wee with his leg in the air. He never complained. When he did bad things, like biting the mailman or pooping on his stepmother's bed, Marleen swatted his behind with a rolled-up newspaper just as you would a puppy. Then he'd whimper until she scratched between his ears and gave him a cookie. My daughter said that Dickie-boy seemed to do bad things on purpose so as to get swatted. I suppose he was just looking for attention, given the kind of parents he had. His dad was never around, and the Vamp hated him, so all he had was Marleen and her games.

Dickie-boy wasn't very healthy, but whenever he got sick Marleen made him well again. It was a gift she had. It sometimes worked on others, too. One time, my daughter had a bad case of tonsillitis, and I thought her tonsils would have to come out, but Marleen somehow brought her fever down and she hasn't had tonsillitis since. Marleen couldn't do anything for my ingrown toenail and canker sores, though.

Dickie-boy had gifts, too, and one of them was finding lost things. Once, I lost an earring, and my daughter brought Marleen and Dickie-boy over to the house to find it. He got down on all fours with his face near the floor, and Marleen showed him the matching earring and made a chirping noise that probably meant "Fetch!," because that's exactly what he did. It had fallen into one of my old sneakers in the closet. He also found a nail brush I didn't even know was lost. Hide-and-seek wasn't any fun at all, my daughter said, because Dickie-boy always went straight to where they were. Same with blindman's bluff—it was as if he could see right through the blindfold. And ghost-in-the-graveyard, if you played it at night, could be downright scary, because he could give you the feeling that he was there and not there at the same time.

Marleen could be scary, too. Whenever she was around, staring her wide-eyed stare and talking aloud to nobody in particular, I kept stumbling and dropping things. My daughter said the same thing happened to their schoolteacher, who sometimes sent Marleen out of the room so she could clear her head.

Marleen often played with Dickie-boy the way you'd play with a rag doll, tossing him floppily about, dangling him by an arm or leg, he looking glassy-eyed and like he'd lost his bones. It was funny, really. They could have taken the act on television. Playing with Dickie-boy like a rag doll was my daughter's favorite game.

Then, one day, when Marleen was dragging him around by his soft ankles, his head broke off. That scared my daughter. She came home crying, though eventually she went back again. Marleen told her that her mother hated Dickie-boy and had cut his head off and then glued it back on without telling Marleen, so that the head would come off again while they were playing and she'd be blamed for it. But the police chief, who went to investigate the death, told me that, after talking with the boy's folks, he was convinced it was just a tragic household accident that the little girl was inventing wild stories about.

The boy was buried alongside his mother under the crabapple tree, and that was also sad, but the little boy had never quite seemed part of this world in the first place, so it wasn't as sad as when his mother died.

I'd been seeing the police chief on and off since my husband left me. Even before, if truth be told. He was sweet and was sometimes fun to be with, but mostly he wasn't, being something of a nail-chewing worrywart by nature. I could see why his wife had left him. The fire marshal was more fun and never worried about anything, but he'd already had three wives and he said he didn't want any more. He preferred booze to broads now, as he put it, and—more than either—the weekly football on the box. The police chief had been a senior when I was just a freshman. We did some things together back then, but I was still very young and shy, and I guess, thinking back, he was, too. He was a Catholic and I was a Lutheran, so it wouldn't have worked out anyway. We were both still churchgoers, so nothing was going to work out now, either, but, at this time of life, that was no longer enough to keep two lonely people out of the same bed.

A few weeks after Dickie-boy died, my daughter went out to the farm one day and found Marleen sitting beside a hole in the ground under the crabapple tree, playing with a pile of bones. Marleen said that the bones were those of her stepbrother, whom her mother had cooked up in a black-beer stew, which her stepfather ate, gnawing all the little bones clean before burying them. Marleen had dug them up and was stringing together a kind of horrible life-size Halloween puppet. She was reciting a rhyme about singing bones, and then she warbled like a bird and held up the bone puppet and rattled it. That was when my daughter stopped playing with her.

There has to be a law against those sorts of things, but when I told the police chief what my daughter had said he only bit his nails and said that it was weird how kids could dream up such crazy stories. I asked him if he didn't think it could be true, or at least partly true, and he said no, he knew the parents well, especially the girl's mother, and such a thing could not have happened. I realized then that, like half the town's heroes, the chief had probably been one of the Vamp's quickies, maybe still was. He wasn't interested in any further speculation about the girl he called "that cute little loony with the big eyes." He did promise to drop by the farm to see if the grave had been molested, but he never told me if he did.

The part of Marleen's story that I thought might be true was how Dickie-boy had died. The Vamp, who'd detested her stepson, was completely capable of doing him grievous bodily harm, as the chief would say, in his detective-movie way, and then making her daughter feel guilty for it. There was something monstrous about her—we all felt it. Of course, she'd messed up a lot of our marriages, so we weren't exactly unbiased. I didn't think that Dickie-boy's dad would have eaten him on purpose, but he was often so drunk that he didn't know what he was doing, and maybe the Vamp had tricked him into it. Stews are stews. Who knows what's in them?

The fire marshal told me that he'd been drinking one night with Dickie-boy's dad, who'd complained that people misunderstood his wife. She had her dark side, sure—who didn't? But mostly she was just frightened and needed protection, and he could provide that. Dickie-boy's dad wasn't feeling well, ulcers or something, and he said he knew that whiskey wasn't a cure for it, but he was a farmer who did certain things every day by the clock. Drinking every night was part of that routine, and he couldn't change it now. But it meant that his wife was alone much of the time, and being alone scared her, which was why she was constantly shacking up with other men. *Everything* scared her, he said. The farm scared her, the birds did, the animals, even the damned crabapple tree. She wouldn't go near it. She kept glancing up over her head as if she were afraid that something might be falling on her. Then the fire marshal made the mistake of bringing up the rumor about the black-beer stew and took a nose-breaking blow to the face, and that was the end of their drinking together.

Dickie-boy's dad died a year after Dickie-boy, almost to the day, and joined him and the boy's mother under the crabapple tree. The doctor said that he drank too much and ruined his liver, and that was maybe so, but he got sick and died awful fast. The Vamp didn't even stick around for the funeral, as though admitting what she'd done, but the police chief refused to order an autopsy on the farmer. He said that it wasn't in his jurisdiction, so we'll never know for certain. That the Vamp had killed her stepson, poisoned her husband, abandoned her daughter, and gone on the run was the general opinion, but my daughter said she wasn't so sure. She wondered if Marleen's mother wasn't also out there under the crabapple tree.

At the father's funeral, Marleen told my daughter that she was sorry she'd stopped coming to play with her, but it was all right, because her stepbrother had come back alive from the bones she'd joined up, and they were playing together just like before. The boy's grave was covered over by dirt and weeds and looked like it always did. Maybe Marleen was making up stories because she was lonely and wanted my daughter to be her friend again, but it didn't work. As far as my daughter was concerned, enough was enough. Anyway, she was too grown up by then to play Marleen's weird games. I've never seen any phantom boy, of course, though my daughter said she "sort of" saw him, "in a ghost-in-the-graveyard kind of way," when she was out riding past the farm one night with a boyfriend.

Eventually, Marleen inherited the farm, which wasn't exactly a farm anymore. She had started keeping birds and other animals out there, turning the place into something of a wildlife refuge. Maybe her imaginary Dickie-boy was part of the wildlife. Some of the animals lived in the house with her. In fact, there wasn't much difference between inside and outside.

There was no money in a wildlife refuge, of course, so, as she grew older, Marleen took up what we all supposed had been her mother's trade, but as if living in a story about herself, without awareness or consequence, a sort of rag-doll act of her own.

The fire marshal was getting fat eating carryout from fast-food joints, so he changed his mind about no more wives and agreed to marry me if I'd promise to cook him decent low-cal meals. I could do that, and it gave me a kind of future. His brief attempts at lovemaking were more like ballgame time-outs, always had been, but at least he hadn't abandoned the practice altogether. Marleen had aroused his curiosity, and he decided to try her out as his stags'-night treat before our wedding, and, a wag by nature, he joked about it with all our friends. I told him to be careful, because people had a way of disappearing around Marleen.

He didn't disappear. He came back and we got married. But he didn't say anything about what had happened that night, and, in fact, never said much of anything again. He still went nightly to the bars to sit over his beers, smiling in a nervous sort of way and muttering to himself as if he were running through something in his mind. He retired from the Fire Department. Stopped watching football. Said it wasn't "real," but agreed that probably nothing else was, either.

Over the years, we got used to thinking of Marleen as something eerie but mostly harmless at the edge of our lives. Children would sneak close to the crabapple tree, but, like the Vamp, they'd never go under it. They made up stories about the dead bodies buried beneath it, mostly to scare the younger ones. Once, somebody tried to set fire to the tree—it looked like a professional job, and the fire marshal hadn't had his heart attack yet, so maybe he was involved. To protect the tree, Marleen had an extension built onto the farmhouse, with a hole in the roof for the tree, or perhaps it moved in on its own. Its apples were said to be poisonous, but birds gathered in its laden branches like twittering harpies to eat them, and, if anything, they got louder and bigger, and there were more of them than ever.

Frederic Tuten

Winter, 1965

IN THE FEW MONTHS before his story was to appear, he was
treated differently at work and at his usual hangouts. The bartender at the White Horse Tavern, himself a yet-unpublished
novelist, called out his name when he entered the bar and had
twice bought him a double shot of rye with a beer backer. He had
changed in everyone's eyes: He was soon to be a published writer.

And soon a serious editor at a distinguished literary publishing house who had read the story would write him, asking if
he had a novel in the works. Which he had. And another one,
as well, in a cardboard box on his closet shelf that had made
the tour of slush piles as far as Boston. Only twenty-three, and
soon, with the publication of his story in *Partisan Review*, he
would enter the inner circle of New York intellectual life and
be invited to cocktail parties where he, the youngster, and Bel-
low and Mary McCarthy, Lowell and Delmore would huddle
together, getting brilliantly drunk and arguing the future of
American Literature.

On the day the magazine was supposed to be on the stands, he
rushed, heart pounding, to the newspaper shop on Sixth Avenue
and Twelfth that carried most of the major American literary

magazines, pulled the issue of *PR* from the rack, opened it to the table of contents, and found his name was not there. Then turning the pages one by one, he found that not only was his story not there, but neither was there any breath of him.

Maybe he was mistaken; maybe he had come on the wrong day. Maybe the delivery truck had got stuck in New Jersey. Maybe he had picked up an old issue. He scrutinized the magazine again: *Winter, 1965*—the date was right. He went up to the shop owner perched on a high stool, better to see who was pilfering the magazines or reading them from cover to cover and call out, "This is not a library!" He asked the man if this was the most recent issue of *Partisan Review*, and it was, having arrived that morning in DeBoer's truck, along with bundles of other quarterlies that in not too many months would be riding back on that same truck—bound in stacks, magazines no one would ever read.

He took a day to compose himself, to find the right tone before phoning the editor. Should he be casual? "Hi, I just happened to pick up a copy of *PR* and noticed that my story isn't there." Or very casual? "I was browsing through a rack of magazines and remembered that there was supposed to be a story of mine in the recent issue but it doesn't seem to be there, so I wondered if I had the pub date wrong."

With the distinguished editor's letter in hand—typed and signed and with the praising addendum, "Bravo," he finally got the courage to call. The phone rang a long time. He hung up and tried again, getting an annoyed, don't-bother-us busy signal. He considered walking over to the office but then imagined how embarrassed he would be, asking: "Excuse me, but I was wondering whatever happened to my story?" Maybe Edmund Wilson would be there behind a desk with a martini in each fist, or maybe the critics Philip Rahv and Dwight Macdonald would be hanging out at the water cooler arguing over the respective merits of Dreiser and Trotsky. What would they make of him and the unimportant matter of his story?

Months earlier, he had written the editor thanking him and now he wrote him again: "Might I expect to see my story in the next issue?" To be sure his letter would not go astray, he mailed it at the post office on Fourteenth and Avenue A. And for the next two weeks, he rushed home every day after work to check his mailbox but found no response, just bills and flyers from the supermarket. He knew no one to ask, having no one in his circle remotely connected to *PR* or to any of its writers. For those at the White Horse he was their ticket to the larger world.

The news that his story had not appeared quickly got around. His colleagues at the Welfare Department—avant-garde filmmakers, artists without galleries, and waiting-to-be-published poets and novelists—where he was an investigator since graduating from City College in '63, gave him sly, sympathetic looks. "That's a tough break," a poet in his unit said, letting drop that he had just gotten a poem accepted in *The Hudson Review*.

His failure made him want to slink away from his desk the instant he sat down. It was painful enough that he had to go to work there, as it was, it made him queasy the moment he got to East 112th and saw the beige, concrete hulk of the Welfare Department with its grimy windows and its clients lining up— eviction notices, termination of utilities letters in hand. His supervisor, who had been at the Welfare Department ever since the Great Depression and who now was unemployable elsewhere, tried to console him, saying he was lucky to be on a secure job track and with a job where he could meet so many different kinds of people with a range of stories, some of which could find their way into his books.

But he didn't need stories. What he needed was the time to tell them. And he had worked out a system to do that. He rose at five, made fresh coffee or drank what was left from the day before, cut two thick slices from a loaf of dark rye, which he bought at that place on Eighth off Second Avenue that sold great day-old bread at half price, and had his breakfast.

Sometimes he would shower after breakfast. But the bathtub in the kitchen had no shower, so he had to use a handheld sprinkler that left a dispiriting wet mess on the linoleum floor, which added cleanup time to the shower itself. Thus, he had a good excuse to cut down on the showers and to use that time at his desk to write.

Usually, by 5:45 a.m., he was dressed and at his desk, the kitchen table he made from crate wood that almost broke the saw in the cutting. He sat at his typewriter for two hours and no matter what resulted from it he did not leave the table. At 7:45 he was at the crosstown bus stop on Tenth and Avenue D and if all went well he was at the Astor Place station before 8:15 and, if all still went well, he would catch the local and transfer for the express at Fourteenth, get off at Ninety-Sixth Street and take another local to 114th. Then he'd race to clock in—usually a minute or two before nine. It was not good to be late by even a minute. He was still a provisional and had to make a good impression on Human Resources.

When he got upstairs to his desk and had joined his unit, he'd look over the list of calls to see if any were urgent. They were all urgent: Someone never got her check because the mailbox had been broken into. Someone was pregnant again. Someone needed more blankets. Someone had had just enough and jumped off the roof on 116th and Park Avenue—her children were at her grandmother's.

Today, he finished all his desk work and phone calls by noon and clocked out for lunch, which he decided to skip. Instead, he finished four field visits very quickly, with just enough time to solicit the information needed to file his reports. He had looked forward all morning to his final, special visit.

He was alarmed when he saw a cop car parked in front of her building. An ambulance, too, with its back doors wide open. He was worried that something bad had happened to her, blind and alone. But the medics were bringing a man down in a stretcher. He was in his eighties, drunk and laughing. The cop spotted his black field book and came over asking, "Is he one of yours?"

"Not mine," he said.

"Maybe not even God's," the cop said. "His girlfriend shot him in the hand," he added. "Jealousy, at that age!" He laughed. As he was being lifted into the ambulance, the wounded man laughed and said, "Hey! Take me back. I haven't finished my homework."

He rang her doorbell only once before he heard footsteps and then the "Who is it?"

"Investigator," he answered. She opened the door, smiling. She wore white gloves worn at the tips and a long blue dress that smelled of clothes ripening in an airless closet. Her arm extended, her hand brushing along the wall, she led him through a narrow, unlit hall. From her file, which he had reviewed that morning for this visit, he knew it was her birthday. She was eighty-five.

"It's your birthday," he said.

She laughed. "Is that so! I guess I forgot," saying it in a way that meant she hadn't. "I have tea ready," she said.

She poured tea from a porcelain teapot blooming with pink roses on a white sky. Its lip was chipped and stained brown, but the cups and sugar bowl that matched the teapot were flawless and looked newly washed. So, too, the creamy-white oilcloth that bounced a dull light into his eyes. It was hot in the kitchen; the oven was on with the door open, though he had told her several times how dangerous that could be. A fat roach, drunk from the heat, made a jagged journey along the sink wall.

"Do you need anything today?" he asked. "Maybe something special?" He wanted to add, "for your birthday," but he did not want to press the obvious point. He could put in for a clothes or blanket supplement for her, deep winter was days away. Or a portable electric heater she could carry from one room to another, so she would not have to use the stove. But how would she locate the electric sockets? "Oh! Nothing at all," she said, as if surprised by the question. "Thank you, but what would I need?"

Not to be blind, he thought. Not to be old. Not to be poor. "Well, if anything comes to mind, just call me at the office," he said, remembering that she had no phone.

"Well," she said shyly. "If you have time, would you read me that poem again?"

She already had the book in hand before he could answer, "I'm very glad to."

She had bookmarked the Longfellow poem he had read to her in his previous visits. He read slowly, with a gravity that he thought gave weight to the lines. He paused briefly to see her expression, which remained fixed, serene.

When he finished, she asked him to repeat the opening stanza. "'Tell me not, in mournful numbers, / Life is but an empty dream! / For the soul is dead that slumbers, / And things are not what they seem. / Life is real! Life is earnest! / And the grave is not its goal . . .'"

She thanked him and asked, "Do you like the poem?"

"Yes," he said, to please her. But he disliked the poem because of what he thought as its cloying, sentimental uplift. He did not want to be sentimental, but he had to admit how much the lines had moved him anyway.

They sipped tea in silence. He did not like tea but accepted a second cup, commenting how perfectly she had brewed it. "Come anytime," she said, "It's always nicer to drink tea in company."

She walked him to the door, picking up a cane along the way. He had never seen her use a cane before. He suddenly worried that should she fall and break her hip, alone in the apartment, she could not phone for help. He made a note in his black notebook to requisition a phone for her.

"The cane is very distinguished," he said.

"It helps me hop along." She smiled. "Thank you for reading to me. You have a pleasing voice, do you sing?"

"My voice is a deadly weapon," he said, surprised by his unusual familiarity. "Birds fall from the sky on my first note."

"Does it kill rats?" She laughed. "I hear families of them eating in the hall at night."

He fled down the stairs, having once been caught between floors by three young men with kitchen knives who demanded his money, but when they saw his investigator's black notebook they laughed and said they'd let him slide this time—everyone knew that investigators never carried cash in the field. He sped to the subway where he squeezed himself into a seat so tight that he could not retrieve his book, Malamud's *The Assistant,* from his briefcase. He tried to imagine the book and where he had left off reading. It was about an old Jewish man who ran a failing grocery store and his assistant, a young gentile who lugged milk crates and did other small jobs and who stole from him. It was a depressing novel that pained him, but that had, for all its grimness, made him feel he had climbed out of the grocery store's dank cellar and into a healthy sunlight.

The train halted three times. The fourth might be the one that got stuck in the blackness for hours and he thought to get off at the next station and take a bus or run home or, better, close his eyes and magically be there. But finally the train lurched ahead and when he exited at Astor Place, a lovely light early snow had powdered the subway steps. He waited for the bus.

He waited only eight minutes by his watch but it seemed an hour, two hours—that he had been waiting his whole life. Finally, he decided to walk and hope to catch the bus along its route. But he still did not see it by the time he got to First Avenue, so he decided to save the fare and walk the rest of the way home to Eighth between C and D. By Avenue A, it began to be slippery underfoot and the snow came down in fists. Now the thought of going home and leaving again in the snowy evening to travel all the way on the snail's-pace bus to the White Horse Tavern for dinner seemed a weak idea. Anyway, he was still smarting from the bartender's faraway look and the wisecracks from the bar regulars when he walked in. He decided to eat closer to home, a big late lunch that would keep him through the evening and keep him at home, writing.

Stanley's on Twelfth and B was almost empty, the sawdust still virgin. It was still early and still quiet, with just a few old-timers, regulars from the neighborhood—the crowds his age came after eleven, when he would be in bed. He ordered a liverwurst sandwich on rye with raw onions and a bowl of rich mushroom soup, made in the matchbox kitchen by a Polish refugee from the Iron Curtain, an engineer who had to turn cook. A juniper berry topped the soup. That, the engineer told him, was the way you could tell it was authentically Polish. He always searched for the berry after that—like a pearl hiding in the fungus. Stanley, the owner, balder than the week before, brought him a draft beer without his asking. "It's snowing hard," he pronounced. "Should I salt the street now or later?" He did not wait for an answer and went back to the kitchen to shout at the cook in Polish.

He took two books from his briefcase, so that he could change the mood should he wish: *Journey to the End of the Night*—for the third time—and *Under the Volcano*, which he had underlined and made notes in the margins. "No one writes the sky as does Lowry, with its acid blues and clouds soaked in mescal." He was proud of that note. One day he would write a book of just such notes. Note upon note building to a grand symphony. Then he voted against ever writing such a book, pretentious to its core—worse, it was facile, a cheat. He wanted to write the long narrative, with each sentence flowing seamlessly into another, each line with its own wisdom and mystery, each character a fascination, a novel that stirred and soared. But what was the point of that? What had become of his story?

A girl he liked came in with a tall man in a gray suit. She smiled a warm hello. He returned with a friendly wave and a smile that he had to force. Now he was distracted and pained and could not focus on reading his book or on his sandwich, which, anyway, was too heavy on the onion. He had met the girl at Stanley's several times, never with a plan, although he had always hoped he would find her there; they talked without flirting, which he was not good at anyway, going directly to the heavy stuff of books and paintings.

The first time he saw her there months earlier, she was reading a paperback of Wallace Stevens poems. He imagined her sensitive, a poet maybe. She was from upstate, near the Finger Lakes with their vineyards and soft hills that misted at dawn and had the green look of Ireland. He had never been upstate or to Ireland. He had never been to Europe. She had been, several times, and had spent a Radcliffe year abroad in Paris, where she had sat at the Café de Flore educating herself after the boring lectures at the Sorbonne in the rue des Écoles. She had learned how to pace herself by ordering *un grand café crème* and then waiting two hours before ordering another, and then ordering a small bottle of Vichy water with *un citron à côté*. By then, she was more than twenty pages to the end of *La nausée*. What did he think of Sartre's novel, she had asked him as if it were a test. He hated it, he said. It crushed him, written as if to prove how boring a novel could be.

"That's smart," she said. "If you were any more original you'd be an idiot."

They kissed one evening under a green awning on Avenue A. He kissed hungrily, her lips opening him to a new life. After he had walked her to her doorway and gone home and got into his bed, he felt as if he just had been released from years in prison, the gates behind him shut, and "the trees were singing to him." He did not have her phone number or her address and, over the next few weeks, when he went to Stanley's hoping to find her she was not there.

He buried himself in the Céline and tried not to look at her. But then she was beside him. "Come over, I want you to meet someone," she said, sweetly enough to almost make him forget that there was a someone he was supposed to meet.

"This is George," she said, "my fiancé." He extended his hand and George did the same, a hand that spoke of a law office or some wood-paneled place of business high up, far downtown, maybe in the Woolworth Building.

George asked him if he'd like a drink and, before he could answer, George called out to Stanley and ordered two double scotches, neat. "Johnny, Black Label," he said. She was still on her house wine, white, from grapes in California, fermenting under a bright innocent sky. The drinks came. They had little to say to each other or, if they did, they said little. He made a toast: "Best wishes for your happiness," he said. Not much of a toast, not very original. It would take him a day to think of one better; under the circumstances, perhaps never. He looked at his watch and remembered he had to meet a friend for dinner across town: They all shook hands again, and he wished them both good luck. "You too, fella," George said.

The snow fell in wet chunks that seemed aimed at him. When he got home, his head and jacket were wet and he had to brush off the snow married to his trousers. He was worried his jacket would not be dry by morning when he went to work, and he was on the second landing before he realized he had not checked the mail. He thought it was not worth the bother of going back and checking, but he could not stand the thought that he would be home all night wondering if *PR* had finally written him. There was a letter in the mailbox. But it was not from the magazine. But it was also not from Con Edison or Bell Telephone or Chemical Bank, announcing the fourteen dollars in his savings account. When he got to his apartment, he closed the door behind him with a heavy, leaden clunk and slid the iron pole of the police lock into place. "Home is the sailor, home from the sea and the hunter home from the hill," he announced.

He noticed that his cactus was turning yellow. He had overwatered it, and now it was dreaming of deserts—the old country—as it died slowly, ostentatiously. He thought of getting a cat. It would be great to have company that would be the same as being alone. A black cat that would melt in the night when he slept. He picked up the letter cautiously when he saw there was no return address. It may have come from a disgruntled client who had wanted to spew hatred and threats. But it was not. The note was handwritten with lots of curls that announced Barnard or Sarah Lawrence or some grassy boarding school in Connecticut. "Sorry," it said, "that your story did not appear in the new issue as you were led to expect. Do call, if you like." There was a phone number, each digit inscribed as if chiseled in granite and the seven was crossed. For a moment he thought it a prank by one of the White Horse crowd, hoping he would call and find he had dialed a funeral parlor or a police station or a suspicious, jealous husband. But what if it was for real?

He washed his face in cold water, brushed his teeth, combed his hair, took four deep breaths and dialed, holding back for a moment the last digit. At first he thought, with a little lift in his spirits, that it was the girl from the bar. Maybe, after comparing him to her beau, she had decided to call off the engagement. But then, he realized how absurd that was since the girl in the bar had nothing to do with his story. He let the call go through and on the second ring a woman answered. "I've been calling for a week," she said. "Don't you have a service?"

"I let it go," he said. "Looking for a better one."

"Well, I gave up and wrote you."

"Sorry for the trouble," he said and then in a rush and hating himself for the rush, asked, "Are you an editor at *Partisan Review*?"

"Something like that," she said. Then cautiously added, "We can meet if you like." He wanted to ask if she could tell him right now, over the phone, tell him what had happened to his story but he held back, not wanting to seem anxious and unsophisticated.

"Sure," he said, adding as casually as he could, "When?"

"How's tonight? I live just across town. You name the place."

"You don't mind coming out in all this snow?" he said, immediately regretting he had asked. What kind of man is afraid of the snow? "I mean, I could come to you if that's easier."

"I'll just grab a cab. How's eight?"

He wondered if she had dinner in mind. He would have to offer to pay for it, and he began calculating his finances. But to his relief, she said, "I'll already have had dinner."

"Okay, then, how's the De Robertis' Pastry Shop, the café on First, between Tenth and Eleventh, next to Lanza's?"

"Is that the café with the tile walls that looks like a bathroom?"

He didn't like his café being spoken of that way. "I guess some may see it like that."

They fixed the time at 8:30. Just as he was about to ask whether they were going to publish the story in another issue, the line went dead. There were still some hours to go before meeting her and he had time to write or to review the morning's work. The portable Olivetti, shiny red, hopeful, was quietly where he had left it, waiting patiently on the kitchen table; the two pages he had written beside it, like accomplices. He read over the pages. They were absurd, stupid, illiterate, worthless—and worse, boring. He was stupid and boring, a failure. The Welfare building sailed at him like an ocean liner in the night. "Life is real, life is earnest," he sang, as the ship loomed larger.

He did not want to meet her hungry and he did not want to spend money for another sandwich at Stanley's. He scavenged the fridge. The crystal bowl heaped with Russian caviar was not there so he settled for the cottage cheese, large curd, greening at the top, which he spooned directly from the container. Then he considered taking a nap so he would be refreshed and alert and not stupid or dull but bright when he met her. He practiced a smile but it was strained and pathetic. He tried napping, leaving on the kitchen light so he would not wake in the lonely darkness. The

Welfare building pressed full steam toward him but he blinked it away and tried to clear his mind of all troubling thoughts but without much success. So he rose with the idea of making himself presentable. He brushed his teeth and gave himself a sponge bath; he cleaned his fingernails and brushed his teeth again. He had reached the limit of his toilette and returned to his desk; maybe his pages would brighten at the cleaned-up sight of him; maybe his Olivetti would regard him more favorably and let him turn out some astonishing gems.

By the time he arrived at the café, he had to shake off the heavy snow twice from his umbrella. His shoes were soaked. He had not changed them for fear of getting his second pair drowned as well and thus having to spend the next day at work in wet shoes.

She was easy to spot, sitting in a booth with a pot of tea and a half-eaten baba au rhum. Her black hair was pulled tight in a ponytail; gold hoops dangled from her earlobes; kohl rimmed her eyes; her yellow sweater was the color of straw in the rain. What was she, twenty? She was more Café Figaro on Bleecker with its Parisian hauteur than someone who usually came into his neighborhood. He was sure he had spotted her at the White Horse, men hoping to catch her eye circling her table, where she sat in among other men chattering for her attention. She had never once looked up at him, even when he was ostentatiously clutching *Under the Volcano* in his hand.

She smiled in an anxious way that relaxed him and he took his seat and said, "I hope I haven't kept you waiting." He was ten minutes early, but he had no better introductory words. He felt foolish for having said them.

"I liked your story," she said, as if she too had mulled over her first words to him and now had let them burst.

"I'm very pleased," he said. *Pleased* seemed tempered and not overanxious, showing a proper balance of self-esteem and of professional dignity. But then he overrode his self-control and said, "Are they still going to publish it?"

She forced a little laugh. "I doubt it."

This was bad news, indeed. But before he could ask the cause of this doubt, she said: "He hates me now." She made a high-pitched sound like a young mouse broken in a trap.

"I read him in college. We all did. I never thought I'd become his assistant! Anyway, he has a new assistant now," she said, her eyes glistening.

Johnny, the café owner, brought over the cappuccino, with a glass of water and a cloth napkin. He looked at the young woman and smiled and turning to him said, "*Hai fatto bene.*"

"You know, it's just one of those crazy things that happens. Maybe not so crazy when people work so closely all the time," she added, as if talking to herself.

He wanted to ask, "Please, what thing that happens?" But he was afraid that pressing her would only make him seem unworldly. Instead, he said: "Yes, crazy things do happen," thinking he would offer, as a current example, the story of the shot man who said he hadn't finished his homework.

The café was foggy, steaming up like the baths on St. Mark's he went to once and hated, all that wet heat boiling his blood—and the absurd thing was that he had to pay for it, too. He could leave now, as he had then, with the steam stripping the skin from his bones. But he was listening to her story and was not ready to run. She looked down. "I suppose you can fill in the rest," she said. And then with a little pinched laugh, added, "After all, you're the writer." He waited for her to add, "and as yet unpublished." But he realized it would have been his addition and not hers and that he was bringing to the table the same feeling of defeat as when he went to the White Horse, where the greetings had gone stale.

"Oh! I don't know," he said, with some affected casualness, "I'm not good at realism or office fiction." He was thinking of a popular novel some years back, *The Man in the Gray Flannel Suit*, which he had not read but understood had to do with office politics and unhappy commuters with sour marriages and lots of scotch and martinis before dinner. He knew nothing of that world, making him wonder in what America he lived and if he was an American writer or any kind of writer at all?

She gave him a studied look and in a brisk, businesslike tone said, "Of course, I know that. That's what I like most about your story. I loved that part where a dying blue lion comes into the young blind woman's hut and asks for a bowl of water and how she nurses him to health."

"That sounds a bit corny," he said. "Maybe I should be embarrassed instead of flattered that you remembered it."

He himself had forgotten the passage as well as most of the story. It had seemed so long ago and somewhat like a friend who, for no reason that he knew, had turned on him.

"Don't be silly," she said. "It's an archetype, all archetypes seem corny."

"So," he asked, as if he had not already been told, as if, finally, to invite the coup de grâce, "why won't he publish it?" The steam was clouding him and the wall's white tiles were oozing little pearls of hot water and bitter coffee.

"Look," she said, with an edge in her voice, "I just came to tell you that I'm sorry it didn't work out."

"Excuse me," he said, "I'm a bit slow, more than usual tonight— the steam's getting to me." He wished he could close his eyes and find himself home and, once there, obliterate all memory of the sent story or of having received the acceptance letter that was to have changed his life. The espresso machine was screaming.

She looked about the room and then back at him and smiled. "And frankly, I was curious to know what you were like."

"I hope I met your expectations," he said. That was so lame. He started to revise but she did not give him time.

"My boyfriend also thinks you're a good writer. And he studied with Harry Levin at Harvard."

"Harry Levin's *The Power of Blackness* is a great book." He wanted her to know he knew.

She offered to pay her share of the bill—and a little extra because she had had those two babas au rhum—but he said, in what he thought was a worldly fashion, "Not at all, you are my guest."

He walked her to Ninth and First Avenue and waved for a cab. "Thanks," she said, "I don't believe in cabs, do you? They're so proletarian." They stood on the corner shivering and waited until the bus skidded to the stop; snow blanketed the roof and the wipers swiped the windshield with maniac fury. He wanted to kiss her on both cheeks, as he had seen it done in French films, but thought it was too familiar too soon. In any case, the hood of her slicker covered much of her face. She smiled at him very pleasantly, he thought. On the second step of the nearly empty bus, she turned and said, "I don't have a boyfriend." He waited until he saw her take her seat. He waved as the bus moved into the traffic, but she was facing away and did not see him.

He thought of returning to the café, but he was sick of coffee and the screaming white tiles, or of going back to Stanley's bar for a beer, but was afraid he would run into the girl he had liked—still liked—and she would ask what he had thought of her fiancé and he would have to be brave and swallow it and say how solid he seemed and how he was happy for her if she was happy.

He went home and climbed the stairs. A dog barked at him behind a door on the second floor—Camus, *The Stranger*, the mistreated, beaten dog; the Russian woman on the third floor was boiling cabbage and the hall smelled of black winter and great sweeps of bitter snow, a branchless tree here and there dotting the white expanse—Mother Russia, Dostoevsky, *Crime and Punishment*, the bloody ax, a penniless student. On the fourth floor, not a peep. Then suddenly, a groan followed by a cry like a man hit with a shovel: "*Welt welt, kiss mein tuchas.*"

On the fifth floor, he thought about the groan and the cry on the fourth. He had seen the tattooed numbers on the old man's wrist and knew what had given them birth—hills of eyeglasses, mounds of gold teeth, black black smoke rising from an exhausted chimney. When he finally reached the sixth and last floor, he stopped at his door, key in hand, thinking to turn and leave the building again for a fresh life in the blizzard. But he was already shrouded in snow and was chilled and wanted to take off his clothes and lie in bed and be whoever he was. There was a song coming from the adjacent apartment: Edith Piaf, who regretted nothing.

His playboy neighbor had returned from Ibiza with a sackful of 45s and a deep suntan. He always had visitors, beautiful girls from Spain and Paris and London, who came to crash and who sometimes stayed for a week or two. One had knocked at his door at two in the morning and asked if he had any coke. He apologized, he did not drink soda; she made a face and said, "Where're you from?" Another banged at his door at five in the morning blind drunk; she had mistaken his apartment for the playboy's. "You have the wrong door," he said, his sleep shattered. "Who cares," she said, staggering into his room.

He was down to his shorts and T-shirt and had pulled a khaki surplus army blanket to his knees. He sat up in bed with Céline and read. Ferdinand was working in an assembly line in Detroit. Molly was his girlfriend. Ferdinand was a young vagabond and she was a prostitute. She loved him. There was no loneliness in the world as the loneliness of America. And the two had made a fragile cave of paper and straw against the loneliness. He read until he no longer knew what he was reading. Then he gave up. His mind was elsewhere and nowhere. The day had been fraught with distractions. He was a distraction. He thought of phoning someone. Maybe the assistant he had just left at the snowy bus stop—to find out if she got home all right. Maybe he would call some friends, but he did not know whom and, finally, he did not have anyone he wanted to talk with or who would welcome his call. He thought again of getting a cat. A white one he could see in the dark. The cactus looked healthier in the lamplight; maybe it had had second thoughts and decided to give life another try. "Good night," he said to himself and switched off the light.

But he quickly turned it back on, thinking again of calling the assistant, thinking that perhaps they could soon become friends. They could go to poetry readings at the Y—Auden and other great poets read there, or take in a movie at the Thalia on Broadway and Ninety-Fifth—he was sure she liked foreign films, like Fellini's *La Strada*, or Bergman's *The Seventh Seal*. Maybe on the weekends they would sit over coffee under the bronze shadow of Rodin's giant *Balzac* in MoMA's tranquil garden, and he would read to her his latest work. She would immediately recognize what was excellent and what was not and, with her as his editor and muse, he would write beautiful, original stories and novels. She had already been his champion. Now they would collaborate, nourishing each other on life's creative adventure and they would never be lonely in Detroit or anywhere else. He tried to remember if he had found her attractive, but she was a blur with a messenger's voice.

Maybe he had neglected to see that she was beautiful, desirable. He suspected that she was both. He was sure of it. Maybe he'd invite her for a dinner of spaghetti and salad and house red at Lanza's, where whatever you wanted on the menu they did not have. Maybe at dinner together there, under the frescoes of Sicilian villas grilling in the sun, she would find its prix fixe and soiled menus louche and seductive and thus find him equally, if not more so. Maybe one morning they would wake together in his bed, the raw light from the window on her beautiful, bare, straight shoulders. Maybe one midnight, after a movie and over coffee and a plate of rolls at Ratner's on Second Avenue and under the eyes of the shaking old Jewish waiters, retired from the Yiddish Theatre, they would realize they were in love. Maybe they were already in love.

He could hear the scraping of a snow shovel in the distance—maybe on Avenue C. His own street would not be cleared for days. He went to his window. The synagogue across the way had been locked tight for two years; its smashed windows covered with sheets of fading plywood. The grocery three buildings to the east of him was closed, the two brothers who owned it were still in Rikers Island for fencing radios, so the whole way to Avenue D might be snowed over, impeding his walk to the crosstown bus on Tenth and D. The snow was building on his window ledge and he would let it mount, better to gauge how much of it was piling up below in the street he could no longer clearly see. With all this snow, the morning bus might be delayed and the subway, too. He would have to get up extra early to get to work, and budget himself the time to shovel Kim's sidewalk. The laundry was still dark: Kim was in the back recovering from a mugging and beating three days earlier. "Where is your gold?" the robbers had demanded. "Chinks always have gold," one said, giving Kim a whack on the knee with a blackjack. He would have to shovel the snow for him before he went to work or Kim would get a summons or two. When would he find time to write? Who cared if he did? He would go down in the street and sleep there in the blanketing snow, Céline in hand. Or maybe the Lowry.

He went back to bed, tossing and turning and sleeping a dozen minutes at a time, then waking. He returned to Céline. Ferdinand was still miserable in cold Detroit, but he had no luck in focusing and no better luck with *Under the Volcano*, whose drunken protagonist still reeled about in the hot Mexico sun. He went to the window again. The snow had piled a quarter way up the window and was whirling in the sky like it owned the world. He might be late to work or never get there no matter how early he left his house.

There was a knock at the door, alarming at that hour, but then he thought it was his playboy neighbor or one of his wandering drunk girlfriends, or the one always prowling for drugs. He opened the door to the limit of the chain. It was the neighbor, drink in hand.

"I heard you puttering about and thought it was not too late."

He opened the door, feeling vulnerable in his underwear.

"Just wanted you to know I'm moving out and want to sublet for a year or so. Thought you might like it for your office." He could not afford two apartments, and was scraping by on one, but he said, "Thanks, give me a day or so to think about it."

"The rent's the same thirty-two a month—I'm not trying to make anything on it."

"I wouldn't have thought so." It was cold in the hallway and he thought to invite him in but was embarrassed that he would see three days of dishes still piled up in the sink. And then, feeling he was not cordial enough, he added, "Where're you going?" expecting him to say Ibiza or Paris or San Francisco.

"Uptown, closer to work."

"Sorry you're leaving," he said.

"Well, me too. But Dad thinks it's time to put on the harness and he got me something in publishing."

"Oh!"

"It should be okay. I'm told editors mostly go to lunch."

"I've heard that," he said. He wanted to add, "I'll send you my novel, maybe you'll like it." But he felt humiliated and hated himself for the thought that he would ask.

"Come and lunch with me one day!"

"I'd like that," he said. They shook hands. He shut and locked the door but felt he was on the outside, in the hall, freezing. He checked his Timex. How had it ever become midnight? No wonder he was freezing—at that hour the boiler was shut off and all the radiators turned to ice. He lit the oven, setting it on low, and left the door open. Maybe he would buy a portable heater and one for the blind woman. Maybe he'd drag out the Yellow Pages from the back of the closet and look up the closest animal shelter, like the ASPCA, which he heard was respectable. He would go there on Saturday and would come home that very day with a cat. He wondered what kind of cats they had there. Old ones, sick ones, mean ones, dirty and incontinent ones who would pee on his bed, all ready to be gassed. He would save ten and herd them in a train to follow him as he went from room to room. He'd circle them around his bed at night and keep away Bad Luck. He had Bad Luck. He'd save fifteen. Seven white ones; seven black ones. The other would be marmalade. Would they let him take that many at one time?

He could not sleep. But he could not stay awake another minute. Better than chancing a morning bus and subway failure, maybe he'd get dressed and start walking to work now, fording the snow drifts so to be sure to get there on time. He'd show up at first light, half-frozen, waiting for the doors to open. He would be exemplary. He would be made permanent. He would be promoted and never have time to write again or wait for rejections in the mail. Or maybe he would be found icy dead at the foot of the Welfare Department's still-closed doors. The editor of *Partisan Review* would eventually learn of it and publish his story, boasting that he had been their promising discovery.

The snow had bullied the streets into silence. The building slept without a snore. In the distance, the tugboats owlishly hooted as they felt their way along. He stayed that way for several minutes, chilled under his blanket. But then the oven slowly heated, sending him its motherly warmth. He rose and went to the kitchen table and to the gleaming red Olivetti waiting for him there.

This story is dedicated to Tom McCarthy

Rebecca Evanhoe
They Were Awake

THE LADIES GATHERED FOR one of their potlucks. They brought beautiful dishes. Red cabbage marinated in vinegars and slow-cooked with nutmeg and caraway seed. *Salade niçoise* with basil and thyme tossed in with the greens, the best Spanish sardines in olive oil, and farm eggs perfectly boiled, the orange yolks on the cusp between soft and hard.

The ladies were happy, and they were pleased to see one another. As they took their places at the table, they were quiet and polite, passing napkins and plates and cutlery, spooning the salad and cabbage with big wooden spoons onto plates. After a few glasses of wine, the ladies became chatty, laughing and drawing one another into conversation: "Emma, I thought of you when so-and-so was quoted in today's paper," and "Amy, it seems like you could say a thing or two about *that*."

They began to tell one another about their recent dreams. They'd all been having anxious dreams, every one of them, even though life had been treating them well. Becca began the discussion as she poured dressing over her salad. She said, "Last week, I had this dream that I owed money to the gas company. There was this loud knock on the door, and when I went to the door, there was just this bright-orange notice saying that I owed hundreds of dollars. And then I went to the gas company offices—it looked like the office I used to work in. And the man, who was my uncle Charley—*looked* like my uncle Charley—he was very passive-aggressive with me. I said I wanted to pay him, and I went to my wallet, and it was full of Monopoly money! All those pink and yellow bills. . . . I said that someone must be playing a joke on me, all I had was Monopoly money, and he said in this menacing way, 'Yes, a joke, of course. But where is your real money?' I woke up in a panic, I checked my account balances online, everything had been paid for, but for a few hours I couldn't shake the feeling that there must be some bill I hadn't paid."

The ladies laughed.

"I had a wild dream, too, earlier this week," said Emma. "I don't often remember my dreams, but I woke up in a funk and couldn't forget this one. I dreamed that an ex-lover of mine and I were in his apartment. Not the apartment he has now—the apartment he had ten years ago, when we first met. And it was full of incredible artwork. Actual, beautiful, rare artwork. And I remember him locking the door behind him, you know? I mean, I saw him do it, but then he showed me this beautiful artwork and I forgot the door was locked for a moment."

"Funny how dreams work, isn't it?" Amy said quietly.

"Yes! This dream was so strange. And then he told me I had to authenticate every piece of artwork in his apartment. Somehow, it was my job to do this. And I thought, 'I haven't been trained in this! How am I supposed to know?' And he kept saying, 'I could sell it, I want to sell it, but I don't want to get ripped off. You've got to keep me from getting ripped off.' And I tried to go to the door, but the locks were locked."

"Did you get out?" the ladies asked. "Did he rape you?"

"No, no, of course not," Emma said. "I woke up when I realized the locks were locked."

"I had a dream where I was trapped, too, just last night," Carrie said. "I dreamed that Carl was going to rape me." Carl was her husband. "I dreamed that he came home from work early while I was doing Pilates, and he told me that I had never given him what he wanted. He looked like Carl, but younger. I mean, he was the Carl I'd seen in pictures before I met him, like when he was eighteen. He said, 'You're going to finally give me what I want,' and I thought that maybe he wanted to rape me, so I ran to the glass sliding door and tried to break it, to get away, but it turned into a concrete wall. It wasn't a concrete wall when I ran to it, but it seemed to turn into that, or I realized it was that—you know how dreams are—and so when I realized I couldn't break through it because it was a concrete wall, I had to turn around, and Carl was there, and he was naked. The eighteen-year-old Carl, I mean. And then he shoved me to the ground, and I realized he *was* going to rape me, and so I woke up."

"Oh my goodness!" the ladies exclaimed. Amy said, "Carl would never, ever do that."

Sabrina, gal of the world, who'd traveled to Russia and China and South Africa, said, "I had a nightmare on Thursday. I was helping a woman, in a clinic-like setting, doctors and nurses were milling around, and the woman had just been raped, she was Russian, and she kept yelling at me, 'You did this! You paid the man who raped me!' That's what she kept saying."

"But why did she think you had paid a man to rape her?" asked Liz.

"Because it was a *dream*," Sabrina said. "And anyway, I kept arguing with the woman, I wanted to help her, but she was so upset with me, and eventually she became my sister. I mean, the woman's face eventually started to look like my sister's face. I kept saying, 'I didn't put those bruises on your body. Who put those bruises on your body?' This woman was covered in bruises, all over her arms and her thighs. But then she ran away, and I woke up. I was so nervous from the dream, I called my sister the very next day, but she's fine. She's traveling, consulting for environmental-engineering firms, so she's been a jet-setter the past few months. She's looking forward to being home."

"Good for her," exclaimed the ladies.

"How exciting," said Amy. And then Amy said that she, too, had dreamed an upsetting dream.

"I dreamed I was making popcorn," she said. The ladies nodded; Amy loved popcorn. "And I looked out the window, and I saw my mother. I ran to the kitchen door and opened it, and my mother walked toward me. She looked so old; her hair was gray, her face was wrinkled. And I just took her in my arms and held her. But over her shoulder, I could see my mother, a younger version of my mother, standing in the yard. I was just holding this old, frail woman and looking at my beautiful mother standing out there."

The ladies were entranced. "And then what?"

"And I woke up," Amy said.

"Are these the worst dreams we've ever had?" asked Becca. "I mean, what's the worst dream you've ever had?"

"I dreamed, in middle school, that my face was eaten by a dog," said Carrie.

"In college, I suppose it was a few months into my freshman year, I dreamed that my math professor at the time told me I would never be smart enough to learn math," said Liz.

"Throughout high school, I had this recurring dream that I kept trying to cook dinner for my parents, and I kept ruining dinner—burning it, forgetting to turn on the oven, that sort of thing," said Emma.

"After I got my first job, I kept dreaming that my coworkers were screaming at me, 'You're a fake! You can't do this!' in the break room," said Amy.

"I had this wonderful dream last year, when I divorced John," Becca said, "that I had killed this man with my bare hands, just wrestled him to the ground and wrapped my hands around his neck, strangling him, and as I was doing it, I felt capable of anything, I could do anything I wanted."

The ladies smiled politely. Amy said, "You certainly can do anything—just look at this *salade niçoise*." The ladies tittered now, grateful for Amy. They picked up their forks again, stabbed at their salads.

"I had a dream like that, too, years ago," said Emma. "I dreamed that police showed up at my door, banging, you know, and shoved me into a car. They wouldn't tell me why, and I thought it was a mistake. They put me in one of those rooms, like you see on TV, interrogation rooms, and they asked me why I had killed this man, some man. They kept showing me these awful pictures. They kept saying, 'You beat him! You beat him with a copper pipe, didn't you?'"

"Terrifying!"

"Yes, terrible, just terrible."

"And then you woke up, yes?"

"No," said Emma. "I mean to say, I did wake up. I thought I had woken up. But I woke up in the dream, you see? And then I realized that I *had* killed him. I had beaten him in an alley. I thought he was trying to attack me, so I got the copper pipe out of my purse and I nailed him in the head. And then I kept hitting him, over and over, all over his body, and then I ran away. And once I realized that, I felt proud of myself."

The ladies reached for their wineglasses, scooped lentils onto their plates from the nearest bowl. "Go on," said Sabrina.

"And then I actually woke up," Emma said. The ladies exhaled and laughed. They really thought that Emma's story was going somewhere else, to an even darker place.

Sabrina shook her head. "You know, it's funny how we keep describing our dreams. Everyone keeps saying the word *realize*. 'I realized.' But it's not like that in dreams, is it? It's *knowing*. It's only after you wake up that you use the term *realize*."

"Yes, that's so, isn't it?" said Liz. "I had this dream in childhood where I knew something awful."

"What was it?" asked Sabrina.

"I knew, for certain, that my brother was going to kill himself. And the dream was exactly like our real life at home. It was Thanksgiving Day in the dream. Everything was like a regular Thanksgiving—the whole family eating breakfast, Mom making stuffing, my brothers playing in the yard with our cousins. Like an old home movie, almost. But the whole time it was happening, I just *knew* he was going to kill himself that night by cutting his wrists in the bathroom, and that I'd be the one who found his body. The dream went through a whole day—everything normal, except for what I knew—and as we were all going to bed, I tried to hug him, and he kept saying, 'Not now, Liz. Hug me later. Not now.' "

Liz looked at her plate. "That dream happened almost a decade ago, when I was in college, and I didn't remember it at all until my brother did kill himself . . . let's see, four years ago."

The ladies clutched their wineglasses. Emma asked, "Did he slit his wrists in the bathroom on Thanksgiving Day?"

"Oh, no," said Liz. "He stabbed himself until he bled to death. And it was June. He was in his apartment. This was many years after the dream, you understand."

"What an unusual month for your brother to kill himself," said Becca. "Don't most suicides happen around Christmas?"

The ladies nodded. "Yes, I think I read that somewhere," said Carrie.

"Where's Amy?" asked Liz.

"In here!" Amy called from the kitchen. She appeared in the doorway with a lemon-meringue pie. "I figured we could all use some dessert." The ladies clapped and nodded at one another.

"Perfect timing, Amy."

"That pie looks fantastic."

"I bought it at Publix. It's not homemade, so I hope it's good," Amy said.

Becca went around the table, gathering and stacking the dirty plates and carrying them to the kitchen, and then Amy cut up the lemon-meringue pie. The ladies put the edges of their forks to their soft pieces of pie.

"It's not a bad pie," said Sabrina.

"No, the meringue is good," said Carrie.

"The lemon part is a little gluey for me," said Amy, "but I'm glad everyone likes it."

"We like it fine," said Emma.

"Have you ever had the kind of dream where you're cutting something, like a pie, and it just keeps fusing back together, so you keep cutting and cutting?" asked Liz.

"Or the dream where you're trying to empty something, and it just keeps filling?" asked Amy.

"What about the dream where time stands still?" asked Emma.

"Or what about when actual time stands still, in real life?" asked Sabrina. "I had an experience like that."

"You mean like at work?" asked Emma.

"No, it wasn't at work. It was when I was living abroad in Russia," said Sabrina. "I went on a blind date with this man, and when I showed up for the date, I realized how much older he was than me."

"And the date lasted forever? A bad first date?" asked Becca.

"No, the date went pretty quickly. We ended up back at his apartment, and we started drinking absinthe."

"Absinthe!"

"Nothing happened, really, we just kept drinking this absinthe. He kept telling me that it was very good absinthe, and that something would be happening soon. I kept expecting to hallucinate, really."

"And did you? Did you hallucinate?"

"Time stood still because you were hallucinating?"

"No, not at all," said Sabrina. "We just got very drunk, and when I woke up the next morning he was gone. I was very hungover. I was so hungover I felt almost glamorous, you know. Like an epic sort of hungover."

The ladies stole looks at their glasses of wine. Some were full and warm; some were nearly empty and still cold.

"And so you felt like time stood still when you were hungover," said Becca.

"No, no. I drank some bottled water from the fridge and put my clothes on," said Sabrina, "and then I realized that his apartment was locked from the outside. I couldn't get out."

"Did you go through the window?"

"Had he locked you in there?"

"There weren't any windows. It was a basement apartment. And yes, he had locked me in there. At first I thought I was just hungover and confused, so I took a shower and ate something. I drank all the bottled water. And I looked at his books," said Sabrina.

"But he came home later that day? And realized his mistake?"

"He came home, yes," said Sabrina. "But he'd meant to do it. He kept me locked in that apartment for two weeks."

"Two weeks!"

"Didn't your employer report you missing?"

"Did he rape you?"

"Yes, two weeks," said Sabrina, sipping her wine. "I was working for a newspaper at the time, and they just assumed that I'd quit. It was a dreadful place to work, really. Those long, late hours. And no, he didn't rape me. I mean, we had sex, you know, but it wasn't rape. I fell very much in love with him."

"Where's Carrie?" asked Liz. The ladies paused. They heard the sound of running water.

"Oh, she snuck off to do the dishes!"

"What a sweetheart."

"Let's keep her company."

The ladies grabbed their wineglasses and pie plates and walked into the kitchen. Carrie turned around. "You caught me," she said. "I couldn't leave all these dishes to Liz!"

"I brought your wine," said Becca, setting Carrie's glass on the counter. "We were still talking about dreams. When you're trapped, or when time stands still."

"These dishes feel that way! I'm in a nightmare right now," said Carrie. The ladies laughed. "I'm kidding, of course—the dishes are nearly done."

"Leave the pie plates for me," said Liz. "I should do some work in return for all this beautiful food."

Carrie dried off her hands and picked up her wineglass. "I've had those dreams. Mostly when I'm trying to finish a book." Carrie was a published author. "I have dreams where I'm writing and writing, I'll write pages of stuff on my computer, but when I try to go back over what I've written, the pages only have a few lines on them."

"Oh no!"

"What do the lines say?"

Carrie said, "They turn into lists. Commands, really. Like, 'Tell us about your other father.' Or, 'Have a son with dark curls.' Or . . . or, once the paper said, 'Write the story twice, at the same time.'"

"But how could you do that?" asked Becca. "I mean, no one can write the same story twice at the same time."

Carrie thought. "I suppose you could," she said, "if you put it all in the same story."

"How do you mean?" asked Emma.

"It makes perfect sense if you think about it," Carrie said. "Every story is at least two stories at the same time." The ladies murmured in response.

When the wine was out and the pie plates were stacked by the sink for Liz to finish, the ladies drifted toward the door. For a few minutes, they stood near the entryway as a group, planning the next potluck, clutching their empty bowls, rattling keys and rummaging one-handed in purses. Emma had parked a few blocks over, and as she walked to her car she got the eerie sensation that someone was following her, but when she turned back to look, she saw only a stray cat sitting in the road. At home she stayed up for hours, practicing her favorite Schubert sonatas on her electronic keyboard. Carrie lived nearby and so she had walked, and on her way back to Carl she texted her lover about the upcoming weekend. Becca drove to her studio apartment, where she fed her cat, changed into pajamas, and opened another bottle of wine. At home, Amy made popcorn before she realized she wasn't very hungry, but she ate half the bag out of duty, and made a to-do list for the next day. Sabrina read a novel to kill time until two a.m., and then she Skyped with a friend in China, a former boyfriend whom she was to see on his next visit back to the States. As for Liz, after she shut the door behind her, she left the plates next to the sink, put on a jazz record, and took half a Valium. Each woman looked at her clock and marveled that the dinner had gone so late into the night, and yet when each one grew tired, she fought sleep.

Ottessa Moshfegh
Slumming

Y OU COULD TELL JUST by looking—grape-soda stains on their kids' T-shirts, cheap dye jobs, bad teeth—the people of Alna were poor. Some of them liked to huddle on turnouts or thumb rides up and down Route 4, sunburnt and tattooed, but I never thought to stop and pick one up. I was a woman alone, after all. And I didn't want to have to talk to them, get to know them, or hear their stories. I preferred to keep the residents of Alna as part of its scenery. Wild teens, limping men, young mothers, kids scattered on the hot concrete like the town's lazy rats or pigeons. From a distance I watched the way they congregated, then dispersed, heads hung at midlevel, neither noble nor disconsolate. The trashiness of the town was comforting, like an old black-and-white movie. Picture an empty street with a broken-down car, a child's rusty tricycle abandoned on the curb, a wrinkled old lady scratching herself while watering her dun-colored lawn, the hose twisting perversely in her tight fist. Crumbling sidewalks. I played along when I went up there, slipping pennies in and out of the dish on the counter of the Gas Plus on State Street as though a few cents could make or break me.

I made an abysmal living back home teaching high school

English, and my ex-husband rarely paid his alimony on time. But by Alna's standards, I was rich. I owned my summer house up there. I'd bought it from the bank for next to nothing, full of cobwebs and tacky wallpaper. It was a one-and-a-half-story bungalow overlooking the Omec River, a sloshy mile-long tributary to a lake twice the size of Alna itself. The real estate taxes were negligible. The cost of living was a joke. The teenage boys in the sandwich shop in town remembered me from summer to summer because I tipped them the fifty-cents change they tried to give me. Otherwise I didn't mingle. I'd made the acquaintance of a few of the neighbors—mostly single moms whose teenage children smoked and strollered their own babies around the graveled driveways. An old man across the street had a long beard stained brassy from cigarette smoke. "Hey neighbor," he'd say, wheezing, if I saw him out walking his dog. But I never felt I was anybody's neighbor. I was only ever just visiting Alna. I was slumming it up there. I knew that.

Clark supplied a steady stream of coeds to occupy the house during the school year. He taught computer programming at the community college ten miles away, in Pittville. I paid him to look after my place. I sometimes got the sense he was overcharging me, inventing problems and costs to inflate his monthly bills, but I didn't care. It was worth the peace of mind. If something went wrong—if the pipes froze or the rent was late—Clark would handle it. He'd wrap the windows once it got cold, fix a leaky faucet, a short circuit, a broken step. And I was glad I never had to deal with any of the tenants. Each summer I drove up to Alna, I'd find the house altered—a new perfume lacing the humid air, menstrual stains on the mattress, hardened bacon grease splattered on the kitchen counter, a fleck of mascara on the bathroom mirror like a squashed fly. I mostly didn't mind these remnants. Having a tenant kept the vagrants out of what would otherwise be an empty shelter from September to June. The street people of Alna were notorious for taking up residence wherever they could find it and refusing to leave, especially during the winters, which were, in Alna, deadly.

There was no scenic hike or museum to visit, no guided tour, no historic monument. Unlike where my sister summered, Alna had no gallery of naïve art, no antique shop, no bookstore, no fancy bakery. The only coffee to buy was at the Gas Plus or the doughnut shop. Occasionally I drove to Pittville to see a movie for two dollars. And sometimes I visited the deluxe shopping center on Route 4, where the fattest people on earth could be found buzzing around in electronic wheelchairs, trailing huge carts full of hamburger meat and cake mix and jugs of vegetable oil and pillow-size bags of chips. I only shopped there for things like bug spray and batteries, clean underwear when I didn't feel like doing laundry, an occasional box of Popsicles.

Monday through Friday I kept to my summer diet of one foot-long submarine sandwich per day—the first half for lunch, the second half for dinner. I got these sandwiches from the deli downtown, around the corner from the bus depot at the hilltop crossing of Riverside Road and Main Street, where the vagrant townsfolk dressed like zombies and kept wolf dogs on rope leashes. The town was rife with meth and heroin. I knew that because it was obvious and because I dabbled in both when I was up there. Unless it was raining, I walked the two miles back and forth up Riverside every weekday morning, got a soda and my sandwich, and more often than not hit the bus depot restroom to buy ten dollars' worth of whatever was on sale—up or down.

On the weekends, I took myself out to eat. I had lunch either at the doughnut shop, where you could get an egg-and-cheese sandwich for a dollar, or at the diner on 122. I liked to sit at the counter there and get a platter of chopped iceberg smothered in ranch dressing and a bottomless Diet Coke and listen to the waitress greet the regulars—big men in T-shirts and suspenders, left arms brown as burnt steak. Half the time I couldn't understand what anyone was saying. For Saturday night dinners I hit the Chinese buffet for sautéed broccoli and free box wine, or I went to Char-lie's Good-Time, a family-style bar serving french fries and pizza. The bar was attached to a combination arcade and bowling alley. I didn't talk to anybody when I went out. I just sat and ate and watched the people talk and chew and gesture.

The Good-Time was where I met Clark my first summer in Alna. Through the haze of cigarette smoke and steam from the bar's kitchen, he was the only person who looked remotely edu-cated. I was inclined to brush him off at first because he was nearly bald and wore a knotted hemp necklace. His hand was limp and clammy when I shook it. But he was persistent. He was kind. I let him pay for a pitcher of beer and try to impress me with his knowledge of literature. He told me he didn't—couldn't—read fiction written after '93, the year William Gold-ing died, and he claimed to know the editor of a well-known literary journal in the city, one I'd never heard of. "Stan," Clark called him. "We go way back." I overlooked all the glaring errors in his personality—his arrogance, his airs, his bony, hairy hands. I still remember the humility it took for me to agree to take him home, then the appalling ease with which I accepted his pathetic overtures of gratitude and affection. He wore a cheap white dress shirt and blue jeans, brown leather sandals, and a small gold hoop earring in one ear, and when we undressed in the dark in my empty upstairs bedroom, me crouching under the sloped ceiling, his genitals swung in my face like a fist. Afterward he said I was a "real woman," whatever that was, asked if I had any children, then shook his head. "Of course you don't," he said, cradling my pelvis. I ran my fingers through his soft, thinning hair.

For the next few weeks he helped me sand the kitchen coun-ters, peel off wallpaper, paint, scrub, fix the old stove. He rubbed my back at night while we watched videos we rented from the Gas Plus. He liked to blow into my ear—some high school trick, I supposed. We talked mostly of the house, what needed to get done and how to do it. Things started to feel serious when he got a friend of his with a truck to help move in furniture I bought for pennies from the secondhand store in Pittville. My sister would have called it all "shabby chic," not that I cared. Nobody was judging me in Alna. I could do whatever I wanted.

Clark was the one to introduce me to the submarine-sandwich diet and to the zombies at the bus depot. One morning he held out his long pinky fingernail. "Sniff it up," he said. The stuff threw sex and romance under an immediate dark and meaningless shadow. It blotted out all our "feelings for each other," as Clark had described our rapport. We didn't sleep together again after that first high, but we did spend a few more weeks in each other's company, nibbling the sandwiches and snorting the stuff from the zombies. Depending on what stuff they'd given us, we'd spend the days either cleaning or passed out on the brittle wicker daybed or on loose cushions on the porch, overlooking the Omec. The day I left to drive back down to the city that summer was a strange parting. We hugged and everything. I cried, sorry to say good-bye to my narcotic afternoons, my freedom. Clark offered to keep the house up while I was away, find me tenants, act as "property manager," as he called it. I generally don't like to hold on to loose ends, but I made this exception. If the house burned down, if the pipes burst, if the vagrants made a move, Clark would let me know.

Half a dozen years had passed since that first summer in Alna, and almost nothing had changed. The town was still full of young people crashing junk cars, dirty diapers littering the parking lots. There were x-ed–out smiley faces spray-painted over street signs, on the soaped-up windows of empty storefronts, all over the boarded-up Dairy Queen long since blackened by fire and warped by rain. And the zombies, of course, still inhabited Alna's shadowy, empty hilltop downtown. They slumped on the curb nodding, or else they rifled through dumpsters for things to fix or sell. I often saw them speed walking up and down the slopes of Main Street with toasters or TV sets under their arms, ghost faces smeared with Alna's dirt, leaving a trail of garbage in their wake. If they ever left Alna, cleaned up, shipped out, the magic of the place would vanish. Monday, Wednesday, Friday—I figured three times a week was a sane frequency—I visited that bus depot restroom, my ten-dollar bill at the ready.

Nobody ever asked me any questions. The zombie in charge just handed me my little nugget, my little jewel, kept his face hidden under the hood of his raggedy sweatshirt, sweat dripping off his chin and plinking down onto the dirty bathroom tiles. There was no logic to what was kept in stock on a given day. Each time I got home and tried what they'd given me, it was always the right stuff. It was always a revelation. Never once did those zombies steer me wrong.

Clark never got that about the zombies—their supernatural wonder. He was too concerned with his own intelligence to see the bigger picture. He thought that the drugs we bought in the bus depot restroom were intended to expand his mind, as though some door could be unlocked up there and he would greet his own genius—some glowing alien in glasses and sneakers, spinning planet Earth on its finger. Clark was an idiot. We saw each other once or twice each summer. I'd take him out to eat in Pittville to thank him for his help with the house, and I'd listen to him gripe about how hard the winter had been, the state of affairs at the college, budget cuts, local government, the health of his dog. He quoted Shakespeare too often. And *that's just life* was a common phrase he used to sound deep and wary—a perfect example of his laziness. Still, I didn't hate him. A few times we even tried to recapture whatever odd coincidence of lonesomeness and availability we'd found together that first summer in Alna, but inevitably one of our body parts would fail us—sometimes his, sometimes mine. It was always humbling when that happened. Time was passing, I was getting old, "middle-aged," my sister called it. The truth was undeniable: I'd be dead soon. I considered this every morning I walked home from the bus depot bathroom, a little foil-wrapped turd of drugs stuffed in with the lint and pennies in the pocket of my pleated khaki shorts.

I missed Alna during the school year. I missed the zombies. Grading papers, sitting in staff meetings, I wished I was sitting on my porch, looking down at the Omec and considering small matters—the little birds and where they found worms to feed their babies, the shifting shades of brown on the rocks as the water splashed them, the way the vines fell from the highest tree branches and got tangled tumbling in the rushing, sudsy water below. When the big city was covered in snow, my bones like ice, frozen air stabbing at my lungs, I told myself I'd go swimming in the lake that summer, get a real tan, frolic, so to speak. I owned a bathing suit, but it was pilly and stretched and the last time I'd worn it—at my sister's pool party a few years before—I'd felt droopy and pasty, like my mother. The freckles on my thighs, once adorable marks of health and frivolity, were now like spots of dirt or little bugs I kept trying to scrape away with my fingernail. My sister showed me pictures later on, pointing out how flat my breasts had gotten.

"Do some of these," she told me, pumping the air with her elbows in her stainless-steel kitchen. That was another thing I liked about Alna. Once I'd settled in each June, I could ignore my sister's phone calls, claiming bad reception. I needed a break from her. She had too much influence over me. She only wanted to discuss things and name things for what they were. That was her thing. "Melasma," she said, pointing to my upper lip. "That's what you call that."

One morning on my way home from the sandwich shop and bus depot, I passed a yard sale selling the usual garbage: baseball caps, plastic kitchen utensils, baby clothes folded into tiny cubes spread out on stained floral bedsheets. The only books at Alna yard sales were convenience-store paperbacks or cookbooks for microwave ovens. I didn't like to read while I was in Alna anyway.

I didn't have the patience. That day a tall, gray metal sunlamp caught my eye. The scrap of masking tape stuck to its base was marked in red: three dollars. I didn't care if it worked. If it didn't, trying to fix it would occupy me for at least an afternoon. It was worth the trouble.

"Whom do I pay?" I said to the gaggle of women sitting on the front steps. They all had the same flat, long brown hair, the same pinched eyes, bulbous mouths, and throats like frogs. Their bodies were so fat, their breasts hung and rested on their knees. They pointed to the matriarch, a huge woman sitting on a piano bench in the shade of a large oak. Her left eye was swollen shut, bruised yellow, black, and blue. I gave her the money. Her hand was tiny and plump, like a doll's, fingernails painted bright red. She stuffed the bills I gave her in the pocket of her worn cotton housedress, pulled a sucker from her mouth, and smiled, showing me—not without some hostility—a lone bottom row of teeth rotted down to stubs, like a baby's teeth. She was probably around my age, but she looked like a woman with a hundred years of suffering behind her—no love, no transformations, no joy, just junk food and bad television, ugly, mean-spirited men creaking in and out of stuffy rooms to take advantage of her womb and impassive heft. One of her obese offspring would soon overtake her throne, I imagined, and preside over the family's abject state of existence, the beating hearts of these young women pointlessness personified. You'd think that, sitting there, oozing slowly toward death with every breath, they'd all go out of their minds. But no—they were too dumb for insanity. "Rich bitch," I imagined the mother to be thinking as she plunked her sucker back into her mouth. I lugged the lamp up the street, thinking of her flesh spreading around her as she lay down on her bed. What would it feel like, I wondered, to let myself go? I was anxious to get home, uncrinkle the little fortune in my pocket. If the sunlamp did work, I would bring it back down to the city with me. The light could soothe me in the winter and clean my dirty city soul each night.

It's not that I lacked respect for the people of Alna. I simply didn't want to deal with them. I was tired. During the school year, all I did was contend with stupidity and ignorance. That's what teachers are paid to do. How I got stuck teaching Dickens to fourteen-year-olds is a mystery to me. I'd never planned on working all my life. I'd had this fantasy that I'd get married and suddenly find a calling beyond the humiliating need to make a living. Art or charity work, babies—something like that. Each time seniors had me sign their yearbooks, I wrote, "Good luck!" then stared off into space, thinking of all the wisdom I could impart, but didn't. At graduation, I'd take a few Benadryl to soothe my nerves, watch those tassled caps float around, all the idiotic high fives. I'd shake a few hands, go home to load my car with musty summer clothes and a case of sparkling mineral water, then drive the five hours up to Alna.

When I got back to my house with the lamp that day, a girl was standing in my front yard. She had her back turned, and she seemed to be staring up at the windows, a hand held over her head to block the sun's glare. Nobody had ever come into my yard before. In all my time in Alna, nobody but Clark had ever even knocked on my door. I put the lamp down by my car and cleared my throat.

When the girl turned around, I saw that she was pregnant. The swell of her baby made a tent of her long black sleeveless shirt. She was thin otherwise, a scrawny young mother, the kind my sister abhorred. Her leggings were pastel purple, and her hair was short like a boy's, and blond. She approached me, her hands supporting the small of her back, wincing in the sunshine, trying to smile.

"Is this your house?" she asked. As she came closer, I thought I detected rose perfume. A raised mole on her chin glistened with sweat. I folded my arms.

"Yes," I stammered, "it's my house. I'm the owner." I guessed at who she was then—a former tenant. A Teri or Maxine or Jennifer or Jill, whatever their names were. Maybe she'd forgotten something in the house. Those girls always left things behind—a hairbrush, a bobby pin, empty boxes of crackers, tampons in the medicine cabinet, stray socks and underwear between the washer and dryer. I happily used up their leftover bars of vanilla- and floral-scented soaps, each laced with hairs and gouged by their fingernails in sharp half-moons. "Can I help you?"

The pregnant girl stood before me now, face gleaming, and looked down at the sunlamp. She held up one hand to wave hello. In her other hand she carried a sheaf of flyers.

"I'm a housecleaner," she said. "I wanted to drop this off."

She handed me one of the flyers. It was a hazy photocopy of a handwritten ad that included her name and phone number and a long list of services she provided. "I do laundry. I sweep and mop. I straighten up. I dust. I vacuum," I read aloud. She'd drawn stars around the page, a smiley face at the bottom, at the end of a line that read, "Ask about babysitting." Her hourly rate was less than what a person would make working at a fast-food restaurant. I considered pointing that out to her but didn't. I picked the lamp back up.

"Do you need help?" she asked. I ignored her tanned, out-stretched arms and let her follow me across the yard. "I cleaned your house last year, actually," she said. "After you left, before the students moved in, I guess."

Clark hadn't told me he'd outsourced the cleaning.

"So you know Clark," I said, pulling out my keys.

"Yeah," she said, "I know him."

I didn't bother to wonder whether Clark might be responsible for her pregnancy. He didn't have it in him. Even with me he'd been fiercely dedicated to his fancy brand of condoms. But it burned me to picture him ogling the girl, counting out the cash to pay her for cleaning up my filth. Poor girl. She was pretty for Alna, and tough in a way that came through in her shoulders. They weren't wide, per se, but angular and taut with budding muscles like a teenage boy's. She must have thought I was old and ugly. I could have been her mother, I suppose. I struggled with the sunlamp as we climbed the few steps to my front door.

"Clark should hire you to clean before I arrive, too," I said, opening the door and putting the lamp down inside. "The bathroom especially is always yucky when I get here."

"I can usually do a house like this in an hour or two," she said, still standing out on the doorstep. "But I've been getting slower and slower, with this baby thing." She pointed down at her belly. She looked up at me, as if she would find some sympathy there. Her eyes were clear and blue but hooded and tired. She spoke with the grumbling, rhythmless lilt of Alna talk. Maybe she had a dragon or a devil tattooed on the small of her back, or a Playboy bunny on her lower abdomen, now stretched and mutated by her pregnancy, that "baby thing," as she called it. I studied her face as she peered over my shoulder, into the darkened house.

"Want to clean now?" I asked her.

"Okay, sure."

Then, despite the information I'd just read on the flyer, I asked, "How much do you charge?"

She shrugged, those gleaming shoulders twitching, clavicles glistening in the sunshine. "Ten bucks?"

"For the whole house?"

She shrugged again.

"Come on in," I said, and held open the door.

"Let me just call my mom."

I pointed to the phone on the wall by the fridge and watched her waddle past me toward it. She put the flyers down on the counter. Her belly was huge, nearly ready to pop. What kind of mother lets her pregnant teen wander around outside in the sweltering heat, I wondered. But I knew the answer. This was the Alna way.

I stared at the girl's face as she passed, her tiny pores, her small, upturned nose, oily purple makeup darkening into the crease of her heavy eyelids. She dialed the phone and lifted the collar of her shirt to wipe the sweat off her forehead. I opened the cabinet under the sink and gestured toward the cleaning supplies down there. She nodded. "Hi, Momma," she said, turning away from me, coiling the cord around her thin wrist.

I left her there, went into the den, unwrapped my sandwich on the coffee table, and unscrewed my soda. I was a grown-up. I could sit on the sofa and eat a sandwich. I didn't have to call my mother. I didn't even have to clean my own house. I listened to the girl talk. "I'm fine, Momma. No, don't worry," she said. "I'll be home in time for dinner." After she hung up, I heard her rattling the bucket of sprays and cleaners from under the kitchen sink.

"You must be hungry," I said to her, eyeing her slim calves as she walked past me through the den. I held out half of my sandwich.

"I'm okay," she replied, one arm weighed down by the bucket, the other dragging a broom behind her. "I'll start upstairs," she said, and lugged the stuff up the steps, her face flat and serious, the enormous bulge of her belly straining against her shirt, which was already darkened with sweat down the front. I chewed and watched her disappear up the stairs. Shreds of lettuce spilled out the sides of my sandwich. A slice of pickled jalapeño smacked the hardwood floor. I left it there and ate, happily. It was deadly quiet in that house without the television on. I could hear the toilet flush, the girl grunt and breathe, the scrub brush scrape rhythmically against the bathroom tile. I gulped my soda down, burped with my mouth open wide. I wrapped up the dinner half of my sandwich and set it aside.

Then I took out my zombie dust. I figured I could just test it to see what the zombies had chosen for me that day, a sneak preview of what I had in store. Later, once the girl was gone, it would be nice to take a shower, walk through the clean house, silent and fresh, and sit at the coffee table in my bathrobe with a rolled-up dollar bill. I'd let my soul fly wherever the stuff sent me until it got dark and I remembered the sandwich and the world down below. My mouth watered just imagining it. My hands got hot. That was the best part, that moment, anticipating miracles. But when I uncrinkled the foil and peeled back the plastic wrap, what I found was not magic powder but a cluster of clouded, butter-colored crystals. The hard stuff, I thought, agog. Upstairs there was a loud thud. I put the stuff down on the table and listened.

"You okay?" I hollered, still staring down at the crystals.

"Yeah, I'm all right," the girl answered. The scrub brush started up again, slowly.

What was the meaning of those crystals? They had appeared only once before, with Clark that first summer in Alna. I was still new to the zombies then, still afraid of them. My walks up Riverside with Clark were fraught with nervous thrills. The bus station had been out of operation for a few decades—fake wood veneer benches and an old soda vending machine, empty windows, faded ads with Smokey the bear admonishing smokers and Hillside Church offering day care and asking for charity. Occasionally teenagers would skateboard around, hopping up with a frightening rumble and clack onto the counters at the old ticket windows. The men's toilets were in back, through a short maze of brick riddled with graffiti. A few zombies were stationed back there, sitting on sinks or squatting on the floor, their wolf dogs tied to a pipe in the wall, panting. The zombie in charge sat in a stall with the door swung halfway open. Silently, he took our money and handed over the goods. His fingers were huge and cracked and red, black creases lining his palm, his nails thick and yellow. I hid my face under my hair, lurked and cowered next to Clark, masking myself in false subservience. The zombies saw through all that. They saw everything. But I was clueless still. I was a foreigner. I didn't know their customs. I got more comfortable as time went on, of course. And then once Clark was out of the picture, I was forced to go alone. The zombies rarely lifted their gaze above my waistline. Theirs was a solid, grounding, animal attitude. Each time I met them in the bathroom I felt I was walking in naked, as if I were some pilgrim approaching a saint. I offered ten dollars and I received my blessing.

When the crystals appeared for me and Clark all those years before, I was honored, moved even. It felt like some kind of rite of passage, a sacrament. But when Clark saw the crystals, he crushed the foil back up and jammed the stuff down the front pocket of his jeans.

"What are you going to do with it, Clark?" I asked.

"Flush it, at my house," was his brilliant reply.

Whatever lame affection I had left for Clark was smashed in that instant—it was obvious he was trying to deceive me. I suppose those crystals worked to save me from really getting attached to the man. Such was the magic wisdom of the zombies.

"What's wrong with my house? Flush it here," I insisted.

"I could flush it here," he murmured.

"So flush it." But Clark just sat there, stroking his beard and staring at the television as if the opening credits of *Will & Grace* had hypnotized him, as if he'd become one of the zombies.

"Ahem."

"What?" he asked.

"Give it back," I said, elbowing him in the knees.

"Trust me," he whispered. "This stuff rots your brains." He stood up, scratching his head, his armpit a rat's nest of hair flecked with white gunk from his antiperspirant. "I'm going home," he said. "I'm tired."

I let him go then. I didn't argue. He tried to kiss me good-bye but I turned my face away. I spent the rest of the day bored in front of the television, pining, furious, confused. I tried to go upstairs and scrape the leftover wallpaper in the bathroom, but it was no use. The next morning I went to the zombies alone and received the usual stuff. When Clark called in the afternoon, I told him I needed some time to myself. I sniffed my magic powders while he blubbered an apology that sounded like all his lame professions—foolishly sincere.

After cleaning my bedroom, the girl trudged slowly down the stairs. I'd been lying on the sofa reading a teen magazine left behind by one of the tenants. I stared at articles that told me how to "live my dreams," "score total independence," and "make more $$$." I can't say exactly what I thought I'd do with the crystals. I'd seen movies about people smoking crack out of little glass pipes. I could fashion something, I thought, but I was scared I'd mess it up. I imagined dissolving the crystals like rock sugar in a mug of herbal tea, or grinding them like sea salt over a bowl of canned tomato soup. But I wasn't sure ingesting the stuff that way would work. And what if it did? I still had a life back down in the city, after all. There were certain realities I had to face. I couldn't handle real oblivion. I just wanted a vacation. So I had some doubts. I had some misgivings.

I'd been rolling the little nest of foil between my fingers, pondering all this as I stared at the magazine. When I heard the stairs creak, I sat up and stuck the stuff back in the pocket of my shorts.

"Hot up there," I heard the girl say.

Her pretty, gleaming calves appeared between the rungs of the banister as she came down the steps. She'd folded the cuffs of her leggings up above her knees, which were red from kneeling on the floor. When her thighs appeared, I saw a black stain of blood at her crotch. She seemed not to know that she was bleeding. There was no way she could have seen the blood past the mountain of her belly, I suppose. She gripped the bucket with one hand and the railing with the other as she descended the stairs.

"Oh, shit," she said when she reached the landing, "I left the broom."

"I'll get it," I told her, folding the magazine shut.

"Shit," she said again, putting the bucket down and holding her face with her hands. "Head rush."

"I'll get you a glass of water," I offered. I wasn't good around blood.

"I'm okay," the girl said, bracing herself against the bookshelf. "Just dizzy." She turned toward the wall, leaned into it, said, "Whew."

I got up then, patting my pocket to make sure the ball of foil was safe inside. In the kitchen I let the tap run cold, got the ice from the freezer, took a glass from the drying rack.

"I'm really okay," the girl said.

I plunked the ice in the glass. The cubes cracked as the water ran over them. "See," the girl went on, "you're not missing anything."

"What?" I hollered back. But I'd heard her perfectly. "You're not missing anything," she said again, louder. "My mom says a baby is a blessing, but I don't know." I suppose it unnerved me that she could be so naïve. She had no idea what her life was going to do to her.

"That baby's going to change your world," I said, walking back into the den. She was bent over with her face in front of the fan. I snuck a look at the bloodstain widening down her thighs. "My sister has a daughter," I said. "Gave up her career and everything." I handed the girl the glass. She pushed herself upright, took a long sip, set the glass down on the TV and sighed. "Boy or girl?"

"Boy," she answered, blushing slightly.

"You sure you feel all right?"

She nodded.

I stood around watching her clean for a while, helping her here and there, moving furniture so she could mop. She seemed perfectly fine to me. "I love *The Matrix*," she said, straightening my shelves of VHS tapes. "I love old movies." She beat the sofa's cushions with her fist. She stacked the magazines on the end table. She straightened my framed posters of Monet's *Water Lilies*. Her eyes were clear and blue as ever under their thick, gleaming lids. I went upstairs to get the broom, then I retreated to the kitchen, put away the clean dishes, and did the dirty ones. I put the dinner half of my sub in the fridge and sponged off the counter. I took out the trash.

Outside my neighbors were filling a kiddie pool with water from their garden hose. I waved.

"Marvin died," one of the women said glumly.

"Who's Marvin?" I asked.

She turned to her sister, or mother—I couldn't tell—and rolled her eyes. Clark had chained the lids of my trash cans to the plastic handles on the barrels. For some reason, the people of Alna liked to steal the lids and throw them in the Omec. That was one of their summer recreations, he'd told me. As I stuffed the garbage down, the pregnant girl threw open the screen door and walked stiffly down the front steps. She held one hand down under her belly and the palm of her other hand up in front of her face. When she saw me and the neighbors, she turned her palm around. It was covered in blood.

"Oh, honey!" cried one of the women, dropping the hose.

"Something's wrong," the girl stammered, stunned.

"Well, honey, what happened? Did you fall? Did you hurt yourself?" the women were asking. The girl caught my eye as they surrounded her. I put the lid on the trash and watched as the women guided the girl across the muddy grass. They made her sit down in a lawn chair in the shade. One of them went inside to call for help. I went back into the house and got the girl's flyers and twenty dollars from my wallet. When I got back outside, she was panting. I handed her the money, and she grabbed my forearm, smeared her blood all over it, squeezed it, shrieking, contracting her face in pain.

"Hang on, honey," the neighbor said, frowning at me, her fat hands stroking the girl's smooth, sweaty brow. "Help is on the way."

When the ambulance left that afternoon, I took a walk down to the Omec. Squatting by the edge of the river, I washed the blood off my arm. I took the crystals out and let them plunk down into the rushing water, threw the crumpled foil at the wind, and watched it hit the surface and float away. I looked up at the pale, overcast sky, the crows circling then gliding down to a nest of rotting garbage on the opposite bank. I sat on a hot rock and let the sun warm my bones. My thighs splayed out; my white skin tightened and burned. It was nice there with the cool breeze, the sound of the traffic through the trees, the earthy stench of mud. An empty Coke can tinkled a rhythm against the rock, shaken by the current. A toad hopped across my foot.

Later that evening I dragged the sunlamp out onto the curb, thinking maybe the zombies would find it. The next morning it was still there, so I dragged it back inside. I walked up Riverside Road. I got what I wanted. I walked back home.

Ron Carlson

Happiness

WE HAD TEN PILLOWS. It was the first thing my son Nick said when we entered the motel room and we were tired from traveling all day and surprised by the deep cold as we got out of the rental car, five degrees or so, and the warm room was perfectly cozy, the two big beds and the large television, and when he said we had ten pillows we both just laughed. Most of the time ten pillows are too many, but now with the trip and the dark and the cold, I wanted all my pillows.

It was wonderful to park our small cases on the bureau and turn on the television. It was October and it was game three of the World Series. Things were working out. The bathroom was big and well lighted and there was all kinds of soap and a coffeemaker. "Are we going over there?" Nick said, meaning Wally's, the burger place we'd seen across the street.

"We've got to," I said. "Wear your jacket."

Outside, the parking lot was full of trucks with fans of mud along the doors and bumpers, big trucks with all kinds of oil gear and toolboxes in the beds. If it hadn't been so cold, there would have been dogs in a few of the trucks, but now I knew the motel was full of smart shepherds and collies. I loved seeing the trucks and I loved seeing our little rental car in its place; we arrived late and still got a room full of pillows.

The cold was like metal in our noses and we tucked our chins and walked across the old empty highway to the little glassed building: Wally's, Home of the Wally Burger. In the street Nick kept bumping into me and laughing. On the sign each of the red letters had a big blue-painted shadow and the Wally Burger had been painted there, big as a car, beautiful and steaming and dripping and sort of vibrating by the depiction. Beneath the burger was the phrase: FRESH-CUT FRIES. Nick opened the door for me. He had read it all and was happy.

Inside there was a couple, a man and a woman who were my age, sitting in one of the little plastic booths by a coin-operated video game with a plastic rifle attached to it. It was called Big Game. The man had a huge white mustache, and they were both eating their Wally Burgers in the bright light. They still wore their coats and I wondered if it was a date. They had a paper between them, spread with the beautiful french fries.

The two teenage boys at the counter in their white paper hats were waiting for us. There wasn't a line. It was so great. I wanted to get a bag of this fine food and get back to the ball game. One kid wrote it all down: two Wally Burgers with everything, two cones of fries. When I ordered I said, "fresh-cut fries," and there was pleasure in it. In the old days I would have asked if Wally was around and Nick would have ducked in embarrassment at his old man, but I stopped that years ago. I turned and saw there were fringes of condensation frozen in the corners of the big front window, but it was warm in Wally Burger and I loosened my scarf.

The bag was hot and we hustled it across the dark highway and into the motel parking lot. The cold was over everything, the great arctic cold which had slid over Wyoming. In the warm motel room, we each sat on a bed picking at the greasy brown fries which were heavy and salty and delicious. The Wally Burger took some skill so that the onion and tomato didn't slide out. It was like food from the fifties and we ate without talking while the game unfolded. This was the game in St. Louis in which Albert Pujols hit a home run and then he came up again and hit a home run. Nick was lying on his bed watching the game and I put on my pajamas and was watching the game. After a while Nick said, "Why do they keep pitching to him?"

I was tired and full of fresh-cut fries, so I turned out the lights so just the game was on and I washed my face with great satisfaction and started sorting my pillows. They had been a terrific help while I was sitting up, but now there were too many. I didn't like putting pillows on the floor. Nick's pillows were all on the floor. Nick was sleeping in his clothes and I reached across to his bed and put my hand on his shoulder. I didn't need to say anything; he turned and undressed in one minute and crawled into bed.

I'd been at home in Southern California that morning and Nick had been in Phoenix with his mother. There wasn't a fall in my little beach town. The ocean layer thickened and the air grew damp and the days short. I'd met Nick in the Salt Lake City airport and we'd motored northeast to Evanston, Wyoming, for the first night of our fishing trip. I grew up in this part of the west, Utah and Wyoming, and I'd loved walking across that old highway in the dark. I found the remote control in the covers of my bed and watched the television for another minute. Nick was lost in sleep. They pitched to Albert Pujols and he hit a third home run.

We got up early and even so all of the trucks in the motel parking lot were gone. The sun was clear and sharp, shooting across the sides of things and catching in the yellow leaves in the bottom of the trees and on the street. There was frost in the shadows.

The interstate highway was full of trucks and Nick drove us east among them toward the Continental Divide. The bright sunlight was on the sage hills and the day was opening. At the great valley of Bar Hat Road, we came over the crest to see the highway descend in a straight line and rise up the far side, and Nick said, "Seven point two miles," which is just the distance. I've known it since this big road was just two lanes sixty years ago and my father used to ask how far I thought it was and I'd say twenty miles.

A little farther on we came to the big green fireworks sign in the high desert and the abandoned Fireworks shop where we'd stopped so many times. There was only one building at the exit, and Nick's mother called me the Mayor of Fireworks because I let the kids buy all sorts of armaments in the bright-colored packages. We drove past that summit, both of us now feeling the trip had really begun; we were far from home and would be at the cabin in three hours.

Twenty miles east, we left the interstate and drove into the Bridger Valley and stopped at Fort Bridger, the frontier garrison. The parking lot for the old territorial military base was empty, banked with leaves against the low fences. Nick had his camera and went ahead of me taking his long steps out onto the grounds by the old wooden schoolhouse and the grave of the famous dog who saved the barracks from the midnight fire. Across the lawn I could see the ancient steel bear trap and the antique buckboard; the museum was down the lane. We'd been in it a few times and I remembered they had a Hotchkiss machine gun. Today there was a wind and it was tricky to decide in the fragile sunlight if it was warm or cold. This little town always thrilled me, isolated as it was in the broad valley, and now watching my son drift among the old white-board buildings in the sharp fall day, it was as lovely as it could ever be. I went back and climbed in the rental car and was pleased at the sun warm on the seats.

At the four-way stop in Lyman, where there used to be two buffalo behind the Thunderbird station, we turned south. The buffalo, which Nick's mother and I saw the day after we were married forty years ago, are gone and the Thunderbird station is gone.

The mountains you can see from the town of Mountain View are the great Uinta Range running there along the northern edge of Utah, a thin and magnificent white line along the horizon, all the distant peaks covered in snow. It was a lot to look at and I was excited. You try not to hurry on such trips to the real mountains, but it is hard not to hurry, and as you get out of your car in the parking lot of the Benedict's Market in Mountain View, you walk toward the store with the measured steps of someone who is not hurrying and it is a kind of happiness in the sunny October day. We filled two carts with supplies: rib-eye steaks and big cans of stew and two bags of sourdough bread and big deep-green cucumbers and a block of sharp cheddar cheese and milk and half-and-half and a box of fresh chocolate chip cookies from their bakery and candy and a bag of potatoes and four onions and tomatoes and two kinds of apples and some soda and beer and bottled water and English muffins and salted butter and paper plates and coffee and hot chocolate and tea and a tub of coleslaw the guy spooned up for us and a bag of green beans and two pages of bacon and four of sliced ham and little cans of green chiles and two dozen eggs and a butternut squash. We checked out and I couldn't help myself and I told her we were going fishing and she said, "Good luck. You've got the day for it." Above the front windows of the big supermarket were fine examples of taxidermy, an antelope and a coyote, and above the woman and our groceries was a mountain lion rearing to reach for a pheasant. The big yellow cat's claw was just touching the bird's tail feathers, frozen in the air. The whole story.

We drove south out of town and then east into the badlands above Lonetree. It was on some of these lonely roads in this barren place where we'd set off plenty of fireworks twenty years before. There was an amazing kind of mortar box you could buy at Fireworks and it had six sleeves and six small balls each with a fuse. It was big stuff for our two boys. You light the fuse, drop the ball in the sleeve, and run back. The running back was everything.

From the badlands, Nick and I drove into the low willow meadows outside of Lonetree, the creeks full and amber, the real streams you see on such a drive. The old Lonetree general store closed twenty years ago, but I was in it as a child. It is where we stopped to use the outhouses behind the old school and to buy a lime pop out of the cooler in the wooden-floored store. The last time I was there was with my father and he admired the old clock on the back wall, a clock made in Winsted, Connecticut. The thing everyone remembers about Lonetree is that there is a parking meter in front of the store by the wooden hitching post. Every time I saw that meter in my lifetime, I was with someone I loved.

Now we were up along the northern slope of the Uinta Mountains, a mile from the Utah state line, and we drove along the beautiful hayfields of the last farms parallel to the state line and below the state and federal land. To our right we could see the great white peaks getting closer behind the foothills.

Yesterday, we had met at the airport and we'd rented this Subaru and the October light in my old hometown wanted to break my heart. We drove up past the university and along Foothill Drive and there at Parley's Way Nick pointed and I said, "Yeah. It's the church where I married your mother."

Now the fields were tall with grass and we passed the old ruined trailer and the neat log-cabin house and tiny abandoned cabin as old as anything in the region, and then we rounded a shoulder on the hillside and crossed back into Utah, though nothing changed.

A minute later the town of Manila, Utah, came into view, the scattered buildings and the blue of the lake behind it. We would fish tomorrow on the far shore.

The entire trip in a straight drive takes just four hours, Salt Lake to the cabin, and every town, every turn has a story: the flat tire and the crushed fishing pole, the herd of deer jumping the wire fence in the moonlight, the mountain sheep, the flood, the bear and her two cubs, the moose, the elk. Going through Manila, Nick had tried to find the Mexican restaurant we'd eaten at after coming out of the mountains on the backpacking trip when he was sixteen. It had been a double-wide trailer and the combination platters were killer, so good, but that place was long gone. Now we drove through the afternoon sunlight without talking. After the last hayfield in Manila, we turned in at the tipped stone canyons and there were two Fish and Game vehicles in the turnout with their orange traffic cones. There was a big black Ford pickup parked there and the hunters were showing the officers the buck. We could see the pink tag on the antlers. I had long ago told Nick of the times that I had deer hunted, all of them three-part stories, pretty good, especially the time when I was a kid and my dad and I woke to a snowstorm and decided to break camp and drive home a day early, but ran into a guy who had shot his hand and my father helped him fix a proper bandage. It wasn't a terrible wound, but I remember blood on the man's canvas trousers and my father working quietly with his first aid kit and the medical tape on the man's hand. My father hated accidents and was angry. When he came back to our truck, I asked him what had happened and all he said was, "There are two ends of a gun, always." I never heard him tell the story again.

On the radio, the football game came and went. Nick and I drove up the sage switchbacks above the massive blue lake and stopped at the rest area which was abandoned this late in the year. The big loneliness of the planet was part of it now, and even in the nourishing sunlight I felt the wind tucking at us; it was fall. Farther, the canyon walls that plunged into the water were red and yellow and gave the whole reservoir its name.

After the promontory we crossed into the real mountains and the pines, past the road to Spirit Lake, the place I learned to fish when I was seven. The forest along the back of the mountains is still thick and green, not ruined yet by the bark beetle. It is like a vast garden, a million pine trees, fir and ponderosa and piñon growing down to the road. This time of day and after three weeks of elk and deer hunting there would be no danger of game on the road. The first feeling in this place is always also the last: We're here. Everything else is gravy.

Nick could sense it too. "Where do you think Colin and Regan are?"

"North of Moab," I said, thinking of desolate Highway 191 as it cuts through the wasteland. I could imagine the connector to Interstate 70 and the fifty miles of that before the Loma turnoff. "No, they're farther. They'll cross into Colorado any time now and then climb over the summit." My son Colin and my brother Regan were driving today from Arizona and would meet us tonight at the cabin. "I hope we can get everything working," I said. "If the water is frozen, it will be a tough night."

I hadn't been to the cabin for a year and a half, and nothing was certain. Now driving with the sunlight holding, everything was still rinsed with optimism, but the bright edge of the short day was crumbling and the shadows of the thick tall pines cut at the roadway in a dizzying serrated shadow that wanted to put me to sleep. When we came to the junction for the lake and the lodge, Nick asked, "Are you hungry?"

"Sort of." We were both thinking of the Flaming Gorge Burger with bacon and cheese which had grown bigger in memory; it had been a while. It was always stunning to eat at the lodge, to sit in a chair and have the salty chili fries set before us on a plate. "But let's go set up and make a pot of spaghetti. They'll arrive sometime about eight."

"Root beer float," Nick said as we passed the turnoff.

"I'm going to get one tomorrow."

Now we drove up the long hill which was the eastern shoulder of the Uinta Mountains and at the top we followed the old highway south through the forest and felt the light change. This was a section of road I sometimes imagined when I could not sleep:

each frost heave, turnout, campground, the old corral fence. Nick eased the rental car down to the steel-pipe gate and I stood out in the shadow of the mountain. The sun was golden on the green hills behind us and the brook was talking where it crossed under the road. There has never been in my life a feeling of homecoming like this: unlocking the gate, swinging it wide for the car. When I'd secured the gate again, Nick drove us slowly along the gravel lane. We could see our little cabin from across the loop and it looked like a cabin in a story, a house a child would draw, the window, the door, the chimney. It was sweet not to hurry and Nick drove slowly so that he could point again to each place he'd had a bike accident, and the slash field, and how big the one hill had seemed twenty years ago and so small now. Our entry was marked with the sign my father cut out of stainless steel, the outline of a little moose along with the number 15, our number, set on the cedar post I'd dug in fifteen years ago. The long tree-lined driveway was grown with tall grass, which you want to see in a place, a thing which makes a house look abandoned and full of ghosts, and after driving on the gravel, our approach became very silent as Nick rolled down into the dooryard. The long woodpile lined one side of the grassy driveway, and I had to say again, "I've had every stick in that stack in my hand."

"I know," Nick said.

"Your kids will burn that wood." When I used to say that, Nick would come back, "I don't think so," or "Who are you talking about." But now we stood out of the car and he looked at the wall of stove-length logs and he said, "They probably will. I'll be sure to tell them what you did."

The cabin stood before us shuttered and silent like a big puzzle box we were about to open. There was work to do. Nick opened the front door and we went in and found the old good smell of firewood and burned coffee and the dry smell of the books. Nick opened all the blinds, copper Levelors. I remember the summer they came. Then we carried outdoor stuff: the ladder, the bicycles, the mower, the barbecue, the picnic table and the two butterfly chairs onto the tall grass behind the cabin. I turned on the electricity and the lights came on in the gloom and the radio roared with static and the fridge chugged and began to grind forward. It was forty years old.

Outside against the cabin wall I opened the small wooden lid over the waterworks and removed the insulating carpet and Nick and I looked at the blue valve that held our success. It was all as I had left it two years ago. I knelt and said, "Listen for it," and opened the valve turn by turn.

Nick ran inside and I called, "Anything?" I could not hear water running.

He appeared a minute later. "I can hear it filling the water heater, but no leaks under the sinks." I looked at the old blue valve and the piping in the ground. It was all working.

"Man," was all I could say, standing up. The feeling now was like being airborne. The meadow in front of the cabin was all yellow sage grass in shadow and the high friction of the air moving in the trees sounded like water over a spillway. The sun was still flat gold against the hills to the east and every time I looked up, walking back and forth from the car to the cabin, the line of shade had advanced. When you know your brother and your other son are on their way, it gives you great reason to assess your groceries again and plan out the spaghetti with thick tomato sauce and hot Italian sausage and big wedges of lettuce with stripes of blue cheese and burned toast and ginger ale. They would have now passed through Rangely, Colorado, through the oil field and the antelope, and they'd be driving into the last low angle of sunlight, the shadow of Regan's Blazer sixty yards behind them.

Nick went out and turned the car around, parking it nose-out in the dooryard, and then he came back in the cabin and found me sitting on the couch. I could feel the altitude a little. It was pleasant looking over the meadow though we knew there would be no deer tonight; they were all in the high country. In the summers, there were deer every night and one summer a moose had tried to head-butt our dear dog Max. Max's tags were in an antique mason jar on the bookshelf.

"How soon will they get here?" Nick said.

"Just after eight, if I know Regan," I said. "We'll go down and meet them."

"Do we need to cook now?"

"Not for an hour."

Nick took the kindling bucket and stood in the doorway. "I'm going to get some sticks and start a fire." We could feel the chill now that the sun was gone. He opened the closet and drew out a pillow from the shelf. "Why don't you lie down there?"

The pillow was perfect. I remembered the old pillowcase pattern from early in my marriage, and I laid out on the long couch and felt the blood beat in my knees while I listened to Nick break sticks and open the stove door and start the fire. I'd napped here a hundred times. Max would find me and lay his chin on my stomach for a minute before curling on the rag rug beside the old couch under the wagon-wheel ceiling light.

One November night twenty-five years ago my father and I put the woodburning stove in the fireplace. It was a great stove with a big glass door and the draft vents made lighting a fire easy and then, when engaged, it heated the whole room. Many times during storms when we'd lost power, Nick's mother would move all the pans to the woodstove top and make a pot of a soup she called slumgullion with knots of sausage and thick carrot coins and tomatoes, and she'd set the teakettle there for hot chocolate or tea. The cabin would fill with steam and sweet smells, and there'd come a moment late in the middle of the night in the dark with everyone asleep when the fridge would suddenly chug and the radio spit static and it was always an odd disappointment: the power was back on. We'd made soup and had an evening of card games in candlelight.

Now I lived four blocks from the Pacific Ocean and it was

fresh there, *fresh* being the word I used for the wet cold which captured many an evening at my cottage. The boys' mother had given me an electric mattress pad I used most nights. I had never lived near the coast, and it was a good place. I could hear the concussions of the surf from my room, and I had a good bicycle which I used every day. I once had a wife and two sons and a good dog, and now I had some tenacious plants and that bicycle. I had survived the pinching loneliness and now I was just alone and, I would admit, a little proud of it. I couldn't cook very well, but I got around that by cooking selectively or riding my bicycle out for Thai food or fish tacos or Mexican food or what there was. I carried a book and rode my bicycle to dinner here and there. Some nights when I rode home from the restaurants in the village, I rode down the middle of the empty streets and I breathed the fresh air deeply under the few stars and remembered being a boy in Utah. In some ways they were the same days: I was just independent, a boy with his bicycle, and now I was an old man alone who rode his bicycle everywhere he could.

I woke warm; the yellow flames fluttered in the glass stove front and it was dark. Nick was on the other couch looking at his iPhone in the gloom, his face lighted by the screen.

"Colin called. They left Vernal fifteen minutes ago."

"Okay then," I said, swinging my feet to the floor. I could feel my heart in my forehead, the altitude, and I let it subside before I tied my shoes.

"What's that?" I said, pointing where the big frying pan steamed on the stove.

"I just fried those sausages and cut them up into the spaghetti sauce."

"Smells good."

Nick adjusted the stove to low simmer and we went out into the cold mountain dark. The stars were coming out a million at a time and it was quiet in the meadow. If you stood still, you could sense the heavy layers of worlds above us. Nick pointed and pointed again at satellites sliding among the stars. I said: "That's your phone company making sure you have reception."

"Or UFOs," he said. We got in the car. "I should have warmed it up," Nick said. "Sorry."

"We're good," I said. "The radio stations will be popping up and maybe we can get something."

He drove us up the narrow grassy drive to the circle road and we crept the mile to the gate. I got out of the car and was clamped by the still cold as I wandered back of the car to pee. The stars piled on my shoulders and the great silence flooded the sky. It was a big night in the world and we were waiting for a rendezvous.

They'd been driving ten hours. Headlights came north and Nick, who had the best eyes of anyone I've ever met, said, "That's Regan's Blazer." I felt a tension let go in my back, and I climbed out again and unlocked the gate, waving at Regan's headlights and waving them through.

"Hello, boys," I said to Colin's open window.

"Hey, Dad."

"Go on to the cabin. We'll be right there."

The cabin was warm against the frozen evening, and Nick took two more logs for the stove when we went inside. You want to hear someone say, "Smells good," when you enter the only warm room in the mountains and Regan said it. "That's spicy spaghetti sauce." We were all standing around and Colin peeled off his fleece jacket and stored his gear on one side of the wood box and Regan began to put his gear away, and I boiled the water and dumped in the pasta and fired up the toaster with sourdough bread and unwrapped the butter and sliced four thick wedges off the cheddar. Nick pulled cases on the pillows and after a while we all sat at the old table in the big room. The silverware drawer was an inventory of the ages. The spoons were silver soup spoons from the Ambassador Club, gone thirty years now, forty, and the forks were heavy and perfect for the spaghetti. We ate and talked about the day's travel, and Regan said my chainsaw was in his car, and we decided not to do the tree work tomorrow, but to fish in the morning over by the state line at Antelope Flats. We had two full days and everyone was talking like you do when you're rich that way.

Nick banked the stove and we made a campsite of the room, pulling out the giant sofa beds and throwing down our sleeping bags. The old couch beds had always been noisy and tilted and crazy to sleep on, even when new, but we were all tired, which improves a bed. We groaned a little bit, I did, but it was all show and led the way to sleep. In the dark cabin every edge caught the orange glow of the pulsing fire.

The cabin percolator was a tall silver pot, elegant and sixty years old. It was the kind of thing that in 1958 looked like the distant future. When it first chugged, the water would start to flush into the glass topper, and the smell of coffee filled the room. It was cold now in the cabin in the morning, thirty-nine. I stepped carefully over all the gear and around the couches and out the front door. The day was like a slap; it was twenty degrees outside and the meadow was frosted white. Inside again, it felt warm. Nick had seen to the fire. I fried the big pan of bacon and dropped eight eggs into the hot grease. Colin was up and he loaded and reloaded the toaster. Regan sorted his gear and got his boots on and then he and Nick put the room away so we could do some good. Everyone was drinking lots of water from the old jelly-jar glasses and even so I could still feel the pressure in my head from the altitude. In ten minutes the kitchen table was wall-to-wall dishes and cups.

"Some coffeepot," Colin said. The percolator rocked and a column of bright steam shot from the spout. We already had the half-and-half on the table.

"We'll stop at the lodge and get licenses and drive across to the flats." We all dipped buttered toast into the thick milky coffee and drank orange juice out of paper cups as old as the boys.

"Sounds good," Regan said. "We'll see if that fish is over there." He went out and came back with the chainsaw and set it on the wood box. "You keep this thing clean as a violin," he said.

"I always did," I said. It was a good saw and I'd gone right by the book with it. We were here to cut down one big dead tree and to remove two that the Forest Service had already dropped. Their annual letter outlined what we needed to do to keep the lease. Colin picked up the saw and looked at me. "We can do this," he said.

"Tomorrow you'll be a lumberjack," I told him. It was a weird thing, passing the saw. I'd cut three hundred trees in twenty-five years, half of them standing dead from beetle kill. I'd loved the work in the summers, writing all morning and then a tree or two in the afternoon.

Nick put the big pot full of water on the stove to boil to do the dishes. I remembered seeing his mother there at the big steel sink bathing both boys at once, a naked little boy on each side. Outside the front window the meadow filled with light and now the first gold grass showed the sun. I knew this light as well as any in the world.

All along the drive down the mountain, the sun burned off the frost and the day opened into broad Indian summer. With the deer hunt concluded, the lodge parking lot was empty, a rare sight. With the few yellow leaves in the two maples, it made a lonely place. Summers there were always big pickups hauling pleasure boats. We already had a big bag of lunch in the car, so we bought licenses and candy bars and big cups of coffee. On the store bulletin board Colin studied the dozens of Polaroid photographs of all the big lake trout being held up by fishermen. On the little magazine rack, Nick saw the copy of a sports journal with my story in it and showed it to Regan; it was the story about a trip Regan and I had made three years before and a fish we did not catch.

I went out into the day. The sun on the mountain downslope and the layered plains of Wyoming in the distance filled me with hope. Nick came out of the store with our goods in a brown paper bag, then Regan with a twelve of Coca-Cola, and then Colin reading his fishing license.

The drive to Antelope Flats was a sinuous switchback descent to the big blue lake, past the marina and then over the silver bridge and then twenty miles per hour over the Flaming Gorge Dam. Now there were two highway patrol cars in the visitors' center parking lot, side by side, as part of Homeland Security. The reservoir here was always a stunning sight: the vast blue-water lake brimming against the huge curved dam and on the other side the red-rock canyon drawing down on the Green River way below. The road wound up and over through where the huge forest and brush fire burned ten years before, past the hamlet of Dutch John, and spooling out around the tendrils of the reservoir and between the rock gaps.

A mile before the Wyoming state line, Nick turned our car down the gravel road that runs down the broad ridge to Antelope Flats.

"Look for my hubcap," I said, because I always said it. That was five years ago or six. Nick drove twenty-five miles per hour down the broad washboard track, sun everywhere in the pale sage. The water was bluer than the sky. Across the huge expanse of the lake, we could see the village of Manila. As we neared the lake, we saw the little campground shelters, each with a cooking grill on a steel post.

"Do you even still have that car?" Regan said.

"No, but look for my hubcap."

Colin said, "There they are," and he pointed to the hill beyond the campground where the antelope stood in clusters.

There were more antelope along the top of the big empty parking lot by the boat ramp. They were all lying down and took little notice of us and we stopped and opened all the doors and organized our chairs and the lunch and then we geared up the fishing poles. They watched us for a while but none of the antelope moved. The air was still here and it was warm in the sun. "I'm going to sit in the car for a minute," I told them.

"You feel okay?" Nick asked.

"Good," I said. "I just want to rest. I'm glad to be here. Catch a fish."

Nick led Colin and Regan over the sage hill and down to the water. I'd first fished here forty-five years before on a trip with two friends the last week of high school. There had been no campsites then, just clearings in the sage; the dam and the reservoir were new. I had waded in my Levi's and later dried them by the fire, burning up a pair of good wool socks. It was warm in the car and I lowered the window a few inches; the sun in October was a blanket of its own.

The road from Manila, old Utah Route 43, used to connect to Antelope Flats. It was just one mile straight on the highway. Then the year I was sixteen, they finished the dam and the water backed up and now with this lake it was fifty miles to drive around. The old two-lane road was still down there somewhere under the lake. For years they used it as a boat ramp on both sides.

Sometimes a little nap is just the ticket and I don't know how long I slept, half an hour perhaps, and when I stood in the slanted daylight all the antelope were gone.

At the lake Nick had caught two fish. I loved this desolate place, the ridged mountains rising out of the water across the lake in a way I'd memorized years ago, their geologic layers tipped in a clear display, a place I saw once a year all these years and always unchanged. Regan had his sleeves rolled up in the sunshine and Nick came over to me with the sunblock. "Where's your hat?"

"In the car." I had forgotten it. "It's okay. We won't be here that long. It's October." I tied a swivel on my line.

Colin had his ball cap pulled low because of the late-day glare. The water was silver for two hundred yards.

Spin casting into the glittering lake seemed a perfect activity. We fished for an hour and Regan, Colin, and Nick each took a fish and Nick two more. I unpacked the lunch and handed out the ham sandwiches with the wedges of cheddar and just enough mayo to make the tomatoes slippery. "Too much pepper?" I asked Nick.

He smiled, my pepperhound. We had apple slices and salty chips and bottles of water. Regan and I propped our poles on the shoreline willows and sat in the gravel of the beach. The sun was at us pretty good. "I never caught a fish without the pole in my hand," Regan said, getting up and reeling in for another cast.

"I did," I said, "and I was unhappy about it. He ate the thing, some little fish, and I had to kill him." I reeled and reset my gear and put it out there thirty yards, the lure making a little sound when it hit: *loop!* I stood fishing until my legs ached, casting, and then I walked up and down the bank stretching.

"Three more casts," I said.

"Well, give it a good go," Colin said. "Because this is as far from home as we're going to get and when we turn for the cars, we're headed back."

I knew he was making fun of me, the thing I always said on our trips, but it didn't sound like mockery. It sounded like my son letting me know the news. I'd said it first on our backpacking trip into the Uinta Mountains, Island Lake, a ten-mile hike. It was a magnificent trip and when we fished Island Lake, a deer, a small doe, followed us like a dog. I'd never seen that before. We caught a lot of fish, putting back all we could, and finally we had to stop ourselves. When Nick had lifted the last cutthroat trout from the water, Colin had said, "That's ten we're keeping." The rocks we stood on were wet and Nick had looked at me to see if we should begin hiking back around to our camp. I said then, "Here we go. Every step now takes us toward home and your dear mother." We had a feast that night in the high mountain camp, frying the trout and dropping the filets into the thick trout chowder we made from leek and mushroom soup. How many times in a life do you have a day where the food is a match for the effort?

The sun fell over the broken red cliffs until we were looking at a world that was only silver and shadow, huge shifting sheets of glittering water. Regan said, "Oh oh," the way our father used to and I turned to see his rod bend and start to dance. Regan was walking along the sand being led by his pole.

"He's a big," Colin said.

"Is that the one?" I asked Regan.

"We'll see," he said. "Maybe he'll have your hubcap. Grab that net, Nick."

Regan walked straight back up the bank hauling his fish in, sliding it on the sand and Nick netted him, a silver rainbow sixteen inches.

"A big fat fish," Regan said. "Let's keep him and have a fry."

"Perfect," I said.

Colin pulled the stringer from the lake with the other fish on it and we knelt and began cleaning and rinsing the fish. Nick took a picture of Regan's fish.

"He's not the one, so we'll have to come back next year."

Nick's arms were sunburned. "What a day," he said. "This is like summer."

"We were lucky," I said.

"It's been like this every year, Nick," Regan said. "It's a secret, this last week in October." We were walking up the narrow winding dirt path over the first sage hump to the big parking lot in the high desert wilderness.

"Parking hasn't been a problem for the fishermen today," Regan said.

We lodged the fish in the cooler and Colin passed out some ginger ale and Regan grabbed his Coke. It was a pleasure being in the car, sitting, and Nick did a slow U-turn and eased onto the gravel road.

"Check," Colin said, pointing ahead.

"Slow down and they won't run," I said, and Nick slowed to five miles an hour and we drove through the middle of the loitering tribe of antelope.

As we drove back up the slope into the forest and along the mountain meadow, the evening wind was up and the temperature had dropped fifteen or twenty degrees and low clouds were moving in tatters around the mountains. We were all a little sunburned and we could feel the cold. "This could put a wrinkle in our plans to fish at East Canyon tomorrow," Regan said.

We stopped at the empty lodge and it was dark in the café; they hadn't turned the lights on in the late afternoon. We stood at the counter there long enough for the waitress who had been working at the desk over a pile of motel receipts to come pour Regan and me big coffees to go and set out all the creamers and spoons and we made a little mess and before I could strike, Nick nabbed a Coke for himself and Colin and put three fives on the counter and ushered us back into the changing day. "You are required to overtip in the territories," he said. Having the coffee was like treasure. Nick drove us up to 191 and then turned up the mountain. We had the windows up and Nick had the heater on.

Colin unlocked the gate, and as he bent to it, I wondered again at all of it, of the days before the great lake filled, before I met the boys' mother in Miss Porter's class, where we read *Silas Marner* and I read my poem after which she spoke to me in the hallway of the old Union Building, and two years before the two of us camped above Kamas with the smallest campfire in the history of Utah, and before I ever had sons and now they were grown and one was driving the car and the other swung the gate open and wheeled his arm and called, "Move it out, buddy!" and we drove through. I could see our little cabin in the trees.

The wind bit at us when we climbed out of the car. It was loud in the trees and the sky was banking up with slow-moving clouds in the deep dusk. Regan put the fish in the sink and rinsed them again, and we hauled firewood into the firebox. Any place out of the wind was warm and our sunburns bloomed when we went indoors.

"We'll bake these trout and my beautiful squash," I said. I looked at my watch. "In about two hours."

Nick banked the stove and in ten minutes the glass front was orange flames and the circulating fan was pumping out waves of heat, a blessing. Colin came in the front door and announced: "It's twenty-five degrees. How can that be?"

Everyone had staked a lamp and part of a couch. Nick was reading a stack of magazines and kids' books that he and Colin had read years ago including an utterly wrong-headed book called *Desperate Dan,* which I had bought in England thirty years before at the seven-story Foyles Bookshop by the Tottenham tube stop, and I had told their mother that I was buying *Desperate Dan* for her kids who were that day still eight years from being people. Regan was sorting his gear, and Colin was going through the floor of the closet to see if there were any boots he could wear should it snow.

"It's going to snow," Regan said. "Can you smell it?"

I'd just put the squash in the oven and could only smell the clean smell of the oven heating up after two years.

"What about these?" Colin said, pulling my old Chippewas out of the tangle of shoes.

"Try them on. They've been here ten years, fifteen. I caught a lot of fish in those shoes. I caught a ten-inch cutthroat on a bare hook in Dime Lake."

I stepped past him and went out the front door in the dark. By the light from the window I could read the thermometer on the porch post: twenty degrees. Now I could smell the dry frozen promise of snow and I could feel the low clouds. There wasn't a star available on such a night. Inside the window everything glowed in lamplight and the fire pulsed.

I peppered the fish and sliced lemon and sweet onion inside of each and laid them on the broiling pan to bake. Nick was reading sections from the scurrilous children's book aloud and laughing and Colin was walking around my father's wagon-wheel coffee table in his new shoes. It was the last Thursday night in October of a year in the mountain cabin with my brother and my sons.

We slathered the steaming squash with butter and we each had a piece big as a cake and a trout which fell apart on our plates and came cleanly away from the bones. The skin was crisp and salty and we ate it with our fingers. Nick wiped the plates with his wadded paper napkin and then slid them into the warm dishwater. Colin opened the couches and pulled out the beds.

"I'm sleeping with my head this way," Regan said, meaning toward the fire. We had already stood four round stove logs on the hearth to load in the middle of the night.

The old poker caddy was full of three kinds of mongrel chips all clay and older than me, fun to handle, and we divvied up four stacks and dealt the old blue Bicycle cards. Nick was talking poker, big blinds and small blinds and being on the button, and Regan said, "Let's just play cards," and so we did that: seven-card stud. Immediately Colin distinguished himself as a bluffer, ten if not twenty every turn, bet and raise, and he got clipped early but wouldn't stop. We played almost an hour. Nobody wanted any ice cream.

"Hey," I said, examining the king of diamonds in my hand. "One of these cards is torn."

"King of diamonds," Nick said.

"You didn't know that?" Regan said.

"A marked deck," I said. I lay the red king on the table.

"That black two has a folded corner," Colin said, and now he was all in and after a minute he showed a seven high, the lowest hand in the history of the cabin.

He stood up. "So close," he said.

Nick and I took a minute and sorted the old chips into the slots and boxed the damaged cards.

"I'll remember that king," I said.

"Wouldn't it be nice if we could," Regan said. "It'll take us an hour next time to figure it out."

"That time, we'll have a big blind and a small blind."

"I'm blind right now," Regan said. He'd put his glasses on the driftwood table beside this bedroll which he was struggling into. "Fire up the stove, Nick."

"I will." Nick was rolling out his bag on our bed. "Think we can get the game?"

"That's right," I said, "they're playing tonight in St. Louis."

It was an old black plastic General Electric AM/FM radio, a small console that had been my parents', in their first kitchen. Days it would get the station from Vernal that advertised auto glass all day long and played eighties songs, but nights the radio stations came out like stars and sizzled against each other, rising and fading.

"Let's see." I leaned against the couch and turned the AM dial up loud and began to drift through the stations.

"They all sound like the ball game," Colin said. And they did, each with its static roar. All the self-help and political bullies were on the clear stations and then just before ten on the dial, I got it. We heard the announcer say, ". . . coming to the plate . . ." and then it faded. I got scientific with my tuning, a whisker, a whisker and we could hear him in there under all the noise, but we couldn't hear what he was saying. I held the radio up and tilted it this way a little and then over there.

"You're a terrible antenna," Nick said. We had done this before on summer nights, the radio dance. Then I tuned in a channel so clear it sounded like someone talking at the table. "It's the UFO guy," Nick said. "Listen."

"What would it take," the baritone voice pleaded. "What would it take to believe they are among us? One convincing crash. Just one. And how many do we have?"

Somebody else, it must have been a caller, said, "I don't know. How many?"

"Fifty-two," the expert said. "We've got fifty-two documented crashes and there are still skeptics. Oh, it's a tough road, my friends."

Regan turned his lamp off and now the cabin was dark except for the fluttering orange glow from the stove fire. I was still holding out the radio.

"Well, let me ask," the caller said. "If these extraterrestrials are so advanced, why are they always crashing?"

The expert didn't miss a beat: "Oh man, come on. Do you think they're sending their best equipment to this planet? They're working with some off-brand airships; it only makes sense."

"Makes sense to me," Regan said.

After Nick and Colin saw the alien visitor movie *Fire in the Sky,* when they were nine and ten, Nick would not sleep outside on the trampoline anymore. His mother had asked him why not, and he said, "It's too easy to get us. We're like snacks on a plate."

I put the radio back on the shelf by the boys' old Lego constructions: jet fighters and battleships. I could feel my forehead sunburned. I was tired in the way you are when a day uses you and it felt good; the room in the muffled light was good.

In the morning, despite the thick gray cloud cover, it was only nine degrees outside. Nick fired up the stove and turned the blower on high while I fried up the bacon and burned a pan of hash browns. We could feel the wind working at the cabin and behind Regan out the front window, I saw the dots commence as it started to snow.

"You guys can tell me how it was at East Canyon," Regan said, stirring cream into his coffee. He was using the white enamel mug we called spidercup, which when you told the story, it made you shudder. "I'll be here reading a book. That place, that trip was as cold as I'll ever want to be."

We'd had a trip four years ago in such wind and snow at that reservoir that I had trouble opening the car doors, and Regan went out to the whitecap water and caught a fish. When he came back up, his eyelashes were iced up. We have a picture somewhere.

"We could do that tree work unless the snow gets too heavy."

Colin had folded his bacon into the sourdough toast, pressed it with his big hands and took a bite. He nodded at me. "Let's do it and learn about this saw."

We laid the saw out on newspapers on the kitchen table and I went through it with Colin. Nick said from the couch, "Teach him and if I need to know it, he'll tell me."

We disassembled the saw and Regan said, "I can't believe how clean that thing is." There were the caps, oil and gas, and there was the trigger and the choke. Regan gave one of the new sharp chains from the bag to Colin. They were lightly oiled and had been in storage for three years. Regan pinched one of the small blades and held it up for Colin. "This is the cutting edge. Set it on the drive rail so this is forward." I stepped back. It was funny about the saw; it was hard not to have it in my hands, but now I knew it was long gone.

"He's got it," Regan said. "Let's do some good."

Nick was wrapping his scarf on and he had his gloves in his hand. We had a lot of gear hanging from the ceiling wagon wheel to dry and I took my jacket off a hanger and pulled it on.

In the meadow, the wind had subsided and the crazy snowflakes were crossing wildly as they descended. It would last all day. We had two hours before it got too deep to work these trees. I checked the toolshed and found the mixed gas and the bar oil right where I put them two years ago. I showed both bottles to Regan knowing he'd appreciate my providence. Colin pulled his glove off to handle the gas and he pulled an envelope out of his back pocket and turned to me and said, "Oh yeah, Mom sent this for you." I recognized her blue stationery and I put the letter in my front pocket, so it wouldn't get wet. We just stood back and let Colin fill the reservoirs in the saw and then adjust the choke and pull the starter rope. He was a big man and made the saw look much lighter than I ever did. It snorted alive on the third pull. Colin stood with the idling saw, adjusting the fuel feed with the trigger. When the rpm dropped to a hum, I said, "You're good to go." There was one fifty-foot jack pine standing dead with its cowl of rusty branches, and he knelt to it. I showed him to make one front cut horizontal to the ground and perpendicular to the fall line, then the angled wedge cut, which he did in less than a minute, kicking out the wedge with his boot easily. We all stepped clear and he ran the saw in the back of the tree and it tilted sweetly, silently in the falling snow and fell alongside of the driveway. Colin looked at me and we talked for a moment about how to limb it up, cutting each branch at the trunk, no hurry. The three of us stood back and watched him walk up the tree, left right left right, sending the limbs into the grass. Nick took more pictures.

"He looks like he's been doing this for a while," Regan said. And it was true. Colin was now bucking up the log, cutting the trunk into stove-length pieces, and we hauled the logs to the old woodpile, the bright yellow ends sharp against the gray wood. The whole job, something that would have taken me two hours, took twenty minutes and we had nothing but a stump and two piles of slash.

There were two more trees, old giants that had been cut down by the power company last summer, and which we'd been instructed to remove. Colin limbed both big trees and we made haystacks of the branches and then he started cutting each log into lengths. They were each almost the diameter of the length of his blade but he didn't force it, letting the saw find its way, and he finished the last tree in half an hour.

We were all red-faced in the snow and Colin turned off the saw and carried a log down to the stack with his other arm.

"What now?" he said, and we all felt it. We wanted more. We needed another tree standing dead or leaning or even downed, but there were none. The trees towering above us had been knee-high twenty years ago. A tree that Nick replanted as a seedling was now thirty feet tall at the corner of the meadow. It was the old feeling: The day is young and we're good for it, and I laughed. The snow was still general, but we could see it wouldn't trap the vehicles or snow us in.

Inside, Nick heated a big pot of Dinty Moore stew, cutting one of our onions into it and simmering it until the brown gravy bubbled, and then he imbedded bread-and-butter pickles in some grilled cheese sandwiches which he fried until they smoked in the pan. The fire had slumped while we were outside and I opened the woodstove and laid in three fresh logs and I closed the glass door and it filled with bright fire. With the fire stoked we ate salty vinegar chips at the table, crunching on the sandwiches, dunking the corners into the potato-thick stew, drinking ice-cold ginger ale. We had one more day.

After lunch, Colin cleaned the saw, taking it apart and wiping it clean and storing it in newspapers in an open cardboard box on the closet shelf. Nick stared out at the snow in the meadow. The snow itself now was not flakes but a steady dusting.

"What do you want?" Nick looked at me. "You want to go for a walk?"

"Yeah, Dad," Colin said. "Let's go. You can show us this place."

Regan had already pulled his boots off and he had his plastic tray of flies on his lap, sorting them for tomorrow. We knew as soon as he lifted his feet onto the wagon-wheel table, he would be asleep. "Have fun, boys."

It was funny going out into the great day. I wasn't sure I was ready.

We walked around the cabin and already the places we had tracked up were covered with snow, the slash piles snowy heaps. The boys would have to haul all those sticks next summer.

"Up the dead end," I said. "And then across the marmot ranch and into the trees."

At the top of the spur road, I led up across the rock spill where all the marmots lived in the summer and they were certainly back in their chambers now. At the far side, I slipped and knocked my knee on the last rock. Colin grabbed my arm and held me up.

"You okay?"

"I'm good." There were no tracks, but across and into the trees, we merged onto a game trail already marked by two deer or three, fresh tracks in the snow. When we were in the trees, Nick said from the rear, "This is just a little weird."

"Not really," I said.

When we approached the big red sandstone boulders, I turned and said, "Do you know where you are? Can you find this place?"

We looked back, marking the grove of trees.

"It's not even half a mile."

"Got it," Colin said.

"We've been here before," Nick said. He was standing next to me and then closer and he bumped me like he always did.

"A couple times," I said. "Remember when we saw the coyotes, the mother and the pups, and we had to stop so Max wouldn't catch the scent?"

"Right," Nick said. "These are those big red-rock rooms." We walked the corridor between the rocks each as big as a bus, and I stopped. It was strange to be here in the snow. Once, twenty years ago, I'd surprised forty elk here and they'd stood and disappeared like vapor. That was when I knew the spot. Now it was quiet in the space between the rocks and the snow fell silently in the odd shelter.

"This is it," I told the boys. "Stand up there on those rocks and let me go." You could see our breath in the spotty snow, the gray afternoon. Nick had come up and grabbed hold of me, just a hug.

"Good idea," Colin said and grabbed me, such big men. "You want us to mark it? Should I make a steel tag, your initials?"

"No need," I said. "You guys will know. That's enough."

"Good deal," Colin said. "We've got it. It's a great place." My son looked at me. "You want to say something? You're the guy with words."

"Not really," I said. "It's sweet to be here." Then I added, "You boys."

"Let's go back," Nick said. "We'll fish that lake tomorrow, but every step from here starts to take us home."

"You lead," I told him. "So I know you know the way."

Reading *The O. Henry Prize Stories 2016*

The Jurors on Their Favorites

Our jurors read the twenty O. Henry Prize stories in a blind manuscript. Each story appears in the same type and format with no attribution of the magazine that published it or the author's name. The jurors don't consult the series editor or one another. Although the jurors write their essays without knowledge of the authors' names, the names are inserted into the essay later for the sake of clarity. —LF

Molly Antopol on "Train to Harbin" by Asako Serizawa

From the story's opening line—"I once met a man on the train to Harbin"—I was captivated. And by the end of the first paragraph, I was entirely invested in the narrator, an old man who had once been a doctor in Japan. I love Asako Serizawa's prose—direct and reflective, lyrical and unshowy—and the utter authority with which she writes about this time and place and her protagonist's profession: bacteriological work at a research unit in Pingfang during World War II, just as his country goes to war with China. For all of the research Serizawa must have done, I never once felt it, was never once reminded that I was reading a story—instead, I was utterly swept up in the world she had created.

Weeks after finishing the story, lines and descriptions (but never scenes—stunningly, this story manages to feel propulsive and immediate even though it's told almost entirely in narration) kept coming back to me. The narrator's poignant relationship with his son, Yasushi. A horrifying depiction of prisoners strapped to planks and gagged with pieces of leather. The narrator's arrival in Pingfang, "still festive with wealthy Russians and a few well-placed Chinese."

For such a short piece, "Train to Harbin" feels epic in its exploration of history, war, loyalty, and trauma. It is also intimate, raw and reflective, as the author examines the psychological effects the narrator's work in China have on him years later. This is a haunting, visceral, and ethically nuanced story, and I was struck by how Serizawa forces her narrator to wrestle with moral consequence on a deeply philosophical level. And by looking so intensely into the deeds of his past, the pain and remorse that define him ultimately become the vehicles that drive the story forward.

In the end, what amazed me most was the story's structure. Rather than telling the story chronologically, Serizawa lets the chaotic nature of memory govern the way the piece unfolds. As the narrator of this heartbreaking and gorgeous tale tells us, "Perhaps it is simply the mind, which, in its inability to accept a fact, returns to it, sharpening the details, resolving the image, searching for an explanation that the mind, with its slippery grasp on causality, will never be able to find."

. . .

Molly Antopol grew up in Culver City, California. Her debut story collection, *The UnAmericans*, won the New York Public Library's Young Lions Fiction Award and a 5 Under 35 Award from the National Book Foundation, was longlisted for the National Book Award, and was a finalist for the PEN/Robert W. Bingham Prize for Debut Fiction, the Barnes & Noble Discover Great New Writers Award, the National Jewish Book Award, the California Book Award, and others. She's the recipient of a Radcliffe Institute Fellowship at Harvard and a Stegner Fellowship at Stanford, where she currently teaches. She lives in San Francisco.

Peter Cameron on "Winter, 1965" by Frederic Tuten

I'm usually very wary of stories about writers, and a story about a writer writing a story is really pushing my boundaries. But I loved "Winter, 1965." Perhaps it was the setting of New York City half a century ago, evoked with such detail and immediacy, that charmed me: Another world, another time, but also achingly real and familiar. The way a snowstorm stills and softens the city is timeless, and its evocation here is beautiful, hushing and finally almost burying the story in its silence. And despite the winter chill, I liked the story's warmth and generosity, its wealth of character and lack of villains, its deft compression of time. As a reader, I felt gently welcomed into this story, and well attended to.

I had exactly the opposite response to another story I admired in this collection, "Slumming" by Ottessa Moshfegh. Although not my favorite, this story startled me. I was impressed by its uncompromising honesty and its scrupulous avoidance of pandering to the reader's sympathies. "Slumming" stuck with me in an unsettling way, and it was good to be moved in such a different direction. It reminded me that stories can work in infinite ways. That the possibilities for good stories are endless.

. . .

Peter Cameron was born in Pompton Plains, New Jersey. He is the author of two collections of short stories (*One Way or Another* and *Far-flung*) and six novels, including his latest, *Coral Glynn*. His novels *The Weekend*, *The City of Your Final Destination*, and *Someday This Pain Will Be Useful to You* have been made into films. His short fiction has been published in *The New Yorker*, *The Paris Review*, *The Yale Review*, and elsewhere. He is the recipient of fellowships from the National Endowment for the Arts and the John Simon Guggenheim Memorial Foundation. Cameron lives in New York City.

Lionel Shriver on "Irises" by Elizabeth Genovise

Ordinarily, I'd resist the conceit that Elizabeth Genovise asks us to accept in "Irises": that our narrator is an unborn fetus whose mother is planning an abortion. On the face of it, this premise sounds either precious, or politically partisan; perhaps we should brace ourselves for a pointed pro-life morality tale. (Typically, given the polarization of this issue, we pro-choice readers resist having our sleeves tugged.) Yet I didn't rebel at that first line, "I am eight weeks in the womb and my life is forfeit," owing purely to the elegance of that second phrase. "My life is forfeit" is such an artful, subtly archaic expression of impending doom, and so efficiently introduces the fact that the mother does not cherish this pregnancy and intends to be quit of it, that my defenses dropped just like that.

I was not disappointed as the story unfolded. The quality of the prose is unflaggingly high, while the style is cut-glass clear. The sentences that stand out as unusually fine do so because they marry formal grace with trenchant content. The mother's husband, Dan Ryan, "shares his name with a Chicago highway that is always thick with cars coming and going to work, and like the highway he is predictable, practical, a man of straight lines." Later in the same paragraph, Dan's frustrated wife, Rosalie, forced to leave behind an exhilarating life as a dancer due to a knee injury and now facing unwelcome motherhood-cum-relocation from Chicago to a nowheresville farm in Tennessee, "sees the remainder of her life in a flash, like a child's flip book, the pages rushing forward and the pencil-thin illustrations slimming down her choices as the years go by." The metaphor is apt and evocative. With Dan, "She is docile with him, a sweetness emerging from some part of herself she hadn't formerly known. It alternately pleases and sickens her." That's in some ways very simple writing, but its meaning is dense, rich, complex.

Though their interests conflict, all three principals in this drama draw on the reader's sympathy: the stifled wife, the good-hearted but limited husband, and the wife's passionate, talented lover Joaquin, a composer who plays the piano for the little girls' dance class she teaches in lieu of being able to perform. We identify with Rosalie's yearning for her more stimulating past—a past that her husband finds suspicious, alien, as much a rival as the lover about whose existence he is innocent—even as we know as well as she does that she can never return to it. Her aspiration to run off to a New Age West Coast cooperative with Joaquin seems unrealistic, and we credit her for the insight that "the singularity of his genius would only cause problems in a commune."

The cuckolded husband works hard, tries to please, and doesn't deserve his wife's betrayal. Especially when getting cold feet right before he and Rosalie have arranged to flee together, Joaquin is sympathetic also. Lost in a museum, he stumbles across an exhibit about the development of the human fetus and suddenly takes on the enormity of what they are about to do. For inevitably in a story whose narrator is an unborn child on the way to the medical waste bin, we're torn about Rosalie's and Joaquin's intentions to dispatch the baby. We're queasy about Rosalie's reasoning, which seems a bit cavalier, just as her conviction that an abortion and a new life with Joaquin in a commune will ease her career disappointment seems delusional.

The story's setup is classic, of course, and has a Chekhovian character, as in some ways does the prose. Yet neither the plot nor the writing feels hackneyed. The tension "Irises" explores is eternal: between the solid, reliable, repetitive life that Rosalie would reject and the riskier, more exciting, but perhaps impractically romantic life that she would embrace with her lover. (Indeed, I wrote a novel about that duality: *The Post-Birthday World*.) Besides, this story takes one of those sudden turns at the end that freshens our scenario, rescues the premise from any danger of cutesiness or political advocacy, and takes advantage of one of the most satisfying techniques that the short-story form affords: the dizzying fast-forward.

More than one tale in this collection commanded my admiration, and my runners-up included "Exit Zero" by Marie-Helene Bertino, "Safety" by Lydia Fitzpatrick, "Slumming" by Ottessa Moshfegh, and "Winter, 1965" by Frederic Tuten—all hugely enjoyable. But Elizabeth Genovise's contribution crossed the finish line by a nose. Both as a whole and line by line, "Irises" is stunningly accomplished.

Born and raised in North Carolina, Lionel Shriver has resided primarily in the United Kingdom since 1987. Shriver is best known for the *New York Times* bestsellers *So Much for That* (a finalist for the 2010 National Book Award and the Wellcome Trust Book Prize) and *The Post-Birthday World* (*Entertainment Weekly*'s Book of the Year and one of *Time*'s top ten for 2007), as well as the international bestseller *We Need to Talk About Kevin*. The 2005 Orange Prize winner, *Kevin* was adapted for an award-winning feature film starring Tilda Swinton in 2011. Both *Kevin* and *So Much for That* have been dramatized for BBC Radio 4. Shriver's work has been translated into twenty-eight languages. She writes for *The Guardian*, *The New York Times*, London's *Sunday Times*, the *Financial Times*, *The Washington Post*, and *The Wall Street Journal*, among other publications. Her more recent novel is *Big Brother*. "Kilifi Creek," which is included in *The O. Henry Prize Stories 2015*, won the BBC National Short Story contest in 2014. She lives in London, England, and Brooklyn, New York.

Writing *The O. Henry Prize Stories 2016*

The Writers on Their Work

Wendell Berry, "Dismemberment"

My story "Dismemberment" is about Andy Catlett's recovery after losing his right hand to a corn picker in 1974. That story was told in a different way, with a different interest, in my small novel, *Remembering*. The question here is whether or not this story is worth telling twice. My own belief, supported by much local conversation, is that a story worth telling is worth telling any number of times.

Wendell Berry was born in Newcastle, Kentucky, in 1934. He is an essayist, poet, farmer, environmental activist, and fiction writer, and has received fellowships from the Guggenheim, Lannan, and Rockefeller foundations and the National Endowment for the Arts, and also the T. S. Eliot Prize, the Aiken Taylor Award, and the John Hay Award of the Orion Society. He is a 2013 Fellow of the American Academy of Arts and Sciences, and has received many prizes and awards in recognition of his long and fruitful career. Berry lives with his family on a farm in his native Henry County, Kentucky.

Marie-Helene Bertino, "Exit Zero"

When my father passed away a few years ago, I found myself in the same position my character Jo does—on my hands and knees, cleaning out a freezer. I had joined the sad club of people who've lost parents, and this distinction, though dubious, made me privy to new information. Ideas about life I had suspected I now knew, and ideas I knew I double knew. I realized my relationship with my father was not, as I'd have guessed, over, but that it continued in a way that felt more intimate. Like someone whispering in your ear.

What I double knew was that there are only so many chances to spontaneously buy a ticket to Paris. So a few weeks after the funeral, I did just that. Thinking back on it, in a place I keep hidden even to myself, I hoped I'd find him there.

I spent ten days walking the Seine but he never showed.

On my last afternoon in Paris, I visited the Musée de Cluny. For the sake of those who haven't read "Exit Zero," I won't name the famous mythological animal I found on the tapestries there. I sat in the room with her for over an hour, casting out my imagination. By the time I returned home, I knew I wanted to write a story that featured her, but I'd have to upend the expectation her presence would bring. Muddy her up a bit. That particular creature enjoys a reputation for being pure and docile, which wouldn't do for what I wanted to say.

What did I want to say?

Fathers can be hard to believe in. Family can be anywhere. Grief, like New Jersey, is a strange place, but that doesn't mean it's without magic. Death, pain, and violence—trauma, essentially— can sometimes act as a portal we do not see as we are passing through.

I suppose I too passed through a portal after my father died, one that delivered me to Paris, and to _____. She gave me a lot of laughter and comfort during a complicated time, not to mention the first scatologically focused scene I'd ever written.

I said my father never showed in Paris. Thinking back on it now, maybe he did.

Marie-Helene Bertino was born and raised in Philadelphia. She is the author of the collection *Safe as Houses*, winner of the Iowa Short Fiction Award and named Outstanding Collection by the Story Prize; and the novel *2 A.M. at the Cat's Pajamas*, a Barnes & Noble Discover Great New Writers Pick. A Pushcart Prize recipient, she has received fellowships from the MacDowell Colony and the Center for Fiction in New York City. She lives in Brooklyn, New York.

Ron Carlson, "Happiness"

I was on a fishing trip one recent fall with my son. We were on our way to a mountain cabin to meet up with my other son and my brother. We were the only vehicle on Wyoming Route 414, driving past Lonetree, a road which every time I'm on it fills my heart with the ages. I was first there with my father sixty years ago. In October the sun had fallen away but was still trying, and the lonely world lay empty. We had the radio on and the announcer in a football game said that the team had good field position. Seriously, that was it. I thought we had good field position. To the north we could see a river wandering between the cottonwoods and haystacks in the fields. I had a feeling under my ribs and I realized I was happy. The affection for the moment took and I began writing the story when I got home the next week, wanting to stay close enough to each small event that I could feel each again in my ribs. The ending of the story was a surprise to me.

Ron Carlson was born in Logan, Utah. His most recent novel is *Return to Oakpine*. His short stories have appeared in *Esquire*, *Harper's*, *The New Yorker*, *The Atlantic Monthly*, and other journals, as well as *The Best American Short Stories*, *The O. Henry Prize Stories*, the *Pushcart Prize*, *The Norton Anthology of Short Fiction*, and others; they have been performed on National Public Radio's *This American Life* and *Selected Shorts*. He teaches at the University of California, Irvine.

Adrienne Celt, "Temples"

A few years ago I reread Vladimir Nabokov's novel *Pnin* and became interested in the way Nabokov disguises his first-person narrator as a third-person voice for most of the novel, telegraphing the true point of view only in small breaths. I also (more simply) loved the character Timofey Pavlovich Pnin, who is so vulnerable and doughty—indeed, noble—despite the tyranny of the voice telling his story and trying to make him look like a fool. One of my interests, then, in writing "Temples," was to play with the idea of hiding a lovely person behind a less lovely speaker, and in that way playing with audience expectations of whom to be closest to, whom to trust.

Of course, as is the way with most fiction, the story didn't exactly stick to the plan. (Most stories, after all, are bigger on the inside.) For instance, I couldn't have guessed, at the outset, how important the church would be to these characters, or how the narrator's voice would bleed into the first person whenever she began relinquishing control. But mostly, I was surprised by how much I ended up loving my judgmental narrator—quite as much as her aunt Marjorie, perhaps because the narrator ended up being the really fragile one in this case.

Adrienne Celt was born and raised in Seattle, Washington. She's the author of the novel *The Daughters*, and her short fiction and comics have appeared in numerous publications, including *Esquire*, *Kenyon Review*, *Epoch*, *Prairie Schooner*, *Bat City Review*, *Puerto del Sol*, and *The Rumpus*. The recipient of residencies and awards from the Ragdale Foundation, the Virginia G. Piper Center for Creative Writing, the Willapa Bay AiR, and the Esquire and Aspen Writers' Foundation Short Short Fiction Contest, Celt lives in Tucson, Arizona.

Diane Cook, "Bounty"

The idea for the story originated with the simple desire to look at the last two neighbors after an end of the world flood. Neighborliness and the forced interaction of neighbors is a thing I've always been intrigued by.

I wanted the neighbors to hold differing opinions as to how to live out the end of days. I love Robert Frost and especially "Mending Wall." The neighbor in the poem likes doing what has always been done and the speaker has a bit of disdain for that. A flood that wipes away all of our man-made boundaries can be a stand-in for the loss of the fence that makes good neighbors in the poem. It puts a familiar pressure onto two people living out an unfamiliar nightmare.

But this was all in the beginning. An idea, a scenario, a voice to get started. Early ideas just give you a framework. They aren't a story. Once I began writing, I discovered more of what I really wanted to write about and I got to a place with the writing where I was surprising myself with things. For instance, with Gary.

I love Gary. He was not a planned character, but he must have shown up when I lost steam just playing around with the scenario and the voice. Gary brings out the humanity in the narrator. And he brings out the real conflict, which isn't between the neighbors but within the narrator. Companionship or survival, our narrator ponders. Which is more important? That quandary has no stakes without Gary. To me, Gary is the star of the show. He presses on the narrator to change, but it's Gary who changes.

Last note of possible interest: the narrator is a man. A number of readers have gotten this wrong, but I think it's fairly obvious. You be the judge.

Diane Cook is the author of the story collection *Man V. Nature*, which was a finalist for the Believer Book Award and the Los Angeles Times Art Seidenbaum Award for First Fiction, received Honorable Mention for the Pen/Hemingway Award, and was longlisted for the Guardian First Book Award. She was awarded the 2012 Calvino Prize for fabulist fiction. Her stories have appeared in *The Best American Short Stories,* and in *Tin House, Granta,* and elsewhere. She was a producer for the radio show *This American Life.* She lives in Oakland, California.

Robert Coover, "The Crabapple Tree"

Began with the desire to set the Grimm brothers story, "The Juniper Tree," on the American prairie. It's a story about cannibalism, murder rewarded, brutality of the "good" people, punishment by millstone, and a blasé acceptance of the extraordinary, which seemed about right for such a setting. The narrator is an old Midwestern girlfriend of mine.

Robert Coover was born in 1932, in Charles City, Iowa. He attended Southern Illinois University, Indiana University, and the University of Chicago. His many awards include the William Faulkner Foundation Award for *The Origin of the Brunists*, REA Award for the Short Story, Lannan Foundation Fellowship, Clifton Fadiman Medal for *Pricksongs & Descants*, and Independent Press Storyteller of the Year, 2006. His most recent book is *The Brunist Day of Wrath*. He divides his time between Providence, Rhode Island, and Barcelona.

.   .   .

Joe Donnelly, "Bonus Baby"

The only way I ever finish anything is if I can feel the guillotine of a deadline hanging over my neck. As for "Bonus Baby," I promised my wife I'd finish it before the birth of our daughter, Olivia, as a gift for her. True to form, I read a just-finished draft to my wife just after her epidural kicked in following twelve hours of back labor.

"Bonus Baby" is obviously a loaded title. A somewhat anachronistic baseball reference, the phrase also denotes to me a late and grateful passage into parenthood. For Olivia, I suppose I wanted to commemorate how her parents bonded over watching the Dodgers and listening to Vin Scully. Part of our connection was a mutual affinity for a pitcher who had old-school style, obvious intelligence, and a deep talent he couldn't quite master. The story was inspired by imagining what it might be like to be alone on that mound attempting to come to terms with oneself and the game of baseball at the same time. As I got into it, the story showed it could contain a lot more than the game itself . . . much like the game itself.

Joe Donnelly was born in Syracuse, New York. He is a journalist and fiction writer. He lives in Los Angeles, California.

Rebecca Evanhoe, "They Were Awake"

My MFA fiction cohort happened to be all female. Right away, the six of us felt a kinship with one another. It was incredibly good fortune to be grouped with these women, all of them smart, talented, honest, and kind. We had potlucks together, and after one where we talked about our dreams, I wrote most of "They Were Awake."

Like us, the six women in the story met up for a potluck, and like us, they shared stories in turn. (Of course, the story's tone is darker than our lovely potluck was.) As they sit around the table, eating and describing their recent dreams, the conversation creates little cycles of dread and relief—dread that something bad is about to happen, and relief that it never manifests. What keeps the tension cycling is the women themselves. They talk eagerly, they listen earnestly, and they spur one another on. But they also make one another uncomfortable and pull back from the unsettling dreams they're sharing, returning to affirmations and the food and wine at hand.

The best stories render something truthful about the human experience, good or bad. This instinct to resist, to gloss over terrible things, felt true to me, and it also felt honest to expose the kinds of disturbing events—nightmares—that threaten women disproportionately. The women in the story are safe for the duration of the dinner party, but as they peel off and reenter the world alone, they are susceptible to anything the world can dream up.

Rebecca Evanhoe was born in Wichita, Kansas. Her stories have appeared in *Gulf Coast*, *Bat City Review*, *New World Writing*, *Gigantic*, *NOON*, and elsewhere. She earned her MFA from the University of Florida, and lives in Gainesville, Florida.

Lydia Fitzpatrick, "Safety"

I'm a big believer in the "write what you're afraid of" advice, and, for me, that's usually an organic process. As the story evolves, my fears surface, and my job is not to shy away from them. With "Safety" that relationship was reversed: it began as a fear. I started the story just after the one-year anniversary of the shooting at Sandy Hook Elementary School, when that tragedy was very much in the public eye. I'd just had a baby, and all of a sudden, my fears involved this new person and the safety of her current self, over which I had some control, and her future self, over which I have way less control. I didn't have any connection to the victims at Sandy Hook, but I couldn't stop thinking about them, and this story was the best way I could find to express those fears.

I also used the snippets I remember from elementary school as a way into the story, and especially into the children's interiority. The first line came from this memory: The gym in my school had skylights and high ceilings, and all this dust floating up there in the light, and I remember being little, lying on my back during the wind-down, staring up into space, and feeling completely relaxed and safe. I wrote the first couple lines hoping to tap into that emotion and transfer it to the reader before it's broken by the sound of the gunshot.

Lydia Fitzpatrick was a Stegner Fellow at Stanford University from 2012 to 2014, and a fiction fellow at the Wisconsin Institute of Creative Writing. Her fiction has appeared in *Glimmer Train*, *Mid-American Review*, and *Opium*. She received her MFA from the University of Michigan, where she was a Hopwood Award winner. She's also received support from the Elizabeth George Foundation. She lives in Los Angeles, California.

Elizabeth Genovise, "Irises"

Two years before I wrote "Irises," my mother took me to the old Fine Arts Building in downtown Chicago, where she had taken dancing lessons before beginning her career as a ballerina. A year later, I was wandering the city alone, remembering certain chapters of my own life and questioning where to go next. I came back to Tennessee and dug up an ancient draft of a story about a woman deciding whether to abort her child. Chicago was still vivid in my mind, as was this unborn child and her young mother, but someone was missing. He turned out to be Joaquin. I fell as much in love with his character as Rosalie did, and the story took on newfound complexity. I was so deeply lost in the story that the ending surprised me, though it shouldn't have. Regret intertwined with revelation is a place many of my characters find themselves on the final page.

Elizabeth Genovise grew up in Villa Park, Illinois, and studied in the MFA program at McNeese State University. She is the author of two short-story collections—*A Different Harbor* and *Where There Are Two or More*. She lives near Knoxville, Tennessee.

Charles Haverty, "Storm Windows"

The summer I turned twelve, my family moved into a big old brick house not unlike the Detweilers', and the putting up and taking down of storm windows became a ritual even more perilous than the one described by Lionel. These windows were massive, and every spring and fall, my daredevil father would haul them up or down an impossibly high ladder, like Jack climbing the beanstalk, while I stood at the bottom, looking on in terror, "spotting" him. In time, this memory (or its mythification) rubbed up against a remnant of an earlier Lionel story—a version of what became the front end of the second act of this one (the pumpkin carving, the phone call, the flight to Chicago, the hospital burlesque)—and spawned a pattern of near misses, real and imagined, which I called "Father's Death in Three Acts and an Epilogue." Though that title didn't survive the first draft, it suggested a structure that did.

Charles Haverty was born in Flushing, Queens, and grew up on Long Island and in the far west suburbs of Chicago. He is the author of the collection *Excommunicados*, which won the 2015 John Simmons Short Fiction Award. His stories have appeared in *Agni*, *The Gettysburg Review*, *Ecotone*, *Colorado Review*, *Salamander*, and elsewhere. He lives in Lexington, Massachusetts.

. . .

Geetha Iyer, "The Mongerji Letters"

There is a fascinating article in *The New York Times* about glacier mice—little moss balls that roll across Arctic ice flats, within
which live tiny animals like springtails, water bears, and nema-
todes. The discovery captivated me. I must have shared the article
with friends and family, but what I really wanted to do was seize
someone off the street and place a little glacier mouse in their
hands and say—*"Look, look closer, isn't this wonderful?"* I wanted
to keep a glacier mouse under a bell jar and tend to it like a house-
plant. I wanted to put the entire polar cap under a protective
bubble just so these delicate micro-ecosystems could live on.

Instead, I wrote the first letter of "The Mongerji Letters."
Almost immediately, I realized that by using an epistolary structure, I could re-create what I found most compelling about the
glacier mice article in the first place—the tactile desire to hold a
whole world in my hand. Letters became literal vessels of experience, the words within coming to life.

And the thing is, this is always true. When you read fiction, to
make sense of words you must enact them inside your head. Even
if it's just for the briefest of moments, you have to believe what
you read to understand it. The great joy of writing "The Mongerji Letters" came from pushing and playing with that idea. As it
grew, it also became a way to explore the tension between protection and possession—something that impacts social relationships
as much as it does the natural world.

Geetha Iyer was born in India and grew up in the United Arab
Emirates. She received an MFA in Creative Writing and Envi-
ronment from Iowa State University. Her fiction and poetry has
appeared in journals including *Gulf Coast*, *Ninth Letter*, *The Missouri Review Online*, and *Mid-American Review*. She's been the
recipient of the James Wright Poetry Award, the Calvino Prize,
and the Gulf Coast Fiction Prize, and has attended the Bread
Loaf Writers' Conference. She lives in Panama City, Panama.

David H. Lynn, "Divergence"

This story, like so many of mine, came about as a collision, as it were, between different events and topics in my life. A close friend was badly injured when her bike hit a groundhog in the middle of a road. Her helmet cracked neatly down the center, as it was designed to do. Unlike the character in the story, however, she suffered no lasting damage. I've also been aware of, and fascinated by, the profound changes in personality, in character, in sense of self, which have been brought about by car crashes and illnesses. I have known some people affected in this manner. The lasting, haunting lesson for me has been the fragility of our selves. We are used to thinking of ourselves as vulnerable physically. But we also tend to assume that "who we are" is solid as bone. The notion that a relatively minor switch in our internal chemistry or neuron circuits can radically alter our identities is deeply and fascinatingly unsettling, at least to me.

David H. Lynn has been the editor of *The Kenyon Review* since 1994. He is the author of the novel *Wrestling with Gabriel*, the story collections *Fortune Telling* and *Year of Fire*, and *The Hero's Tale: Narrators in the Early Modern Novel*, a critical study. His stories and essays have appeared in magazines and journals in America, England, India, and Australia. A professor of English at Kenyon College, he lives in Gambier, Ohio.

Ottessa Moshfegh, "Slumming"

The rural landscape in "Slumming" was inspired by central Maine. In 1999, my mother took over an abandoned Girl Scout camp on a lake near Bangor. I try to spend time there every summer. It's a safe space in which to look at the delusions and brainwashing I've experienced during the year living in the "civilized" world. The urban neurotic, such as the narrator in "Slumming," is a great character for me to use in describing the damage done to the human psyche when it's disconnected from nature.

Being at the camp in Maine challenges me to face myself more honestly. The place isn't home to my archive of past selves, and that is liberating. I feel that I know myself better after a few days up there. I do get scared at night sometimes when I'm alone—the wind in the trees, the loons on the lake, the stars, the darkness. I begin to feel inconsequential, just a little human life in the midst of so much nature. I suppose that's behind my impulse to be creative.

Ottessa Moshfegh is the author of *McGlue* and *Eileen*. Her forthcoming story collection, *Homesick for Another World*, will be published in early 2017. She lives in the Northeast and in California.

Sam Savage, "Cigarettes"

This story began the way all my stories begin, with a sentence or two and an image. In this case the image is of a woman standing in an open doorway looking down at a man who is sitting tipped back in a chair. They are smoking. From that image the basic elements of the story flowed easily, and it was finished almost as fast as I could type it. This is the way it usually goes for me, and is probably the reason my stories are so short. Writing a novel is just the opposite—a laborious, slow, and sometimes excruciating accretion of word upon word.

I was thirteen when I started smoking. I can vividly recall the manifold pleasures of cigarettes, moments of intense calm and satisfaction, the sense of release, leaning back and exhaling slowly, and I can also recall sucking smoke into burning lungs, scrounging ashtrays for butts that could be relit and smoked, and even, on one occasion, picking a butt up from a sidewalk in Paris, my reluctance eased by a smear of lipstick on the filter tip. Even today, with ruined lungs, I sometimes, sitting over coffee in the morning, feel a tug of the old craving, though the cigarette I crave is not the final scorching Gauloise I smoked when I was thirty-six but the Chesterfield I held in a hand I had posed with studied nonchalance on the steering wheel of a 1954 Pontiac Chieftain when I was fifteen. I suspect that my own fraught relation with cigarettes contributed to whatever power this story possesses.

Sam Savage is the author of five novels. His first, *Firmin*, was a Barnes & Noble Discover Great New Writers selection. Originally from South Carolina, he lives in Madison, Wisconsin.

Asako Serizawa, "Train to Harbin"

To talk about "Train to Harbin," I have to talk about its companion, a story called "The Visitor," which I was lucky enough to have included in *The O. Henry Prize Stories 2013*. Both stories belong in a collection of interconnected stories and are literal companions in the sense that the man in "Train to Harbin" is married to the woman in "The Visitor." Like husband and wife, who are relegated by war to the margins of each other's lives, the two stories are written to complement each other, each furnishing a part of the world the other shares but has no access to; together, they are set up to speak to the symbiotic way in which war affects seemingly discrete groups of people living in varying proximity to it. The stories were conceived this way, as a pair, and I wrote them in succession, though revision took its own time and separated their births by a couple of years.

"The Visitor" is a compact, linear story, confined to one domestic arena and spanning just a few hours; "Train to Harbin" is a more expansive, elliptical story, inherently undomestic, and spanning several decades. "The Visitor" is basically all current action and one long scene; "Train to Harbin" is its inverse, almost all backstory and exposition, with one scene that can properly be called a scene. "The Visitor" is a kind of ghost story that takes place at home; "Train to Harbin" is the ghost, the murky context that haunts the private everyday. The two stories are worlds apart—two autonomous pieces written to be read independently—but juxtaposed, they are meant to line up like a photograph and its negative. "Train to Harbin" is the negative, rarely exposed to the light of day.

Asako Serizawa was born in Japan and spent her precollege life in Singapore, Jakarta, and Tokyo. Her stories have appeared in *The Southern Review*, *Prairie Schooner*, *The Antioch Review*, *The O. Henry Prize Stories 2013*, and the 2016 Pushcart Prize anthology. A recent Fiction Fellow at the Fine Arts Work Center in Provincetown and a recipient of a Glenna Luschei Prairie Schooner Award, she has received grants from the Ludwig Vogelstein Foundation and the Vermont Studio Center.

Shruti Swamy, "A Simple Composition"
Mainz, Germany! For many years, I had been trying to write this story, but got stuck every time at the moment of departure. Whenever Arundathi and her husband arrived in America, I could find no way forward. It was just too familiar for me to depict it with the strangeness Arundathi felt. Mainz was a random Internet find (I think I just Googled "physics university Europe"), but as soon as I saw pictures from that carnival, the story ran ahead, and I followed it home. "A Simple Composition" is perhaps the ugliest story I have ever written, and many scenes unnerved me as I was writing them. ("Oh no," I said aloud, genuinely dismayed, when I realized what would happen between Arundathi and the professor.) But each turn of the story presented itself in an undeniable way, and I felt I had to be faithful to it. The oddest thing about this story was that though I felt a mild horror—sometimes physically—at some of the situations I was depicting, I also took a

true pleasure in the writing of it, every part. Over and over again, I had the feeling of stepping forward into darkness, and finding that though I couldn't see the way forward, my feet kept falling on solid ground.

Shruti Swamy's fiction has appeared in *Prairie Schooner*, *Agni*, *Black Warrior Review*, and *New American Writing*, and she has received residencies and fellowships from Hedgebrook, the Millay Colony for the Arts, Vassar College, and Kundiman. She received her BA from Vassar College, and her MFA from San Francisco State University. Born in California, she lives and writes in San Francisco.

Elizabeth Tallent, "Narrator"

Years ago a box of love letters came from FedEx, very kindly returned by their recipient, who had written to say they were coming, and I had a bad feeling about those letters and how nakedly needy the girl who wrote them was going to seem. I got as far as nicking the brown packing tape with a knife before putting the box away in a corner of the closet it ended up never leaving. Whenever I thought of it that box gave off a quiet radiation of unresolved trouble and sexual shamefulness. Sometimes I tell students that shame is a compass needle pointing to a potential story, but, in a clear case of *Do as I say, not as I do*, I so hated the actual feeling of shame aroused by the box that I had trouble tolerating it long enough to see whatever story it promised or obscured. Only when I gave up and tried a slantwise approach, a draft whose narrator falls in love with a writer purely on the basis of having found his work beautiful, did I get a narrator who seemed the right mix of bold and scared, of insight and self-deception. The risk was that her fool-for-love naïveté seemed to solicit a plot that would be a series of deserved disillusionments, and I wanted a more volatile progression, a kind of narration that was going to keep sabotaging itself as it went along. Then, too, I really love stories that carry the marks of having scraped into being past resistance, that sound like they cost something to tell, and I tried to get that in.

Elizabeth Tallent was born in Washington, DC. *Mendocino Fire* is her fourth and most recent collection of stories. She teaches in Stanford's Creative Writing Program and lives in California.

Frederic Tuten, "Winter, 1965"

In 1962, I found myself adrift. I had just returned to New York from having dropped out of a PhD program in literature at a frosty upstate graduate school. I found a job clerking in a bookstore that paid by the hour, and I needed to work long hours and six to seven days a week to pay my rent and to live. My hopes of finding time to write or ever becoming a writer were vanishing. A year passed this way before I received official word that the social worker job I had applied for in the New York City Welfare Department was mine.

I lived in the Lower East Side—as does the character in my story, "Winter, 1965"—in a six-floor walk-up—one room, a kitchen with its own bathtub, a toilet and stand-up shower. I was happy because I worked only five days a week and was now free to write and to dream.

But many of my dreams were haunted by the stories, the hard lives and worries—which often became mine—of the sixty or more people on my welfare caseload. Every day there was some new emergency: evictions, utilities shutdowns, suicides. Sometimes in my sleep I would confuse and blend the stories of my clients with my own history of childhood impoverishment in the Bronx. In that Welfare Department period, which lasted a charged year, I never wrote about those people or my life with them: I wanted to escape from them; I wrote anything that was far away from what I was then living.

Fifty-three years later I woke up one morning, having had a dream about a former client, a blind Jamaican woman in her nineties who wanted me to read poetry to her—Longfellow, her favorite. And I began writing this story.

Frederic Tuten, Bronx born, has written about art, literature, and film in several periodicals, including *Artforum*, *The New York Times*, and *Vogue*; was an actor in the Alain Resnais movie *L'An 01*; taught with Paul Bowles in Morocco; and cowrote the cult-classic film *Possession*. He earned a PhD in literature, three Pushcart Prizes, a Guggenheim Fellowship, and an Arts and Letters Award from the American Academy of Arts and Letters. Tuten is the author of five novels: *The Adventures of Mao on the Long March*; *Tintin in the New World*; *Tallien: A Brief Romance*; *Van Gogh's Bad Café*; *The Green Hour*; and a book of interrelated short stories, *Self Portraits: Fictions*. He lives in New York City.

Zebbie Watson, "A Single Deliberate Thing"

This story and I had chemistry from the start. I like to approach a story not with a plot in mind, but by throwing together a few elements to see what happens as a result. A drought, a sick horse, a boy. Like the character, I did not quite know the end until it happened. The epistolary-like address presented itself within the first paragraph, long before I realized it was a story about telling and not telling. It is by far the most intuitive story I have written. There are lines that I did not write, I just knew.

Notes (and his haircut) is based on a pony named Snowflake, who lived and died at a farm where I worked. I grew up with horses and sometimes I find it easier to populate my writing with believable equine characters than human ones. I have heard many comments about the connection between the name "Notes" and the theme of letters, but I must admit that I did not notice that myself until the story was already finished. I just thought it was a memorable name. His friend really was a horse named Otter; that one was too perfect to change.

Zebbie Watson is from Elverson, Pennsylvania. She is a graduate of Bryn Mawr College. Her stories have appeared in *Breakwater Review* and elsewhere, and she received a 2016 Pushcart Prize. She lives in Athens, Georgia.

Publications Submitted

Stories published in American and Canadian magazines are eligible for consideration for inclusion in *The O. Henry Prize Stories*. Stories must be written originally in the English language. No translations are considered. Sections of novels are not considered. Editors are asked not to nominate individual stories. Stories may not be submitted by agents or writers.

Editors are invited to submit online fiction for consideration, but such submissions must be sent to the address on the next page in the form of a legible hard copy. The publication's contact information and the date of the story's publication must accompany the submissions.

Because of production deadlines for the 2017 collection, it is essential that stories reach the series editor by July 1, 2016. If a finished magazine is unavailable before the deadline, magazine editors are welcome to submit scheduled stories in proof or manuscript. Publications received after July 1, 2016, will automatically be considered for *The O. Henry Prize Stories 2018*.

Please see our website, www.ohenryprizestories.com, for more information about submission to *The O. Henry Prize Stories*.

The address for submission is:

Laura Furman, Series Editor, The O. Henry Prize Stories
The University of Texas at Austin
English Department, B5000
1 University Station
Austin, TX 78712

The information listed below was up-to-date when *The O. Henry Prize Stories 2016* went to press. Inclusion in this listing does not constitute endorsement or recommendation by *The O. Henry Prize Stories* or Anchor Books.

A Public Space
Brigid Hughes, editor
general@apublicspace.org
apublicspace.org
quarterly

Able Muse Review
Alexander Pepple, editor
staff@ablemuse.com
ablemuse.com
semiannual

Agni
Sven Birkerts, editor
agni@bu.edu
bu.edu/agni
semiannual (print) / biweekly
(web)

Alaska Quarterly Review
Ronald Spatz, editor
aqr@uaa.alaska.edu
uaa.alaska.edu/aqr
quarterly

Alligator Juniper
Skye Anicca, editor
alligatorjuniper@prescott.edu
prescott.edu/alligatorjuniper
annual

American Short Fiction
Rebecca Markovits and Adeena
    Reitberger, editors
editors@americanshortfiction.org
americanshortfiction.org
triannual

Antioch Review
Robert S. Fogarty, editor
Christina Gabbard, managing
    editor
cgabbard@antiochreview.org
review.antiochcollege.org
    /spring-2015
quarterly

Apalachee Review
Michael Trammell, editor
mtrammell@cob.fsu.edu
apalacheereview.org
semiannual

Apt
Carissa Halston and Randolph
    Pfaff, editors
carissa@aforementionedproductions
    .com
randolph.pfaff@gmail.com
apt.aforementionedproductions
    .com
annual (print) / weekly (web)

Arcadia
Chase Dearinger, editor
chase@arcadiamagazine.org
arcadiamagazine.org
quarterly

Arkansas Review
Marcus Tribbett, editor
mtribbett@astate.edu
altweb.astate.edu/arkreview
triannual

Baltimore Review
Barbara Diehl, editor
editor@baltimorereview.org
baltimorereview.org/index.php
annual (print) / quarterly (web)

Bellevue Literary Review
Stacy Bodziak, editor
info@BLReview.org
blr.med.nyu.edu
semiannual

Black Warrior Review
Zachary Doss, editor
blackwarriorreview@gmail.com
bwr.ua.edu
semiannual

Bomb
Betsy Sussler, editor
betsy@bombsite.com
bombmagazine.org
quarterly

Booth
Robert Stapleton
booth@butler.edu
booth.butler.edu
semiannual (print) / weekly (web)

Border Crossing
Julie Brooks Barbour, Mary
    McMyne, and Jillena Rose,
    editors
bordercrossing@lssu.edu
lssu.edu/bc/index.php
annual

Bosque
Lynn C. Miller, editor
lynn@bosquepress.com
bosquepress.com
annual

Boulevard
Richard Burgin, editor
richardburgin@netzero.com
boulevardmagazine.org
triannual

Brain, Child
Marcelle Soviero, editor
editorial@brainchildmag.com
brainchildmag.com
quarterly

Bridge Eight
Coe Douglas, editor
coe@bridgeeight.com
bridgeeight.com
semiannual

Carve
Matthew Limpede, editor
editor@carvezine.com
carvezine.com
quarterly

Chautauqua
Jill Gerard and Philip Gerard,
     editors
clj@uncw.edu
ciweb.org/literary-arts/literary
     -journal
annual

Chicago Quarterly Review
Syed Haider, editor
cqr@icogitate.com
chicagoquarterlyreview.com
quarterly

China Grove
Luke Lampton and R. Scott
     Anderson, editors
chinagrovepress@gmail.com
chinagrovepress.com/china-grove
     -a-literary-journal
semiannual

Cimarron Review
Toni Graham, editor
cimarronreview@okstate.edu
cimarronreview.com
quarterly

Colorado Review
Stephanie G'Schwind
creview@colostate.edu
coloradoreview.colostate.edu
     /colorado-review
triannual

Confrontation
Jonna Semeiks, editor
confrontationmag@gmail.com
confrontationmagazine.org
semiannual

Conjunctions
Bradford Morrow, editor
conjunctions@bard.edu
conjunctions.com
semiannual

Copper Nickel
Wayne Miller, editor
wayne.miller@ucdenver.edu
copper-nickel.org
semiannual

Crab Orchard Review
Jon Tribble, editor
jtribble@siu.edu
craborchardreview.siu.edu
semiannual

CutBank
Billy Wallace, editor
editor.cutbank@gmail.com
cutbankonline.org
semiannual

Dappled Things
Meredith McCann, editor
dappledthings.editor@gmail.com
dappledthings.org
quarterly

December
Gianna Jacobson, editor
editor@decembermag.org
decembermag.org
semiannual

Denver Quarterly
Laird Hunt, editor
denverquarterly@gmail.com
du.edu/denverquarterly
quarterly

Descant
descant.ca
CLOSED

Ecotone
David Gessner, editor
info@ecotonejournal.com
ecotonemagazine.org
semiannual

Eleven Eleven
Hugh Behm-Steinberg, editor
elevenelevenjournal@gmail.com
elevenelevenjournal.com
semiannual

enRoute
Jean-François Légaré, editor
info@enroutemag.net
enroute.aircanada.com
monthly

Epoch
Michael Koch, editor
mk64@cornell.edu
english.arts.cornell.edu
    /publications/epoch
triannual

Event
Shashi Bhat, editor
event@douglascollege.ca
eventmagazine.ca
triannual

Exile
Barry Callaghan, editor
exile2@sympatico.ca
theexilewriters.com
quarterly

Faerie Magazine
Carolyn Turgeon, editor
submissions@faeriemag.com
faeriemag.com
quarterly

Fairy Tale Review
Kate Bernheimer, editor
ftreditorial@gmail.com
fairytalereview.com
annual

Fantasy & Science Fiction
Charles Coleman Finlay, editor
fsfmag@fandsf.com
sfsite.com/fsf/index.html
published six times a year

Farallon Review
farallonreview.com
Suspended Publication

Fence
Rebecca Wolff and Paul Legault,
    editors
rebeccafence@gmail.com
fenceportal.org
semiannual

Fiction
Mark Jay Mirsky
fictionmageditors@gmail.com
fictioninc.com
semiannual

Fiction River
Kristine Kathryn Rusch and Dean
    Wesley Smith, editors
subscriptions@
    wmgpublishingmail.com
fictionriver.com
published six times a year

Fifth Wednesday Journal
Vern Miller, editor
editors@fifthwednesdayjournal.org
fifthwednesdayjournal.com
semiannual

Five Points
David Bottoms, editor
fivepoints.gsu.edu
triannual

Fourteen Hills
Heather June Gibbons, editor
14hills.net
semiannual

Gargoyle
Richard Peabody, editor
rchrdpeabody9@gmail.com
gargoylemagazine.com
annual

Glimmer Train
Linda Swanson-Davies and Susan
    Burmeister-Brown, editors
editors@glimmertrain.org
glimmertrain.com
triannual

Gold Man Review
Heather Cuthbertson, editor
heather.cuthbertson@
    goldmanpublishing.com
goldmanreview.org
annual

Grain Magazine
grainmag@skwriter.com
grainmagazine.ca
quarterly

Granta
Sigrid Rausing, editor
editorial@granta.com
granta.com
quarterly

Green Mountains Review
Elizabeth Powell, editor
gmr@jsc.edu
greenmountainsreview.com
semiannual

Grey Sparrow Journal
Diane Smith, editor
dsdianefuller@gmail.com
greysparrowpress.sharepoint.com
quarterly

Grist
Helen Stead, editor
hstead@vols.utk.edu
gristjournal.com
annual

Gulf Coast
Nick Flynn, editor
gconlineeditor@gmail.com
gulfcoastmag.org
semiannual

Harvard Review
Christina Thompson, editor
info@harvardreview.org
harvardreview.fas.harvard.edu
semiannual

Hayden's Ferry Review
Chelsea Hickok, editor
hfr@asu.edu
haydensferryreview.com
semiannual

Huizache
Dagoberto Gilb, editor
editor@huizachemag.org
huizachemag.org
annual

Hunger Mountain
Miciah Bay Gault, editor
hungermtn@vcfa.edu
hungermtn.org
annual

Indiana Review
Peter Kispert, editor
inreview@indiana.edu
indianareview.org
semiannual

Iron Horse Literary Review
Leslie Jill Patterson, editor
ihlr.mail@gmail.com
ironhorsereview.com
published six times a year

Isthmus
Ann Przyzycki, Randy DeVita, and
    Taira Anderson, editors
editor@isthmusreview.com
isthmusreview.com
semiannual

Jabberwock Review
Becky Hagenston, editor
jabberwockreview@english
    .msstate.edu
jabberwock.org.msstate.edu
semiannual

Kenyon Review
David H. Lynn, editor
kenyonreview@kenyon.edu
kenyonreview.org
published six times a year

Labletter
Sarah Marrs, editor
thelabletter@labletter.com
labletter.com
annual

**Lady Churchill's Rosebud
    Wristlet**
Gavin J. Grant and Kelly Link,
    editors
150 Pleasant St., #306
Easthampton, MA 01027
(no e-mail submissions)
smallbeerpress.com/lcrw
semiannual

Lake Effect
George Looney, editor
gol1@psu.edu
behrend.psu.edu/lakeeffect
annual

Literary Imagination
Archie Burnett, editor
litimag.oxfordjournals.org
triannual

Little Brother Magazine
Emily M. Keeler, editor
info@littlebrothermagazine.com
littlebrothermagazine.com
semiannual

Little Patuxent Review
Steven Leyva, editor
editor@littlepatuxentreview.org
littlepatuxentreview.org
biannual

Make
Kamilah Foreman, editor
info@makemag.com
makemag.com
semiannual

Malahat Review
John Barton, editor
malahat@uvic.ca
malahatreview.ca
quarterly

MĀNOA
Frank Stewart, editor
mjournal-l@lists.hawaii.edu
hawaii.edu/mjournal
semiannual

Massachusetts Review
Jim Hicks, editor
massrev@external.umass.edu
massreview.org
quarterly

Meridian
Emily Temple, editor
readmeridian.org
semiannual

Michigan Quarterly Review
Jonathan Freedman, editor
mqr@umich.edu
michiganquarterlyreview.com
quarterly

Mid-American Review
Abigail Cloud, editor
clouda@bgsu.edu
casit.bgsu.edu/midamericanreview
semiannual

Midwestern Gothic
Jeff Pfaller and Robert James
    Russell, editors
info@midwestgothic.com
midwestgothic.com
quarterly

Mississippi Review
Andrew Malan Milward, editor
msreview@usm.edu
usm.edu/mississippi-review/index
    .html
semiannual

Montana Quarterly
Scott McMillion, editor
editor@themontanaquarterly.com
themontanaquarterly.com
quarterly

Mount Hope
Edward J. Delaney, editor
mount.hope.magazine@gmail.com
mounthopemagazine.com
semiannual

n +1
Nikil Saval and Dayna Tortorici,
    editors
editors@nplusonemag.com
nplusonemag.com
triannual

Narrative
Carol Edgarian and Tom Jenks,
    editors
narrativemagazine.com
triannual

Natural Bridge
Mary Troy
natural@umsl.edu
blogs.umsl.edu/naturalbridge
semiannual

New England Review
Carolyn Kuebler, editor
nereview@middlebury.edu
nereview.com
quarterly

New Letters
Robert Stewart, editor
newletters@umkc.edu
newletters.org
quarterly

New Ohio Review
David Wanczyk, editor
noreditors@ohio.edu
ohio.edu/nor
semiannual

New Orleans Review
Mark Yakich, editor
noreview@loyno.edu
neworleansreview.org
annual

Nimrod International Journal
Eilis O'Neal, editor
nimrod@utulsa.edu
utulsa.edu/nimrod
semiannual

Noon
Diane Williams, editor
noonannual.com
annual

North Dakota Quarterly
Kate Sweney, editor
und.ndq@und.edu
arts-sciences.und.edu/north
    -dakota-quarterly
quarterly

Northern New England Review
nner@franklinpierce.edu
facebook.com/Northern
    -New-England-
    Review-724349747695453
annual

Notre Dame Review
Evan Harris, editor
notredamereview@gmail.com
ndreview.nd.edu
semiannual

One Story
Hannah Tinti, editor
hannah@one-story.com
one-story.com
published every three to four weeks

Orion Magazine
H. Emerson Blake, editor
orionmagazine.org
published six times a year

Overtime
David LaBounty, editor
info@workerswritejournal.com
workerswritejournal.com/overtime
    .htm
quarterly

Oxford American
Eliza Borné, editor
info@oxfordamerican.org
oxfordamerican.org
quarterly

Pakn Treger
Aaron Lansky, editor
pt@bikher.org
yiddishbookcenter.org/pakn-treger
triannual

PEN America Journal
M Mark, editor
journal@pen.org
pen.org/pen-america-journal
annual

Phantom Drift
David Memmott, editor
phantomdrifteditor@yahoo.com
phantomdrift.org
annual

Pinch
Tim Johnston, editor
editor@pinchjournal.com
pinchjournal.com
semiannual

Ploughshares
Ladette Randolph, editor
pshares@pshares.org
pshares.org
triannual

PMS poemmemoirstory
Kerry Madden, editor
poemmemoirstory@gmail.com
uab.edu/cas/englishpublications
    /pms-poemmemoirstory
annual

Pointing Dog Journal
Jason Smith, editor
jake@villagepress.com
pointingdogjournal.com
published six times a year

Post Road Magazine
Jaime Clarke and David Ryan,
    editors
postroadmag.com
semiannual

Potomac Review
Julie Wakeman-Linn
potomacrevieweditor@
    montgomerycollege.edu
blogs.montgomerycollege.edu
    /potomacreview
semiannual

Prairie Fire
Andris Taskans, editor
prfire@prairiefire.ca
prairiefire.ca
quarterly

Prairie Schooner
Kwame Dawes, editor
prairieschooner@unl.edu
prairieschooner.unl.edu
quarterly

Prick of the Spindle
Cynthia Reeser, editor
pseditor@prickofthespindle.com
prickofthespindle.org
biannual (print) / quarterly (web)

PRISM International
Christopher Evans, editor
prose@prismmagazine.ca
prismmagazine.ca
quarterly

Pulp Literature
Mel Anastasiou, Jennifer Landels,
    and Susan Pieters, editors
submission@pulpliterature.com
pulpliterature.com
quarterly

Raritan
Jackson Lears, editor
rqr@rci.rutgers.edu
raritanquarterly.rutgers.edu
quarterly

Redivider
Lise Haines, editor
editor@redividerjournal.org
redividerjournal.org
semiannual

River Styx
Richard Newman
bigriver@riverstyx.org
riverstyx.org
triannual

Room
Rachel Thompson, editor
contactus@roommagazine.com
roommagazine.com
quarterly

Salamander
Jennifer Barber, editor
salamandermag.org
semiannual

Salmagundi
Robert Boyers, editor
ssubmit@skidmore.edu
skidmore.edu/salmagundi
quarterly

Saranac Review
J. L. Torres, editor
saranacreview.com
annual

Slice
Beth Blachman, editor
editors@slicemagazine.org
slicemagazine.org
semiannual

Slippery Elm
Dave Essinger, editor
slipperyelm@findlay.edu
slipperyelm.findlay.edu
annual

Smith's Monthly
editor@wmgpublishingmail.com
smithsmonthly.com
monthly

South Dakota Review
Lee Ann Roripaugh, editor
sdreview@usd.edu
southdakotareview.com
quarterly

Southeast Review
Erin Hoover, editor
southeastreview@gmail.com
southeastreview.org
semiannual

Southern Humanities Review
Keetje Kuipers, editor
shr@auburn.edu
southernhumanitiesreview.com
quarterly

Southern Indiana Review
Ron Mitchell, editor
sir@usi.edu
usi.edu/sir
semiannual

Southwest Review
Greg Brownderville, editor
swr@smu.edu
smu.edu/southwestreview
quarterly

Story
Travis Kurowski and Vito Grippi,
editors
contact@storymagazine.org
storymagazine.org
semiannual

StoryQuarterly
Paul Lisicky, editor
storyquarterlyeditors@gmail.com
storyquarterly.camden.rutgers.edu
quarterly

subTerrain
Brian Kaufman, editor
subter@portal.ca
www.subterrain.ca
triannual

Tahoma Literary Review
Joe Ponepinto, editor
fiction@tahomaliteraryreview.com
tahomaliteraryreview.com
triannual

**The Asian American Literary
Review**
Lawrence-Minh Bùi Davis and
Gerald Maa, editors
editors@aalrmag.org
aalr.binghamton.edu
semiannual

The Briar Cliff Review
Tricia Currans-Sheehan, editor
tricia.currans-sheehan@briarcliff
.edu
bcreview.org
annual

The Carolina Quarterly
Lindsay Starck, editor
carolina.quarterly@gmail.com
thecarolinaquarterly.com
triannual

The Cincinnati Review
Nicola Mason, editor
editors@cincinnatireview.com
cincinnatireview.com
semiannual

The Fiddlehead
Ross Leckie, editor
fiddlehd@unb.ca
thefiddlehead.ca
quarterly

The Florida Review
Lisa Roney, editor
flreview@ucf.edu
floridareview.cah.ucf.edu
semiannual

The Georgia Review
Stephen Corey, editor
garev@uga.edu
garev.uga.edu
quarterly

The Gettysburg Review
Mark Drew, editor
mdrew@gettysburg.edu
gettysburgreview.com
quarterly

The Hudson Review
Paula Deitz, editor
info@hudsonreview.com
hudsonreview.com
quarterly

The Iowa Review
Harilaos Stecopoulos, editor
iowa-review@uiowa.edu
iowareview.org
triannual

The Literary Review
Minna Proctor, editor
info@theliteraryreview.org
theliteraryreview.org
quarterly

The Long Story
R. P. Burnham
rpburnham@mac.com
longstorylitmag.com
annual

The Louisville Review
Sena Jeter Naslund, editor
louisvillereview@spalding.edu
spalding.edu/louisvillereview
semiannual

The Massachusetts Review
Jules Chametzky and Jim Hicks,
    editors
massrev@external.umass.edu
massreview.org
quarterly

The Missouri Review
Speer Morgan, editor
question@moreview.com
missourireview.com
quarterly

The New Yorker
David Remnick, editor
fiction@newyorker.com
newyorker.com
weekly

The Paris Review
Lorin Stein, editor
theparisreview.org
quarterly

The Saturday Evening Post
editors@saturdayeveningpost.com
saturdayeveningpost.com
published six times a year

The Sewanee Review
George Core, editor
sreview@sewanee.edu
review.sewanee.edu
quarterly

The Sierra Nevada Review
Laura Wetherington, editor
sierranevada.edu/academics
    /humanities-social-sciences
    /english/the-sierra-nevada
    -review
annual

The Southern Review
Jessica Faust and Emily Nemens,
    editors
southernreview@lsu.edu
thesouthernreview.org
quarterly

The Strand Magazine
strandmag@strandmag.com
strandmag.com
monthly

The Sun
Sy Safransky, editor
thesunmagazine.org
monthly

The Thomas Wolfe Review
Paula G. Eckard and David
    Strange, editors
twostrange2000@yahoo.com
thomaswolfereview.org
annual

The Threepenny Review
Wendy Lesser, editor
wlesser@threepennyreview.com
threepennyreview.com
quarterly

The Worcester Review
Diane Mulligan, editor
twr.diane@gmail.com
www.theworcesterreview.org
annual

Third Coast
Thisbe Nissen, editor
editors@thirdcoastmagazine.com
thirdcoastmagazine.com
semiannual

Tin House
Rob Spillman, editor
info@tinhouse.com
tinhouse.com/magazine
quarterly

Tweed's
Randy Rosenthal and Laura Mae
    Isaacman, editors
tweedsmag.org
semiannual

upstreet
Vivian Dorsel, editor
editor@upstreet-mag.org
upstreet-mag.org
annual

Virginia Quarterly Review
Paul Reyes, editor
editors@vqronline.org
vqronline.org
quarterly

Weber
Michael Wutz, editor
mwutz@weber.edu
weber.edu/weberjournal
semiannual

Western Humanities Review
Barry Weller, editor
whr@mail.hum.utah.edu
ourworld.info/whrweb
semiannual

Willow Springs
Samuel Ligon, editor
willowspringsewu@gmail.com
willowsprings.ewu.edu
semiannual

Witness
Joseph Langdon, editor
witness@unlv.edu
witness.blackmountaininstitute.org
annual (print) / semiannual (web)

Workers Write!
David LaBounty, editor
info@workerswritejournal.com
workerswritejournal.com
annual

Yellow Medicine Review
Jerry Brunoe, guest editor
editor@yellowmedicinereview.com
yellowmedicinereview.com
semiannual

Your Impossible Voice
Keith J. Powell, editor
editor@yourimpossiblevoice.com
yourimpossiblevoice.com
quarterly

Zoetrope: All-Story
Michael Ray, editor
info@all-story.com
www.all-story.com
quarterly

Zymbol
Anne James, editor
hello@zymbolmag.com
zymbolmag.com
semiannual

ZYZZYVA
Laura Cogan, editor
zyzzyva.org
quarterly

Permissions

O. Henry Juror Acknowledgments

"Molly Antopol on 'Train to Harbin' by Asako Serizawa," copyright © 2016 by Molly Antopol. Reprinted by agreement of the author.

"Peter Cameron on 'Winter, 1965' by Frederic Tuten," copyright © 2016 by Peter Cameron. Reprinted by agreement of the author.

"Lionel Shriver on 'Irises' by Elizabeth Genovise," copyright © 2016 by Lionel Shriver. Reprinted by agreement of the author.

Grateful acknowledgment is made to the following for permission to reprint previously published materials:

"Dismemberment" by Wendell Berry first appeared in *The Three-penny Review*. Copyright © 2015 by Wendell Berry. Reprinted by permission of the author.

"Exit Zero" by Marie-Helene Bertino first appeared in *Epoch*. Copyright © 2015 by Marie-Helene Bertino. Reprinted by permission of the author.

"Happiness" by Ron Carlson first appeared in *Ecotone*. Copyright © 2014 by Ron Carlson. Reprinted by permission of the author.

The O. Henry Prize Stories 2016 /

Oct 2016